HEROES NO LONGER
A novel by Lewis Eyre

Michael

Hope you enjoy the book! Good luck with your own!

Eyre

CONTENTS

PART ONE
THE ESCAPE
1.   Woodville Estate

"What a load of…," exclaimed Hex Croft, nine years of age. His first curse word.

The way the word Hex uttered was pronounced could not be described using that word. Plosive, explosive, like spit in a fruit bowl, the perfect expletive. When signing up to the position as a teacher, monosyllabic mocking and the occasional unmotivated tantrum should be taken for granted, but not this abuse. Many of his peers, aged between four and thirteen, erupted into a cavalcade of shrill laughs which worked together to mock her authority. Winona would have been disheartened by their response had she not accounted for their age. These younglings, who picked their noses like a gardener picks berries, swearing remained a novelty spared for the adult kind, so to hear the blonde ragamuffin speak in such foul tongue served as a novelty.

The Unblessed Bible, which his teacher had been reading to their congregation of twenty-six, claims that the minority must remain in their compounds for the sake of the masses. It states that if the unblessed leave these bases, their skin will malt, their spittle will become crimson, and their shoulders will jet above their heads to create a monstrosity of unmounted proportions. It reinforces that if the unblessed even so much as touch the blessed, then the blessed will lose their precious abilities. Yes, as Hex implied, it was 'Codswallop', 'Balderdash', a real work of fiction, but this nonetheless came as a shock for Miss Barton.

Whether she liked it or not, Winona Barton - English teacher, Maths teacher, whatever teacher the school needed that day - would be stuck in the grip of tedious employment until the sweet release of retirement. Until then, she would have to make do with being treated on par with the devil by dozens of judgemental children. She straightened herself to regain control, towering above her youthful disciples like a despot. Her sharp features - including a crow-nose (akin to a Terrahawk's snout) - assisted her domineering disposition to construct a love child of pure authoritarianism and remorseless vexation. Her narrow eyes merely dabbled with kindness, unfit for an occupation reliant on approachability. Her colleague, seated on the spartan blue poly chair behind her, rolled his eyes and palmed his face. The freckled specimen knew what was coming. Winona was about to pick a fight with a child. Good god! She could never win! Kids are smarter than the rest of us.

According to Miss Barton, Hex's tight squirm was too smug to ignore. The blonde lad was right. It enraged her that a child possessing intelligence beyond his years, like him, would never amount to anything beyond the stuffy jail they called home.

She, however, with her tight lips and narrow squint, dismissed the brief warnings Francis issued about a verbal conflict she could never win, and…

"Language!" She blasted, carrying spittle in her stormy voice. "It's Hector, isn't it?"

"Hex," the nine-year-old corrected, despising the name his parents had bestowed upon him. Hector made him sound like an OAP, so he opted for 'Hex', forgetting that 'Hex' made him sound more like the Devil's spawn.

"Tell me, Hex. Where did you learn that word?"

"Which word?" "*That* word." This could have gone round in circles.

"It don't matter."

"*Doesn't* matter," corrected the notorious Grammar pedant.

"I know it, that's all, and I'm not gonna say sorry for using it."

"What do you think is…" careful, Winona, "…Baloney, about this situation? This is a primary school. We don't use words like…"

"What's wrong with that word?"

"Lots of things! We're using baloney today."

One nitpicking student raised her hand. "Actually, we had beef stew today. There was no baloney on the menu."

Winona felt like hailing insults on the child from Hell's grim rainstorm, but she opted to keep her job. The salary may have been measly and the conditions poor, but she was lucky to have one. She tapped on the crimson-coated bible ahead of her, instigating a steady clamour.

"I think they're keeping us here because they're ashamed," cried Hex. Hector? Hex. It had to be Hex.

"You're mighty mature sounding for a nine-year-old!"

"Uh-uh. I don't think it's true. Do you think it's true?"

These were the stories Winona had been raised on, fed to her like fine meat and which the generations

4

were hooked on as if these spun yarns were opioids. Her experience with the fairytale began with her secondary school teacher, the tweed-jacketed teacher stereotype Mr Farrow, known to the masses as Shaun, in that same sweat-tinged mini-hall. Of course these were not just stories, but researched, definitive facts, or so the time travellers and the government all seemed to state.

"We're here in this compound to protect ourselves and to protect the blessed," Winona reinforced, "and there's nothing more to it than that."

For every child, there must come a time when they are exposed to universal truths. Every child must learn about divorce, about desire, about death, about their disease.

Of course, to label it a virus would be erroneous. They were just like everybody else; Walking, talking, breathing, thinking human beings, many of which with the capacity to accomplish more than the borderlands could accommodate. That was not the way the world perceived them. To those outside the gate, they were 'abnormal', 'unwanted', even unknowing, besides what the front page of their local newspaper could inform them. They were the glitches in the system, the one percent, the unfortunate few deprived of the luxury of substance and superpowers.

For Poseidon was in fact real, a man who could control earthquakes and sandstorms. For Icarus did indeed fly too close to the sun, and Medusa did have locks of death. For they would never be the same as the gods in a godless world, where everybody else was divine. From the looks of it, Hex had been enlightened to the inequity of this perfectly imperfect (or imperfectly perfect) society long ago.

Winona blew a whistle purchased from the scraps of their scant budget. This signified the end of the assembly. There had been enough cruel realities for one day.

"Not you, Hex," she drew him back as he attempted to join the crowd, led off by Francis, the shepherd of the student flock. He grunted like a bedraggled teenager, four years too premature, forcing his way to her pillar. "What's gotten into you, eh? You're a smart lad. You don't want to let yourself down by wasting your intelligence."

"Mummy says that I'm smart too, but that's what Mummies are meant to say. She says that I won't be able to do anything about it. I'm stuck here, aren't I? There's not much you can do here."

"What would you like to do with your life, if you didn't have anything confining you?"

His lips curled into a grin; a welcome sight more characteristic of his age than prior behaviours. "I'd like to look after animals. You know, real, proper animals. You can't have seen them either. I've only seen them in picture books. Well, apart from butterflies and spiders. They're hanging about all the time. I'd love to work in a zoo.

The mere phrase 'Spiders' was enough to send shivers down Barton's spine. Winona thought his dream was sweet but dismissed his dreams as implausible.

"You can tell me who taught you *that* word," Winona insisted with the softest gear in her vocal engine, testing out benevolence despite the crossed arms that made connotations of hostility come naturally. "It wasn't your mummy, was it?"

"I ain't no snitch."

"You *aren't* a snitch."

Hex sighed. "It was Aggie, all right." Thus rendering himself a grass, giving into a miniscule amount of pressure. "Aggie from the newsagents."

Of course it was Aggie. It was always Aggie. All Hex's parents heard was Aggie this and Aggie that, as if it were healthy for somebody under the age of ten to be best friends with a sixty-eight-year-old woman. Agatha helped him, though, and that care was genuine, by no means anything for his parents to be concerned about.

"She thinks it's a load of…that…too?" She asked, and he chortled. "What's so funny?"

"Why don't you say it? It's funnier when a grown-up says a swear!"

"Grow up," she said, even though he was nine. "I'm gonna have to have a chat with her. You'd think the mayor's wife would have more faith in this regime."

"Isn't a regime a bad thing? I think I'm right. What if I am right?"

"Well…I don't know what I'd do. It'd mean my whole life had been a lie and I don't want to imagine the repercussions. You'd better go. You'll be late to class. What's Francis teaching you today?"

"*Charlie and the Chocolate Factory.*"

"You have fun, alright?"

Hex skipped along, leaving Winona with nothing more than a self-administered despairing groan for company. Tired of the ennui which defined every instinct, the lithe lady marched into the staff room. This was nothing more than a store cupboard painted in misty green, and she rammed a sequence of numbers into the phone, which she had transferred from a straggled strip of A4 she had collected from her classroom. Two vibrations preceded the urgency of a hand clasping against a ringing call which the woman on the other line took almost no time to answer.

"What's up?" responded a sweaty Hull-born voice with a larynx as rough as tar.

"Am I speaking to Eva Croft?"

"You sure are! Come on, Winona, it's hardly a big place. We all know each other."

The muted response suggested Winona did not recognise the voice on the other end of the line. "Oh, hello…you! It's about Hex."

"Of course it's about Hector," she wheezed, "It's always about Hector."

"Natural troublemaker?"

"A bit beyond his years, but a troublemaker? No, I think that would be unfair."

"Has he said anything to you about thinking that it's all a lie? This community, I mean. Life hinging on what's behind these gates."

"Not particularly," though there was apprehension in Eva's cadence.

"There are people who thought the same as him. You remember Kelly, don't you?"

"No," Winona responded. Eva's reply was exact and blunt: "Exactly. Neither do I."

"I'm worried Hex, and maybe some others, are starting to think about getting out."

"He wouldn't! He couldn't! He's a kid! Nobody with half a brain cell would heed his warnings."

"I can't be sure. I need you to keep an eye on him. It's one thing for an adult wanting to take the risk of leaving, but I don't want him to go through with whatever he's planning."

"Yeah, of course. Thanks for letting me know." Eva put down the phone right away as if she hadn't acknowledged a single word.

Winona locked the phone back into its metallic grip. In spite of whatever her boss believed, she cared about the children and their wellbeing. She expressed that in her anguish as she slammed her head against the nearest desk she could find.

*

At home, Hex's home, another unemployed day had elapsed in a city of the jobless. After all, there were only so many vacancies for a place as small as Woodville. Alongside Eva on that tall October morning was Eva's wife, Maeve; equally thin, almost as dishevelled, though with a greater pretence of effervescence. Within those brave, wide cheekbones of hers was a hidden sense of depredation. Perhaps their means of finding hope was in each other, in their son, but certainly not in their home.

They resided on the second to top floor of Apartment Block A's aesthetic jigsaw, below 'Aggie' and the mayor, above the rowdy family below – the insomniac's worst nightmare, whose furious cries could still be made out by the Crofts in the premature hours of the day. At night, rats and mice would claw against the wall with their rampant talons, replaced by other, equally repulsive rodents while the nocturnal beasts slept. The stench of hobo's urine smell made air fresheners imperative, but their meagre salaries could rarely afford such luxuries. Leaks with patches of soil and excrement dripped from the damp ceilings, but no resident was knowledgeable enough to do anything to stop the downpour.

Any room tour conducted would be complete in a matter of seconds. From the door, a brief and crumbling carpeted hallway which preceded a flight of two stairs, one lone bed, with slight space to the right for sleepers relegated to the floor (Hex, most often, because he found innocent excitement in the grounding). Before the bed was the stove, a small table, and a coat hanger, while a sharp turn to the left immediately after entry would lead a person into the bathroom. If one envisions the living area as the antithesis of glamour, then that hypothetical individual should first endeavour the bathroom. It contained a toilet encrusted with brown stains, a soiled basin directly above the bowl, and a mirror with a mustardy light that died long ago, plunging the chamber into almost incessant darkness.

When the promise of 3PM emerged, Eva wrapped herself up in her piteous rags, which barely contained her against the scathing chill of these December months, while Eva stayed behind to read Dolly Turpin's latest piece of academia, a new find in the Newsagent's about the American Civil War.

Lights out, television off, conversation exhausted, their morning had been spent in relative silence. Eva enjoyed few activities more than sitting on her rough as rocks armchair and reading while Maeve and Hex were absent. It helped her escape from the sight of broken plaster and constant musk of decay. Those precious pages of escapism, which she could flick through and beam herself to another world or another time. This was the one instance where concerns about money or her constantly rumbling stomach would not be able to catch her. Eva tuned out the slammed doors from Elijah and Elaine barking at each other downstairs, refusing to let anger overcome her.

*

During the cursory jog to St Joseph's, Maeve discovered a reminiscent release to the dozens of children in identical cobalt jumpers escaping from the institution. Hex, too, was excited to liberate himself from his scratchy straitjacket-like shirt, even if that would involve a sudden transition into the one item of clothing Eva had ready, washed and ironed, his dressing gown. It wasn't that she didn't have the time. She had nothing but. The costly expense of running a washing machine could be held accountable instead.

Mrs Croft bobbed down the hallway of grass and concrete, a straight line made of nothing more than green and grey, until she reached her darling son. She unlocked her wings when he came bounding towards her, leaping into her with an abrupt collision. Maeve chuckled briefly as she recovered from his flight, making the most of his embrace before, inevitably, there would come a time when he would be too old to want to hug his old mum. Watching them, naturally, was Winona, whose hawkish features were acknowledged by Maeve through vague hints of windowpane. From the other side, Maeve waved briefly, but Winona drew the curtains and retreated to the din that was her classroom.

When they returned to Apartment Block A – five minutes away, they made careful steps to prevent the staircase from collapsing in on itself, since the structure leading up the tower was fragile enough that a heavy enough step could shatter the baluster. Upon entry, Hex threw his microscopic bookbag onto the lone armchair at the dining table and jumped into the arms of his other mother, after which she nagged him for being 'a bad boy'. Dinner that night would consist of a can of tomato soup distributed evenly between three people. Breakfast had consisted of an apple each, picked locally from the orchard downtown, and lunch had been a butter sandwich deprived of all other fillings.

If anybody could pass through the bodybuilder of a gate which secured the community, then the orchard would be what they encountered first. The gardens would infuse Woodville with a deceptively edenic quality, with trees that sparkled with Autumnal tangerine and vines which remained kempt despite the generally unkempt aura of the settlement's greater expanse.

Before the gate, outsiders would face the label in all its glory: Woodville, a sign rusted and bronze with vowels falling from the ledge. Perched on the cusp between city and village were two men in obsidian overcoats with rifles at their sides. They had more meat on their bones than most, matching with their bald-headed gruffness, indicative of their fairer pay packet. Kenny exchanged his gun, his stopwatch, his binoculars, to Elijah – changeover time! While Elijah was eager to get to work, Kenny had the promise of returning to a desolate household with an evening ahead to fill.

At least Elijah was out of the house for the time being. That meant Eva could concentrate on her book, properly this time. Part of her felt she should have trickled down the staircase to keep Elaine company. Elaine had Steven, and Eva would much rather be in the company of a good book, waiting for the turn of the key to indicate the return of her wife and son.

2. <u>Dayetime</u>

7.30. 7.30PM, it must be clarified, because there was no way that Isla - keeper of her own time - was ever going to wake at 7.30AM.

She woke to her alarm clock's unrelenting howl; a shrill, repetitive bark which plugged the eardrums. Drizzling out of the mattress – the rare place where reality could not harm her – her fingers scuttled in a desperate crawl to quell the siren's raging scream. Alas, the alarm was a worthy opponent, so she had to climb out of bed to force the machine's wheezing croak into surrender.

Where possible, she tried not to use her abilities, but abusing them was too tempting a proposition. If she was running late to work, for example, the cacophony of rush hour would be the last resort. If you have the power to control time, why wouldn't you use it? An alarm clock may have been a petty investment for somebody who could spin time backwards and forwards at will, but part of her liked feeling 'ordinary'.

Her groans became increasingly persistent as she cleaned the sleep dust from her eyes, curling her fingers into a ball and spiralling her arms to and fro. Downstairs, the swift rumble of pots and pans indicated that her roommate was making dinner. Sapphire may have been a professional chef, but the prospect of another inadequate pot pie was too much for Isla to bear.

"I've won awards for my cooking," Sapphire would brag whenever Isla squirmed at the cooking she pretended to enjoy to spare Sapphire's emotions. She'd become a rather skilled actress when it came to the fake yummy noises that were expected of her.

"Your restaurant relies on the gimmick," Isla would want to say. "You can do anything five times quicker than most. People only come to your restaurant because they get their grub slapped on a plate thirty seconds after ordering it."

Instead, the cockney would cry: "And Speedy Sapph's deserves the michelin star!"

Whenever Isla wished to avoid consuming the mushy content slapped onto her plate, she rotated the clock again, and she could escape the nightmare scenario. Claiming she was in a rush, she skipped the meal and hopped to the bathroom. After a thorough shower and a ridiculous quantity of push ups, she drew open her wardrobe to reveal clothes she only held onto for emergencies, beside the sequined white and gold cape which served as her usual workwear.

All she had to do to reach her destination (In this case, ironically, the local club they called *The Destination*, which, thanks to the tumbling neon vowels of its sign, now heralded The Dstntion as its title) was place on her pocket watch and concentrate. Complete concentration, focusing on the short-hand first. The clock's hand initially progressed at its stationary pace, but a few seconds allowed the wristwatch's metal fingertips to rotate freely, spinning at their own volition. The spiralling wheels became unsteady, as if the hands would collapse from their hinges. Isla's head went spinning with it, allocating time the impression of unmatchable speed. Day faded into night, and the salmon walls of her bedroom contorted into the outskirts of night-time Hull where hoards of immaculate women lined up to feign rapport with the grubby bouncers in hope of an easy entry. One bouncer, a chubby ogre with a naked head, offered hand sanitizer which sprayed from his fingertips. The other similarly meaty footsoldier promised to equip his iron fists if any misconduct occurred.

High heel clitter-clatter indenting against the pavement made the woman in leopard print the subject of their shared gawps, as she swayed her vermillion hair in coquettish circles and let cleavage run free between the gaps in her coat.

"Howdy, gentlemen," Isla said, batting her fluorescent eyelids, unconcerned that they might recognise her from her considerable reputation as one of Hull's greatest superheroes, the notorious 'Quickfix' of Defence E.

"Howdy," they chanted in hypnotic unison, hypnotically, letting her strut into the obnoxious disco-ball glare, which combined with the throbbing hip hop propulsions to make the place inexcusable. A censorious groan reached her when she entered what her mother would call 'the last place God built', but she flashed a grin back at the vile attendants, taken aback by their blatant misogyny. Her censure, amidst their overt objectification, shifted to revulsion.

All she could smell was vinegar and vomitus, and all she could see were people kissing and heaving. These were people she had to fit in with, so she let the drum and bass music play her like a fiddle, lugging her eyes across the perimeter as if they were tracking devices. If they were indeed tracking devices, they would have beeped when they met the gentleman at the bar with his lurid flock of blonde hair. As her heels descended from the platform, she waited for his attention to retreat from the whisky in his grip onto the patter of her shoes. Naturally, once she secured the seat beside him, his arctic-white teeth shone at her, as did the glint of gold from his nine-carat bracelet. She handed a ten-pound note to the mixologist who poured her a contraption which came out in a concerning colour. He drowned his throat in whiskey, as if to prepare himself, before handing the bartender money of his own.

"Here, let me," he gestured, leading Isla to giggle.

"What a gentleman!"

"A girl as pretty as you shouldn't have to pay for her own drinks!"

When the bartender shifted to the other side of his station, Isla's stool croaked as she budged closer to him, detecting a stiff vineyard scent which crept from his armpits.

"I hear you can offer me favourable odds for the game tomorrow night," she whispered.

"How did you hear something like that? I wouldn't peg you as a sports fan."

"A girl can always surprise you," she chuckled.

"It's right what you hear. I'm Russ, by the way."

She did not need his introduction, of course. Isla knew all about Russ Conway.

"Isla," she shook his sweaty mitts. "You can predict the future, can't you?"

"That's my deal. See that guy over there?" Russ pointed to a bumbling oaf on the furthest table to the right. "He's going to bump into that wall in a minute. He's so drunk. Just watch." He paused. "You're interested in sport?"

"I'm interested in money."

Russ released a notepad from the mahogany duster draped over his seat, slipping it into the woman's grasp with a sly hand.

"Norway's set to win against Gibraltar. Here's how this works. You lay down some money now. I do the dirty work for you. Two hundred quid. If Norway wins, which I guarantee they will, you get the money."

"They're not going to win though, are they?"

"Eh," he remarked at the sudden shift in her tone.

"You think you're the modern Nostradamus, but if you were so skilled at predicting the future, you should have seen this coming."

The bumbling oaf bumped into the wall. Isla pulled a pair of handcuffs from the one pocket in her dress, and heads turned when she grappled with his neck, smashing his face onto the oak bar before he could reach the next swig of whiskey. With the beat of a drum, the chains wrapped around his wrists as she pulled him up. The grip of the cuffs was loose, so he managed to run, but no worries, because…One click of her finger later…The steely bite of metal crunched against his veins, and no amount of hip thrusting against the purple glaze could liberate him from their stronghold.

"Who's the snitch, huh?" he asked, as his former debonair was replaced by grinding teeth and snarling vocals. "Name him!"

"You gave yourself away, mate."

"You're Defence E, aren't you?"

"Damn right. Isla Daye. People call me Quickfix. Why? I'm sure if I clicked my finger, I could show you." And flash!

A sleek brown Edwardian courtroom. Jury to the left, judge in the centre, Russ in the defendant's box, with his back turned, at first, to Isla, chuckling in the front row. The Judge's gavel slammed against the oak podium with reverberating ferocity. The furious discharge of a guilty verdict - so brief yet so destructive. He swivelled around, noticing Isla tightening the polyester bow on her changed outfit, much to his chagrin. Sighs of relief, mixed with groans of despair, erupted across the court as the fraudster discovered his punishment entailed having to pay back every penny he had taken from those whose trust he had exploited, though at least he could avoid a stretch inside. He waved his fists at her cartoonishly. This was a promise of retribution. His mouth cursed Defence E with words shaped but never spoken.

Another snap returned her to *The Destination*, a few seconds after the arrest. Explosions of indigo light flashed past the dingy street as Russ was carried away by green vested bobbies. She found great satisfaction in moments like these, turning the clock, letting time do its work. Time bobbed away on her wristwatch as she concerned herself with returning home. Sapphire would be waiting for her, perhaps watching TV, perhaps doing something more important. What she didn't expect was a grand swishing noise to come from the skies. Was it a bird? The rumble would suggest something more manmade. Was it a plane? No, it was Carim Shafiq.

His steel capped boots landed on the pebbles directly outside Isla's doorstep as he descended from his airborne home. Isla's grin would indicate she was pleased to see him. Having just completed a day at work, Carim held onto his outfit, a tin suit of armour from which vague sunlight bounced, and the steel staff in his left hand. In his right, the helmet that had been removed from its regular position, fully padded with a crimson feather flowing from the headpiece and holes for where his pretty brown eyes would fall.

"I hope I am not disturbing you," asked a voice which retained its crooked charms, matching with his expression's morose attributes. His hands were to his side, while hers were posed honourably at her hips.

"I just got back from taking down a con man. I'm feeling in the mood for celebration. Would you join me?"

"If you refer to partaking in an alcoholic beverage, then you should know I do not drink."

"You drink hot chocolate though, don't you?"

"Have you eaten yet?"

"You're just here for a slice of Sapphs's Shepherd's Pie, don't you?"

"Of course I am!"

"God knows why."

A delicate throat cleared itself, alerting Isla to their eavesdropper.

"Something wrong with my cooking?" asked the roommate.

"Nope," Isla bumbled. "I was talking about…a different woman's cooking."

"Which woman's cooking have you been sampling?"

"I'm digging myself in a bigger and bigger hole here, so Carim, I'll turn my attention to you. What brings you here outside of working hours?"

"I wanted to talk," Carim replied.

"And to eat Shepherd's Pie!"

"Of course."

"I have some leftovers," Sapphire announced. "Why don't you come on in?"

This was a home, unlike the flats at Woodville, with three neat and tidy bedrooms, no mould in sight in the ensuite, and a great deal of materialism which the pair of hard workers believed they deserved. Sapphire plated up a hearty plate of batch-cooked swill, sliding the dish over to Carim, who had removed his armour to reveal a plain white T-Shirt. Isla, meanwhile, grappled with a wine bottle, having already distributed cocoa into Carim's mug, but even the corkscrew did nothing. Carim's chair squeaked as he excused himself, making his way to the kitchen. His eyes gathered momentum, lighting forlorn brown into roaring amber, and a ray of golden light extended from his golden peepers. The cork clicked as the beam forced it from its place, allowing Isla to dispense the fluid into two equal portions.

"Two superheroes at my dinner table!" Sapphire chortled when they reached the spherical seating area. The redhead always gave away the most awkwardly eager expressions. "Should I feel intimidated?"

"You'll be in a great position if anyone tries to hurt you," Isla remarked, "so you should probably feel safer than you've ever felt before."

"Wonderful! The Knight and Quickfix. Do people call you by those names?"

"The papers do," Carim replied.

"Oh, the bloody papers. Exquisite wine by the way!"

"Any wine is nice wine," Isla commented. She'd purchased the bottle herself on payday.

"The press gives the police a hard time, but I've seen how hard Isla works."

"Bloody hard! On top of that, I've got my parents to contend with."

"How did you two meet?" Carim asked as he poked his fork around the last inches of his meal. Before he could finish, a guest joined them at the table, a tabby Persian longhair with more fur than whiskers. She leapt onto Carim's lap, and a sneeze exploded from the superhero's lips, leading Sapphire to spit blood (well, a glass of delicious red, but an outsider may perceive it to be blood) onto the table which remained there for the rest of the night.

"What is so funny?" asked Carim as he shooed the creature away.

"What sort of a superhero is allergic to cats?"

"We all have our vulnerabilities!"

"You can fly and you can punch steel and nothing will happen but Whiskers Galore comes over to you and it causes you to sneeze! Blimey, that's ludicrous."

Isla stroked the cat when it brushed against her legs, and Carim felt its aflame eyes burning into his, making him shudder. Unlike Sapphire, Isla restrained her laughter.

"Anyway, as I was saying, back in Aldgate, I wanted to learn more about my powers, and they split us off into groups. People with cognitive abilities, temporal abilities, then there was us, the ones who played with time. Me and Isla were both cockneys, and both bored, so we got talking."

"And then you made me lasagne," Isla intervened.

"A lasagne that you said you liked! Little white lies still hurt."

"Don't take it personally, mate." Then to Carim, "What did you come here to talk about then?"

"The new boss starts tomorrow," Carim declared. "Are you ready to meet him?"

"I'd say I'd think Petula had chosen the right man for the job, but I have my doubts after Morris. I hear the new guy's a military man."

"Indeed he is. At the end of the day, as long as we get in there, and do our jobs, save the North from criminals and hoodlums, then what more can they ask from us?"

"You should know by now that they will always ask for more."

Carim left his knife and fork in the correct correlation and rubbed his full belly. The lack of leftovers, Carim suggested, was "A sign of a good meal." Isla did not agree.

"Did you see that documentary on TV last night?" Sapphire asked them both. Without the strains of meal prep, Sapphire occupied much of her time watching television, simply to cure the boredom.

"What documentary?" asked Isla, after collecting a newly decanted glass of rosé.

"They say the light's going out. At Stonehenge. They say it's only a matter of time before it starts taking its toll. People are losing their abilities."

"It's all hocum," Isla declared. "The light has been a part of our lives since…what was it…1350, or something?"

"1347. Black death. It was a documentary by Billy Chapelle."

"It's all something to generate conversation between people like us, intended for when we drink. Who is Billy Chapelle?"

"You wouldn't have heard of him. He says more people are becoming unblessed each day. Scientists have always feared it might happen."

"I can't see that it's anything to get our knickers in a twist about!"

"Believe it!"

At the doorstep, about two hours after Carim's arrival, The Knight returned his steel plating to his body and prepared to whisk himself into the skies. It was while Sapphire sped through the washing up that they had the opportunity for covert conversation. She slammed the door and led him into their back garden, where night's globe let reflections bounce off the trickling water feature. In said mirror glass, he encountered the image he sought to escape, his dearly departed brother. He shook his head, shaking it away.

"I didn't want to ask in there, because I didn't think you'd want Sapphs knowing," Isla said, "but how's it going with the…" whisper.

"I am getting closer."

"I can't believe you're gonna be a dad! It's ace!"

He shushed her. "I thought we were meant to be keeping down!"

"Yeah I know, but how are you feeling?"

"Excited, of course I am. It is what I have always dreamed of, but can I do it right?"

"You'll smash it, mate!" She grazed her knuckle against the bed of his arm. "You're a literal superhero."

"I just want to give a child the life I was never able to have. I can do that now. I just need to convince the adoption agency that the perils of my job will not stand in the way."

"You'll find the right kid," she promised with a gentle smile. He nodded and fled into the pale mist of the night. Isla waved at him as if he was close enough to see her.

Isla had skipped backwards and forwards already, and she had only been awake for an hour. Time was making her head numb, so she felt the need to sit down. She retreated to her chamber, meeting Sapphire's vehemence, and tucked into the next sip of wine, which made up her supper.

A day in the life of a superhero is an exhausting one, and there were still sixteen hours left of it. She would skip sleep, skip breakfast, and take herself forwards twelve hours, where Deansgate fire station promised an encounter which would change her professional life.

3.   The Guards

Back at the orchard, Kenny remained by Elijah's side while Elijah, as instructed, rocked back and forth, each foot slightly ajar, sipping water at regular intervals. Never did anger reach his indifferent expression, even when he considered what his densely built friend had once done.

The moment replayed in his mind which everybody else forgot. The bullet went off like a confetti bomb. His father showered in the lead he fired. Back to the present.

Certain areas of the orchard had been better managed than others, so stray vines kept certain less admirable hidden. Among them was the west corner, where a bushy limb protruded from its base, unseen. Elijah's attention was instead focused on the screen that embellished the gate, akin to a ring doorbell on which a live recording played while Kenny glared aimlessly into the wilderness. Sometimes the Ottomans would patch through, at other times the Soviet Union, but today the chief of Hull's resident police force, Petula Wednesday, was on the line.

"Excuse me, a second," Elijah said to Petula – a reliably miserable woman, as could be expected from somebody with a weekday for a surname - and pulled back the bramble which had obscured Winona. Miss Barton brushed the ashes of the surrounding grass from her trouser legs, bumbling as if to pretend that she had not been peeping on them. Petula's grey solemn snarl indicated that she was watching on, while Kenny, lost in whatever daydream ensnared him, remained inattentive to the boss's impatience.

Winona pulled herself from the bushes with a slight skip.

"Kenny, there's a woman in this bush!"

With that, Kenny broke his trance's hold, swaying his neck back and forth. "What? Where?" He could not have turned quicker, but his elation morphed into disappointment when he noticed the scrawny destitute.

"Oh, it's only Winona Barton," wheezed Kenny.

"Yes. Winona Barton, spying on us through the hedges."

"You seem disappointed," replied Winona. "You lost your bachelor buoyancy ever so suddenly, you sexist pigs."

"Big words there," Kenny grunted. "Harsh words."

"Is there something disappointing about me, Mr Farrow?"

"You're gonna think I'm a misogynist or something if I explain my disappointment."

"You're running that risk either way!"

Kenny, speaking in a macho cadence so deep that it was practically fabricated. "Elijah said there was a woman in the bush."

"Digging yourself in a hole here, mate," Elijah warned.

"I ain't saying you're not attractive. You're a teacher. You know, like a typical teacher. You'd probably grade a rump in the sack once it was finished."

"You won't have to worry about that," Winona replied.

"Don't anger him," Elijah joked. "He's got a rifle."

"A bloody big rifle too," the misogynist winked.

"Excuse me while I heave!" exclaimed Winona.

A brief but husky cough reverberated behind them as Petula's speech patterns bobbed up and down like a heart monitor. "I haven't finished yet."

"I had a few questions," stated Winona.

Then came Petula's voice, "I said I hadn't finished yet!"

"What, are you a journalist now or something?" Barked Kenny. "What is it you want?"

"Have you ever thought about leaving this place?" Winona asked. "Surely you'd have the authority."

Kenny twisted his head back to check that Winona and Elijah would be engaged enough to not turn their attention back to him, and their eager mutters suggested as much.

"Nobody has the authority, ma'am," Elijah insisted.

"There's a boy in my class. I'm worried about him. He's starting to have doubts about this place."

"Keep your voice down! You know who that is on the screen, don't you?"

"The woman with the cane? The head of Defence E."

"Exactly!" He drew Winona's shoulders towards him. "You can't let her hear us! You should know how serious she takes the safety of this place, and particularly the people outside of it. Of course I've never thought about leaving, and if I ever wanted to, I wouldn't be able to. These gates are too stiff to ever be opened, and Defence E would be called by the alarm if we ever could."

"If it's so impossible to escape, why did Kelly have to die?"

Kenny's head bowed in shame. The noise of the ricochet rang out in his head once more. Shaun's death, his father's murder, replayed in Kenny's mind. Petula had wiped this from the history books, alongside all the others who were murdered. Kenny couldn't recall anyone called Kelly ever living in Woodville, but he did know that Winona's secondary school teacher died and everybody thought a heart attack caused it. No, it was the bullets from his rifle.

"If Hex tried to get through…"

"Hector Croft?"

"Yep. If he tried, would you shoot? If he caused a scene, I mean."

"I'm here to deal with crime. Luckily, in this place, we don't get much crime. I only shoot to kill if there's a threat to life."

In that Dickensian 'utopia', crime rarely saw the light of day. Everybody chuckled and ate soup together to overcome the boredom. The shortage of weapons minimised the opportunity for dissent. Whatever Elijah and Winona had been discussing did not matter, because the conversation had resolved itself. Elijah joined the pair, wrapping his hand around the stock of his firearm.

"You best get home," Elijah demanded.

"How long is your shift?" Winona asked.

"Ten hours. Might be longer yet. It's baked Alaska night, and Mum will probably make too much when I get to the fridge at 3 in the morning. I don't want to have to deal with that again."

"Can't beat baked Alaska night." Elaine cooked for the resident cafe, and her baked alaska was top of the dessert menu, which Winona treated herself to every Christmas Eve. "What is the secret ingredient again?"

"You'd have to ask her! My guess is marmite."

"We'll keep an eye on Hector for you," Kenny promised. "Come on, I'll walk you home."

"I'll be fine," Winona skipped the chance to walk home with the "altruistic gentleman" who offered out his arm. "What were you talking to Petula about anyway?"

"She's just making sure everything's tickety-boo," Elijah replied. "She tells me there's a new boss at Defence E."

"Oh, better be better than the last one." Kenny added. "The scandal!"

He referred, of course, to Morris Bridges, the man who could manipulate people's minds to suit any agenda he deemed fit. You can assume that this power went to his head.

Winona approached the boundary, grazing her palm against the bronze structure. Before she could discern a means of unlocking the gateway, Elijah pulled her back.

"Home time," Elijah said, snapping her out of her haze. "Suzie will be waiting for you."

4.   Late Home

The clock on the mantle kept on ticking. Suzie, thirty-seven years of age, didn't seem the type to own a mantle. Agatha and Gordon did, being older citizens, but not her, with her luscious but unruly hazelnut hair and delicately lined visage. These qualities were attributes of youth, which she somehow retained in a place free of manicurists and skincare. To the side of the mantle was the alarm that would ring out if ever her attention was sorely required, and beside that alarm was a first-aid kid, fully stocked, as much as their stocks would allow. In case she was required, Suzie wore her blue Nurse's polo shirt with he white striped collar, ready for the worst, waiting in a home that was identical, almost brick for brick, to the Crofts' grim abode.

Already that morning, she had been called out to the butcher's, a man who wouldn't make another night. Later that evening, there would be further calls of great importance, but for now she only awaited Winona, who promised to be back by five. They had planned an evening run, to burn off the calories they had not yet consumed. Instead, Winona made her next priority the Newsagents, which also - thanks to the shortage of buildings - functioned as the grocer's, the supermarket, the florist's, and the free bookstore, with its books donated by unblessed charities. Deliveries came every Wednesday, following an intricate procedure involving outsider goods shipped to the front gate without the blessed ever making contact with the unblessed. By

Tuesday, even the lesser explored sections of the store – health foods and lottery tickets – would be ransacked. People stole and there was nothing the elderly manageress could do to stop them. Not even the men with the rifles intervened, because they understood the plight of their peers and their poverty. In fact, even Elijah had resorted to pinching supplies so he could profit his mother's business.

The Crofts refused to resort to such low methods, especially since Eva worked the stock and wished to avoid Aggie's stone-cold glare whenever possible. That Tuesday was Eva's day off, so it was up to Agatha to become an agent of the news in Woodville's poky store. There, Francis purchased a carton of milk and some cheese as a Tuesday night treat, before handing the machine his card. A grinding cross marked the transaction.

"You'll have to tap again," insisted Agatha. "Perhaps try putting in your pin this time."

Following a third failed attempt, Francis finally agreed to pop his card into the reader. Declined, again. Francis placed the block of cheese back and distributed a collection of coins onto the table to purchase the milk. When he swung around to swiftly depart, his chest collided with the body of his colleague, pushing his bowline specs back to his brow with an anxious twitch. They needed no more than a nod to acknowledge one another before parting in their separate directions, leaving Winona to drum her fingers against the counter. Agatha preoccupied herself with the refreshment counter, behaving as though she did not notice the wannabe customer.

The desk bell chimed with a clang that at first felt immortal, forcing the baggy-eyed cashier to turn her attention to Ms Barton. "I assume you can afford the transaction?" Agatha scowled. "I'm not the type to gossip, but your colleague couldn't."

"Sounds like gossip to me," Winona replied.

"How much do they pay you down at St Joseph's?"

"I don't think that matters."

Agatha returned to the stocks but kept her mind on the natter. "I don't have to work anymore, you know. I'm not a spring chicken anymore. You don't mind if I stack the shelves, do you?"

"I can wait." Forgetting Suzie was anticipating her return. "I've got nowhere to be."

"Aren't you going to buy something?"

Winona stopped, scanning the aisles. "Not what I came here for."

"It's a shop…"

"Yes, it's a shop, but a shop's not just for shopping."

"Of course it is! Otherwise it wouldn't be called a shop now, would it?. Buy something, or leave. I say this in the most polite way possible."

"Doesn't sound polite to me!"

"Buy something," she repeated, "Or leave. *Please*."

"Not much better, but I'll take it…I came here to speak about Hex."

Colour sprung into Agatha's muted complexion. There was something about the ajar manner in which she composed herself, hunchbacked, bent-chested, which should have sparked concern. With her abrupt pivot, a can within Agatha's fingertips crashed to the ground, accompanied by a fatigued groan. Winona picked up the dropped goods and handed it back to the till worker, but Agatha exhibited no expression of gratitude.

"Are you alright?" Winona asked.

Agatha grumbled. "Like I say, I'm no spring chicken anymore. It's my back, you see."

"My roommate's a medic. If it's something to be concerned about…"

"Gordon thinks it is, but he's making a problem when there's no need for one! You know what men can be like!"

"Unfortunately…But your Gordon has always seemed like a half-decent guy."

"What did you want to tell me about Hector?"

"You spend a lot of time with him, don't you?" They were making eye contact at last.

"Sweet boy. Very bright. I've been helping him out where I can."

"He said something concerning in today's assembly. He used a word he shouldn't have even known. Says he got it from you."

"You think I would be so vulgar?"

Yes.

"I'm going off what he said. I thought I'd ask: Do you think it's a lie? That we're only locked away in these compounds because the government is ashamed of us?"

Agatha leaned forwards, arching her back, something she should never do. Suzie, the only medic in the village, would be on hand with one phone call. Then

Agatha would have to face reality. Then she would have to question why she coughed blood on sleepless nights.

To answer Winona's question, Agatha reached for *The Morning Manifesto*'s latest edition. The headline: *The Old Bill comes for Old Phil*. It must have been a headline devised by Ruth Mayor and her encyclopaedic mind. How clever she was!

Agatha tapped on the photograph of the well-groomed chap on the front page whose practically plastic skin shone through even the confines of the front page.

"The politicians, the government, they're sleazebags and liars," Agatha spat. "Our Prime Minister could be arrested for syphoning off money from unblessed charities. The Shoreditch community went without bread last month because of him. Sure, the Queen wishes us a happy Christmas and the Tories pass a law every now and then to suit us, but is that really enough? We've got rotten lives here, and they're refusing to do anything about it."

"And that makes the disease fictitious?"

"It's a possibility."

"What about Hop?"

"Wha*t about* Hop?"

"He visited 1347 when the disease first spread. When the one percent became unblessed. It was true that there was a disease at the start, even if there isn't now. We're born weapons. The Unblessed, that's all we are. Weapons."

"The Police are puppets for the regime. You can believe me, or you may not."

"I'll choose not to, if I were me, which I am, thank God!"

"I'd say the same about the way the government treats the unblessed. I don't see the logic in there being a gate where, if we step beyond it, we melt away, but if we stay behind it, we're all dandy. It makes no scientific sense."

"It's for their sake, just as much as ours."

"More so. If you'll excuse me, I need to stack these shelves."

Winona followed Agatha around the store. She wouldn't let the old mare get away that easily. "I'm worried that if Hex believes you, he'll do something stupid."

"He's a bright chap."

"Chap! He's nine!"

"He knows better. If this fusty old bird isn't worth listening to, then he'll choose not to listen. Buy something or leave. I'm trying to run a business here and we hardly have a constant influx of customers."

Gifted with that choice, Winona left the vacant Newsagent's empty-handed. Taking the back route home through the cobbled street which were antiquated enough to warrant the lamplights which should theoretically have been prohibited by low expenditure, and along that path, only one thought rested in Winona's mind, a mind hardly exposed to enough experience to accommodate constant stimulation: What if Hex was right?

Winona saw Shaun Farrow's widow, Kenny's mother, wandering through the streets. She still cried every day since she'd lost her husband to an alleged heart condition that had previously gone unnoticed.

There had never been a body. The way Catherine Farrow grieved didn't seem right. None of it did. That's because Shaun Farrow was murdered when he tried to escape Woodville Estate. By his own son. Suspicious of this, Kenny's mother hadn't spoken to her son in many years.

Winona stormed back to the orchard when the wind began to settle, carrying herself in a strop. Elijah rocked back and forth to the rhythm of the evening while he hummed that song from The Meaning of Life, and then came the schoolteacher, in all her miserable glory. Kenny had popped up too. Maybe Kenny had never left. It wasn't like he had a life.

"What's up?" Elijah asked.

"Don't you want to know?" Winona questioned.

"Not this again!" grunted Kenny. He was the sort to have a cigarette lodged between the gaps in his teeth, if he could afford to have a cigarette lodged between the gaps in his teeth, that was. "She's going on about wanting to see what's beyond the gates again."

"You don't want to know what's out there," Elijah insisted.

"Maybe I do," Winona replied. "I can tell Hex that way."

"No, because you'll be dead." Kenny replied. "Dead as a…"

"Doornail?"

"I was going to say Dodo…"

"Winona, you've got to get this idea out of your head," Elijah's voice softened and his face became warmer. "There's nothing out there for people like us. Nothing besides death."

Winona arrived at the screen, plugging her dumpy fingers into every slot they would fit, instigating a few murmurs from the mechanisms. A slight click. Elijah's rifle.

"You're not going to shoot me," Winona muttered with her back turned. "Not after what happened to your father."

Kenny shuddered. "How did you know? Nobody can know."

"Educated guess. If they wanted us all to forget that people had tried to escape before - wiped those people off the face of the Earth - then the ones responsible must have something to hide, and the answers are beyond those gates."

"I'll do it," Elijah replied. "You know I would."

"You won't," Kenny said. "You're shaking too much for that."

"You've always thought I was a coward!"

"Never have I called you a coward."

"You don't have to. You just have to look at me and show it."

Kenny lunged at Elijah, and the rough expressions of the two alpha males collided.

"You two!" Winona snapped. "Cut it out!"

"You're not gonna hotwire those buttons," Kenny said. "I'm not going to help you."

"Yes you are, because you're as intrigued as me, Kenny, and there's nothing for you here."

"There's...That's not true!"

"You want a purpose? We can find purpose. We can step out those gates and we can find it. Jobs, homes, you name it. Escape this half life and enter a whole one."

"We'd die. End of story."

"How long have you been here now, doing this job?"

"Four years," Elijah responded.

"Six years," Kenny followed.

"A long time," Winona replied.

"Too long."

"You've never wanted to open that gate and see what's beyond the walls? Don't lie to me."

"No, we've got brains."

"But have you got guts? I just need to know, and it needs to be me. Someone with nothing to lose. I can't let it be Hex."

"You've got a job," Elijah remarked. "And a house, and friends. Could be worse. And you've changed your tune too!"

"Then let it be worse. Who knows what will happen if I don't take this chance? What could we be missing out on?"

Winona let impulse ride her, and it appeared Kenny was about to do the same. Brash, but rarely impressionable, the apish attendant unbuttoned his black jacket and hurled it onto the grass. Elijah couldn't believe his eyes.

"To hell with it," he said. "Let's see what's out there."

"Kenny!" Elijah grumbled.

Winona smirked. "Why the change of heart? Doesn't it make you a hypocrite?"

"It's what Dad would have wanted."

Elijah, embracing the mood of rebellion, flung off his overcoat too and swung down on the iron door's steel grip. It was stiff, but he ushered his comrades to help him, so they huddled around him, bringing all their strength to the proceedings. The gate creaked open, exposing the unrestrained sunshine which they had been hidden from for so long; its glare forming in their eyes. It felt great to be free.

They could have done this long ago – anybody could – but the prospect of bullets prohibited them. The exterior unravelled, revealing a field of grass and hay which stretched on for miles. Storms caused blades of grass to whimper, but blue remained the mood of the sky. Leaving their coats behind them, the march commenced. Elijah's industrial boot stepped from concrete into meadow. Freedom reached them. The air felt fresher than it ever had before.

The gate light flickered vermilion. A hounding alarm shrieked, bellowing to itself. Too late to turn back now.

5.   <u>The Gathering</u>

Deansgate Fire Station - Defence E's temporary headquarters.

There was once a time when they met in abundant towers and stylish abodes. For whatever reason, they had become the runt of the litter. Isla arrived at the swank and scarlet exterior a few minutes late. For somebody who could control time, she was surprisingly poor at keeping it.

There were mumbles coming from upstairs which conveyed signs of life. She dressed in full regalia, as instructed. Her white top was branded with a large, three-dimensional 'E' on the chest. Behind her, a sequined cape that carried white and gold behind her. Chalky trousers and arctic monk shoes completed the ensemble. She looked ridiculous, although she guessed that was the point. Petula, their former boss with the black cane, had the luxury of civilian clothing while they put up with ludicrous dresswear.

The first person that greeted her was a lady with glasses who was too small to be of average height. She perched behind a coffee table with her mouth against the phone. The language of the day was Italian, presumably, from the ciao's and arrivederci's passed down the line which Isla recognised from her languages degree. Beth was the faithful receptionist who could speak any language without thinking. This allowed her to establish Defence E's national and international contacts. To date, she was the only person on record with this ability, surprising her parents when her first word at eighteen months was 'Madre' and not 'mummy'. Isla asked where she needed to be, directed by a left-facing hand up a staircase composed of industrial blocks. Beth was too busy speaking to the Carabinieri to embark on a conversation.

For somebody so able, a staircase shouldn't have been so difficult to climb. The colossal steps made her breath wheeze, and she became tempted to skip time to the point where she reached the summit. Overusing her abilities would only drain her more, and she could do with the exercise. Rumbles of conversation became more perceptible once she reached the peak. Defence E, all dressed in colourful iterations of her uniform, appeared in a blank room deprived of everything other than a coffee table. On that table rested a stash of untouched brownies and a jug of water. Isla's first action involved suffocating a cup with an ocean of Adam's ale.

"You're late," grunted Hop in his signature, thick as clotted cream, Scottish tongue.

Hop remained in his chair, palms clasped, back rested, with his blonde hair and blue eyed combination. Carim, the more approachable of the pair, rose from his seat to shake Isla's hands. His mitts were sweaty from exercise, which didn't calm Isla's escalating nerves. He forced her into a hug, the sort of embrace two best friends would exchange. His lips twinkled, delighted to see her.

Carim was a model-like man with skin so smooth that anyone would think he had been carved. Syrian and twenty-seven, with eyes that sparkled with such a bright shade of azure that the colour must have been artificial. His attire was made from blue steel, as opposed to the silk fabric of Isla's dresswear, and a metal rim surrounded the central 'E' on his chest. His hands were at his hips and his stance allowed him the image of being innately dashing.

Three seats were occupied, but two were empty. This was a meeting of five where only three people were present.

"Where's The No Man?" Isla asked as she sat down to Carim's right.

"Right over here!" announced an unidentified voice. Isla faced the direction the vocals had come from. A cactus rested on the third chair, green and prickly like any other cacti but, unlike other cacti, had a voice. Most oddly of all, it also had a Northern accent.

"Don't tell me he's in the cactus," asked Isla.

"Of course he's in the cactus," replied Hop with a roll of his eyes.

"I could've been the glass of water, but you'd drink me then," said The No Man. "Have you tried my brownies?"

"I'm on a diet," replied Isla.

"You're always on a diet when I bring in food!"

Hence his name, The No Man didn't have an official title, or he'd kept it secret for the six years that he'd known his associates if he did. Only his backstory - that he had spent his early years in a mental asylum for superheroes - had been disclosed. It was either that he was ashamed of himself, or that he thought his identity was none of their business.

"I dread to think what's happening to his carrot and peas when he switches," Isla said.

"Is that some sort of cockney rhyming slang?" asked The No Man.

Carim swiftly changed the subject. "When's the boss getting here?"

"The boss is sunning it up in a lakeside resort in Crete," said Hop, rolling his R's like a bowling ball.

"Petula's not our boss anymore," replied Carim. "You need to get used to the idea that she's gone." He reverted to Isla's question. "Very soon, apparently."

"Oh, goodie!"

"You can't miss Petula so much that you've resorted to that degree of sarcasm," Isla remarked.

"Sarcasm defines me. Besides, she changed our lives, so I think it's only fair."

The walls were thin enough to make every conversation transparent. Beth was nattering away with gentle oscillations fit for a receptionist. She spoke to Defence A, an organisation based in London which was established in 1829. Defence B was in Edinburgh, Defence C in Dublin, Defence D in Cardiff, and Defence E in Yorkshire. On top of that, international organisations - top secret which everybody knew about, were hidden in plain sight.

The fire station entrance flew open to the point that it almost left its hinges behind. Despite being upstairs, the quartet heard the steady gust of wind and the boastful Arabic conversation which followed. One voice in the discussion belonged to Beth. The other - a low, well-measured organ - was alien to them all. Footsteps followed, agile as a feline.

"He's coming up the stairs," announced Carim.

"I can hear that, Mr Exposition!" replied The No Man.

For the superheroes, the climb up the mountainous staircase culminated in a breathy halt. These dense footsteps, however, detected no struggle in reaching the top. A shadow lingered at the aperture. The white gateway that Isla had entered through came to house their new leader. He was a tall but contained dark-haired and dark-mannered figure who wore his open-collared suit as if it were the only facet that made up his identity. Reinforcing his industrial persona were the hands clasped behind his back and the bend of his tortoise neck. His presence commanded such silence that it felt wrong for Carim to clear his throat. Ethan sauntered for some time, until he stopped, right ahead of them, gaze steely and fastened. Fastened on Isla, whose heartbeat was rising. Fastened on Carim, who felt the remote attributes of fear, an emotion foreign to him these days. Ethan's navy jacket was adorned by a splattering of gold from the medals he boasted. His boots were steel capped, and his shoulders were densely built like a weightlifter's. The indifferent posture of his lips rarely wavered and his facial muscles seldom twitched.

"Introductions are unnecessary to me," Ethan announced, in a thick, gravelled moan. "I know what I need to know about you. I should hope you respect this job enough to have taken the time to read up on me. My role here is to keep you on a leash. I am more than capable of that. You should know that if you completed your reading."

"It's like being in year one at school again," Isla murmured.

The No Man raised his hand. Nobody could see it, so the gesture made no difference. "What if we didn't do the reading?"

"I know I didn't," said Hop, still slouching.

"You will receive a demonstration." He clicked his fingers at Carim. "On your feet, soldier!"

Carim rose, mimicking Ethan's undeviating posture. Ethan approached, pacing steadily until he reached Carim. Ethan's breath hovered over Carim's face and his nostril hairs saluted. His heart rate was well above average. Ethan remained silent for about half a minute, waiting until Carim appeared disciplined enough to lose his immaculate stance.

"You call yourself the Knight, don't you?"

"Yes, sir, yes I do."

"Don't whimper in front of me! Knights don't whimper."

Ethan, of course, was referring to the salute which Carim was about to issue. Carim didn't issue a salute which would have been indicative of subservience. Instead, he nodded.

"I want you to race towards me as quickly as you can," Ethan said.

"I beg of your pardon?"

"So British! Such fear! Come on, quickly!"

Carim didn't hesitate. Ethan, from the way he authorised his commands and positioned his stance, wasn't the sort to issue orders only for them to be dismissed. The Knight's hand rested on the iron plate on his heart. The 'E' on his chest inflated, converting into silver. No longer was his top a steely blue, as his entire body twisted into metallic armour. Everything was made from tin except for his head and his hands, which preserved his natural complexion. His cloak danced behind him like a butterfly. His arms bent into a sprinter's pose. First, he geared up by sprinting on the spot. Then, his stationary jog transformed into a mad dash. His eyes raged with a golden yellow expression. A wooden lance formed at his side which became his companion. The closer Ethan got, the more obscured he became. A slight lump of vomit formed on his palate. Ethan's hand extended to Carim, and Carim halted in his place. No amount of acceleration could keep the North's greatest hero moving. Carim had read the files - he knew what Ethan was capable of. Ethan didn't have to explain how his eyes changed from oak brown to daylight yellow, nor why his eyeballs captured an inferno. An identical lance formed in Ethan's fingers and glistened with red rage. Carim was forced to the back wall when the weapon targeted him, and the vinyl surface pummelled his skull.

Hop burst out laughing, pleased to see Carim's default look of valiance wiped from his face, with a tear to wipe away instead. Hop's mocking cackle was slow but succinct. Carim didn't have an ego, but Hop was jealous of his unmatched strength, so this pleased him considerably.

Isla was next. Again, Ethan weaponised eye contact and staggered breath to display ascendency. She slouched on her chair, but he throttled her wrist, forcing her to stand, chucking her down.

"Let go of me," she protested, wrestling against his muscular grip. She faced the watch on her wrist, spiralling the short hand with a glance alone. Time was freed from its linear asylum. She entered a vacant room. Her limbs felt limp. The faint waft of burning hovered around her nostrils. No colleagues, no cactus. Just Isla and Ethan in limbo.

Isla wasn't like Hop. She rarely worried about the rules of time. So many alternative versions of events existed on the same plane thanks to her manipulations. Time ran by her rules, but not anymore. Ethan placed his palm on her wrist, creating a tumbling spiral.

The building was gone, replaced with a pile of bricks which surrounded her and a blaze encircled them. A flame abundant with smoke, too late to be expunged. Beyond the horizon was Hotel Hilton – a local rip-off of a familiar chain - standing at half its former size. Her hands were before her eyes, observing a hideous sight. Her formerly pristine complexion had vanished, replaced with wrinkles and warts which reeked of age. Any mirror would place her at eighty-five. Her hair was grey instead of scarlet. Her fluorescent grin was replaced with permanent cynicism. The blaze was all around her, but she was powerless to move. Her leg was held by a cage for the arteries - a boulder amongst the debris. Ethan leered over her in his intact uniform while Isla's clothes were fit only for a slave.

"Where the ding dong bell are we?" Isla asked, cockney accent withered to mush.

"Somewhere beyond the reach of your abilities," Ethan announced. "The far future."

"I ain't no time traveller. That's Hop's thing."

"You're right. Hop's a time traveller. You could be too, but you choose not to use your powers to their full potential."

"Help me up!"

"You know how we get out of here. We turn back time as we turned it forward. You're not strong enough, though, are you? You can turn back time in hourly instalments, two hours at most. But in years? You could be so much more than a quick fixer. You could be a god."

"You like the sound of someone with that much power?"

"On my team? Of course I do. I can't say I trust you with that immense responsibility. Let's take you home."

A whirlwind returned them to their former habitat, and Isla was relieved to see the talking cactus and the wounded knight. Isla's leg remained stiff, but was free from the boulder, though bound by the memory.

The same process followed for Hop. Intense staring, intense breathing. Hop refused to stand or surrender to fear. He crossed his legs and waited for Ethan.

"Transport yourself back in time," Ethan demanded.

"What if I don't?" He grunted.

"You're too much of a coward to run the risk of finding out."

Hop closed his eyes and shot through the colour vortex of simmering purple and green. His body remained still but he felt himself traversing eternity's protracted avenues. He felt the icy breath of winter on his neck, causing him to rub his nape. The desolate sky became free from colour and disposition.

Bass groans droned at an inescapable low pitch. Foghorns rumbling, misty lights flaring He was alone amid the battleground, surrounded by incoming Luftwaffe. Screaming soldiers raced across impromptu settlements to reach their trenches. To the North of him was a bunker, a concrete vault of bricks and mortar. He picked up his pace, following the soldiers to escape the bombardment overhead. Sprinkles of smoke crowded behind him and nearly caught his feet on the rocky terrain. It was like one of those nightmares where moving is impossible no matter how much you try. His loosened laces caught on the gravel. He noticed the bombs from above, forming into tangerine clouds. A figure towered above him, immune to the discharge of ammunition. Ethan, like a ghost, extended his hand for Hop to clasp, and every speck of sky formed anew.

He was high in the mountains, nearly touching the sky. He felt as though he was moving, but it took time to understand how. Rocks of mouldy orange were eclipsed by the sun. Hills of dusky grey soared over him. The rare patch of linear ground promised to scatter into instability in time. The glory of Kuju at sunset was distilled by an infantry of armour-clad, spear-wielding soldiers. Their horses were galloping towards him, as were those of the opposition. He was in the middle of two armies, with their swords pointing in his direction. He had only just noticed that he too was on a stallion's loin, metal shield over his forearm, galloping at racing momentum.

The Mongols were masked, except for one, who removed his helmet to reveal Ethan's visage. Two hordes of horses sprang at one another. The Mongol's axes were glowing with luminous pink which showered from the tip like water from a hose. Hop's fellow men were drenched in death; skin burning, flesh rotting. Their screams ignited. Neither side could win this battle. One side had a flame-breather, and the enemy was armed with a human bomb about to detonate. Hop didn't have to worry about the resolution. Ethan returned him to the colour vortex and before he knew it, he had better things to worry about.

A rope throttled his neck, fastened so stiffly that he thought his Adam's apple might burst. A ripple of gasps erupted across the audience. His pulse accelerated. Oxygen defied him. The executioner didn't need to cut the rope, because one regal hand gesture would do the job. To his left, three bare-boned prisoners who smelt of decay simpered through whatever energy was left inside their brittle bodies. Their sternum was visible through their skin, their legs and arms as thin as matchsticks. They were the unlucky ones, the one per cent, the prisoners of a civil war motivated by their existence. Hop worried that the crumbling sign, 'Andersonville', would be his eyes' final feast. Ethan was dressed in a uniform fit for a guard, expression unbroken. With a click of Ethan's fingers, Hop was back in the room. The right room, to be precise, where Carim had returned to his feet and Isla had caught her breath. Hop was the sort of time traveller who only used his abilities when he needed to. The future was a mystery to him, while any visit to the past was motivated by obligation. Hop wasn't an adventurous person like his father had been. Ethan had just made him grateful he wasn't.

Only the cactus remained. Ethan felt ridiculous puffing in the face of a barrel cactus in a soiled ceramic pot. The No Man acted on the cue of a glare. No longer was he inside of the cactus. He was the jug of water, exemplified by the irregular ripples in the potable pond. It only took a few moments for Ethan to disappear too. The other three, preoccupied with their traumatic endeavours, failed to question his withdrawal.

Suddenly, the walls started to shake. The floor began to tumble. The tables and chairs appeared to shudder. Cracks dawned on the vinyl surfaces, diminishing the deception of untarnished white. The others lost their footing as the floor indicated its collapse. Isla, formerly at the room's centre, was whisked to a nearby wall.

"Oh no," said the jug of water.

"That doesn't sound like an optimistic 'oh no'!" Isla cried.

"When does 'oh no' ever sound optimistic?"

"Good point!"

"Ethan can mimic our abilities. He's proving to us that he can reign us in. At the moment, he's using my abilities."

"Then why's the building shaking?" Carim asked.

"Because he *is* the building."

Ethan had infiltrated the bricks, the structure, and he was tearing it to pieces. One scream from Carim ceased the vibration. The property, less sound than it had been moments earlier, returned to its bygone stability, a few creases aside. Ethan brushed the cinder from his trousers, straightening his well-ironed outfit.

"Please know that it would be futile to refuse to follow any demands I issue," Ethan declared. "I can match your abilities and surpass them. Defence E is under my command now. Any opposition to my declaration of control will be met with punishment akin to a permanent rendition of what you each experienced. Do as I say, when I say it, how I ask it to be done." The others were frozen into cooperation. "Any questions?"

6.   Isla's Story

I won't ever forget the day I first met Petula Wednesday. Her matted grey hair was wrapped up into a bun, making herself known down the cobbled alleys past Brick Lane by her leather-bound black cane which foreshadowed every step she took. Her croaky voice should have been expected from a sixty-two-year-old, but I expected a woman of that much power to look more youthful. She surprised me – a dead-average Londoner - with the offer to join Yorkshire's defence force. That ain't an offer you pass on.

"What sort of a name is Petula Wednesday?* I asked her during our first of many encounters. "It sounds like some character in a film or TV show." I sort of thought that was the point.

I'd been ordinary before that. I had abilities like everybody else, but I took them for granted, like everybody else. Some wouldn't call me ordinary, because of how privileged I was. I went to Oxford and got a degree in Philosophy and Modern Languages. Not bad for a chick from Whitechapel, eh? When I was young, I'd see pompous ignoramuses bragging about their Oxbridge degrees, thinking of themselves as superior. I'd always muse that they weren't better. They couldn't save a life, or build a house, or find world peace. All they could do was drone on about Shakespeare and all the other nutters. Pop wanted the best for me, and when I got three A's, he forced me to scrap any other plans I had and shipped me off to Oxford.

Pop was a fishmonger; Mum was a hygienist. I use 'was' as if they're past tense, but they're still clinging on, if you consider living in a retirement community life at all. If it wasn't for my generous salary, Pop wouldn't have received the treatment he needed, and he might have died long ago. Apparently he was lucky. People don't usually go into comas when they've been stabbed. They usually recover pretty much immediately, or they die straight away. Pop was an exception, because

52

the mugger's blades were latched to his fingertips - a rather twisted superpower.

When I was seventeen, a bore of a man in a dapper suit interviewed me to ask why I thought I'd fit in at Oxford. I was lucky, because I didn't have to lie. They asked me about my extracurricular activities, and I told them about my training. I glared at the bronze walls, the bookcases, the fireplace, and even they were pretentious. I didn't feel I belonged there, but the bearded fossil disagreed. Moving out of London wasn't something I imagined for myself. Three years later, no wonder why, because I was back.

My parents had always wanted me to aspire to greater heights. Fair to say, I didn't get on well in Oxford, as I'd aspired from a young age to flex my more physical muscles, where my true talents lay. I told them that their trades were admirable and required a considerable amount of skill. My abilities were one of a kind and, according to them, so was I. I'd skip past the middle of bitter films just to relish in the joyous endings. I'd rush through the embarrassing nativities just to bask in the applause. Meanwhile, my parents had the most vanilla abilities there were: Lightning speed and underwater breathing. Abilities are a lucky draw, and they'd removed the shortest straws.

There's always been a museum at the end of my childhood road, which I visited at school. It's dedicated to the unblessed. I hear that inside of their compounds, they call themselves powerless. I visit now and again, whenever I want to learn more about them. We learned about the Civil War of the fourteenth century between the blessed and unblessed back in school, and I was always glad that the blessed won. Who knows what we'd be like if we didn't have abilities? I wouldn't be out there saving lives, for one. I'd probably be stuck in a stuffy office or serving ice cream in a van - not that there's anything wrong with either occupation.

Visits to the museum allow me to feel grateful for what I have. I don't visit often, because the paparazzi always follow me, demanding to know the inside story about Defence E's latest screw-up. I wish I could tell them to clear off, but Petula and Ethan care about my reputation too much.

I inherited my childhood home when my parents moved into the retirement community. They didn't want to, of course, but I told them it'd be good company. I sold the house right away and bought a joint with Sapphire right away.

Tending to the three-bedroom abode in Ripper territory became too much for them. Hampstead would suit them better. They're grumpier than they once were, and they hate that they've lost their independence. I vowed to look after them, which is why most of my money goes on their half-decent lives.

My home isn't anything to write home about, but it's enough for Sapphs and me, our Jack Russell terrier, Tracy Barker, and our Persian longhair, Whiskers Galore. Every week I visit them. Sapphire would bake a chocolate cake that would always make Pop – the diabetic – salivate. I'd bring the newspaper, and Pop would shower me in praise for what he'd read about me that past week.

Mum, on the other hand, I'd never been close with. We argued a lot when I was a teenager because rebellion is programmed in teenage DNA. Pop had always understood me, and any praise he offered made my lips twinkle. Pop would inevitably get the two bob bits and leave me and Mum alone. We wouldn't know how to talk to each other. Every compliment Mum gave was most likely a thinly veiled criticism about my hair or my weight. She'd always remark on how handsome Carim was, and whether he was my boyfriend yet. I'd tell her Carim wasn't attracted to women, or indeed anyone, which baffled her close-minded worldview.

I remember one exception to the rule, when we went to 'Ability Tower', the amusement park near Windsor. Basically, the whole gimmick is that the rides simulate how it feels to have different superpowers. There's a log flume where you can see what it's like to fly, and one where a guy stretches out your skin for you, so you feel like you're elastic. The worst was one where you could see what life was like for people with the ability to resurrect themselves. Nobody is immortal, but some people can die and then come back, say, seven times across their lives. They bring in some dude who can resurrect others, and they drown you, then they bring you back to life. You basically pay twenty quid to die. Entering the eternal black, and knowing it's more than sleep, really changes everything. You appreciate it all, and that's why me and Mum went out and got candy floss and we talked for hours. It only happened because we'd had our near-death experience that didn't come anywhere close to actual death, but it was the only time I felt anywhere near as close to Mum as I did to Pop.

The years following Oxford were dull except for the hours I'd spend at the Dojo. Like Jackie Chan, one leg would be lunged while the other extended and ready to kick. My palms were straight with the touch of death. Punching 'Aik', I'd scream as I released my inner rage. Take that, Mr Grimsby, the gym teacher who'd always branded me lazy! Bags, dumbbells, all to flex my muscles to maximum capacity.

My degree amounted to little more, in the end, than a few months as a transcriptionist and two years as deputy manager of a fast-food branch. Extracurricular activities and the grind of endorphins must have been what caught Petula's attention. The head of Defence E selected me because of the strength of my abs and the robustness of my mind. I suppose my fortunate, if a little average, upbringing did me wonders. I attended the gym every night. I became an exercise addict. I owed Pop that.

Thirteen years old, I made my promise. Alder Street. Pushed into a position no thirteen-year-old should be. Down the shop with Pop – or the lollipop, as we'd call it. We'd collect the paper, the groceries, any yellow sticker items we could find. We never went without, maybe because I was an only child and my parents had sustainable incomes. Tea and dessert on the table every night, snacks in the evening, and I never thought to be grateful because I never knew anything less. Whitechapel, despite receiving its reputation for obvious reasons, is a lovely place, but like all lovely places, not everything about it is sublime.

One man proved this: one with a tattoo of a skeleton scorched across his neck. You wouldn't need a degree in psychology to work out he was a victim of parental deprivation. I could relate him to some philosophical theory if I'd cared to remember anything I learned in my three years of study.

We strolled in swift paces, oblivious to the shadow forming behind us. We moved into a back alley, deprived of all but us three. The click of the finger knife was the only warning I had of the blade entering Pop's back. I would describe how it felt for him. His blood gushed, and his breath clambered, but I couldn't describe what he experienced because I didn't experience it. A thirteen-year-old without a clock on hand was helpless. We weren't underwater, so his aquatic breath was useless, as it was in any scenario other than his brief stint as a lifeguard in his late teens. The mugger pinched the wallet and rushed off so hastily that a few coins trickled on behind him and marked his path.

I rushed to the nearest phone box, conveniently only seconds away, to insert the coins we'd planned to spend on broccoli and marmite into the money pit. Pop was bleeding out by the time the aggressor we never caught had dashed away like a constipated penguin. Pop spent three weeks in temporary death in a hospital ward where even nurses with healing hands failed to soften the blow. He remained in a vegetative state for twenty three days, and a victim of Mum's never-ending concern. He still isn't quite right now. Sometimes when I speak to him, I can tell my words aren't reaching him. He looks at me and his expression is empty. He often stops speaking halfway through a sentence. He walks like his bones are about to shatter and I think about what could have happened if I wasn't there to call for help. Furthermore, I think of how different he'd be if I managed to discover the true potential of my abilities sooner.

This incident at Aldgate motivated my desire to save people. I'd failed Dad, so I resolved to never fail anybody else again. By the age of fifteen, I'd punched enough bags and released enough endorphins to complete a choir's annual quota of exercise. Academia claimed to be my strong suit, but physicality was my drive.

Pop woke from his slumber within weeks and recovered quicker than I did. My entire life is compensation for that moment when I failed to save Pop from what could have been his final moments. I considered myself a failure, but Petula Wednesday didn't agree. I could have rotated the clocks so that the attacker had never gotten to Pop, but I needed a clock to rotate time, and I hadn't been carrying a watch that day, nor had Pop.

Our schedule was rigorous but effective. We'd rise at five when thrushes still tweeted and when the dusty sun hadn't yet risen past the horizon. We'd shower in Antarctic chambers and gorge on a hearty bowl of muesli. An hour's run down a mucky field would follow. Then, three hours of uninterrupted cardiovascular activity. Never did my Oxford degree come in handy, not that Oxford is to blame. Philosophy never steered me, as it would some academics, scholars, or journalists.

I found my passion, and that's fighting crime. I'd spend my days tuning my abilities to their optimum capacity with Petula, in front of a clock. She'd become my motivational speaker, leaning over me with her iconic platinum cane firmly in situ. I'd squint to allow the clock to become a fugitive from time. I'd travel backwards seconds, sometimes minutes. If Ethan had been my teacher, maybe he would've told me how to go back far enough to stop the mugger. Petula didn't want another time traveller. She already had one of those in Hop. Hop always thought he was Petula's favourite, but the admiring look she often issued me with indicated otherwise

Never did the blank face of the mugger leave me behind, even if it became a blur. They never caught the man with a knife for an index finger and a machete for a pinkie. Our unit features a colleague who can access memories to decipher a criminal's identity and match those features to a current location, and that identified the mugger as Julian Clarke. Turns out he died of an overdose in Bradford. It irked me that he hadn't fallen at my titanium fists. If I could travel back, I'd kill him myself.

The first case I solved alone involved a woman capable of reducing victims to dust. She may have been difficult to catch with her single touch that could corrode a soul, but I caught her by pushing time backwards and forwards enough to confuse her. One kick forced her to the floor. One wrench of the handcuffs and she became an ordinary woman. Husband killer, son killer, dust bunny. Abilities are nothing in jail, taken on sentencing, and allocated back when the convict is released. I knew what I could do for Defence E. I made my parents proud, even if Pop's gotten to the stage of forgetting what he had for dinner last night.

To make up for my failure to catch the mugger, I devoted my life to catching criminals and saving lives. Maybe I could prevent another little girl from having to live with the same pain that has always defined me.

7. **Incoming crimes**

The vault which held the future crimes unit smelt of durian, and durian does not smell nice. Workers rarely left their computer desks. Visitors seldom stayed long enough to help out with cleaning. It was easy to see why. The curtains were down, and the eyes of the occupants were square. These were people who spent enough time indoors to be surprised when they discovered the outside world was made from atoms and not pixels. They knew no better than the darkness, so the miasma rarely bothered them.

The role of the future crimes unit was self-explanatory - to identify the attributes of given crimes before they were committed and passed information down to Defence E, granting ample time for the organisation to prepare their response.

Two siblings, Jack and Alison Naylor, plugged their minds into the system through a single prick of the temples. An extensive wire stretched from their brains to the CPU. They would close their eyes - watery and burning from indulgent quantities of screen time. Metallic green integers would surface to form a date and a time in which a crime would transpire. Their Puerto Rican associate, Jake Latimer, then emailed the details to the necessary contacts.

The Naylors were identical, especially when their thoughts bobbed along like capillary waves. Caucasian, with blonde pudding bowl haircuts, bald philtrums, and amber eyes. His face was feminine, but her shoulders conveyed masculinity. Their thin physiques and empty looks would imply exercise which they rarely resorted to. Jake, on the other hand, lacked their trim figure. Despite vague hints of good looks, Jake's baggy stomach undermined him. Staying in that one room, and gorging on pop chips every afternoon, must have caused the problem.

The image box was empty at first. The pixels clubbed together and convened into an imperfect correlation which formed a woman of pallid complexion, bird-like in appearance. On the other monitors scattered across the suite, the faces of two males, sharpened by patience. Latimer scribbled down their details on a pad of A4. Their names were appearing on the screen as he recounted the numbers that the Naylors recited in their trance-like condition.

About a quarter of an hour later, Ethan stormed in, making his presence known from the cyclone which his boots designed. Ethan was dressed in a crisp dinner suit, while Carim followed in more farcical attire. The pair discovered nothing other than dust and dusty people. Carim's stomach churned upon the sight of cheese strips eroding on the floor from lunchtime, adjoined with the cheddary waft of exposed feet. Calling this den bilious would be complementary.

Upon their arrival, Latimer's fingerprints chuntered across the computer keyboard. His slight shudder proved he was fearful of the leader's simmering scowl. Latimer knew, after a demonstration days before, what Ethan was capable of.

"I trust that everything's in order here," Ethan said, clearing the newfound cheddar coating from his footwear.

Latimer issued a sickly salute. "Yes sir! It's a pleasure, sir!"

"Don't be a suck-up, Latimer! I sense trepidation in your eyes. I only hope that anxiety will not affect your work ethic."

"No, sir. Of course not."

"This place should be spotless! What do we hire cleaners for?"

"We do not hire cleaners," Carim replied.

"Then you should be the one cleaning, Latimer! What is your purpose here anyway?"

"To assist with the mapping out of future crimes," Latimer revealed. "I can discover information about criminals through access to certain memories."

"I'm fascinated by your abilities, if not by you."

"How are the twins?" Carim questioned.

"As talkative as ever," Latimer sighed, glaring at the silent superbeings. "They've not said a word since their release."

"What have you got to report for me?" Ethan asked.

Carim's attention was fixated on the inseparable twins in the corner. Ethan, meanwhile, leaned over Latimer. Jake was slaughtering the keypad to retrieve the information they required. On a clean green page, those three faces appeared again. Latimer handed Ethan the slip of paper he had scrawled notes onto, attempting a curtsy which led Song to groan.

A Polynesian rat, hunchbacked, buck-toothed, had entered through a mould hole fashioned from penetrated brick. Two squeaks led Carim to shudder. He could blast the rodent's tail with his laser peepers, leading it to scurry back through the burrow it created. He didn't want to harm it. He definitely didn't want to kill it. The bloodshot eyes of the Naylors opened in unison while the twins gasped. The male partner's hand reached out into a grasp, ceasing the creature's infernal yapping. Silenced but not burst, the vermin descended into dusk before Ethan's head could even turn to notice.

Ethan's bark brought Carim back to focus. "Over here, Shafiq!"

Carim drifted over, dreamily, so used to self-powered flight that he only walked when there was no other option. "What crime have they been accused of?"

Latimer took the lead, adopting a formal tone. "All three are residents of the unblessed compound in Hull. They will escape from Woodville tomorrow, at approximately 6PM."

"It's finally time," Ethan muttered.

"Not a fan of the unblessed, I gather?" Carim asked.

"The moment they escape, they risk contaminating the rest of the world with their disease. The moment that occurs, everything we have built will be thrust into jeopardy. All abilities will be placed at risk. I dread to imagine a world where the blessed are wiped out."

"An epidemic of death and destruction?"

"There's no doubt about it. They must be stopped."

"What unrealistic command are you about to issue me?"

"Are you a pacifist, Carim?" A half-nod formed a response. Have you ever had to resort to violence? Radiation sprouts from your eyes yet I know you have never abused your abilities. You'd never wish to take a life?"

Carim turned to the hole which the rat had scurried through. He gulped. "I trust you are not calling me a coward."

"I can call you what I like, Shafiq. You're my property. The same applies to the rest of you." Reluctant nods from fellow apostles summarised the mood. Ethan turned back to Carim. "I expect you are aware of what I want from you."

"I'm worried that I am."

"We must be seen to be strong, Shafiq. The world is looking at us to become its salvation."

"If I do this, is it absolutely certain that the results will be free of consequence?"

"I can't predict anything beyond the next few hours," Latimer replied.

"Please, do not make me do this."

"Kill them on sight," Ethan demanded, in front of Latimer and the Naylors, fearless of the witnesses. "If you don't, everything humankind has worked for will be destroyed."

8.   The Reckoning

Shift workers woke like zombies forced to retire from their slumber once the grinding alarms gnawed every earbud in the district. Screens turned from soap operas to grassy knolls in no time.

Agatha, agent of the news, was busy shutting the community express at the time. The screen was on the news, discussing some scandal about petrol hikes, irrelevant to a community populated with pedestrians. Agatha expected the electricity bills must have accompanied a high upkeep, but it was in the legislation that the television in the Newsagents must remain on from open to close.

The same schedule as always: Spray, wipe, dry, reprice. Suzie was her assistant for the evening until the store closed at 9. It wasn't like Winona would be joining her. Eva was at home, on her sofa, son and wife in arms, watching a game show.

Sometimes Agatha forgot why she still worked there. Day in, day out, for fifty-odd years, her father's business, and his fathers before him. For the sake of legacy, she kept going. In need of a pastime, she kept going. The newsagents was all Agatha had and would ever have. Other than that, all she had was Gordon, husband of several decades, whose Shepherd surname she rejected so that she could keep the Churchill legacy alive.

Francis Swallow was their last customer for the day. He'd forgotten to purchase plasters earlier that evening when he'd come for milk and cheese. The machine faltered as usual. Francis swiped his bank card over the machine again.

"What do you think of the surname Swallow?" Agatha asked again. They had this conversation almost every time he came in. Agatha's memories were a mess. It wasn't that she was senile. Everybody in Woodville found it difficult to keep their memories intact.

"It didn't do me any favours in the playground, I'll tell you that," Francis edged into a laugh. "I don't suppose you have cigarettes?"

"You can't afford cheese, but you think you can afford cigarettes?"

"I can afford cheese. I've just bought cheese."

"Well, it's the plasters you can't afford then," she declared as she snatched the plasters from his grip. "Your card declined."

Francis noticed the screen's rejection, so he swiped again. Alas, no response.

"Excuse me a second," Francis said.

Francis retreated to the alleyway outside, and when he returned, he'd swipe his card again and it would accept his purchase. His neck tilted to the screen. Suzie's gormless expression dropped into a gawking grimace. Agatha's affect hardly changed, crossing her arms as usual.

"What's happened to the TV?" Suzie asked.

Agatha whirled back to observe the display, occupied by a wobbly recording of an open pasture. It resembled the grassy expanse beyond the gates. "It's giving me a migraine, whatever it is!"

"At last!" Francis exclaimed as the machine registered his payment. "Thanks, Agatha."

"Yeah," Agatha grunted abruptly, hardly an ambassador for customer service.

"To answer your question, it's difficult being called Francis Swallow, but I make do, as I've made do my entire life. The amount of times I've been asked if I suck or swa...Well, let's not be vulgar."

"You can go now. Shop's closing!"

A twinge of Agatha's back. She grasped her spine. A twang of pain.

"Are you alright?" Francis inquired, as if he knew for a fact that she was not.

"Dandy."

Suzie was right about the peculiarity of the broadcast. The camera was unsteady. A croaking breath became the soundtrack for the footage. The live recording turned to the right, painting an image of a dark soldier, rushing at more of a tempo than he could handle.

"Who's recording that?" Suzie asked as her tone became rickety.

"Must be Kenny," Agatha remarked. "Gordon says Kenny and Elijah have cameras built into their jackets in case of emergencies. This is probably broadcasting to every TV in the city. Surprisingly the government isn't keeping tabs on the broadcasts."

"Should we be worried?"

"If it's an emergency," Francis interjected. "Then of course we should be."

The recording focused itself again, focused on a blank canvas of opulent blue skies and ripe grass. Never was the camera completely set on its target. A swift head wobble hinted at Winona's presence. Suzie's ostrich neck leaned into the screen.

"That's Winona!" Suzie declared as her bony-faced friend appeared on the screen.

"I can see that," Agatha replied. "Hollow as a twig."

"Don't tell me they've got past the gates," Francis remarked.

"Good on them if they have."

"Are you serious? They're goners!"

"Oh, flipping hell, Barton," Suzie murmured. "*That's* why you didn't come home."

Screens beamed these images to every active screen in the city. Take the Crofts, creating a groove on their sofa. A distant recording replaced the game show they were engrossed in. Fearing the worst, Maeve wrapped her arms around Hex's upper face. She knew what would happen. He shouldn't see this. Eva glanced over, less concerned about their son. Agatha was right - shielding him wasn't the best option. The truth was favourable to shower-free mornings and boiler-free nights.

"I hope everybody is seeing this," Kenny said to every waking soul in the community. The camera lingered on heaving palisades of iron that stabbed the heavens. Attention sat on the crumbling sign at the entrance to Woodville Estate, directly outside the orchard. "That's where you all are, the unblessed community, and look at us. We've been outside for three minutes now. No boils on our skin. We haven't become lepers yet. I don't know how long they say it's meant to take."

Elijah continued. "They, as in the blessed, always claimed we'd die the moment we stepped beyond that gate. We'd collapse, burn, combust, whatever. Look, here we are, perfectly fine. It was all a lie."

Hex turned to his mother. "See?"

Maeve dived for the remote, but Eva snatched it before her wife could take it. Maeve felt like fighting, but she knew she could never beat Hull's taekwondo champion.

"He needs to see this," Eva retaliated.

"You've changed your tune. Then again, so has Winona."

"I'm just trying to protect you. All of us, for that matter."

A practically vacant landscape stretched as far as the eye could see. No unblessed escapee could reach the precious blessed from that distance. All that could be seen were sky and grass. A long walk was ahead to reach the city, but the trio's sighs retained stamina. If the community had a pub, the patrons would have cheered at their courage. Alas, no pub, because nobody could afford to drink.

"They're ashamed of us," Winona cried, the trembling lens now on her. "They've locked us away because we'll interfere with the government's statistics. So what? They don't want their world to be imperfect. That's what we are, imperfect. Isn't everybody?"

"Abilities may not even be beyond our reach," Elijah remarked. "I reckon there's a way we could get superpowers. That way, we could fight anyone who stands between us and what we want."

"I don't think I'd want abilities even if they were on offer. Look how much they've corrupted people. I believed the propaganda for too long. Hex, if you're watching, you were right." Hex smirked. Maeve groaned. "I need you to know that. I had to know. I'm the only one with nothing to lose. Sorry, Suzie."

"No problem," her roommate grumbled in the corner shop.

Elijah's family were watching on too, in the house below the Croft's. Thin floorboards made their panicked shrieks all the more audible. Elijah issued a wave to his family, even though the snarling rage heard at night from their abode indicated anything but adoration. Maeve wished she could see their faces to know if their expressions were anywhere near as frightened as hers. Terrified, not just at revolt, but at how quickly Winona had changed her mind.

The terrain was no longer empty. Clouds fluttered in the sky from where God made his impressions. Brown leaves danced in the wind's swift tumble. Something was coming, and it was a man in spandex. At first, he swayed with the skies, refusing to let his feet drop to the grass. Eventually he descended, allowing the steel lance to form in his fingertips, and his blue steel dresswear transformed into an outfit befitting a Knight.

At the end of the grassy expanse, one look blurred the gate they'd escaped from. There was a hilltop on which Carim had landed. His eyes melted with volcanic red, ready to blast with sunshine yellow. Elijah and Winona took a handful of steps backwards. Kenny's camera displayed Carim at a distance. Faces of terror, deep gulps.

Carim expected to be met with monsters with bulbous heads and oozing flesh. Instead, he faced three people who were very much the same as him. Sure, their grubby fingernails and flaxen teeth left nothing to be desired, but they had noses and mouths and thoughts and feelings, and they were frightened. Carim couldn't murder these people. Murder - that gruesome word rattling about in his head. He knew killing would be monstrous, but he had no other choice but to follow

Ethan's orders, for the sake of his team, whose lives would be endangered if he refused.

A gust of amber from Carim's illuminated pupils later, and Elijah burst into ash. The layers of Elijah's flesh rotted away until only particles remained. A scream erupted as his skin degraded. His exoskeleton became transparent for one single second. Black cinders remained in the air for moments after his body became no more than atoms. His clothes died with him. Carim wiped away a tear and told himself he was doing what was necessary. Winona and Kenny exchanged a terrified expression under the impression that this fate would soon befall them, and Carim gained no pleasure from the sight of their distress. He didn't want to be the antagonist, the killer, but as far as he knew, he was only keeping matters under control.

Winona wanted to run, to sprint, but people don't always run when they are afraid. Sometimes they stick into frozen frames of grief.

Carim was sliding closer, ajar feet hovering above the ground. Kenny raised his rifle, releasing several bullets in quick succession from the muzzle. Shards of lead ricocheted off Carim's suit, striking the silver plating with a bullet bubble before they retired into the atmosphere. Kenny tugged the rifle upwards, aiming at the face unprotected by metal. Aiming at those eyes, the glow that killed Elijah. His fingers started to shudder, unable to pull the trigger. One blast later, he was ash. His final scream crushed Carim's soul as much as it did Winona's. The gun collapsed to the floor with a rusty clang. The echo of his scream lingered for some time.

Winona was the last one standing. She had to run. Every step she took was so rapid that her crumbling trainers crunched with the grass. Every ray he issued was a misfire as her speedy step refused to be caught. She continued to sprint until a rock collided with her toes. She tumbled over, landing on the sweaty grass, sweating herself. She tugged on her ankle as if one pull would cure the sprain. Carim was approaching her. A blast to her left, followed by a blast to her right, but she kept bobbing her head so he couldn't catch her. Truth was, he missed on purpose, delaying the inevitable. Her feet wouldn't let her get up. Ash surrounded her, mocking her, telling her that she too would become nothing more than dust in time.

Winona noticed the rifle in the corner of her eye which Kenny had dropped. On her back, only one stretch away from clasping at the weapon. Her muscles weren't flexible enough to allow her to grab the firearm. Carim ascended into the skies before drifting back to his feet. On her hands and knees, she crawled back, but Carim was trudging at twice the pace. Winona swung for the weapon, but her claw cane failed to reach its target. Carim hovered over her, ready to fire. With Kenny and his uniform vaporised, the community had stopped seeing events play out live.

"Please don't do this," Winona begged him as all her strength turned to vulnerability.

"It's what has to be done," Carim said. "I am sorry."

If he refused to follow his leader's orders, who knew what Ethan might do? Maybe he and Isla would die. These were criminals. Not worth losing everything for them, he thought.

"You're a puppet for them, aren't you? So was I, just this morning, but I got out."

Carim swam through his tears. "I didn't want to kill them. I'm only following orders because I've been given no other choice."

"Doesn't matter. You're still the one who followed the orders. You're just as much a killer as the one who issued them."

Winona returned to her feet, but Carim managed to grab her before she could escape, his hand touching her exposed skin. Winona struggled, but she couldn't release herself from his firm grip. He felt the perspiration dripping off her back and the terror pulsating through her veins. Nobody other than Carim saw Winona reduced to ash, by which point the broadcast had stopped airing. He watched as embers drifted into nowhere.

The screen cut to black. The stage fell to silence. The revolt was over before it had even started.

9.   Lifelong Lies

The quizmaster returned to the TV screen. The Crofts returned to watching a game show where contestants used psychokinesis to push counters down an arcade machine. The answers to the questions were meaningless. As with any gameshow in this world, the contestant's abilities were all that mattered. Experts on gameshows relying on intelligence were often born with brains the size of continents. Maeve's particular favourite followed players whose minds operated faster than the speed of light.

Nobody paid attention to the white noise of the gameshow host. Maeve rocked Hex back and forth to quell his tears. Eva watched on without sympathy. The image on the television may have been blurry, but she saw enough of it. Her terror should have matched Maeve's. Maeve became a shaking, wailing wreck. They hadn't known Winona well, but she'd been a continuity through each of their lives.

Eva kept cradling the remote like a baby Maeve couldn't reach. Blood and ash had never traumatised anybody quite as much as it did Maeve.

Hex, too, was about to burst into tears. Endless, whining screeches, akin to a supermarket tantrum. No child should have to watch their teacher die. The image had cut off before Winona's death but, still, the after effects could be viscerally understood. Eva stroked his hair, keeping her attention on Maeve. Maeve's eyes were blank and worn, terrified enough to desire never opening again. Her palms were firmly fixed on her knees. She hadn't moved since the broadcast. She had to keep strong, for Hex's sake, which Eva somehow managed with ease.

Maeve's chest swerved in and out while Eva flicked off the television screen and surrendered control of the remote. She grasped at Hex's icy mitts to drag him over to the kitchen where, in silence, they prepared that night's soup. How Eva could even think about eating was beyond Maeve.

"I knew what was coming when the broadcast began," Eva justified her indifference. "They'd call in Defence E and the insurgents would be dealt with. It's happened before."

Eva distributed a glass of spring water into a decanter, finishing it off with a few impromptu ice cubes from the freezer ledge. Maeve, recalling the mother in herself, surrendered her seat so she could offer Hex a place in her embrace, and let the liquid drown her throat.

"Miss Barton's dead, isn't she?" Hex asked.

Maeve didn't know what to say, so Eva took on the responsibility of answering. "She did something she shouldn't have done. She was naive, too brash. She should know that we have to make steady movements, not rash ones. Slow and steady wins the race."

"Is she dead, mummy? Is it all my fault that she's dead?"

Maeve gulped. "You should have turned the TV off."

"Why don't you go and lie down, sweetie?" Eva said. "I need to talk to Mummy."

Without hesitation, Hex dashed out of Maeve's clutches and over to the bed in the room's corner. Every word they spoke would have been audible, but Hex tuned them out by plugging in a set of half-broken headphones. Simon and Garfunkel's melodic harmonies calmed him down. He shut his eyes to make the bad memories go away. He knew what they'd be talking about. Part of his fear was only an act. Hex knew more than he was letting on, as did Eva. Now and again, he pictured Elijah's body bursting in his head like the television had hinted at. Skin melting, face corroding. He'd only seen bits, fragments in the few seconds he'd fought past his mother's restraints. They were enough to make him shudder.

Maeve leaned against the fridge to catch her breath. She didn't want to cry. She couldn't afford to look like a fool, especially when her wife was downing water with unbroken serenity as if nothing had happened. While Eva prepped the tea, Maeve composed herself. Gaps through the floorboards made the wailing below more pronounced, breaking Maeve's already fragile heart. Elijah's brother, Steven, even punched a wall, preceding a groan prompted by knuckle injury. Maeve took her water to her seat. Maeve didn't once look at Eva, too focused on her water and the drywall in her view.

"Why aren't you more affected by this?" asked Maeve, the question she had longed to ask.

"I knew it was coming," Eva replied. "I prepared for this. So should you have done."

"Come to mention it, you weren't surprised earlier when I mentioned what Hex said. This is different. People have died."

"We'll pay our respect to the victims."

"I'm not denying that. First time somebody's escaped here, first time somebody's been murdered. That's what this is, murder. The Knight murdered Winona and the others, and you aren't shocked in the slightest."

"At least we can stop pretending that Defence E is perfect now."

"What's up with you, Eva?"

Eva retreated to the bathroom, pinching her chasmic nostrils, which were wide enough to fall into, to circumvent the stench. Above the basin, there was a mirror, where she conducted an observation of her scatty appearance every morning. The mirror contained a door which secured any toiletries they could afford. A scuffled comb, a wrinkled flannel, a half-empty bottle of shampoo, and behind these were a stash of papers. Some were notices about upcoming community events parcelled through their letterbox. Among the books stored there in the place of bookshelves was *A Guide to the Outside World.* The cover contained a picture of a globe, and a pink sticker bulged from the middle page. Eva slammed the book onto the table, flicking through the page with her forefinger, fragile from where she'd chewed her nails. Maeve wiped leftover tears onto her bare arm, too impoverished to deserve a tissue.

"Do you think we should go down there and pay our respects?" Maeve asked, picking up on terror-stricken screams of grief from Elaine downstairs, so detectable that the noise may as well have come from that room. A knock at the downstairs door. A creak of the downstairs door. A voice they recognised but couldn't quite place.

"Too soon," Eva replied. "We really shouldn't be able to hear them."

"Give them a rest, they've just lost a loved one."

"Haven't most of us in our time?"

"Jesus, Eva," Maeve said. "How can you be this insensitive?"

"I knew it was coming."

"You keep saying that. Somebody just died on our TV screen. How could you possibly be prepared for that?"

"People die all the time. That's Gordon speaking down there, isn't it? He's comforting the Norths, unaware that he recently lost as much as them. Do you really think this is the first time somebody's disappeared? No. They've covered it up before. The others found out the truth, just like Winona did."

"You say that with certainty."

"Come over here and take a look at this."

Maeve crept over with water at hand. She thought she had wiped off the tears, but her face reeled from a flood. Hex was crying too, but they were too preoccupied to notice. This was trauma fit to make a person or break them.

Maeve leaned over the book, observing a four-leaf clover-shaped map. France. Eva planted her index finger on a green blob just above the centre.

"Paris," Maeve said.

"Yes, Paris," Eva replied. "You need to calm your tears. I know you've always been an emotional person."

"Excuse me for showing a little bit of human emotion!"

"It's unfortunate what happened, I know, but I'll save my tears for the next one."

"It hasn't happened before. It won't happen again."

"We've always wanted to go to Paris." Eva scrolled through photographs on the following pages of the Eiffel Tower, the Louvre. "You wanted to go there once. I expect you still do."

"If I could leave this place, then France would be the first place I'd go, money permitting. Drink wine, eat cheese, and see the landmarks. So romantic, from what I've seen in the films."

"*Before Sunset*? *Amelie*?" They'd watched both movies together on a quaint night in the orchard's three-time open cinema.

"Beautiful! You know as well as I do that we'll never get to go."

"Winona's sacrifice would suggest otherwise. I was looking through this book one day, ahead of the pub quiz in the community hall. Remember?"

"I wondered how you became such a boffin!" Maeve chuckled, forgetting for a moment that three people had died. "You knew the capital city of Tanzania was...what was it?"

"Dodoma."

"I thought it was shocking because you've never been good at geography."

"Tell me about it! I found something. A slip of paper. Here."

A scruffy notepad page, occupied by lines that raced down the sheet. Scribbles of adjoining words. Arthur Trent, Lewis Shepherd, Kelly Summerhill. Eva clicked a biro from a pen pot with only one pen, adding three names to the list. Elijah North, Kenny Farrows, Winona Barton. She took her time when clicking the thrust device, waiting for Maeve to catch up. She turned the page, revealing a hastily written note in Eva's disjointed handwriting.

I'm unsure if I will remember this. Somebody close to you harbours superpowers. I overheard a conversation between two people whose voices I didn't recognise and faces I didn't see. They brought up the names of people I have never heard of and claimed they once existed among us. I've written them down here.

They were our friends. Our minds were wiped of the very memory of them. Go-

The page ran out of lines. Definitely Eva's handwriting, the penmanship unmistakable, but the message was bewildering. Maeve paced back and forth, scraping her hair back, finding the matter overwhelming.

"Somebody in this community is hiding superpowers," Eva said. "The ability to wipe away memories on a colossal scale."

"The blessed can't be here. They'd lose their powers if they interacted with us."

"That's what we've been told. The 'Go' must have led to something but I must have been interrupted. There was a conversation I must have stumbled upon, but they found out I was onto them before I could complete the note. It won't be long before they make us forget. I expect they're working with Defence E. If news of tonight's deaths gets out, The Knight's reputation will be tarnished, and Defence E don't want that."

Maeve wheezed. "So you think they were right about the lies?"

Eva heard Gordon's voice coming from downstairs. "I told you he lost someone. That was Lewis. Lewis was his son, and Gordon doesn't even know Lewis existed. We're told people like Winona are criminals that are a danger to the majority. They must be killed, otherwise, the consequences are catastrophic. If it's not true, and they know it's not true, then there's no way they can justify these deaths. If there's a way to cover it up, they'll take it. They - the government, whoever's been doing this - are the true criminals."

"Our whole lives have been a lie?" Maeve's mind was swelling. Everything was going too quick. Hex carried on listening to his album.

"This whole community is built on a lie," Eva continued. "Maybe that wasn't the case once, but it is now. We'll get to Paris one day, Maeve. Their sacrifice won't be for nothing. Even if Winona and Kenny and Elijah are forgotten, their names never will be. We've written them down now. We need to find Defence E's undercover agent and stake them out, otherwise it will keep on happening. It's likely that if they find out we have this, they'll wipe us off the map. Anybody who gets close to the truth is in danger. Luckily, or unluckily, in the morning, we'll probably be distant from it."

They dedicated the rest of the evening to mourning. Weeping resumed downstairs which lasted throughout the night. Maeve wanted to go down to pay her respects, but Eva enforced a curfew. They ate tea which Maeve only picked at. Whenever Maeve wept, Eva's frosty grasp clasped onto her. Eva slept well on her igneous mattress, while Hex and Maeve kept their eyes wide open on the ceiling. When they shut their eyes, darkness could cloud their minds. In the morning, they might have forgotten who Winona even was.

10.   Carim's Story

Waking up with blood on my hands reminds me of back then. When I look in the mirror, I no longer see myself. I see the ash and bones of those who I have killed. They howl at me, begging me to stop, yet I act regardless. *Please don't do this*, Winona's plea reverberates in the dark. I see destruction. I am destruction. Fear me.

My semi-detached cottage home is an outcome of hard work. I would not have it if I did not follow orders. Then again, nor would I have my guilty conscience. My Yorkshire terrier, Crackers, forms my only source of consistent company, although being alone has never bothered me. A kitchen with a stove, a living room with a fireplace, a chamber with a bed. I have not always been blessed with these luxuries.

Three nights of mine were once spent on a rickety ocean in a dinghy without even an orange high vis jacket to protect me. Before that, I lived in a rundown shack in the back streets of Damascus, waking every morning with the throb of fear.

Sometimes I still hear the screams from the night it happened, just as fresher cries will curse me forever more. Occasionally my image flickers in the mirror as if I am someone else, the one who deserves this body. To this date, Abbas remains at the mercy of Poseidon. I do not even have a picture of him. At least I see him in the mirror, even if he only taunts me.

There was once a time I was much less than a superhero. In those days, I could only fly from one stretch of Earth to another. I could not fly over rivers back then, or sail one country's skies to reach the next. If only I could save him now.

I wash my face to clean off the dirt. Dirt that is not there, imagined, metaphorical. Afterwards, I feel no cleaner. I remove my outfit to escape the shame. Every silent stage allows those four panicked words to tunnel through my synapses. *Please don't do this*. First, my wired helmet is removed from my fore. Brief pain greets my agitation with one jolt of the brow. I remove the plates which contain my shoulders and pelvis. Blood is not sent wheezing through my body as it must have rushed through theirs. Only one scar marked my fingertip from where I had swiped at Barton. I left myself panting, just to let the pain sink in. I deserved that. Three lives that could have carried on instead of mine were lost. Maybe I will still face the bite of my actions yet.

It takes me back to the times when I was with Abbas. I cannot think of them as the glory days.

Abbas was a skinny chap used to the company of vest tops. His lips were pale but boundless. His tongue stuck out from his mouth no matter what he tried. Aside from a few freckles of facial hair, his brown physiognomy peaked purity. Thin enough that his back arched like a bow and his chest was a spring waiting to be uncoiled. foul-tongued but well-meaning. Fundamentally, kind.

We lived together for thirteen years in a shed reminiscent of a fallout shelter outside a puddled swamp with only one door for decorum. Six of us slept on exhausted sofas that we had no choice but to share. People out there had the ability to make food and alter infrastructure with a singular finger click. None of those people came to us.

Poverty makes one appreciate the most trivial of comforts. Every weekly loaf of bread divided out between our sextet always instigated ravenous smiles. Walking two hours each day may have wilted our legs under solar humidity, but we returned with an ewer filled to the brim. I equip words such as ewer and brimful now, only because Petula hired the finest language professionals to teach me English, taking me from hello to salutations in a fortnight.

Our motivation to flee was initiated by those unmistakable thumps of the knock of an ability guardian in the shack next door. Two taps preceded a doorstep quake. Screams like howls were followed by the ruthless ripple of bullets shattering spines. Those left behind were taken. We had heard the stories, but we had never thought those legends could apply to our fates. The stories told around our campfires said that if an ability guardian finds you, you must not hesitate to run. So we ran. They were next door, which meant they would come to our settlement next.

Abbas broke a window in the cardboard walls, allowing the partition to tumble. Light mass and petty height played to our benefit. The other four remained under the decision that they would rather fight for their home. They would never win, and we never saw them again. We escaped Damascus before we could hear them face the bullets. Their deaths are not confirmed. Reassurance resides in the knowledge that they *may* still be out there.

I could not make out much more of the ability guardians than their shadows, brooding and hollow reflections of death. They steadied their guns, clicked in the triggers, and screaming silhouettes fell to the barrels before them. My brother and I were cowardly enough to leap in our haggard van and only take stuttering glances back through the windscreen mirror at the friends we had left behind. Their black cloth uniforms were accompanied by dark tin helmets with self-drawn sockets for eyes, not too dissimilar in aesthetic to a certain white supremist group who would, in a different time, be the threat us Syrians were running from.

Third world countries are those deprived of powers by the extractor guns of the avaricious ability guardians. One tug of energy and our powers would be theirs. They would take a life just to spread terror and strap up the survivors with a bobbing apple in a straw-tied chair, and plunge the hardware against the temples of their victims, draining their body of all abilities. A new class of unblessed were subsequently created. The created unblessed, not prone to disease like those in the compounds, hence they could continue living in a world they no longer wished to reside. That is why we had to run. I would not let them take my laser eyes, or my brother's elasticated skin.

We travelled to the borders where migrants were sprinting toward indigo yachts in the gloomy Mediterranean Sea. We had already embarked on half a day's drive in our exhausted van. The wheels were tired, the petrol tank enervated, and the engine fizzled under the promise of combustion. Still, we made it to the shore, and in good time. Sprees came from all directions. A great deal of pushing. The most violent participant in the beachside boxing match would secure a place on the dinghy. I had to push and pull and tug for the sake of my brother. Somebody tripped Abbas up, forcing me to take a few steps backwards to offer him my hand.

Unlike those unfortunate victims of the ability guardians, our proficiencies were conserved. One traveller leaped off the pebbles from the sand into the raft. Another acquired their telekinetic abilities to edge the sailboat closer to the shore to avoid contact with the poisoned lake. The presence of water in such dry land would suggest that this ocean was constructed by the blessed and was probably a product of the water wars.

I could have equipped my powers of flight to reach the yacht, but I had to be selfless and help Abbas recover from his fall. Clusters of stragglers were crawling on hands and knees as the vessel set off to Marseille. I blasted into airspace without a jet on my back. My crash into the rower affected little more than a shimmer of local waves.

Abbas mustered the strength to accompany me. He positioned himself into a bear crawl, with his palms pressed against coarse sand with hands directly beneath his shoulders. His table-top back straight, his legs behind himself, progressively curling. He released his hands from the surface and his legs tumbled over him. Releasing his head from the dirt, he spiralled into the dinghy. One bold, unrelenting leap, letting himself become free with nature, and he was on the boat. I landed too after being unsure whether I would. At that time, I had yet to tune my abilities to their maximum potential, so I could only fly meagre distances. If I had the abilities I boast today, back on that fateful day, Abbas would still be alive, but ifs and buts solve very little.

We cradled each other upon our reunion. The leisurely drift dragged time on enough so that we could feel the pain of the anguished expressions of onlookers whose lack of dexterity prevented them from reaching the dinghy in time. They begged on hands and knees for us to stop, but we had to leave so the guardians did not catch up with us.

Our journey to France commenced on tranquil waters, and the foreknowledge of the storm that would greet us once we hit Herzegovina was unbeknownst to us. The sea remained silent for the first night, and Abbas and I remained together. Thanks to the constant stomach upset and the lack of drinkable liquid, vomiting became a frequent activity. Our yacht was unstable enough that it often rocked, though we generally avoided the black stormy skies that defined the remainder of our journey. If there is a God, lightning was his means of exhibiting shame at us for leaving our peers behind. Allah once owned my faith, but now I find the matter of religion more dubious. For if there is a God, he would not condemn good people like myself and Abbas to a city of liquid death.

On Day Two, waves became more white than blue, and the clouds coughed with raucous phlegm. The gentle swaying on Day One was a distant memory once we reached the tumult on the border of Serbia. Beetle black skies, confused seas. The river of tears would contain the droplets of everybody on board.

Never did I count how many people accompanied us. The nausea instigated dizziness and the vertigo manufactured confusion. We each told our stories, our battles with the ability guardians. Whether they could control minds or strike lasers from their eyeballs, they each spoke as if they were powerless because, despite our advantage over the unblessed, we were merely mortal men. There is no such concept as immortality in the real world. The surrounding waters were daggers waiting to stab us and prize us open. Once the boat capsized on day three, its desire was fulfilled.

We were just a few miles from Marseille. Our destination had almost been reached. None of us were more than anybody else. No lifeguards or drivers; just a dozen or so strangers travelling on open seas with rudders. There were children, too, some as young as five, snatched from makeshift homes. They were hungry and thirsty on a boat devoid of sustenance. Some of them did not make the trip.

The dinghy caught on an accelerating tide when some of us were in the middle of sleep. We took it in turns to guide the boat, but nobody was to blame other than the chaotic tides. Wind led the yacht to jolt. We managed to hold onto the edges at first. The rivers were deep, cruelly so. The boat dragged along until it could not restrain the disarray. It flipped diagonally with little warning, taking us with it. Three of us - me, a middle-aged gent, and a young woman with a headscarf - managed to hold on while the less fortunate entered the waters. Parents dived in to catch their children but none of them returned.

And Abbas. His bleak hands swung up from the waves in disconcertion. His head bobbed to the surface; his strength defeated by the brisk sprint of undulation. That is the sight I see every morning in the mirror, as one wave held his throat until another crashed over his head and absorbed him. Then he was gone.

I now have a fresh curse to haunt me, to take the place of those wounds. Could I have rescued him? I could have dived in and been a hero. Small fry hero, without the fame, without the guilt. What more could I have done? If his virtuous heart still existed on this plane, the same contrition would be displayed, except he was destined to never escape the icy tentacles of the tide. Jumping in there to play the saviour would have killed me too. If Allah does exist, he decided I had a place in this world, and it was a place that I needed to earn.

Visiting France for the first time should have been glorious. To many, the towns were quaint and the rivers luxurious, but not to me. I could not bear to look at water in the same way again. If I was not the one who killed my brother, then the sea was his assassin.

Eating became a chore, while sleeping transformed into an involuntary exercise. My eyes were so black and dusty with remorse that I rarely wished to close them. I was housed in a shack not too dissimilar from the Damascus settlement I had abandoned, alongside the 'lucky few' who lived another day that their families did not. His oval head kept crawling back to the glass whenever I looked in the mirror. Those shattered eyes, that unbroken wail. To escape him, I turned to exercise. Each day, five miles walking, five miles running, twice-daily sessions of bench pressing and weightlifting to build muscle. Random acts of kindness became a daily fixture, from helping a senior across the road, to picking litter by our French home. The more I exercised, the fitter I became. The fitter I became, the more in tune I got with my abilities. I joined the gendarmerie soon afterwards, which required me to train more rigorously.

The Telegraph found enough in our story to unite the three survivors from the dinghy to speak about those lost on the French border. Petula must have heard the story, because she approached me in the police headquarters about two years into my time as an agent of the corps to ask me to join Defence E. Perfect backstory, exquisite track record. They didn't remember me for my cowardice. To them, I was a victim. I could have saved Abbas, just as I could have declined Ethan's orders. In both cases, my cowardice undermined me, and I acted in the sake of deceptive goodwill.

Petula interviewed me, and it did not take me long to accept her offer. The least I could do to repay my debt was move to England to save lives to make up for the ones I had not saved back in Damascus. She offered me a visa, and my cottage home. This was six years ago. They loved me then. My reputation is at threat now, and rightly so. Maybe I should tell them that I am a fraud. Defence E would not have found me if Abbas had not died. Should I keep telling myself that he had to die, for the greater good, or own up to the knowledge that we are in a godless world where the only fate is injustice? He did not die so I could live. He died so he could die, and I just happened to keep on living. I fought crime, enforced laws, and I became property of Defence E. Maybe the world should know who I really am.

PART TWO
COVER STORY
11.   Breaking News

The Morning Manifesto claims to be there for you. Like all newspapers, *The Manifesto* was a breath of fresh air amidst a world awash with fake news and cancel culture. They achieved this through false reports and hate mobs. Their tagline indicated otherwise, but they were exactly the same as the rest. They were propaganda in a boxed office. Rule breakers who followed every regulation.

The dull grey office provided little room for interaction between colleagues. Everybody was blocked off into isolated cubicles built for introverts. Chrissie, a reporter who was anything but introverted, escaped the colourless sterility by basking in walled kaleidoscopic prints and photos of her ragdoll cat. Chrissie was the sort who opted for aesthetics, which was why she chose contact lenses over glasses. This did not strike her comrade, Ruth, whose eyes were grouped by browline specks. Ruth and Chrissie knew more about one another than their first names. That was a lot for a place where the staff rarely spoke to one another.

A knock emerged at a cubicle as the computer screen ahead of her made her eyes turn sour. She swivelled around to respond to the soft knock, banging the white wood wall with her swivel chair. She faced Clive, her frosty-bearded, snowy-haired boss. He fostered a constant frown on a face already defined by wrinkles at the age of fifty-one. His muscovado scent was credited to all the sugar he had consumed. He always applied too much moisture, for no good reason. His excessive weight meant he could never look fresh. His managerial caboose occupied the olive chair opposite Chrissie.

"Anything new?" He sighed. He sighed a lot.

"I can check if you'd like!" swift-speaking Chrissie responded.

"It's probably best if you do." Another sigh. He had lost all motivation, and the moon wasn't even waning yet. "We don't have a cover story yet. I've got to find a headline by the morning."

Chrissie fought through mounds of paperwork on her chaotic desk. Her organised mind didn't correspond with the disorganised layout.

Incessant ringing from neighbouring phones was enough to spark a headache. She flicked through each drawer on her three-storey container as recycling drowned each plastic floor. Pictures of gurning interviewees in courtrooms were in front of what she needed - her memory stick - key to her abilities. Once she retrieved the device, she slammed the drawer with conviction and uncapped the lid. Chrissie placed the connector plug into her mouth as the metallic edge scraped her gullet until she found a connection. Clive shielded his eyes to avoid the disgusting sight of somebody attaching a USB stick to their oesophagus. A clicking noise sounded as alloy met trachea. Her eyes slammed shut whilst she launched her journey across her membrane. Her mind became binary. Letters and numbers in a perpetual abyss, no personal thoughts and feelings intact.

Swimming through that memory index resembled the grace of a breaststroke. The arms needed to be direct, and the legs needed to crab behind. Only goggles, which may have helped dispel the dust atoms that drifted into her eyes and her ajar mouth, were absent from the procedure.

Memories were like doors in the binary kingdom. Opening these doors required more effort than turning a handle. First, she would need to form the door. Chrissie locked her vision on constructing a handle that she could grip onto so the blackness would face an obstacle. All she had to imagine was that shape. Spherical, bronze, polished. She was used to it by now. She remembered the first time - aged nine when the doctors discovered her idiosyncratic abilities. How intimidating it had been back then, compared to the somewhat relaxing sensation of bathing in memories these days.

The handle was there, and the door formed around it.

The first door led her to a family of three on the beach in Swanage. Waves wrapped around the ankles of the euphoric child. Meanwhile, her parents sipped pina colada on the golden sand. Lights glistened on the sea to brighten the imperial skies. A bearded guy in a hoodie came at them. A carving knife sharpened in his grasp, but the family were too busy laughing to notice. The killer took a swing at the mother's back first. Her cheap deck chair with a frayed back made her stern accessible. One swing and she would be oozing with blood. He pulled the chair back, forcing her to the sand. She crawled away. The dad wrestled with the assailant but fell into the knife's steel arm. The footage paused on a freeze frame of the grieving mother turning her head. She'd felt his breath on her nape like she herself was there.

"Boring!" she heard Clive say. His grinding cynicism made him difficult to please. "*The Mirror* reported on that yesterday, as did *The Standard*. Family of three murdered by a man who could make nightmares a reality. Has a ring to it but there's nothing special about the story. *The Sun* branded it a page five story. A headline about a Kardashian's breast enhancement surgery made page three."

Clive kept his arms folded and his legs together, but Chrissie was too abstract to notice. The screen ahead of them showed everything Chrissie was seeing inside of the memory house. Clive's impatient disinterest encouraged her to advance to the next room. Her mind was a mansion connected to a computer database. Her abilities allowed her to sniff out and grab any stories that the world had to offer.

Another handle formed a door made of dust ahead of her. She reached out to twist the shaft and entered an endless, tunnelling labyrinth of windows and doors. This would have constituted a house if darkness was all that made a home. All she could discern were entrances and exits which she used her signature scissor step to scurry through. A proper breaking news story had a distinctive smell. Good news usually smelled like caviar or fine wine, whereas bad news reeked of cigarette butts or rotten eggs. Luckily - lucky in theory, anyway - decay was the trademark whiff of Room 26B. One snatch of the doorknob followed by a few imaginary steps, and she would be inside. No other tabloid had anybody like Chrissie Young, who could stake out crime by digging through her intellect. Her thoughts were not like others. They were not linear, but a hive mind, connected to every other event and person without consent. Clive knew Chrissie had stumbled upon a story when pixels of The Knight's laser eyes moulded on the monitor. Rarely did he smile, but once the footage played, his grin was born.

"We've got a live one!" he exclaimed. He was not a natural shouter, as his unnatural inflexions indicated.

Chrissie became the omniscient third party. It was as if she was a ghost on the field, there without being there at all. Two uniformed brutes were on open greenery next to a raven woman in threadbare cloth. Flora and fauna surrounded the human bird in the sky. Elijah collapsed into ashes first, and then Kenny. Minutes followed before Winona faced the same fate. Clive watched in glee as Winona wrestled for her life in the dirt and grime of the soiled plane. Carim departed the scene by shutting his laser eyes. He collapsed to the floor in a battle with frenzied tears.

Chrissie's eyes may have been shut but her jaws were wide open to the point that the soft scarlet palate of her mouth was visible. A memory stick dangled between her gnashers, at risk of falling into her cavernous inlet. Clive hauled the rod from her throat, triggering a scream akin to a gasp waking from a nightmare. Even the dim light proved unbearable following the darkness. The off switch on her database had been pressed, software off. Clive seized her computer, which contained the recording. The three-minute clip was then emailed to every workstation in the office. A choir of pings suggested that the message had been successfully distributed.

Most of Clive's time was spent in his spacious office with the door locked. He'd introduced a podium in the office, however, to house his lectures. Any person not facing the stage would only have to conduct a brief swivel to let their eyes meet with the editors. Rolls of blubber were beginning to spill over his stomach, exposed by the short black waistcoat he opted to wear that day. To catch their attention, he clapped his hands. Dominic Driver, a comic illustrator, listened to UB40 with plugged ears while he animated a cartoon rodent. Clive ambled over to clap in front of Dominic's dopey face and Dominic shuddered.

"Quiet, listen up everybody!" He bellowed as if a hall of introverts would be midway through a conversation. "Thanks to Chrissie, we have access to a story that may make tomorrow's Manifesto one of the best-selling editions to date. I've emailed you each a copy."

Chrissie's database not only recovered footage but also sound. When everybody watched the recording in unison, Winona's echoing screams twisted the earbuds. Applause bounced from hand to hand upon the collective realisation that a salary increase was incoming. An exclusive story would sell more copies, ergo their incomes would be greater. Chrissie's face twisted into a humbled smirk. Her soft skin and bobbed black hair bowed with her.

"No need to applaud!" Clive insisted, and the room immediately fell to silence. Life was reaching the voice of this listless fellow at last. "Work must be completed on this story by the morning." He pointed at a tall stick of a dandruff-coated woman. "Sandra, ensure the footage reaches Instagram and Twitter no earlier than midnight. We can't let the other papers find out before we print. Ruth, produce a sparky headline to ensure the copies sell."

"Righto, boss, boss!" Ruth said. No, that was not a syntactic error. Ruth had a tic which always made her repeat the last word she said.

"Adam, I want you to cut down the footage. We'll sell more copies if we make it look as though Carim presented no evident signs of empathy."

"Are you suggesting we bring down Defence E?" Adam asked.

"No paper can get far without lampooning someone. Our duty as journalists is to exhibit a unique perspective. Why should anybody buy our paper if we cannot bring our own signature slant to topical affairs? Everybody considers Defence E to be heroic. Rightly so. Nobody dares to dissect their heroism. What if we dare? It presents us as honest, and bold, and people appreciate that in a day and age when everything's censored and shepherded. Why should people buy *The Manifesto* if we're the dead spit of *The Times*? It's 2p more expensive. Let's get this out there, and copies will sell."

"He's right," Chrissie remarked. "The most successful journalists and papers are those which are unafraid to be bold."

"We're declaring war on the Police," Adam said. "That's a war we can't win."

"You're more outgoing than I thought you were, Adam," Clive responded. "You know what they say? Any press is good press. We'll face the backlash in the morning. Until then, we get this story out into the world, and we do it before anybody else. Nobody else has anybody who can find stories anywhere through thought alone like Chrissie can. The likelihood is, that's the only recording that exists of the incident."

"What actually happened then, then?" Ruth asked.

"Likelihood is that three unblessed people tried escaping from Woodville," Chrissie said. She spoke at lightning speed like a 1940s movie star. "The Knight was called in to restrain them so that the disease they carry does not spread."

"That must make him more heroic, heroic?"

Clive shook his head. "Not if we word the story right. We need to antagonise The Knight. That's the only way we can sell copies. Rip his reputation to shreds."

"I'm not sure I like that idea, idea."

"Tough! My paper, my rules. If you didn't want to test the waters of morality, you shouldn't have entered the journalism field. Rules are cruel here. Simon, continue working on the sports pages. Neve, on copy! Driver, on Ricky Rat! As for the rest of you, get working on our top story. Chrissie, find the names of the victims. We'll print at 2AM." Clap clap, chop chop. The relentless pounding of rollicking keyboards commenced. "Our top story: Defence E's most prestigious killer strikes again! Just you wait. We're gonna make so much money!"

12.   <u>Ordinary Morning</u>

Nobody should be able to sleep on a guilty conscience. After much tussling with the bed sheets, however, Carim got some shut eye.

5AM was when his bladder called. His alarm would usually wake him with a sharp bleep at 6, so he was early. An empty brain woke him in an optimistic mood which descended into oblivion once his bleaker memories returned. His exhaustion was simultaneous with his inability to sleep. Part of the issue was that he had slept with the duvet thrown off and the curtains open. Sunlight had only recently reached the windowsill, but the dark exterior was bright enough to penetrate his resting state. It struck him that he couldn't remember going to sleep. Then again, can you ever?

He spent moments alone in his single bed. He thought he could restrain the liquid that trickled through his system. He launched into an awkward bed dance but, unfortunately, he failed to resist the temptation, and sprung from his bed to rectify the problem.

He dashed into his polished lavatory, which was squeaky clean and cream walled, but not for long. He waited for his personal hose to drip. Those difficult few seconds of waiting for the waterworks to stop while he glared into nothingness. It was too early to engage in intelligent conversation with his mind. He snapped off some tissue paper from the half-empty dispenser. Believing his abilities equated to an Olympian shot-putter's aim, he chucked the wetted paper into the bowl. The sheet fluttered to the floor, drenching the ground in his own contents. A sigh. Life should be better than this for a superhero.

Except when he looked in the mirror, he reminded himself that he was not a hero. He killed people last night. Heroes don't kill. Vigilantes kill, and the police don't hire vigilantes. Vigilantes are scum, fishing the streets for blood while the police pick up the pieces. Carim was a vigilante now.

He reached the mirror and watched Abbas's woes and wails transform into Winona's unremitting howl. The reflection was transparent enough to resemble a recording. Part of him forgot it was a hallucination. Four faces haunted every waking moment. Only in sleep could he escape, and even then, escape was never guaranteed. He couldn't take the pain any longer. He looked away, head groaning. There would be ibuprofen he could consume downstairs to cure his headache. Those words repeated in his head with each hurried step: *You're a puppet. Please don't do this.* His mind raised the pitch of his victim's exclamations, and the urgency, for dramatic effect.

Crackers waited for him at the bottom step. Carim had been dashing to escape the screams. The faster he went, the less clear those noises were. He almost forgot about his poor dog and could have trampled on his little lodger, who was fast asleep and snoring and not responsible for a single cent of rent. The dog's draggled face twinkled beside an alligator chew toy coated in spittle. The door above Crackers had a house key firmly situated in the lock. He wasn't ready to leave yet. First, he had to get rid of the headache that was crushing his mind.

He consumed the tablets in his metallic bronze kitchen in a glass branded 'Defence E' (four of a kind). He always closed his eyes when he ingested tablets. Another type of tablet - a mobile device - was beside him, suffocated by wires, screen soul black, with the promise of becoming more.

Every day required a nutritious but busy breakfast to prepare for his duties. His cupboards were sparse, containing only the necessary materials. A bowl, skimmed milk, oatmeal, bananas, berries, and nothing more. He distributed these ingredients into a dish, collected a spoon, and indulged in groans of pleasure with each bite of the succulent dish. He ate slower than usual in the knowledge that work was hours away. Once he finished, he washed up without washing up liquid, and realised he needed to conduct an online shop. Only two minutes passed after entering his payment details when a flash of lightning shot past his window. Two bustling cardboard boxes emerged on his doorstep. Hull's only delivery man had arrived! He had superpowers, like most people - lightning speed, and the ability to be in more than one place at once. At the same time as delivering to Carim's Yorkshire household, the footman was also shooting off to deliver a speaker to Whitby. At 5AM.

Carim decided it would be premature to suit up this early. His morning routine continued with a trip to the bathroom, where he stripped the delicate hairs looming on his chin. He brushed and flossed and used the mouthwash to override the minty Colgate aftermath. His body was deprived of all but boxers, making him conscious of his rising chest fluff. He chucked on a shirt - Led Zeppelin '77 - and pranced past the Yorkshire terrier's cutting yap. From a distance, the kitchen tablet was trembling against the table as it barked a beep. When he reached the kitchen, the screen accompanied an image of Ethan's uninviting mug above a green button that demanded to be pressed. He swiped up the footer, revealing an encased soundwave that bobbed up and down alongside their humble leader's measured speech.

"How long have you been awake?" Ethan asked.

Carim rubbed his eyes. "About an hour, probably." He turned to face the 5.30 clock. Time does *not* fly when you're not having fun. "Scratch that. Half an hour."

"You've been awake that long? You must know by now. You didn't think to call me?"

"How long have you been awake? You do not sound tired."

"I tend not to sleep much. Forty winks suit me fine."

"You know what happened last night?"

"How did you know?"

"The tone of your voice. It is slightly different."

"Of course I know! The entire world knows! The Manifesto published a report on last night's events. What have you been doing with your morning?"

Carim hadn't yet processed what Ethan had said. "I have been getting ready."

"You don't read the papers? Or watch the news?"

"Watching television as soon as you wake up is harmful for the eyes. I rely on them to thrive."

"Put on the television, immediately."

Ethan was the boss. Their whole relationship relied on Ethan barking orders and Carim accepting them. The Knight switched on the 35" TV that hung framed on his wall and waited for the image to load. *Northern Hero kills unblessed fugitives*, cried the scarlet banner. He fell to the settee in his industrial living room with a palm to the face and a groan in the throat. Crackers leaped up beside him, expecting a massage, but Carim was too busy to tend to the dog's needs. *Kills.* Those five letters stabbed the heart.

"Are you still there?" Ethan's carcass of a voice barked. For Carim, thoughts were racing at such a pace that nothing else mattered.His sight became coated by dark reddish polkadots which were ordinarily symptomatic of delirium. All his eyesight missed was the footage of Winona's death playing over and over, taken from Chrissie's memory stick.

Carim's feet wobbled, and not from the pins and needles he woke with. He used his coffee table for balance to force stability as he staggered through unsteady footsteps.

"Yes," he said, once he finally reached the gadget. "I apologise."

"Don't apologise about the orders you followed," Ethan demanded. "Apologise for the way in which you followed them."

"I am sorry about the way I followed your orders, sir."

"You're frightened of me. It's unhealthy." Saying this, Ethan quite liked being feared. At least he knew where he stood then. "A reporter called Chrissie Young reported the story this morning in *The Manifesto*. Are you watching BBC News at the moment?"

Carim peeped his head through the doorway that connected the living room to the kitchen. "Yes."

He noticed that the focus had changed. That shot was playing where Carim reached out to restrain Winona, touching her unadulterated skin. He had touched her plain, unguarded flesh. The journalist remarked on the scandal, and Ethan was furious too. One could always tell when Ethan was incensed from the subtle rise in his vocal modulations.

"You touched one of them, Shafiq," Ethan said. "Do you know what that means?"

"I may have risked becoming one of them."

"Have you checked on your abilities this morning?"

Carim usually tested his laser eyes in the mirror as part of his routine. Today was not like any other day. He would ordinarily pamper Crackers and ignore the press, yet he had to do the opposite. He pranced to the door where his reflection occupied a vacant mirror. Usually, the thought of his optical rays would be enough to spark the amber floodlights to glow. Not this time. His eyes were like anybody else's. Flying may have caused him to bump his head on the lampshade, but a thought always made flight achievable. Not this time. Carim tried again, though yielded no result. He rushed back to the device, drowning out the white noise that droned on from the TV set. In fact, he decided to flick off the small screen, opting for silence over censure.

"I hear your footsteps are louder than usual," Ethan remarked.

"You can hear my footsteps?" asked Carim.

"I can detect the exhaustion from the movement of your feet in comparison to their usual conviction. I know what that means. You've lost what makes you special."

"I believe I may have."

"You were meant to complete your task without physical or emotional entanglement. Not only have you risked yourself, but you have risked the lives of everybody in this city. You know we cannot let this disease spread."

"What if this is not contagious?"

"If it wasn't contagious, there'd be no reason why those three fugitives needed to die. They knew what they were doing, and the risk they were taking. The only life you've destroyed that doesn't deserve it is your own."

Carim was thinking to himself, I do deserve this. He didn't verbalise this sentiment.

"Are you aware of what this means?" asked Ethan.

"I have endangered everything," Carim replied.

"It means you're riddled, Carim, with the same disease that they are."

"Have I signed my own death warrant?"

"You've issued yourself a prison sentence. We can't have you interacting with the outside world. People will be with you shortly to remove you from your premises. They will take you to Woodville Estate immediately."

"You cannot do this. This is my home."

"Your home is property of Defence E, and so are you. You gave us permission to do what we wanted with you when you signed up to our initiative."

Carim gulped. "I killed three of their people. How could I consider living alongside them?"

"You'll have to prove you did it for the greater good."

"Should I tell them you issued the order?"

"You didn't have to accept it," Ethan said. Carim felt like throttling Ethan, but Ethan was nothing more than soundwaves on a screen. "Your role in this society is to be a hero. *The Manifesto* have attempted to strip that from you. As a reward for your services, the least I can do is rectify that. Unfortunately, you have also become a threat. My role is to administer national security, and I cannot let your perilous existence endanger the world we have built. It's been an honour serving with you, however limited our time together has been."

"There must be a cure."

"If there was, don't you think we would have distributed it?"

"Surely my abilities cannot be lost forever."

"You shouldn't have gotten close to them, Carim," Ethan said.

Knocks hammered at the door. Crackers growled at the foreign knock whilst embarking upon a frantic sprint across the lounge. Carim felt like hovering in the corner so they couldn't reach him. More strikes from figures dressed in white whose silhouettes could be seen from a brief head jolt. They knocked on the glass even if there was a doorbell. Their knocks became heavier, from taps to hammers.

"Answer the door, Shafiq," Ethan commanded.

Three men adorned in rubber hazmat suits approached him upon answering the door. Masks covered their noses and mouths, leaving only their stark eyes and hints of hair to distinguish them from one another. One was blonde, one was a woman, and the third was ginger. They barged into his home, carrying tasers in their gloved palms, and kept their distance at all times. The blonde one pulled out a leash which shot out to grab Carim's neck. Carim suddenly became fastened to the man's grip like a dog. Meanwhile, Carim's dog watched on with empty eyes full of terror. The ginger gentleman kneeled down to stroke the black and gold creature.

"Cute!" The ginger male exclaimed. His breath wheezed through a support tank. More suspirations than audible syllables were present. "It's exactly like my mum's dog."

"Don't touch it!" The pessimistic female in the group squawked. "We're under strict orders not to touch anything within this household."

"Especially not the subject," The man carrying the leash concurred, "Or his dog."

"You do not need to do this," Carim insisted. "I will be fine."

"Sorry, fella. You may be a national hero, but we can't run the risk. Say you're a secret coward, and you decide to run. That's an entire town contaminated, and from there, the disease will spread to other neighbourhoods and cities, everywhere."

"You sure I can't touch it?" The kneeling ginger asked.

"*Him,*" Carim interjected with as much rage as a pacifist could muster.

"You touch it," The leader's tone started out promising, "and you run the risk of joining Carim, even with gloved hands. What abilities do you have?"

"Don't you know by now?" His colleague asked. "I can see the future."

"You could've warned me! Two-dimensional vision would be a curse after what you've been used to. Don't touch the dog. We don't know how infectious this thing is."

"I can't see myself losing my powers in the future."

"Can you see yourself touching the dog?"

"No."

"Then don't touch the dog."

"This cannot be permanent, surely?" asked Carim.

"Say farewell to your home, because this will be the last you see of it."

Carim looked at this house of luxury. A high rise oak dinner table, plasma TV, glistening fireplace. He had never deserved this place. A life of punishment was what he deserved. Carim tugged on the leash with his neck to push the men forwards.

"We do have an eager one today!" The leader exclaimed.

"Just look after Crackers, won't you?" Carim asked.

"I've always preferred my cheese on toast," The redhead replied.

"I mean the dog!"

"Oh, the dog! That's his name? Strange name. Dogs are usually called Bella, or Molly, or something. Only if they're a girl, I suppose. I'm afraid you've had contact with him. He's contagious. We'll have to put him down."

Carim questioned intervening, by which point the woman had already injected a stiff needle into the dog's neck and put him out of his misery. Carim's heart shattered. Needless cruelty.

Carim was outside in the darkness which obscured his view of the twee cottage. Night-time hardly did the place any favours. Owls tweeted as if to rub in that they were free and he was not. While Carim waited, the woman was tending to the device which held Ethan's soundwaves.

"The subject has been contained, sir," she said militaristically.

"There will be reasonable compensation for your sacrifice," Ethan replied.

On cue, the female soldier, who was thin beneath her suit but looked plump with all the padding, flicked a switch to terminate the conversation. Following this, she flicked off all the light switches in the house. The broadband, the television at the wall, the chargers that leached off their sockets, shut all the doors. Every manoeuvre was conducted under two layers of gloves. By the time she vacated the premises and locked the door, the other three were in the minibus. This minibus was labelled 'Defence E,' was white but almost grey, and had enough seats to house sixteen schoolchildren. Space was necessary with somebody as dangerous as Carim. He may have been powerless, but he was more of a threat than ever. They forced him into the backseat while the three custodians perched at the fore. The blonde man was driving. A rev of the engine. Next stop: Woodville Estate. Carim's new home.

They removed Carim's collar but handed him a mask to place over his mouth to contain the germs. Windows, while murky, allowed him to observe the entire journey. The woman kept a constant eye on the windscreen mirror. The other passenger scrolled through Instagram while singing along to Billy Joel on the radio.

Billy Joel was right. Only the good die young, and this fate was as good as death. Carim drifted into dread, and guilt, and all the normal emotions, as he realised that Ethan was right. He was one of them now. One of the monsters.

13.   Everyone has their price

Clive spent lunch hour in the company of a beef dripping sandwich and a can of full-fat coke and wondered why his heart was hurting. A flabbergasted wave of commotion emerged from the chilly, radiator-free suite outside, stirring him from his daze. Frenzied natter kept the minds of the journalists distracted from the cold while Clive enjoyed the warmth. Clive, in a Monday-born suit, felt comfortable in a building where the conditions rarely became anything better than wintry.

He crunched down on his sandwich at 11.30. An early lunch, because the ennui was starting to sink in. Despite the healthy salary, his job involved nothing more than barking orders and writing the Page 2 column each morning.

Although boredom may have permeated, this was far from a boring day for *The Morning Manifesto*. Every convenience store in the country had a copy of their paper front and centre. Every oblivious eye would turn and stare in wonder. Tills would pop open across the globe and the contents would line Clive's pockets.

Meat juice dribbled onto the manager's navy tie but wiping it took too much effort. For the rest of the day, the flesh stain placed his quality of professionalism at stake. A yawn busted past his tongue even if he hadn't yet been awake for three hours.

Approaching the conclusion of his roll, he tossed the wrapper in the bin and felt his stomach still growling. One button on his shirt remained unfastened from where he had fought to tug the fabric over his balloon belly. He'd tried Weight Watcher, but his mind never let him succeed with the diet. The only option left was to visit somebody with the ability to hypnotise him, but he knew how much it would cost, financially, and spiritually.

After a quick check of *The Manifesto*'s feed on the computer ahead of him, he lifted himself from his chair. The move required the effort that any ordinary person would face benching 150 pounds. Before he could reach the vending machine, a knock reached his door, and he breathed a sigh of relief when the visitor burst through. Thank God - he didn't have to get up! He enjoyed sitting down, not because it was easier, but because interlacing his fingers and arching his back gave him authority.

While he may have expected a bobbed brunette or a jittering redhead to dawn on his doorstep, the presence of a stranger was somewhat reassuring. They were empty-handed, without a name badge to instate his status. He emanated Clive's more assertive attributes, without the excess baggage or tedious definition. This well-dressed man swiped at Clive's Newton's cradle, allowing the spheres to ripple off one another. The medals on his military regalia rattled as he moved. He waited for the clamour to stop before he spoke. The rotating chime became the soundtrack to intense eye-led interchanges.

"Clive Mannering," Ethan said. "That is who I am meeting with, am I correct?"

Clive nodded. "Unfortunately for you, that is correct."

"I gather you're a glass half empty sort of man?" Ethan asked. He rose, inspecting a coke can from the multipack which Clive had purchased. "Or a coke half empty sort of fellow? You should be careful, you know. 137 calories in one can."

"Do I look like a dieting man to you?" asked the chubby-faced boss.

Ethan flicked the coke's pull tab to prompt the drink to open. While Clive's super-hearing had its advantages, exercises such as these were excruciating. The harsh click of the can as the tab flicked its heel. The effervescent fizz of the bubbles and the ring scraping against his throat. Even the brown liquid slinking down Ethan's gullet was audible. Ethan made himself a hypocrite, savouring the refreshment he had recently denounced.

"Do you mind not drinking my coke?" Clive asked.

"Yes, I do mind."

Clive popped his index fingers in each ear, even if his distal finger was too dumpy to fit. "I hear what you hear now," Ethan remarked. "I'm just better at controlling your abilities."

Working in an environment like theirs was chaotic enough to drive anybody with enhanced hearing insane. The constant racket of the clanging telephone. The grating hubbub of water cooler rambling. Every word was audible from every mouth in the house, and it drove Clive crazy. Ethan heard as much as Clive did, thanks to his ability to mimic, but squinting tuned in the noise to areas of focus. He heard Chrissie speaking on the phone to another paper about the Carim incident. Then, he made out Ruth wittering on a call to her mother about her date with a lunatic magician the night before. Ethan shut his eyes and returned to focus. Back in the room. All he could hear were Clive's amplified words.

"Did you just come here to torment me," asked Clive, "or do you have another reason for being here?"

"The receptionist let me in. Nice girl. She had powers of persuasion, I believe, but, well, I ended up being the one persuading her to let me in."

"Am I meant to know who you are?"

"I'm not insulted that you don't. I'm new to the scene, you see. Sure, I worked on Defence J, but Orkney's so distant that I wouldn't expect you to know that. I'm Ethan Song, captain of Defence E. I resumed the position from Petula Wednesday."

Clive sunk back into his chair, locking his hands, equal parts thrilled and terrified. "You're here to talk about the article on The Knight, aren't you?"

"*The Morning Manifesto* declared war on Defence E when it went to print this morning. I rose with a cup of oolong tea and a slice of marmalade on toast to an alert on my phone that one of my agents had been branded a murderer. Slander against a hero, as some papers have declared, and as you will soon enforce."

Ethan rose, not used to sitting down for such extensive periods. He leaned over the table and snarled.

"Let me get this straight," Ethan continued. "Do you think that by attacking us, you will sell more copies?"

"I believe the financial benefits of my decision will soon become clear."

"We have power over you," Ethan warned. "We will soon, at least."

"You're here to buy us out, aren't you?"

"I was about to make that proposition, yes. How much is your paper worth?"

"None of your money!"

Ethan crossed his arms and released a momentous groan.

"You believe you have a gimmick on your hands. Attacking heroes who put their lives on the line on a daily basis isn't a gimmick. It's defamation, and the public will hold you accountable. Without people like The Knight, our country will be doomed."

"Heroes don't kill people. Vigilantes kill people."

Ethan ignored this. "Name your price. Everybody has their price."

Clive shook his head. "No dice. This is my paper."

"I did my research on you," Ethan said. "Surely you've learned not to reject offers by now."

"I only reject offers that aren't worth accepting."

"You were formerly an employee of Firefox, an advertising agency. You'd raid competitive firms by eavesdropping on board meetings. You'd steal any client worth taking and provide them with better offers. You rose up the ranks, becoming director of communications. Those companies called you out, and Firefox fired you. Somebody gave you another chance when you were at your lowest point. Alan Pye offered you a job as a columnist on *The Manifesto*, the paper he owned. It was much more prestigious back in his day. Much better known. He knew how to make the paper stand out without resorting to slander. Then he retired, and the man who had been there longest replaced him."

"What's this got to do with anything?" asked Clive.

"You were corrupt, untrustworthy, but Alan Pye gave you another chance. I'm giving you the opportunity to make *The Manifesto* into the paper that Alan always wanted it to be. More money, greater independence."

"We're a threat to you, that's all. You're trying to remove said obstacle."

"Quarter of a million pounds."

Ethan removed his wallet from his pocket and divulged a cheque for £250,000. Clive's eyes sparkled as Elizabeth Windsor's face reflected on his irises.

"Again, I insist, we're not going to be bought out," Clive insisted.

"Half a million pounds."

Outside the office, the hustle and bustle conquered a room of sharp voices. Chrissie spammed text onto a word document. Ruth watched her, with little better to do. Ruth, a short red-haired woman, petite, and with a wart for an eyelid and freckles for a cheek. She hung off Chrissie's desk like a schoolgirl chuntering about romantic trivialities.

The gateway to Clive's out-of-bounds office hurtled open, and the boss emerged with as much swagger as a dad at karaoke. Mannering returned to his podium and heard faint whispers about the size of his tummy and the beefy blubber on his tie. His ears stood up, as did the hairs on the back of his neck.

"An announcement!" Clive exclaimed.

"Not another one, one," Ruth remarked.

"We're still dealing with the aftermath of last night's announcement," commented Chrissie.

"This is Ethan Song, leader of Defence E," said Clive, to a collective eye-roll. "*The Manifesto* is now the official paper of Defence E."

"He's brought us out?" Adam questioned. "How much for?"

"A price you will be seeing none of because it will go to improving the quality of the paper, not the quality of your salaries."

"I bet it will improve yours though."

"Have some respect for your boss!" Ethan barked. "What's your name, son?"

"Adam Mortimer. I'm the social media coordinator for this paper."

"You don't seem to be coordinating much. There's work to be done."

"Let me introduce you to the staff you will be working with," Clive said to Ethan.

"I won't be working with anyone. Carim will."

Ethan's domineering footsteps had the intention of frightening them. Ruth felt a lump form in her throat. Chrissie didn't flinch. Ruth was the pussy cat and Chrissie was the daredevil. He marched around the room, taking heavy footsteps and fear-inducing eye contact with him. He noticed everybody stunned to silence, apart from Chrissie, who he paused at.

"I did my research on you too, Chrissie," Ethan said. "I was dazzled by your work at the power complex in Edgehill."

"Thank you," Chrissie replied. "So was I, quite frankly!"

"You're a bold person, releasing that story on The Knight this morning."

"I found the story. Clive was the one who told me to go through with it."

Ethan looked at Clive, who blushed frenetically. Ethan tutted. "Do you realise the damage it caused? Carim has now been taken from his home, lost his powers, and incarcerated in a community with the unblessed."

"He shouldn't have killed three people then, should he? Or were those your orders that he was following?"

Ethan smirked. "A tough cookie."

"One that you'll struggle to break, even though I'm sure your macho ego will try."

"What about you?" Ethan asked as he turned to Ruth. "Did you have any role in the story?"

"She does the words, I do the wit, wit," Ruth replied.

"She's got a speech impediment," Clive interposed.

Ethan began to trot around the room where silence had replaced commotion. "I have chosen you to complete a very special task."

"Me, me?" Ruth asked.

"Not just you, you, but her, too."

"I expect the answer will be no," Chrissie replied.

"You've always been an ambitious woman seeking opportunity, so I guarantee the answer will be yes. This morning, The Knight was stripped not only of his abilities but his reputation. Our new deal seeks to rectify that."

"A deal is a two-party agreement."

"You enjoy a challenge, don't you? You've been searching for challenges ever since you started at this place. You've never been one for the rigmarole of 9 to 5 monotony. I have a challenge for you. I invite you to join the community in Hull where Carim currently resides. The pay will be agreeable enough to meet your standards. Your role would be to record Carim's every movement to prove that he is redeeming himself in light of his recent behaviour. That way, we can restore his reputation as a hero."

"You expect me to give up my life, my family, my career, to go and live alongside the unblessed? Granted, I have nothing against the unblessed, but I have a life here."

"You are your career. It's all you live for. Think about how challenging this would be. It would get your brain working, and it's more money in the bank." He turned to Ruth. "What about you, Ruth?"

"I'm hardly Chrissie, Chrissie," Ruth said.

"I know you're not, but you're like gin and tonic, sweet and salty. Great alone, but better together. This is the first time any blessed hero has lost their abilities since 1347, and the first time any unblessed person has escaped. Look at the historical event you've broken here. This is an opportunity to make history."

"Carim isn't part of Defence E now," Chrissie thought. "Why would you go to this effort to restore his reputation when you could just replace him?"

"People still associate him with our organisation. Perhaps one day there will be a way to cure him so he becomes part of our organisation again. If we show him working with, and for, the people of the community that he's allegedly opposed to, we can scrub out the blemishes on his, and our, reputation."

"That's what *The Manifesto* is now? Your weapon. Your propaganda tool."

"This is the best thing that could ever have happened to us," Clive claimed.

"That's what you said yesterday about us declaring war on Defence E, and now that's apparently the worst decision we could have made. I'll wait until tomorrow to make up my mind on this one."

"You should be flattered," Ethan said, "That of all the journalists in the world, you're the one that has been chosen for this task."

"I'm just the first fool you could find."

"You're one of a kind. You can stake out any story using nothing more than a memory stick."

"I'd rather not do your bidding, thank you."

Ethan rotated to face Clive. "Get Dawn up here, please."

Dawn was the receptionist with the powers of persuasion, who still wore her hair in pigtails even though she was thirty-five.

"Tell me to do something," Ethan demanded when Dawn arrived.

"I don't know what you mean," Dawn replied. "Who are you?"

"You let me in earlier, remember? Just tell me to do something."

"Erm…"

"Tell me to pick up that set of pens over there."

"Okay…Pick up that set of pens over there."

Ethan responded to the self-inflicted imperative by collecting the tub of stationery. It rattled about in his grasp. Dawn didn't like having that amount of power, which was why she chose to be a receptionist.

"Thank you, Dawn," Ethan said. "That'll be all." He turned to Ruth and Chrissie. His eyes were more hypnotic than before, having harnessed Dawn's abilities. "You will accept this opportunity. This is a chance of a lifetime."

Chrissie tried to resist, but she shook her head and shook all the apprehension away with it. "I suppose you're right. This will do wonders for my career." She held out her hand for Ethan to shake, which he did, with a pompous simper. "I accept your proposal."

"I suppose that means I accept too, too," replied Ruth.

He turned back around to Clive. "See what I mean, Clive? Everybody has their price."

And with that, Ethan grinned with the satisfaction of knowing he had won , andClive smiled profusely with the satisfaction of knowing what his pay packet would look like at the end of the month. Chrissie and Ruth, meanwhile, were unsure what they had involuntarily signed up for.

14. Remember, Remember

They didn't forget Winona in the morning, nor in the many mornings that followed. They remembered Winona in the afternoons and the evenings, too, when the memories were just as unwelcome.

Do not mistake this for a funeral. There were no bodies to bury. Carim had already cremated them. Even if there were bodies, it would have been too early for a full-on, coffin-clad, obituary-laden burial.

Depriving them of cremation happened to be a godsend for the residents. Most deceased locals – under the government's paranoid orders – had their bodies burned in a ritualistic ceremony while friends and family watched on. Only a fortunate few received the luxury of burial in unmarked graves beneath the orchard. The ashes of the cremated, following the funeral service, would usually be broken down until nothing remained. That way, no risk of contamination to the blessed could surface.

This, on the other hand, was more of a memorial service than a funeral, held in the community hall, orchestrated by the man who opened it.

That man was Gordon Shepherd, husband of Agatha Churchill. The community mayor had stolen the place of Bishop Tomlinson at the altar and had carried leadership in his visage. There had been a time long ago when he had, anyway. Decades ago, he'd been dashing, assertive, front-facing. His age was showing now, and he had enough wrinkles to prove it. Where a handsome face had once lived was nasal fluff in place of a moustache, damp skin, oblong glasses, and a balding scalp. He perched at an altar centred around a golden cross, conflicting with his devout atheism.

Tomlinson, withering into a smoky grey twig, had been working there long enough to get his way. Tomlinson, a physical gremlin, looked old enough to have been around in the century when they built the community.

Gordon dressed all in black, and so did everybody else, except for Maeve and Eva, who failed to receive the dress code menu, in their tattered navy dress and grey cardigan, respectively. Glistening with gleaming gold tapestries and bronze skies, the chapel was a tutorial in elegance. It was ornate with idolatry and stained-glass windows patterned by the face of the lord himself. The only inelegance came from the weathered posters left behind from the Harvest festival.

In the front row sat Elijah's haggard brother, Steven, who left his home so rarely that the permanence of his dilapidation was under question. His mother and father, Elaine and Caleb, wrapped one another in their grieving arms. Elaine was even more weedy and unkempt than she had been prior to her son's demise, starving herself to negotiate with her sorrow, but Caleb remained naturally dense in build, despite the lack of sustenance. Caleb argued the previous night that Elijah's escape attempt had been foolish – Maeve and Eva had heard every word through the narrow floorboards – but they weren't angry. Quite the opposite. They understood why Elijah wanted out, and that was why their faces exhibited pride whenever Gordon mentioned Elijah's intentions. What angered Elaine was that Elijah hadn't told her first. He hadn't even mentioned his doubts about the community, to her knowledge. Not to mention that he was twenty-five and they were without the child they had never truly appreciated. Seeing his picture at the front of the hall, alongside Winona's hawkish profile and Kenny's thuggish visage, brought them each to tears with the recognition of missed opportunity. It wasn't like Elijah had planned this spur of the moment sort of deal, encouraged by his elders, Winona and Kenny, who should have been wiser. Then there were all the kids who turned up to pay their respects to their teacher. Barton, no longer with them.

Beside them was Suzie, the trim and scowling friend of Winona who carried grief in every expression. Misery became the substitute for her carefully curated beauty, and any aspiration she had to be blessed died with her best friend after witnessing firsthand the terror that abilities could cause. As a kid, she had wanted to be like the superheroes from the books she read, making a difference, with proper training, proper powers. Now, she'd acknowledged she was blessed to be unblessed, and would rather save lives in the way she knew how: With a first-aid kit by her side.

Both parties had fallen victim to the glares of early arrivals as they traversed down the chessboard aisle. The accompanying music originated from a morbid tune played by a child who had used rogue materials to construct his own harmonica. A harpist would have been preferable to the jagged melody, but authentic musical instruments were beyond their price range.

Agatha dressed in a knitted sable cardigan that was so fickle that it barely contained her. She had been punctual enough to class as the first one to arrive so she could pry on everybody who stepped through the double doors. Her husband's speech about the tragedy was

GOULDS

EST. 1902

22 - 23 South Street
Dorchester
Dorset
DT1 1DA
01305 217800
VAT No: 274249192

02/09/23   11:46

1x Heroes No Longer by Lewis   £8.99
Eyre @ £8.99
      9798854371377

Subtotal (Ex VAT)   £8.99
        VAT   £0.00
Total   £8.99
        CASH   £10.00
Change Due   £1.01

R008080700107000101

For Hygiene reasons swimwear, hats, hosiery
underwear, pierced earrings and
pillows and duvets cannot be returned.

Thankyou for shopping at Goulds

drowned in inaudible tears, while Agatha's dampened tissue extracted the makeup she had sacrificed time to apply that morning. Suzie's mood sat somewhere between anger and upset. The Norths - Elijah's clan, comprising his ramshackle father and virile brother - were quiet. This was surprising for a family that could never shut up when they were at home, arguing. Nobody was there to mourn Kenny, so mentions of him in the speech were fleeting.

Eva's attention became transfixed by the identity of the secret superpowered enemy. Could it be Francis, dinky with his hands clasped and eyes shut in mute prayer? Or Agatha, nails shaven and facial hairs extracted, under the same roof as the mayor, so spywork would be no bother. Maybe the mayor himself was the one they were looking for. 'Go' for Gordon. Nobody was beyond suspicion, not even Hex, the one who had implanted the idea of rebellion in Winona's mind. What if he were Defence E's weapon? Hex looked so empty. He'd been holding back the tears, but Maeve mistook that emptiness for callousness.

Suzie kept turning back to face the Crofts. Another glower. Maybe she was the spy, or maybe she was regretting ever having given up her baby to the Crofts in the first place. Hex was Maeve and Eva's now, not Suzie's. Vexation opened Suzie's expression to fresh realms of inaudible anger once she returned to face Gordon. Gordon ranted away about how much they would all miss the deceased. He warned the crowd not to take a similar risk, and anybody could tell that most onlookers wanted to ask the questions they couldn't. Eva wanted to interrogate Gordon about how much he knew. She felt it would be the wrong time.

By the time the service was over, hands were shaken and condolences were exchanged. The pianist droned out a groaning rendition of Be Still My Soul. Maeve approached Suzie to distribute sympathy, but Suzie thrust her head left and traipsed away. Eva held Hex by the oak doorway while Maeve ambled down the aisle. Her hands clasped onto the frills of the dress which was crumbling around her waist. Her clicking, clacking heels made every move as emphasised as a mare's.

"She chose to give up that baby," Maeve grumbled to herself.

"What are you talking about," Hex, the boy who didn't know his birth mother, asked.

"Nothing, sweetie. How are you both?"

"I'm having so much fun," Eva murmured. "Funerals are a real Mardi gras."

"It's awful, isn't it?" Maeve asked as she watched the North family cry away to themselves alongside Suzie, who batted away the tears.

Eva nodded. "Suzie looks awful."

"She's grieving. I don't think we can expect her to look like Grace Kelly."

How did Maeve know who Grace Kelly was? Too much time spent in front of the television, one would imagine.

"Can we go now?" asked Hex, who was by no means unaffected by the experience. He'd cried himself to sleep the previous night. Most people had.

"We should stay for a while," Maeve suggested. "Pay our respects?"

With that, Gordon approached, accompanied by the shadow of his more unwelcoming wife. Agatha had tissues stuffed in her breast pocket which she often dived into. She blew her nose with such vehemence that her nostrils almost eroded.

"Beautiful service, don't you think?" Agatha provoked, to which Maeve inclined.

"Beautiful," Elijah's mother repeated, not sure what more to say.

"Certainly so," responded Gordon. He spoke in received pronunciation, which made his meandering speech passive to a fault. "We'll be holding a wake in the community centre if you'd like to join us."

Suzie lingered in the backdrop, listening in case they talked about her, and muttered. "People are dead, but at least there's a buffet." There wouldn't be a buffet. The community was too skint for that. Francis knew that, but his ears still stuck up at the mere promise of food, forgetting for a moment that his colleague, and friend, was dead.

"I thought this wasn't a funeral?" Eva responded. "Why are we having a wake?"

"It *is* a funeral," Gordon replied.

"Make your mind up! You said it was a memorial service!"

"Eva!" Maeve squawked.

Strike one. Eva had always been the more rebellious member of their double act. Maeve was the goody-two-shoes parent who instructed her son to do his homework and eat his vegetables. Eva was the rowdy one who'd let Hex do what he wanted when he wanted.

As a teenager, Eva had been more conventional, staying out late with friends even without a nightclub in sight. She'd nourish freedom by tattooing her armpit with a love heart while Maeve stayed at home with an easel. Eva's husky smoker's breath confirmed the rebellious habit that defied the laws of finance and reason. Only her newsagent job confined her to a lifestyle of domesticity which her parents never believed she could accomplish. She only agreed to settle down because of her love for Maeve, and because there wasn't anything more to do. Otherwise, she would have escaped, like Winona, and off to Paris she would go! The rebellious sides of her must have been rubbing off on Hex who, the previous day, had displayed an attribute that eventually amounted to insurrection.

But nobody could know about that. If they found out, Hex could be in danger, and so could they. After all, if Hex didn't plant the idea in Winona's head, she would never have thought anything wrong with the way they were living. If Winona never rebelled, neither would Kenny or Elijah. They would be branded the ones responsible for Winona's death, and then they would lose everything - not that they had much to begin with.

The last time they had been in the community centre was Hex's eighth birthday party. A bleak affair, with sugar cookies instead of birthday cake and handwritten posters instead of balloons. The falsetto happy birthday wishes of Hex's shrill school friends. The shallow ball pool. This had been enough to brighten Hex's murky expression. Throw in a large paper mache pelican, and he would be just fine. He'd reflect fondly on the gathering, even if it had motivated an epidemic of typhus due to the spread of lice amongst the unclean. None of Gordon's extravagances, after all, could cure the innate issues, such as the lack of cleanliness and spread of disease, which the blessed refused to assist them with, despite the tools at their disposal. Gordon prevailed through death and disease to brighten community spirits, usually employing the same bitter mustard yellow hall to do so.

There were weddings (including the Croft's), bar mitzvahs (for Kenny) and funerals (like this not-really-a-funeral funeral). Bishop Tomlinson used it for Sunday service, where he'd be forced to preach the gospel of the unblessed bible which had instigated Winona's rebellious urge. The community centre wasn't anything special. It was only a room with nothing other than a kettle and a table to say for itself, but it was theirs.

Suzie trailed on after the precession with ears piqued by obsession. Maeve and Eva, acknowledging their enemies' pursuit. let her follow Agatha out of the building. Agatha employed baby talk to mollycoddle Hex. She clasped his hand and treated him like her own. He'd talk about dinosaurs, and dinosaur birds, and she'd try to pretend to care.

"Come along, Hector," Agatha embarked on the argument she had with him every time she encountered him.

"*Hex*," he corrected.

"Your mothers shouldn't even humour you by calling you that. It's a dirty nickname!"

"It's not my nickname. It's my name."

"You're a bright child. You deserve a better name than *Hex*." Jesus, she practically spat the word.

"It's not like anybody else has a name like it," he beamed, "It makes me stand out and I'd like to stand out. Nobody else in Woodville even tries."

Agatha's husband stayed behind to watch everybody leave. Francis left with the Norths, and Maeve hoped she would be next. When she noticed Eva standing stationary in the altar, Maeve acknowledged that they wouldn't be leaving anytime soon. She tugged at Eva's hand. Gordon was at the altar, ruffling together papers he'd compiled for his speech the morning before.

Eva hauled the note from her polyester pockets and observed it again. Somebody in this compound had abilities. Go. Maeve's initial hypothesis was that the fragment referred to the aforementioned infinitive. Go, as in leave. Eva, instead, believed she had been cut off from writing 'Gordon'. It made sense for the mayor to have abilities. Perks of the job and better than anyone else in a community of equals. The emerald wedding ring that graced his finger was one of a kind in a place where most survive on one meal a day and four pounds an hour. He was the one with the means of contacting the outside world, making him apt for espionage.

Gordon didn't notice Eva's furious stride down the aisle because his scrawled notes preoccupied him. Maeve wanted to pull her back, but there was no pulling Eva back, and Maeve sort of admired that.

Take the old days, for example. They met in primary school. Best friends forever, friendship bracelets, double Dutch, two broken souls who became one. Maeve, an only child with an unidentified father and a mother with cystic fibrosis. Eva, neglected by parents who cared more about themselves than their offspring. They kissed in secondary school and fell in love in college and had never looked back since.

College operated in the same building as the nursery and always had done. It comprised three rooms which each arranged separate curriculums. Maeve's art class was housed in the same place as Eva's performing arts block; not that anybody could aspire to be an actor or dancer, of course, in anything other than amateur productions in the village hall. Eva was too diseased to go to Hollywood. She'd have to make do with being a stock assistant instead.

Back at college, Eva had cared more about a play they were performing than her teacher did. Eva's teacher - God rest his soul - - went off sick on the night of their proposed adaptation of King Lear. Eva, on top of a mesmerising performance as Cordelia that dazzled Maeve's lovestruck gaze, prepared the lights. She distributed the pamphlets and orchestrated the show so it wouldn't fall apart. It went ahead and she'd never heard such passionate applause.

Maeve expected the same audacity from the confrontation between Eva and Gordon. Gordon looked up, not at her, but to the ardent gasps and spirited screams that fought through oak to be heard. Gordon ignored the Crofts, swinging open the weighty wooden gateway that stood between them and the squawks. A ray of sunshine poured into the chapel as the explosive heat stifled their thoughts. Eva and Maeve, enraptured by God's torch, snuck up behind him. Eva hid the pamphlet away. This wasn't the time to ask Gordon what he knew.

At first, Gordon only saw spines under suits through the gleam of daylight. All the Crofts could see were gravestones in a drained field and the humidity from the Western sun. A pandemic of gasps was spreading as the residents reacted to the sight of somebody they had only seen on the small screen. Please welcome Woodville's latest resident, Carim Shafiq! A knight without armour. Instead, he wore a white hoodie and grey trousers. A hero like him could have embraced the moment by waving and expecting people to cradle his ego. The solemn look upon his face refused to indulge himself. No longer was he a hero, because he was an ordinary man with average eyes beating down on him as if he were a God – or the devil incarnate.

Suzie headed the crowd, of course. The Crofts would have expected the Norths to be the more expressive ones, after all the sleepless nights they had left Maeve and Eva with. Suzie, in theory, was trained to be tamed. A medic should never resort to violence, at least not violence of action. Violence of words, however, was a different matter, and she approached Carim with contempt. She never brandished her fist. She was better than that. Gordon pushed through the crowd to reach Carim, extending his arm, and Carim took his time to shake back.

"What a pleasure to have you here," Gordon said, mechanically enough to bring into question whether or not he meant it.

Eva took mental notes about their reactions. Those who responded too well, or not well enough, were the prime suspects. Eva, a former actress herself, knew theatrics when she saw them. She hadn't yet noticed any theatrical cues.

"You knew about this?" asked Suzie.

Gordon nodded. "We must welcome Carim into the community as our latest resident."

"He's a killer!"

"I know," Carim acknowledged. "I am sorry."

"Sorry won't bring them back, will it?"

"No."

"I thought the blessed weren't allowed near the unblessed," Eva noted.

"I am one of you now."

Suzie chuckled, with makeup so smeared that she resembled a circus performer. "That's why you wish you could reverse all this. You've lost your precious, prized powers that you can't live without. Guess what, mister? We've had to cope without abilities for our entire lives, and now you do too."

"I know. I will have to adjust. It is my punishment."

"You deserve a prison sentence for what you did."

"Isn't that what this is?" Agatha muttered, much to her husband's disapproval.

"What happened yesterday was a tragedy," Carim remarked. "I was only following orders."

"Children lost their teacher," Suzie pointed at Elijah's family. "People lost their loved ones."

Francis bobbed his head. "Him being here isn't right."

"Defence E have instructed us to accommodate him," Gordon droned.

"It's as if it's more their community than it is ours. I expect you had no say in this."

"I accepted their proposition."

"Because you were too frightened to decline it. We are all too frightened of them."

"And for good reason," Agatha said. "They killed three of our people yesterday."

Suzie, much shorter than Carim, had to raise her toes to face him. "Whose orders were you taking?"

"It was all for the greater good," Carim responded. "To protect those on the outside."

"Who thought that a schoolteacher and two security guards needed to die 'for the greater good'? What sicko thought that?"

"The greater good of the majority. 99% of people live outside the compounds. It may be a horrific fact, but it is the truth, that they must be put first, ahead of the 1%. That is how the world has always worked."

"Well, the world needs to change then, doesn't it?" Eva interjected, to which Maeve groaned. Maeve admired Eva's courage, as long as it never endangered them. "You superheroes have the power to achieve remarkable things," she continued. "I've read about Defence E in the papers. Quickfix can play with time, and Hop can time travel, but neither can go back and rewrite what happened. Neither can go back to when it all started and cure that virus which locked us all up in here. Neither of them can bring our friends back to right your wrongs. Why not? Because none of you want to. You like us being here where you know we always will be, so you have somebody to control. Humanity wouldn't be able to cope if somebody wasn't lesser."

"What is your name?" Carim asked.

"Eva. Eva Croft. I've got a ten-year-old son who had to watch his teacher die yesterday."

"Your son is there?" Carim pointed to a cluster of three children. "Is he among those children?"

Hex waved, releasing his hand from Agatha's grip. "Hiya!"

Carim kneeled down to pat Hex on the head. Eva was unhappy with a murderer making contact with her son, but Maeve pushed her back. For all they knew, Carim still had laser eyes that could kill them in an instant. "I apologise, son. I am here to make everything better."

Hex felt like ranting again. He inherited that rebellious streak from his mother. He restrained himself.

"Rewriting time is not the answer," Carim declaimed, back to the masses. "Death exists for a reason. Mistakes are made to be learned from. I am here to learn from my mistake."

"I know why you're really here," Suzie replied, as her snarl collided with his face.

"For what reason is that?"

"To strike terror into our hearts, so that we know that insurrection isn't tolerated."

"You know as well as I do how futile it is to attempt to escape this place. Our sacrifice in confining ourselves to this compound is necessary. The people of the outside world will lose their abilities if they come into contact with us."

"Wouldn't that be better?" questioned Agatha. "Equal people in an equal world?"

"The world's unfortunately never been that simple," Maeve remarked. "And never will be."

"So you're powerless now?" Francis asked. "Just like the rest of us?"

"That is correct," said Carim. "My abilities were stripped away from me after I made physical contact with Winona."

"And what will be his purpose in the community?" Suzie asked Gordon.

"He will be taking over the duties of Kenneth and Elijah."

"You've got to be kidding me! He's replacing the people he murdered!"

"His background in military and public service provides him with the perfect resume to act as a security guard."

Elijah's brother, Steven, churned a tear. "How ironic."

"It's like letting Jack the Ripper run a brothel," Suzie mocked.

"I will make it clear to you that I am not a bad man," Carim stated, although even he didn't believe himself to be a good one. "And that I did what I did for the sake of humanity if not for the sake of this community."

"Are we not 'humanity' enough for you?" Eva asked.

"Please don't be too harsh on him," Gordon said as his monotonous voice trickled out words. "Carim will become the cornerstone of this community."

"Whether we like it or not," Agatha murmured.

As the crowd dispersed, Suzie passed Carim with a scowl and released a ball of saliva from her glands. Hex laughed to himself once the spit collided with Carim's face. Suzie sauntered away, taking a look of disdain from Eva and Maeve with her. Gordon offered a handkerchief to allow Carim to remove the contents of Suzie's mouth from his cheek, and he diligently wiped it away.

"Let me show you around," Gordon remarked, and Carim followed.

Agatha strayed behind them, leaving Hex to return to his parents. For some reason, he enjoyed the company of the old woman, whose idea of fun was scrabble and bingo. His parents, meanwhile, were loving but drifted off at any sign of conversation about birds or football. Agatha at least tried to care about his principal interests.

Maeve and Eva hadn't noticed that Francis had strayed from the pack to waddle down the street to catch up with Suzie. She'd marched in a tantrum past the graves through a beachless city made of only grass and cement.

"Hold up!" Francis cried once he reached Suzie, far away from the weapons cupboard where Carim was headed.

"I don't want to talk to anyone," Suzie wailed. "Not even you, Francis."

Suzie shed a tear at last. Her face was finally dark enough to match with the drab colour scheme of her attire.

"There's something you should know," Francis said, breathy from the speed walk, clasping his hands over his knees to control his puffs. "It's about the Crofts."

"I don't care." She clicked her key into the lock of the apartment complex. "Shouldn't you be grieving? You knew Winona as well as I did."

"She meant a lot to me. One of my closest friends."

"She didn't like you much."

"I know," Francis replied. "I bet she talked about me all the time."

"The past is irrelevant now."

"I take that as a no."

Suzie wiped her feet against the matted carpet which approached her upon entering the apartment complex. "Go to the wake. I shan't be attending. Not if Carim is going to be there."

"Shouldn't you be paying your respects?"

"I shouldn't. I'd only cause a scene." Suzie prepared to slam the door. "Enjoy yourself, Francis!"

Francis locked his boot into the doorway so it wouldn't close. "Wait a minute!" Suzie turned. "Hex is the reason why Winona is dead. That's what I wanted to tell you."

"I'd say that was Carim."

"Hex planted the idea in Winona's head that the government was lying to us. From there, she decided to rebel. I was there in the assembly."

"The son they stole from me," Suzie spat.

"The one you adopted from them because you didn't want him...but that's beside the point. Maeve and Eva must have put ideas in Hex's head. If he didn't exclaim in assembly that the unblessed bible was lying, then Winona never would have been tempted to find out whether Hex was right."

"I can't blame her for it. We all want to know. She did it because she had nothing left to lose. It broke my heart a little, since she was my best friend, and she didn't really care about losing me."

"She didn't like you much," Francis said.

"I know. I bet she was talking about me all the time."

"Aren't you angry with Hex?" he questioned.

"Fuming," Suzie replied. "But I'm angry enough with the Crofts that it isn't possible to be bitterer."

"I'll let you leave then," Francis said. "I thought you should know."

"Enjoy your evening, Francis. I need to get away from it all, and away from Carim. If I stay around him too long, the fists may come out."

"What are you going to do about the Crofts?"

"They're not to blame for Winona's death, but Carim is. There's not much to be done."

"They're to blame for so much more though," he exclaimed, by which point the door was already shut. Francis's face turned, and he started to curse himself. What Eva had failed to notice when investigating her cohort was that Francis was investigating too. Francis knew what Eva was thinking. He knew what everybody was thinking.

He could report back to Defence E every rebellious thought that anybody was thinking. Later that night, he would inform Ethan that the Crofts believed there to be a spy within the community. His secret superpowers were under threat of being discovered.

Francis's abilities brought him pain since an artillery of thoughts bombarded him whenever he approached a person. Suzie's mind, for example, had been as uncontrollable as a wildfire. What she thought of him - the freckled freak. What she thought of Carim, the murderer at large. How much she despised Maeve and Eva, and Francis wished to capitalise on that. They were a threat to him. They were getting closer to the truth. The Crofts had to go.

14.   Recorded Letters

The Knight, a man who once had impenetrable armour and felt indestructible indifference, wallowed away in a pit of tears that he had dug for himself.

Carim's new home was on the sixth floor of Apartment block C. It was a far cry from the opulent cottage he'd been used to for six years. Mould on the ceilings and rat droppings on the floor made the stingy, mildew-smelling abode irredeemable. The walls were bare except for a 'welcome home' banner implemented three hours earlier and drawn in a rush by a child. Suzie wouldn't be happy if she knew that Carim was living in Room 66C, Kenny's home, the man he killed.

A fly buzzed around the ceiling, steering clear of his clean, blemish-free face. It was, however, attracted to the dirt which amassed in every other corner of the pit. Anytime he attempted to swat it away, it flocked over to the window and rested on grime.

Cubes of patchy yellow highlighted photograph shapes where pictures of Kenny and his late parents had once been. Carim didn't have any photographs with him to replace them. Even if he had time to prepare, he didn't have pictures of his family. He couldn't remember his mum, and he and his dad had always lived distant from technology. Abbas may have been photogenic, but no photos of him existed. Their primitive home avoided all tech, which made his mind the only place he could remember them.

Before Carim could settle down on his bed, a knock announced a cleaner at the door and Carim's gentility gave him little choice but to answer. The hag of a woman swept up all remnants of Kenny. His stray hairs were dotted around the floors. The couch groove he made whilst watching the television which was still in place. The permeating sense of masculinity that his masculine odour carried with him. Two sprays of Febreze and a dash of the broom later, and Kenny was gone for good. Once the cleaner had vanished, Carim deemed it time to sleep.

He had all the intention of sleeping, but neither guilt nor duty allowed him uninterrupted rest. Noises through thin walls from the community centre one block away kept his eyes open. It was the evening of the funeral, and the wake was going ahead. Carim liked getting eight hours, which his restless mind never let him have.

Gordon had propped a rifle by the door like a broom. What if he would have to use it to kill more people? Had he become Ethan's weapon? He hoped they were as frightened as he was so that they would choose to be subservient.

There was not much to do in the community other than sleep. Only to watch television. A sitcom was on, and he needed a good laugh, even though he knew he wouldn't get American humour, which he'd never found funny. What he failed to notice was that his phone - A swish Samsung, as opposed to the Nokia Bricks of his neighbours - was ringing with the name of Isla Daye. He was too distracted by the televised farce to notice.

The sitcom became background noise to suffocate the pain that accompanied his thoughts. Carim distributed the content from the bags the blonde leader, ginger man, and brunette woman had packed for him. The unblessed may have been wearing smart and rich clothes at the funeral, but that was only because grief commanded them to. Any ordinary day would dress them in tattered rags or roughened uniforms, but this was a special occasion. His wardrobe was busier, comprising a reasonable supply of socks, pants, and other essentials.

A quick check of his phone revealed one voicemail. He typed in his password, switched off the television, and listened to Isla's sweet voice, in mourning of the life he would never return to.

Only me! Hope you are missing me too much. I'd like to think I've had enough impact. I hear that people leave good memories in their friends' heads to lessen the impact of the bad ones. Remember when we went to New York to take down the industrial giant, and the Sushi we had afterwards? Salmon skin roll. Yum. Or when we fought off Eclipse in Cumbria using nothing but our wits? I expect you're not having a good time now. I wish I saw you last night before you left because Ethan tells me that I may never see you again. Not only that, but I wanted to beg you not to hate yourself, and that it wasn't your fault. Ethan told me earlier that I couldn't go back to change what happened. I wanted to be able to turn back time so that you didn't get taken away. We know what Ethan is capable of, and what he could do if we break his rules. He wanted those three people dead, at whatever price. It pains me to see The Manifesto ripping into you the way they have. Again, Ethan's dealing with it. He's brutal, but he'll get the job done. When you hear this, let me know what life is like down there. The No Man said he'd call at some point. I'd like to say Hop is missing you too, and that he'll send you a call, but you know Hop. He keeps himself to himself, and he's never been too fond of any of us, or of the Unblessed. Anyway, I'm rambling, and the bleep is going to cut me off-

The bleep cut her off. Carim gathered his thoughts with a shower in alloyed water, a drink of tap water, and a stress-chomp of a Hershey's bar. The three operatives had smuggled in plenty of treats for him which would make the unblessed jealous. He waited through five firm trembles before the operator told him to leave his message after the tone. *Beep.*

Carim here. Sorry I missed your call earlier. I was watching a sitcom! Yes, I watch sitcoms now! It was that one about the teacher with the power to read his students' minds. I also eat peanut butter cups, and that is a novelty for a man who once refused to eat any sugar-based products. I would promise to start the diet again tomorrow, but what have I got to lose? I cannot put into words how elated I am to hear from you. I am sure that elation will turn to desperation in the coming days as I adjust to life in this place. How do I describe it? The antonym of luxury. Dozens of flies are currently circling my lampshade. I lack the resources to remove them. The shower sprouts arctic cold sewage, and the people see nothing but the murderer in me. I wish you could turn back the clocks too, not that your powers, or the abilities Hop possesses, would allow you to do so.

Hop cannot change time, and Ethan would not allow you to break it. You do not have to justify your actions. It is I that must justify my own actions. Ethan may have issued the order, but I was the one who accepted it and administered it in an inadequate manner. Defence E will continue to serve Hull and I am sure you will do it proud. You will receive a new member who will put me to shame with their diligence. Besides, I will come to adjust to this place and prove that I am a better man than they have seen. Their first glimpse of The Knight provoked nothing other than pain. Kindness and goodwill will be my gifts to these people wherever I can provide them. I remember the good old days well. One day we might be able to work together again. Hopefully by me escaping this place, and not you coming to it.

The tone cut him off before he could continue his lecture. Only a few minutes later was the line clogged up by the warning that The No Man was about to bombard him with a call.

"Is this Carim?" The Northern ignoramus asked.

"I'm currently inside a table leg."

"As you do," Carim's glum face brightened. Nostalgia would be his downfall. "How are you doing?"

"Could be better. I'm trying to chase down a teenage arsonist. I shouldn't have disguised myself as wood…"

Commotion rested on the line as The No Man chased after the criminal. Groans followed hasty punches and the click of handcuffs. Hearing events that he could not see infused them with an almost comical vibe. Carim tapped his fingers against the wood while he waited for his ally to return.

"Can I put you on hold?" The No Man asked.

"Certainly," Carim responded.

The No Man returned twelve minutes later. "Bloody teenagers! What buggers, especially when they can set things on fire with their teeth."

Carim recalled how exciting it once was catching criminals - the thrill of the chase, the satisfaction at restoring justice. He would never get to experience that excitement again.

"So, how are you doing?" asked the Northerner.

"I could be better," Carim responded, "Why did you call?"

"I missed you, and I wanted to catch up."

"I have not been gone for long at all."

"Still, we're quite close."

"Are we?"

"I'd hope we were!"

"Even your first name is a mystery to me."

"My enigma is part of my charm, not that I've ever been charming enough for any man or woman to dig me!"

"You could morph into the body of a more charming person?" Carim chuckled.

"You're really helping with my self-confidence there! Thanks! How are you doing anyway, mate?"

The No Man was one of those people who couldn't make 'mate' sound natural. Carim had not announced it yet, but his arm was numb with pain. "Ow!" he exclaimed.

"You alright, chief?"

"Chief? My upper arm has been providing me with a sort of stabbing pain."

"Nothing compared to the emotional pain of being there, I suppose. Do they have Netflix?"

"Yes, they have Netflix. Is that all you care about?"

"Mostly," he said. "Hey, do you want me to come and see you? I could morph into a food lorry or something and infiltrate the place."

"It would be too risky. We do not want another hero to lose their abilities," Carim paused. "You know what you could do to cheer me up?"

"No," The No Man said.

"You could tell me who you really…"

"No, not no as in, no, I didn't understand, but no, as in, the negative."

"There is no need to be ashamed of yourself," Carim insisted.

"I'm not ashamed of myself. It's that I'm less ashamed of everything else." He changed the subject. "What is there to do in that place, anyway?"

"Eat peanut butter cups. Watch TV. Go to work. That is all."

"You eat chocolate now? You must have changed!"

"I have no other way to spend my days."

"I bet having to live without powers is like having to adjust to single life after a long-term relationship ends. Not that I've ever been in a long-term relationship."

"I expect it is reminiscent of that!"

"Ethan's kicking up a stir. I bet Isla's told you."

"I left a voice message for her," Carim replied, although one look at the clock indicated it had been half an hour since he had sent the message. How time flies, sometimes. "How is Hop coping with losing Petula?"

"Hop's a berk," The No Man hissed, hardly the chief of Hop's fan club. "Hop ain't happy because he was in love with Petula."

"Do you think so? What about the age difference?"

"Apparently that's not important when it's true love, although she was a bit of a hag. A lot of a hag, actually. So's Hop, in a way, I suppose. She's probably the only person who would put up with him."

"Hop is quite a conventionally handsome individual."

A northern chuckle. "Ha! He wishes. Best dash. Got to stop a burglary."

"You must be busy!"

"I bet you're missing it!"

"Yeah," Carim sighed, and smirked in a sombre fashion. "I guess so."

When the call dropped, the phone revealed she had left another message. He dialled 901 and awaited the call. He could still hear people at the wake in agitation with the awkward feeling that most have at such events. At the community centre, Agatha was squirrel biting a homemade quiche, aggravating the Crofts with her patient gnawing. Meanwhile, Carim still had the pleasure of more than a slice of cheese and leak since both his stomach and cupboards were full.

Carim waited for the voicemail to dial through. Isla's familiar modulations returned a smile to his face, almost making him forget the decaying husk of an apartment that encircled him. He had never appreciated his friends so much.

Nice to hear that you're finding it nice to hear from me. I suppose that shows I mean something to you. I'd like to think I've made an impression on all my colleagues, even Hop, even if he hates me. Even hate is better than indifference if it means you're remembered. Know that I'll always be here when you need me. Give me a call when you need it most. Maybe this time we'll be around at the same time. I best be going because I'm in the middle of speaking to Ethan. It's an appraisal sort of thing.

With that, she departed from the conversation, and Carim felt like he needed her then, but he decided to save their next conversation for another time, whenever he would need her most. He opted instead for the sound of robins nestling on nearby branches, and uncertain emotions from the village hall.

15.   The No Man's Story

"I'm a slipper!" I screamed at me Mam, on the day that I became Mam's slipper.

Every evening, she'd have a bath. Every single bloody evening. She were obsessed with being clean, which were strange for such a dirty person. She'd lather her hair in soap, sling on her dressing gown, go downstairs, watch a soap opera, and place on her slippers. She had never screamed as much as when she heard her slipper speaking to her in her son's voice. She threw the slipper to the wall and threw me fragile Northern soul with it. I felt all the pain that the shoe would have felt if it were animate as it collided against the drywall, and her general lack of care didn't help. She'd been so used to ignoring me by that point that she didn't notice I'd disappeared and become a slipper instead.

Conversations between me and Ma were never more profound than: "I wonder what percentage of our lives we spend going to the toilet? I bet it's not as large a percentage as how much time we waste talking about it!"

Ma knew I were a shapeshifter from birth. Everyone I met thought me abilities were mint. Try living with them, mate! I'd always been able to change into what I wanted to when I wanted to. I'd wake up in the morning sometimes and felt like being a traffic cone. It weren't unlike waking up and thinking you want to wear that nice blue T-Shirt you haven't worn in a while. This were the first time I shifted against me own will, but it weren't the last time.

Mam weren't winning Miss Grand International, I'll say that much. What am I talking about? /Were. She's still very much alive. Unfortunately. More often than not she's hogging a ventilator while claiming she's got some chronic illness that she really don't have. She scoffs two packs of digestives down her gullet and never drinks a sip of water and wonders why she has a chronic heart condition. Dad, well, the less said about him the better, so let's say nothing about him at all. I bet you're thinking, "Oh great, another effing origin story about mummy and daddy issues!". Don't be an eget and wait for me to get to the good bit, eh?

Mum had strangled dandruff blonde hair and wore the sort of tan and fake lips that made her look like the Bride of Wildenstein. Her clothes didn't do the fifty-year-old any favours. I ain't painting a pretty picture of her, am I? Don't tell me Mam I said all this because I'll probably be kicked out!

I let people see me for who I really were as a kid. Me large fod were ridiculous and I were lanky as hell. We'd been skint, you know, so that were probably why. I got bullied because I were lanky and meek. I don't want to reveal too much about me age or me appearance. Part of me superhero gimmick is that I'm an enigma.

Mam may have been a drunk and she stayed in her underwear on every unemployed day, but she definitely weren't abusive. She just liked chucking me to the wall when I became her slipper.

Luckily, I weren't the slipper for long because I became the wall - a beige wall. Then I were me mam's fag. Then I was a raspberry doughnut. Then I were an Asda catalogue, and one of Darren's dirty magazines. A picture of a woman concealing her naughty-sporties under two well-placed palm tree leaves. For the first decade of me life, I could choose when I changed out of me ordinary body and what I changed into. In the second, I lost control of me powers.

It could've been some kind of body dysmorphia for all mam knew. Luckily, it were just a life-changing, chronic disease that ruined every chance of happiness I could have had. Not a big deal then, really! Mam only started caring when I became a wine bottle and wasted her pinot noir when I needed the can. For any other person, rose red urine would be a cause of concern, but for me, it were just another part of living.

After this tragedy - a waste of five quid, a blood-red mess of a bathroom, and a waste of a decent bottle of booze - she sent me to The Institute. This were a place for messed up people like me who couldn't control their powers, or whose powers harmed them.

Among them - a guy who could pop in and out of existence but could never control when; a compulsive liar whose tongue extended every time she lied (her tongue eventually took up most of The Institute), and a woman with a melted face. The latest sod to come down those ends were a shapeshifter who could choose what they shaped into as a kid, but puberty sent me hormones skyrocketing, and I started morphing into all sorts against me own will.

Being a shapeshifter is an odd sensation, because you feel like you're still human, no matter what you morph into. I might be a keyboard, or something, but I can still curl me fingers and roll me eyes and feel me tongue moving. It's just like being human, in every way but not at all.

The first few months were painful. Me sticky, ashy childhood home weren't Villa Aurora, but it were home. At least I didn't have to worry about money. They fed me, even if it were muck. We had mushy cabbage slapped on a plate for every meal with a side of peas, and I always saved the peas for last. We had to keep strong, they kept saying, but true strength comes from a sirloin steak and a glass of rum.

The Institute was split into three demographics. The adult part were a proper loony bin, with madmen psychos and Nurse Ratchets. The kids had a playpark and adolescents had the exercise yard. They'd occupy us with team building, pattern finding, memory training. Everything kept us in line, and we'd get control over our minds in a jiffy. Every morning we got given a chalky pill that tasted of, well, chalk, and a crisp glass of water. Some got painkillers to curb the insanity. It's probably not too dissimilar from the life that Carim's living out now, but the opposite, because everybody had powers in The Institute.

The doctors were only unpleasant on needle day, but needle day were only unpleasant because of the needles. It came twice a month, regular as clockwork, with a jab in the arm that they said wouldn't hurt at all. It always bloody hurt. They wouldn't have to feel the twang themselves, so they could easily tell us it wouldn't hurt and they wouldn't know they were lying.

I wish I could say I didn't know how long I were there, but I put a tally in white chalk on a black chalkboard for every day I spent there. It ended up being somewhere between two and three thousand days. There weren't much to do other than mill with your own thoughts in the evenings. Every room were a blackened cube with a toilet and a bed, like a prison cell, but not just like a prison cell, because it were a prison cell.

Unlike most teenagers, I loved school, and exams because it were something to do. I scraped a passing grade but only because I worked. I'm dumb as trash but I got lucky. Is trash dumb? See what I mean!

In the later days, chores kept me company. Folding up the laundry, collecting the laundry, placing the laundry into the wash, removing the laundry out of the wash. Bored you there? Made your eyes gloss over the page? Good, because the job were boring too, but it were something to do.

No interaction was allowed with the other nutcases. When the pills wore off, before breakfast medication, I'd be bouncing into beds and peoples' noses without realising it. I hope none of them found it erotic! Focusing me mind on something allowed me to stop jumping. Me hormones wore off in time, and I returned to me former status of being able to leap into whatever I wanted. Petula must have scanned through The Institute resident list and been impressed by how far I had come. It weren't me 'I'm Rubber, You're Glue,' quick wit that led her to hire me, that's for sure.

Petula weren't young when I met her, but she were younger than she is now. So were I, I suppose. I wish I could say I am wiser now, but I'm still a numpty. Sometimes I'd get on with her, then sometimes she'd bark orders at me, and I'd go off her.

Mam didn't care about me returning home. Gran called me that evening, but only to talk about herself. Grandad invited me over to his retirement home, only to brag about his new, 'uber-hot' girlfriend, who weren't uber-hot at all, because she were seventy-six. Mam hadn't thrown a surprise 'welcome home' party because she were out cold on the sofa in front of a documentary about the SAS.

Home would have been nice, but I don't like how much it smelt of vinegar I popped out for a takeaway with the mates I don't want to name, for confidentiality reasons. We ate out in a cheap curry house which, following me cabbage and pea diet, were much appreciated. Unlike me last meal out, I didn't have to worry about becoming a korma! Petula approached me there after finding me after doing very little digging. It were all part of her abilities, apparently.

She were looking for four people to join Defence E and I were one of them. Only four defence groups existed before that, and now there's dozens! Carim were the level-headed one, Hop managed the History - not very well, of course - Isla took care of the future, and I were their top spy. We met over a few alcoholic drinks while Carim avoided anything that weren't orange juice. Petula liked the sound of her own voice, and her own morals, but at least she were better than Ethan.

Our first mission were a training one where we had to defeat a bloke the size of a skyscraper. One moment he were the size of an ant. The next, the size of Goliath. The scenario said he intended on achieving world domination, and we had to stop him. He'd been engineered in a factory, and I should've guessed because the animatronics were shite. I wobbled and whizzed at first, not sure if the job were for me. I held myself together and told myself, "Right, get a grip, you arse, and get to work."

I would provide the first blow to the being stomping on the people who surrounded the Empire State Building. High enough for his features to be obscured, all that could be heard from the Goliath creature were his 'Look upon me works, ye mighty, and despair' laughter. I raced up to him, leaped into his large legs, past the leg hair and into the bones. His insides were disgusting, but I needed to sprint up and down the tendon track. I started at his foot and ended at his pelvis to destabilise the circulation in his legs. His blood gushed down like an uncontrollable fountain. When I released myself from his skin, like the tick I were, he felt the blood pumping through his system so quick that his heart couldn't catch up. He collapsed to ordinary size, and Isla and Carim cooperated to punch blows in his cheeks and stomach until they could force him down. Hop did bugger all, really.

I weren't quite as involved as that, but I think I deserve to be the hero for once, don't you? People never take me seriously. It's always "The Knight's a hero" or "Isla's a hero", but I'm the laughing stock. I'm a shape-shifting class-clown with a junkie mother and *redacted* father, so let me be the hero because the others sure as hell get enough chances.

The President himself sent us a video message and said how wonderful we were. God bless the orange buffoon! There was some joke about one duck that looked right like Keith Harris, and we were all in hysterics, for some reason. Isla and Carim didn't know who Keith Harris were, which was why the joke were so funny.

Carim and Isla had their own jokes that I were never brought in on, while Hop grunted and groaned whenever we broke the serious mood. Five-star hotels and sushi bars made it into a first mission that we'd always remember. Isla and Carim always say New York were the start of their lives. This were when they truly started to live and feel as though they were truly a part of the world. I think I'd probably agree with them.

16. Interview with the Superhero

Two knocks at the door in quick succession brought Carim's attention to a pair of visitors. They were too cocky and spunky in their stance to have been anything other than journalists. The pointy-faced woman and her minuscule red-headed accomplice held notepads in their chests and pens in their hands. Their mouths would have revealed disgust at the sight of the rundown apartment if their mouths were not covered with surgical masks.

Induction had hardly been welcoming for Chrissie and Ruth. The unseen looks of dissatisfaction on their profiles said as much, hinted at from their eyes alone. The double act had been commissioned to a home in the field where the man they were trying to defend had committed the act they were trying to defend him for. Their new home was not a home at all, nor a house, but a shack that resembled a latrine, built in fragile white plastic. The interior consisted of a mildew-laden, dark red painted outhouse with nothing other than one all-in-one room, comprising a toilet, a shower, and a window to observe the unengaged scenery, and a camping bed and a desk with papers stacked on top. Chrissie slept in one hut while Ruth resided in the other. The night terrors made Ruth unbearable to sleep beside, so Chrissie was thankful they were separate. Ruth joked that they should have been humbled the place was built for them. Chrissie wasn't willing to keep her glass half-full, because the wine had run out long ago!

Chrissie tried her best to look elegant in her linen black suit and pampered lipstick one shade redder than scarlet. All that effort was futile, as nothing showed beyond her white hazmat cushion and dainty high heels. Ruth, anticipating the protective gear, opted for more of an everyday T-Shirt approach. The smell of the air had an earthy, mossy quality to it which their visors let them avoid. Ruth's boots made an indomitable impression, as every step she made required an emphasised step to bypass the padding, while Chrissie's hooves came with a clitter-clatter. Ruth revealed a detergent spray and cleaning cloth which she acquired to wipe down every surface. First to fall victim to her spray were the wooden chairs where they would plant their posteriors.

Saying goodbye to their loved ones had been excruciating. Ruth, planting a kiss on her ailing mother's crumpled forehead, knowing there was a chance it would be the final time. Chrissie, telling her boyfriend she would be back soon even though she knew this could have been a forever deal. The farewells were elongated enough to make them regret deciding to leave, but this was the opportunity of a lifetime. Besides, the goodbyes weren't even the most agonising part. That accolade went to the rigmarole of clean-down upon entry.

First, a conveyor belt would scan for any items inside their pockets. Phones and wallets needed to be stored out of reach until the blessed were out of the unblessed zone. Then, a bellowing voice insisted they proceed to the showers and rinse themselves down with unalloyed water. Afterwards, they'd place on their handpicked replacement attire that they found draped over the rail. In the meantime, their old clothes would be sterilised relentlessly and returned at a later date. Two anonymous workers placed the radiation suit over their legs to roll up their bodies. They lifted each arm and removed the impression of excess weight provided by the cushioning by patting the suit down.

Ethan had surveyed the process like a hawk to ensure they would avoid running the risk of contamination. His glares and sneers would dissuade them from reneging on their task. The cleaners provided Ruth with detergent in a backpack containing enough spray to clean a city.

Chrissie wriggled to station herself at Carim's desk - which became her own - cupping her chin to look clever. Biro snapped on the verge of rapid squiggles. Usually she would use a laptop, but she decided to spare the staff from the strain of the decontamination process which would ensue to get her one.

"How did you sleep last night?" Chrissie inquired.

"Not well at all," Carim replied. "Voices are still swirling through my head."

Some of these voices were not imaginary and had originated from the nearby village hall. There was always something going on down there - cooking classes on scarce materials, acapella groups, Yiddish chants. Others were imagined voices that refused to vacate his mind. Chrissie jotted down notes as if her life depended on it. Carim wasn't sleeping? She knew she could twist that into a story. The man lived and breathed guilt, and that would redeem him.

Ruth, looking ridiculous since the only part of her not covered by mask or glasses was her strawberry-red toupee, remained oblivious to her purpose in the scenario. Chrissie does the words, Ruth does the wit, but a bleak situation like the proverbial left little room for humour.

"Whose voices do you hear?" Chrissie asked.

"I hear the voices of those I have killed," Carim said. "They stay with me."

"Good," she remarked as she scrawled information and haemorrhaged words as a consequence of her pace. "Well, not good, it's horrible, I'm sorry, but we can turn that into a sympathy story since it proves you're remorseful for your sins."

"I realise that we have been denied a formal introduction."

"Did Ethan not tell you?" Carim shook his head at Chrissie. "We're from *The Morning Manifesto*. We wrote a story that announced you had killed three people and cast a shadow over your reputation. Let me be honest with you. You're a murderer, and I'm not happy with defending you..."

"I recognise you from an interview you conducted with me and Hop three years back. I admire your honesty. Most are too afraid to tell me what they think of me."

"You're Unblessed now. What reason would I have to fear you? If you had your laser eyes and automatic lance, I'd be saying the same thing. I'm not the type to fear."

"So why are you defending me?"

Chrissie couldn't answer without twitching. Ethan's voice still rested on her mind's surface. "It's my job."

"Our job, job," Ruth interjected.

"Yes, our job, and we've been sent here for a purpose, and that purpose is to defend you."

"Defend me?" Carim jolted. "How come?"

"Your reputation is wounded."

"Well, maybe it does not deserve to be healed."

"You must have fun at parties, parties!" Ruth jabbed.

"What separates me from the villains that I have apprehended? The murderers I have arrested all believed their crimes were justified, as did I."

Neither woman could give him a straight answer. Ruth proceeded to unleash the blue spray again, sprinkling liquid dots onto whatever surfaces Carim had touched. She worried she'd lose her abilities if her gloved hand came into contact with the table it had rested on. One squirt was allocated to the table before she foamed up her hands with soap and water, after spraying the tap.

"Why do you keep spraying everything?" Carim probed.

"We've been told to ensure the disease does not spread," Chrissie replied.

"My friend, Helen, tells me I've got OCD, OCD," Ruth said. "You'd like her, her. She can fly, so she's just like you, you."

"Poor woman," Carim remarked.

"Don't be so self-deprecating, deprecating! You're a hero, hero. That's what we're here to show the world, world."

Chrissie's silence spoke volumes.

"By choice, or because you have to? This is all because of Ethan, is it not? Did he buy your paper out? Are you allowed in and out of Woodville, or are you marooned here, just like me?"

Chrissie smirked. "It seems I underestimated your intelligence."

"Why would you have a reason to do that?"

"All of Defence E are typically handsome, physically strong. Usually typically handsome, physically strong people aren't the most intelligent types. Nobody's lucky enough to have both brain and brawn, or maybe I've met the exception."

"What do you want from me?" Carim asked, his empty expression fading into the scorching light that flickered on the oven which he couldn't work out how to switch off.

"I want to start by building up a picture of you as a hero so that our readers will sympathise with you."

"*The Manifesto* has become the paper which people believe will speak candidly on matters such as these. Your disposition exhibits nothing other than reluctance."

"Did you read the story we wrote about you?"

"I expect anything you said has already been uttered by my mind."

"So I suppose that makes the answer 'no'?"

"I was swept away from my home early that morning. I did not have time to sit down with a cup of tea and a biscuit, let alone to read the Manifesto's denunciation of my behaviour."

Carim rose from the seat he had occupied and shifted to the nearby basin. He filled three bottles full of water and collected two biscuits from the bags and offered them to the pair. When the glasses slammed on the table, creating two rings, Chrissie and Ruth each revealed their canteens of water. He'd forgotten that he had a disease and couldn't touch them.

"We can't take those, I'm afraid," Chrissie explained. "Doctor's orders."

"I am not like the rest of you anymore," Carim sighed. "I keep on forgetting that."

Carim returned the two untouched glasses to the scant cupboard, which was basically a drawer of four cups. Each of the three crates below contained clothes, food, and assortments. Ruth's eye wavered over the digestive which Carim dissected. Soon enough, he'd have eaten enough confectionery to lose his muscles. He no longer cared.

"Tell me, what abilities do you have that you are so desperate to keep hold of?" Carim questioned in mouthfuls distorted by cookie clusters.

"It's meant to be us asking the questions," Chrissie replied.

"It seems to be you asking the questions. Your friend has hardly said anything."

"She has a name, you know, know," Ruth barked.

"And it is not a name you have entrusted me with yet."

"Oh right, right! My mistake, mistake! I'm Ruth, and this is Chrissie, Chrissie. She does the words, and I do the wit, wit. Excuse the repeated words, words. I've got a tic, tic."

"You poor thing."

"I usually try to avoid short sentences and fragments as much as I can because I know people will judge me when my sentences come to an end, end. I've gotten used to it, it."

"You spoke in fragments only moments ago."

"That's beside the point, point! Answering your question, I'm like a walking dictionary, and they hired me because my mind has access to niche references and information which makes me the perfect headline writer, and Alan Pye used to say that every writer lacked the spark that I have, but that's only because I know everything, everything. I went on Mastermind once and won, but they sued me when they found out why I was so smart, smart. Chrissie here can smell stories, stories. She can access this matrix thing by placing a USB stick in her mouth, and it's rank, but that's how she found your story, story."

"I'm not even sure how it works," Chrissie said, "So don't ask."

"I expect you are the bold type then," Carim declared, "If you were willing to declare war on Defence E, you must possess very little in the way of consternation.

"I've been commanded to take on this story so I can keep my job. It doesn't mean I won't tell it on my own terms. I've set myself the challenge of defending you, but that doesn't mean I can't be honest."

"Be honest, then. What is your fully-fledged verdict on my actions?"

Chrissie's head rotated to face her notes. "Perhaps you'll find out when you read my article."

"How are you going to condemn me and defend me at the same time?"

"I'm not interested in doing this to defend you. I want to use you to defend the one percent. Look around this place. The walls are rotting, the ceilings are leaking."

The cavalcade of clicking claws against the walls sounded at the right moment. They turned their heads in unison, and the noise of mice was enough to make Ruth shudder.

"Nobody on the outside would want to live like this, yet they turn the other cheek. All my life I have done the same, but only because they never show you what this place is like on the news. We're meant to forget about the unblessed. Seeing the community today and knowing that there are children here, families, just like the rest of us, it enlightened me to their plight. I'm going to paint a portrait of this place as being a punishment; one you believe you deserve, but they do not. Positioning you as an advocate for unblessed rights would allow you to make history. Is that what you'd like?"

"I agree that the conditions here are far from adequate, so I would take on that opportunity."

"What time will you be guarding the gates today?" Chrissie asked.

He glared at his wristwatch. 10.50AM. "Midday."

"And who's guarding the gates now?"

"The gates do the guarding for themselves. Everybody has been frightened off from revolting by what I did."

"How do you feel about being placed in the same position as the man you killed?"

"I will not allow it to distract me from my duty."

A long pause cursed the room while Chrissie raced down notes. "What are you writing?"

"I've got a memory like a sieve."

"We both do, do," Ruth remarked. "Must be the journalist's curse, curse!"

"I thought you had an excellent memory?" Carim recalled.

"I can reel off every shade of blue or every leader in Russian history, but I can't remember what I had for dinner last night, night."

Chrissie ripped the paper from its elastic hold, revealing another notepad sheet. She distributed the written piece into her luggage. "Tell me about what you had to leave behind when you came here. That will get the readers teary."

"My home…" Carim muttered.

"I expect your home was a lovely place that most would be jealous of?"

"A quaint cottage in a reasonable neighbourhood. I expect that would be enough to spark the jealousy of many."

"We won't put that down then."

"I left my dog, Crackers. He is a Yorkshire terrier. I do not know who is looking after him, if anybody." He dared not mention what happened to Crackers next.

"What about a girlfriend? Boyfriend? Significant other?"

"I tend to not feel the way a girlfriend or boyfriend must feel to ever have one."

"You've been stripped away from your life and placed in this prison - and it is a prison - to ruminate on your actions. I think that's enough for people to feel sympathy for you."

"People will believe I deserve the fate I received. I am a murderer. I have come to acknowledge that as objective fact. That is why Defence E brought out your paper. My actions ihdicate that they rely on murderers to enact their dirty work, and that does not paint them in a particularly favourable light."

"I would've thought you'd believe that you did what you did for the greater good?"

"Like you said," Carim replied, "You underestimated me."

"Then why did you do it?"

"I was too afraid of what would happen if I refused. At that moment, I believed I was doing what was right. Now, I acknowledge that my decision was ill-fated."

Carim discovered her tepid smile while she distributed her notes to the page. She turned to face Ruth. "You are recording this, aren't you?"

"Oh bugger, bugger!" Ruth exclaimed, rushing through her backpack to reveal a disposable tape meant for backup notes. Her maladroit mechanisms left the bag's contents on the floor, forcing her to crawl onto the dusty matted carpet to collect the equipment. She took the spray with her to dot cerulean squirts wherever she placed her hands. Once she had grabbed the device, it dropped out of her hands, and she returned to the floor once more. Ruth flicked a green switch to launch the tape. "My flipping butter fingers, fingers! I'm as clumsy as Ivan the Terrible, which isn't that clumsy really, really. Shepherds Pie, pie! I remember now, now!"

"Right," Chrissie composed herself. "What have you thought about experiencing firsthand the way that the unblessed have been treated, Carim?"

"Their living conditions?" Carim asked, to which Chrissie nodded. "Insufficient to say the least. The water comes out as sewage. The rooms are unkempt. No flowers can grow where life cannot. Everybody lacks the necessary money to survive. I expect a well-cooked meal is difficult to come by amongst the deprivation."

"They have restaurants, don't they? And cafes?"

"One cafe, which nobody can afford to dine in. I have usually confined myself to my room out of fear of how I am regarded. Last night, the opportunity to walk around arrived when the streets were silent. I observed the school, the apartments, the orchard, the newsagents, the bank, the church, and the café. This is all they have. I expect unemployment is epidemic because of the lack of employment prospects. The unemployed receive as much money as the employed - a fixed rate - meaning the only incentive for work is that jobs are a means of occupying their time. The employed are the lucky ones because I am already bored of this place. I am unsure if they set everything aside to be less antisocial and embrace the community spirit. I have not been here long enough to say that for sure. I am sure you will find out when you investigate this place further."

"Which I intend to, once I have left you."

"I expect that will not be for a while. You will want to observe me at work, will you not?"

Ruth unveiled a disposable camera. "Oh yes, yes!"

"Have you experienced any community spirit yet, Carim?" Chrissie queried.

The night before, Carim heard a clamour from the community centre. The walls were so thin that he could hear every rising note and fading melody. Choir practice - tuneless, the works of the inexperienced. The prospect of company led him there, forgetting this was not the outside world. He wasn't accepted here. He wasn't their hero.

When the unlocked doors to the centre opened, Maria stood at the front with lyrics they repeated. *When the night has come...* Agatha lingered in the backdrop, refusing to participate in the festivities. It was fun, after all, and Agatha did not subscribe to merrymaking. Plus, her back hissed with agony. Suzie relished the opportunity to escape from the grief. When Carim entered, their happiness resolved in awkward silence for everybody other than Tony the bank clerk, who kept singing for one note longer than anybody else.

"We don't welcome your kind here," Maria said, despite being so elderly that hostility should have been beyond her interests. "I'll have to call somebody if you don't leave this instant."

"I thought everybody was welcome."

"All Woodville Estate residents are welcome. Not you."

"I am sorry," was all Carim could bring himself to say, and he bowed his head in shame as he left without dispute. He didn't recount this story to Chrissie, to spare himself the embarrassment.

Although community spirit may not have been high when he was around, the months and years preceding Carim's arrival had brought plenty. Whenever there was a fire - one had struck Apartment Block B in 2006 - the entire community would gather together with hosepipes in tattered rags. Many fetes had taken place in the orchard, at Harvest and Summer barbecues. Thursdays, for example, would usually be home to market day. That Thursday was an exception, for obvious reasons, but usually the hustle-bustle of archaic community spirit would ensue. Sometimes there'd be a children's choir. Sometimes the radio would blare out instead. The market comprised a row of lamplit tents which operated from midday to midnight – fish, jewellery, books – which were better to behold than to finance. Everybody came out on market day because it was something to do, but very few had the money to do anything more than browse. Still, they came together to pleasant music and reasonable climates and smiled and laughed as if their lives weren't anything less than wonderful.

"Do you think they're happy here?" Chrissie asked.

"One woman, Eva, lectured me on the abusive treatment of the unblessed from the likes of us."

"Us, as in me and you?"

"Us, as in them out there. We intend to make a difference, Chrissie, and we will achieve that together. I hope that my actions will enlighten people to the segregation which the unblessed fall victim to daily."

"Even if that makes you into a villain? I expect your boss won't be too happy."

"We have all fallen under the tyranny of Ethan Song. Whatever needs to happen to let the unblessed have justice will happen. Is anybody working on a cure to allow the unblessed to enter the real world? No, because nobody wants them to. I saw in Winona's eyes lost desperation that cannot be branded anything other than virtue. Her group sacrificed themselves to spread the word to those inside and outside. Their message stated that the way the blessed treat the unblessed is far from right. The outside world is ashamed of those they believe to be far from righteous, so they look away. We are like a bruise that will not vanish. There is no option to remove the blemish, but there is the option to ignore it.

Once midday arrived, Carim suited up in the uniform gifted to him from the staff wardrobe; a spare left behind by Kenny. One white vest, one black bodysuit, one rifle, one black pair of trousers, except he left the rifle behind. They followed Carim past the orchard to the gate, met with the snarling glares of innocent strangers, who they realised they must ignore. Ruth became waylaid by flowers with complicated names she knew, and wished to brag about knowing. Francis passed, camera for a mind, feigning scorn, despite being one of them.

Carim lurched at the gate, unsteady, unstable, perturbed by the journalists who recorded his every jolting limb. His rocky hands trembled, so his weapon would have trembled also. Luckily, his weapon was at the house. Chrissie was still scratching at her paper.

"Do you think they're afraid of you?" Chrissie shouted past the brewing wind.

"Pardon?" Carim quizzed from metres away, forcing Chrissie to step forward.

"I said, do you think they're afraid of you?"

"Of course they are afraid of me. I was the face of the local police force for six years. I killed three of their people. My purpose is to prove that I am not to be feared."

"How are you going to achieve that?"

"I have left my firearm behind. My face will always be engaged by a smile."

"I don't see a smile on your face right now."

Carim sighed. "Give it time. I am still mourning what I have taken."

"That's a good sign, trust me. People will support that."

"I do not need the support of people. I need the support of the Unblessed."

"Do you not consider the Unblessed to be people?"

"I consider the Unblessed no less human than the rest of us."

The gate button buzzed green with a clink. "Do you mind if I take this phone call?"

"Certainly, certainly," confirmed Ruth.

They observed Carim's call with the cube-eyed, dark-haired stranger that flashed up on the screen. Even Jake Latimer, remote enough in his pungent hovel, appeared afraid of Carim. Bleeps and whirrs of machinery distorted Jake's monotone voice. Ruth and Chrissie were too distant to discern anything beyond murmurs anyway.

"What do you think of him then, then?"

"He's not a bad man," Chrissie replied. "That's the best I can give him."

Chrissie approached Carim in her hustle stride, while Ruth remained behind to admire the flowers.

"I've got everything I need for today," Chrissie alerted. "I'll be back tomorrow."

"Do you not wish to know what we are discussing?" Carim questioned. "Jake and I are conversing over the security of this place."

"The Twins haven't detected anything in the next twenty-four hours for us to worry about," said Jake. "That's not to say nothing's been missed."

"Thank you for your time, Chrissie." Ruth hacked from afar. "And you too, Ruth!"

"It's a pleasure, pleasure!" Ruth exclaimed.

"Same time tomorrow?" Carim asked, to which Chrissie hesitated.

"Depends how people react to the story I release about you tomorrow. If your reputation is restored, our work is complete. I'd like to come back regardless to prove how charitable you're being. You will be charitable, won't you?"

"Come back this evening, and you will see."

17. Goodwill

That evening, Chrissie returned to find that Carim had donated most of his belongings. Food, clothes, his expensive wristwatch, labelled only by an anonymous banner: 'Help yourself'. Carim was left with only a few T-Shirts, two Digestive biscuits, and some toiletries. Suzie may have hated Carim, but she didn't recognise the handwriting. Her hunger forced her to swallow her pride and snatch the peanut butter cups on display. Carim collected what was left behind the next morning and took it back to his apartment. Chrissie noted his sacrifice, and a smile reached her face upon acknowledging that she was defending an innately decent man.

Before all that, Chrissie skidded from location to destination to chronicle the community. The cafe was desolate except for the disgruntled staff, who deterred any potential customers by freeing savage snarls. The reasonable prices (One pound per cappuccino) were still unreasonable for those on minimum wage. The bank was a ragtag exterior of malting brown brick which she wanted to enter, although a hostile typeface announced it was 'CLOSED'. Entry to the school was also forbidden, but she gauged the rotten building had the potential to be better than it was. Ruth's recording device picked up merry muffled screams from nearby children. They reminded her of the merry screams of any child in any playpark.

A sharp ping of the bell at the Newsagents. A haggish grey creature surfaced, whose frown went so deep that smiles presumably never reached her face. Eva stacked apples and trousers into adjacent compartments from tin trays which almost collapsed. Chrissie pinged on the receptionist's bell, by which point Agatha had migrated into the store cupboard. Ruth skimmed through a gossip magazine and Chrissie rattled her fingers like an impatient child. Chrissie noted the prices on the counter on her work pad: 45p for a chocolate bar, 90p for soap, and 90p for milk. Ruth trickled through the magazine pages in an empty store. Turning the page revealed Eva ogling over the cover, slapping the publication from her gloves. Ruth ensured she sprayed her hands down after she returned the issue to its habitat.

"You have to pay for those," Eva said. "And I expect from the gear you're wearing that you're financially stable enough to afford it, unlike the rest of us."

"If I was allowed money here," Ruth replied, "I'd give you it, it."

"Can people afford these magazines by any chance?" Chrissie asked following a pivot.

"Are you journalists or something?" Eva questioned.

"Yes, *Morning Manifesto,* at your service!"

A craggy voice emerged at the till. "Nobody can afford these magazines, nor the lottery tickets, or the fancy clothes, but we put them on our shelves for show regardless. Most of it just goes back into general circulation for those on the outside."

"They're journalists," Eva hissed.

"I have ears, Eva! Get back to work, my dear!"

Eva returned to her station, stocking stationery and gizmos aplenty. There wasn't much to stack, but she needed to fill the time. Agatha reached for a Manifesto in her eyeline on the top shelf, slamming it onto the counter.

"Sorry about that," Agatha continued. "She's a lovely girl usually or most people would consider her lovely, anyway. She's in a grump at the moment."

"You're one to talk," Eva muttered.

"I know what you've come here to ask me. It's about Carim, isn't it?"

"Yes, but probably not what you're thinking."

"You're Chrissie Young. I admire your chutzpah."

"Most people do!"

"My husband's mayor of this place. Gordon Shepherd, know him?"

Chrissie shrugged. "I haven't been here for long."

"I can't be honest around him much. I'm paranoid about my own husband dobbing me in! Yet, seeing that story provided me with relief. This place isn't good enough." This was a field day for the notetaker. "You're declaring war on Defence E?"

"We *are* Defence E. We've been brought out now."

Agatha sighed, preparing to return to her cupboard. "No further questions!"

"Wait!" Chrissie cried, preventing Agatha from retreating. "Just a few minutes of your time."

"Fine. Are you one of those journalists who needs to build up a profile of the people they're interviewing?"

"It always helps."

"Well, you wouldn't find much interesting about me. I'm like most old people. Rarely do I talk about anything other than the weather, or politics, or who's died this week. I run this place to entertain myself. I have done since I was a teenager. I don't need to go to work. Working only gets you a bit more money than not working, and I'm sixty-eight, so I could retire, but that wouldn't make any difference. Some people here have been retired their entire lives."

"The Community Express is a cure for your boredom?"

"The evenings can become lonely, but they're short. I can read a book. Gordon and I both work, so I can afford books. I can't complain, because we're more financially stable than most people here, but I enjoy complaining. It's a nice pastime."

"What is this place like to live in?"

She sniggered. "I could tell you it was terrific, but I'd be lying."

"Then don't tell me that."

"Let me provide you with an example. Two minutes down the street, there's our rubbish bins. Every Tuesday, they come to our gates to collect the waste. We don't have crates to transport materials. Our men aren't strong because there's not enough food to feed them. The bin men can't come in to collect the rubbish, nor can their vans, because they don't want to run the risk of infection. So, our men carry the rubbish by hand, and they end up dropping some of what is inside. One week makes very little difference. Over time, the leftovers pile up, and create a mess. If you hear rats and mice at night, that's why they're here."

"I'd like to speak to your husband."

"You wouldn't find him or his job particularly exciting," Agatha replied.

"He has more of an insight into this place than anybody else does."

"Let me call him to see if he's busy. He might be able to pop down for a chat."

Agatha picked up the 60s landline phone, and rolled across the analogue digits, waiting for the vibrations to stop. Chrissie waited at the desk. Ruth couldn't bear to wait around any longer and occupied the wait by leaning over Eva. Ruth was like a child when considering her meagre attention span and hyperactive tendencies.

"Whatcha doing, doing?" Ruth inquired. The more perspectives they had of the community, the better.

"Stacking shelves," Eva grumbled. "You're recording me, aren't you? You've got a microphone?"

"Are you satisfied with life in this community, community?"

"That's a yes then? No, I'm not satisfied. I'm pretty sick of it. You know why? I go to work, do the same thing, every day, and I get four pounds an hour for it. I go home, and it's the same every evening. Outside, you get to do what you want. You get your vacations, your night outs, your parties, but what do we get? We get television and water, and that'll be all. I've got a child to support."

"Son or daughter, daughter?"

"A son and a wife," Eva looked as though she was about to break down. "They're all I keep living for, and now I don't even know if I have them."

"What does that mean, mean?"

"It doesn't matter. I've always wondered, as I'm sure we all have: Why us? Why do people like you have all these remarkable powers while our bloodlines have never been able to do anything more than walk or talk? Why do we have to live in poverty while you get your fancy houses and your fancy ways of living?"

"I...don't know, know," Ruth stuttered, overwhelmed by the gravity of it all. She wanted Chrissie back. "It's not fair," was all she could say in response.

"I know it's not! I don't want Hex to live this life of restraint."

"What does your wife do, do?"

"She's a teacher at the local school. I'll tell you she worked with Winona Barton, as I'm sure you'll ask. They weren't close."

"Are there many jobs on offer here, here?"

"Occupations are hereditary. The Bush family - they live down the way - have always been accountants. Agatha's family have always had the newsagents. I never had that, really."

"What are your thoughts about Carim living here among you, you?"

"I don't hear much work being done," Agatha barked.

"If she'd leave me alone then I'd be doing it," Eva lied, because she was grateful for the intermission. "You're working for Defence E. Anything I say could get me killed. I'd rather not comment on that."

"We're writing an article about the plight of the unblessed, so we'd quite like to hear your thoughts, thoughts.."

"Like I believe that! Nothing's changed since the 1300s, and it never will. My wife doesn't believe it's all a lie. My son does, but Maeve's adamant about believing the lie they've always weaved. I've never known whether to believe it. I guess I thought I had to, until Winona came along. What Winona and Kenny and Elijah did - please publish their names - was an act of heroism that altered all our standpoints. You believe, and do I, that Carim was proof that the so-called heroes are the villains in fancy clothing. Out there people like The Knight are heroes, but here, he's an antagonist, just as we are to them."

"I thought so too, but I got to know him, and he's not a bad man, man."

"That's the popular consensus," Eva responded. "You don't have to believe it."

Agatha popped up with percussive hands. "This interview's outstayed its welcome!"

"Sorry, ma'am, ma'am," Ruth trembled.

Agatha giggled. "Nobody's ever called me Ma'am before, and certainly not twice!"

"It's my tic, tic."

The bell chimed once again. It was Gordon, the damp-skinned mayor topped by a sleek Panama hat, buckled jaw, and expiring suit. Chrissie turned to the gust of wind that carried him. The wind was unpleasant, so The Weatherman must have been having an off day.

"Apparently I've been summoned," Gordon said.

"Thanks for coming," Agatha replied with a peck on his cheek. "Defence E has sent some journalists in to talk about the unblessed."

"I see. I suppose you know who I am."

Chrissie answered. "As I said to your wife, I'm new in town."

Gordon may not have had a walking stick, but he was hardly vigorous. He plodded to the furniture aisle, collected a wicker chair, and plopped himself down. Although it may have appeared discourteous not to offer his wife a chair, nobody could accuse Gordon of not caring for her. He looked at her with eyes more loving than at the sight of any other.

"Love's old dream is what we are," Gordon grinned, speaking at one pitch lower than his voice had been when he first met Agatha. "Aggie and I met at school, and we haven't looked back since."

"Is this place usually busier than this?" Chrissie asked.

"A surge of customers usually come in around lunchtime," Agatha answered. "There aren't enough people living here to allow a constant stream of business."

Back to Gordon. "You're the mayor. Do you think Woodville is a good place to live?"

"It's as fine a place as I could imagine it being," Gordon answered without hesitation.

"That seems like an empty answer to me."

"We've got a real sense of community spirit. Employment for adults, education for children, hobbies for everyone else. We've taken what little we've got here and adapted it into something special."

"You have regular contact with the outside world, don't you?"

"I'm the one who enforces all the decrees which those higher up have insisted I do. My role is to do as they say and attempt to serve the people's needs in line with that."

"People aren't happy with the way things are run, especially not after Carim's arrival."

"That will change over time once people get to know Carim. He's a nice chap. People lost loved ones. Part of the grieving process is looking for someone to blame."

"Don't you believe Carim is to blame?"

"I believe in forgiveness," Gordon declared. "I believe Carim will earn our trust."

Afterwards, Chrissie and Ruth convened in the orchard to compile their notes from Chrissie's scribbles, with the slight help of Ruth's mumbled recordings. Ruth heard the children in the school playground again. She could even see Hex dashing around the field in his ragtag uniform.

Meanwhile, Francis played the onlooker from a picnic bench. He hoped they would speak to him, but they had everything they required. Once he realised they didn't wish to interview him, he poked his glasses back to his glabella and moved along. Maeve had been approached for an interview too, but her nerves led her to claim she was busy, and she skipped along before they could catch up with her.

Following steady decontamination, the reporters returned to their shacks. They'd been given a laptop and Ruth lingered in the background at all times. Chrissie's version of the story was as follows: *Yesterday, we reported on the scandalous and somewhat erroneous allegations that Carim Shafiq, known to many as Defence E's flagship superhero, The Knight, was not a hero after all. After I and my colleague, the excellent Ruth Mayor, were allowed access to Hull's Unblessed community, we were enlightened to a side of Carim that very few are aware of - one of deep, emotional turmoil. Carim is a man who plans to earn his redemption, and he will do that by standing up for the rights of the unblessed, with charitable due diligence.*

Carim told us himself that the voices of those lost as a consequence of his actions "Stay with him." He feels guilt for following the orders of those above him. Carim was doing what was asked of him, aware of the consequences for if he refused, and he felt ashamed. Perhaps we should blame the ones who issued the orders, and not the one who followed them.

When asked to describe the living conditions of this community, Carim described them as 'insufficient'. That is a sentiment that I, from personal experience, would agree with. I sit here in accommodation laid out like a prison cell, yet that is still preferable to the lowest standard of living. The unblessed have shelter, but inadequate shelter. They are exposed to standards with which we on the outside world would not tolerate if we were the ones living under these roofs. Perhaps everybody believes that is fair because they are inferior. They are not lesser. They are just like the rest of us.

I spoke to numerous people in the community. Gordon Shepherd, the Mayor, argued that he was trying his hardest to fix the community to serve more in the interests of its people. He has a wife, who runs a newsagent. Eva Croft has a family and a son who plays hopscotch and sings nursery rhymes. These children have to go back to rancid houses that are falling apart and that the residents have no way to repair. Everybody earns the same paltry sum of four pounds an hour. This will not suffice when residents have to pay bills, pay for food, pay taxes, and pay to keep their families alive. Taxes for a world they do not truly live in, and bills for conditions that do not meet essential human needs.

What is the solution? Regular supply drops into the community or more focus on a cure which nobody seems to be pursuing. Chocolate bars may be 45p instead of 70, but that is only because the maximum wage is over half of our minimum wage. The wages need

*to be raised, the supplies need to be more accessible, and
the Unblessed must be remembered. This is not the fault
of Defence E. Thanks to the graceful leadership of both
Petula Wednesday and Ethan Song, and the courageous
work of its members, the North has thrived. The
Northern compound is far from thriving. We need to
remember the middle man, just as Carim is intending to.
Carim donated much of his clothing and food just to
prove that he is willing to do whatever he needs to prove
he has changed. We need more heroes who act in the
favour of the unblessed, like him.*

*Carim and I will continue our best to spread the
word until change is felt. Change for the one percent is
not just needed. It is deserved.*

This was not the version of the story that Clive
published. It painted Ethan in too negative a way for him
to ever let Chrissie's work reach the light of day. Instead,
he released a doctored article which never once
mentioned injustice. Ethan despised the unblessed and,
as you will come to learn, for good reason.

PART THREE
THE COVER UP
18.   Visiting Hours

The news that broke *The Manifesto* the next
morning was not the story which everyone was
expecting. Not even Ethan's doctored version of
Chrissie's article made the front page. Instead, the topic
on everybody's lips regarded the hospitalisation of Petula
Wednesday. It claimed she had gone into comatose
following a skiing accident in Austria.

"I thought she was in Crete?" remarked Hop when he found this out.

Hop always believed he was Petula's favourite, but she had lost contact with him following her retirement one month prior, and made no effort to reach out. Besides, it was Isla who Petula's Nurse called, not Hop.

Isla had been showering at the time, humming Bill Withers like the dying cat parade. On later inspection, she would find that Petula had been in Austria, not Crete, but now she was in a Hospital in Manchester. Hop rushed to Manchester's Hospital as soon as Isla broke the news.

To claim that a stay in the infirmary was preferable to living in Woodville Estate would have been to lie. Petula may have had three meals a day, nurses dedicated to her every need, and a room all to herself, but she would have rather stayed in Kitzbühel. Not that it mattered when she was in a deep, semi-permanent sleep. She could have been on Snake Island and indifference would persevere on her expression.

Hop traipsed along sterile white corridors that reeked of sanitiser and ill-cooked gammon to reach her. He stopped to buy two coffees from the canteen, but this move underestimated her condition. Upon entering the room, he placed one cup next to her, kept the other in his grasp, and planted a kiss on her moist forehead. Wires strangled every vein across her body, and he knew then that she wouldn't want coffee. He thought he saw her wrinkled eyelids fluttering, but this had been dramatic licence on his imagination's behalf, alongside the flickering mustard lights playing their tricks.

Her croaky voice and matted grey hair may have implied extensive age, but the cane propped against her bedside was for show, and she was far from infirm. The eternal optimist that we call Hop looked for somebody to blame for the accident. Nobody was to blame but Petula. Petula had been riding down the fleecy mountains, getting too carried away with herself. She plunged off the top of an unmountable summit, since her ambition believed she could make it. Her helmet flung off her head. Jaw cracked on the ice; skull shattered by a rock. That was why they shaved her hair and encased her head in a strip of white plaster cast.

Hop waited beside the bed in morbid silence. Is any silence not morbid? He crawled down the side of her bed to grasp her cold, limp hand, feeling the weight of emptiness in her palm. He clasped her with such ferocity that would instigate pain if her ability to feel remained intact. He needed to hold on, believing she would stay in this world if he didn't let go. The plate of soup beside her bed was getting cold, and so was the coffee. He consumed a dose of his beverage with his left hand while maintaining his grip on her in the right.

A tap on his left shoulder. The nurse? Another visitor? Nobody. He could have sworn he felt a hollow hand touching him. He must have been going insane. Unless it was the wind.

Moments later, after ignoring this peculiar sensation, he felt a breath on his nape accompanied by a gruff and shallow source of suspiration. Again, turning around, the room was empty, and the door was closed. This breath was so clear that it must have come from behind him. He released his grip on her, letting Petula's frail arm collapse over the bedside, shaken by the rush of three breaths in a room of two.

"Martin," came the ghost's first words. A voice he recognised. Fluid, bass, Scottish.

His raindrop footsteps trickled across the floor. A flashing force emerged before him like a flash of lightning on a clement day. A ghost stood before him, glass-like, opaque, with masculine shoulders locked in place and arms firmly situated by his side. His puckered lips repeated: "Martin." Hop's first name.

Hop only saw the figure for a few moments before he dissipated into nothingness and his breath faded into the air. Only the unrelenting intones of Petula's machine chimed to fill the silence the spectre left behind. Hop was losing it. He could have sworn the man was his father, but his father died when he was ten.

Then he remembered something else: *Defence C member branded a coward for leaving Colombian miners under the soil.* He shook this memory away. It was not real. That was what he thought, anyway. Then he looked at Petula, took her hand again, and whispered promises into her ear that were so mawkish that they weren't worth repeating.

A maladroit nurse, young enough for Hop to question her ability to manage her own life, let alone Petula's, tumbled into the suite. Despite the grungy beige walls and urine smells from the adjacent bathroom, it was preferable to any other room in the vast halls of the Royal Infirmary. The woman checked the readings on the screen, updated her paper matrix, and checked the wires were still fastened. Hop, on his fold-up chair, embodied his crankiness by balancing his hand on his chin.

"Jesus," Hop grumbled in his harsh Scotch tongue. "Shouldn't you be at school?"

"I'm twenty-seven, and I'm a fully qualified nurse."

"I trust you're looking after her."

"I sure hope so," The nurse quivered as she checked Petula over. "She's in good hands here."

"She better be. You know who she is, don't you?"

"All I know is she's from an incredibly rich family, considering that her daughters paid money for a private room and transferred her from Austria."

"They did that so she could be near them?"

"Are you family too?"

"A friend," Hop said, refusing to disclose his identity to avoid the fuss, even though he already had disclosed these hardly secretive details at reception. "Any idea yet when she'll wake up?"

"I'm afraid not. Cranial damages from the accident were detrimental enough to ensure that, even if she wakes up, the brain damage will be permanent. She'll likely forget much of her life. A man named Ethan paid a visit and informed us about her powers."

"She can leapfrog from place to place," Hop announced.

The nurse's face looked as though it had said too much, so she backtracked. She busied herself by collecting the cold, mushy tomato soup and coffee cup. "We're still delivering food in case she wakes up. Only nutrients can be passed through the drip." She departed the quarters after promising, "I'll be back in a sec."

Hop continued to clasp her hand, and an idea floated into his mind. He closed his eyes, and imagined Austria, a place he'd never been to, but seen enough pictures of. Tall boulder mountains coated in sugar white snow. The oceanic blue in the sky and the feathery texture of overhanging clouds. Green trees caked in sleet. The ringed flame scorched above the drooping mountaintop. The colour vortex transported him to a rustic hazel wooden two-story shack that overlooked the summit. Ski lines had been indented in the racing track fields beyond the wired carts that swung back and forth along the playing field. Dressed only in the T-Shirt and trousers he had worn to the hospital, he lacked the garb required to battle the gusty wind and steep inclines.

The croaky cabin door snuck open, revealing a thin frame padded by a muted pink overcoat that stuffed Petula's arms and legs with wool. Two skis dangled off her right shoulder, gripped in her gloved hand. Goggles that didn't suit her sat over her nose. She removed them to let the dusty breeze flow into her eyelids. Hop shielded his slim figure from the cold by crossing his goosebump-dotted arms.

"Martin, how curious it is to encounter you in such a habitat as this!" Petula always overcomplicated her speech. Perhaps it was the elocution lessons Father had forked out for her when she was nine. "These penetrating conditions must be shattering your unsheltered form! For what reason have you frequented Austria?"

Hop had not heard a word of what she had just said because the wind was ferocious enough to make audible voices inaudible. As well, it was cold enough to freeze the balls off Hop!

"I'm here to ski," Hop made a lucky guess in forming an adequate response.

Petula grinned, removing a wallet from her coat pocket. "Take the internal coinage to the desk to apportion the necessary costs and accompany me on this particular voyage."

Hop nodded, although he underestimated how long it would take to suit up. Instructors ensured he had the suitable padding, gear and mindset before he could rejoin Petula. And the payments, too, were extortionate, but he cared not about that. You see, Hop had always set the rules that he would never change time. Everything happens for a reason, he believed, or so his bosses had always told him. Today was the exception. Petula Wednesday must live.

Petula was not the hugging type, nor was Hop, so they never embraced, nor did they kiss. In public, they looked awkward together. In private, there may have been some love - atypical love - between them.

Hop's frozen face lost all the tan developed from his pilgrimage across the world in his vicenarian years. He was two decades older than when his journey began, and he had preserved his perfect colour, despite all he had endured.

The ski lift carried them across the landscape. Hop was not keen on heights, especially when the contraption that elevated them clattered to imply instability. Petula was used to heights, for this was not the first time she had been up into the mountains. As the rocky apparatus tumbled and the sky became touchable, Hop closed his eyes and imagined happy thoughts, if his bleak mind was capable of positive machinations. A few jolts and rickets later they were on the mountain top where Petula would lose herself.

From the moment they placed their skis over their boots, Petula's ambition was prevailing. Hop, shuddering, unstable, unable to even distribute the skaters onto his feet. Petula was raring to go with her two ski poles ready to thrust back, but she grazed his shoulder in consolation and helped him apply his gear. How could Hop save her if she needed to look out for the resident coward of Defence E?

He felt the lingering, solemn breath of his father again, and his vision became blurry from the adrenaline. He faced a stoic, bearded, broken, brown-haired man, more complete than before, and as light and hollow as a phantom. Hop reached out to touch him, but his hand went straight through his father, who was no longer made of flesh and blood.

When Petula swung back to check on Hop, she observed the apparition and felt a lump forming in her throat. She skidded over to him and tugged him back.

"Do you see him too?" Hop asked as the pressure pulled him back. A spark of vague euphoria replaced his usual grimace, because his father, his hero, missing for decades, was alive, and standing right before him.

"Do I see what?" Petula pretended to glare into the beyond.

"She sees, son," The former Hop, Wesley Harrington, declared. "Perhaps it is time that you saw her."

Hop looked into Petula's empty, lying eyes, and asked, "Can you see my father?"

"I could be there now, but I am not, because of what she did," his father's booming voice caught on the wind. "I am lost now, because of her."

Hop shuddered, not because of the mountain, but because of the spectre before him. His father was back before his eyes, so why was he not happy?

"I'm out there on the shores of time," Wesley said, "being washed away by the tide."

Petula forced him along, pulling him down through the frozen island, and Hop knew then that it was too good to be true. Wesley followed them by floating along the ice with empty feet that hovered above the ground. Wesley's face was as cold as the conditions that marooned them. Hop's expression was lost, bleak, gone. Petula was facing the same direction, looking away from the peak. They were too busy looking at the ghost to notice they were about to tumble over the cliffside.

They fell back into the cavernous chasm of sandy snow until they could fall no more. Petula released her grip from Hop, and they were sprung into separate directions. Their heads bumped against stones in impossibly incongruous unison. Hop's last sight was of his phantom father. He closed his eyes. Then everything went black, silent.

That stark chill of ice had remained with him until the last moment before he slept, so to feel the heat on his arms and legs from a nearby radiator was relieving. First, he heard the bleep from the machine and the wheeze of the ventilator. His eyelids fluttered onto the sight of a Nurse's stomach leaning over him, blurry at first, becoming clearer by the moment. There was a cannula stapled to his arm. He pulled back and forth in a fitting struggle, but wires confined him to the brick bed, which was warm and congealed. His head was numb, and his brain felt empty, like a completely blank slate. His leg was in a cast which hung above his bed and stretched his ligaments.

His bed faced the desolate white hallways which visitors traversed past. What astounded him was the sound of familiar footsteps as his past self rushed down the hallway. The time traveller was about an hour ago. Water trickled into his system from the funnel that passed liquid from the saline drip. He found consolation only in the acknowledgement that he hadn't consumed any of the stale gammon which formed dinner that evening.

"Don't get up too quickly!" The Nurse urged in her erratic signature style. "Sudden movements won't do you any good whatsoever!"

"Petula," he murmured. "Did I save her?"

"I'm afraid you were both transferred down here together. She suffered a fracture to the skull. Permanent brain damage, I'm afraid. I'll be paying her a visit in a moment."

"Still..." He murmured. She prepared to disappear, but his voice pulled her back. The Nurse presented him with a mirror, displaying his once perfect blue-eyed, blonde-haired face charred on the left side. Hop's eye hung slightly detached from its socket, and stitches gave his formerly smooth complexion a harsher quality than that which he had grown used to. This distilled him with horror as his fortuitous good looks were stripped away from him without warning or reason.

"Wait! I'm a time traveller. I can be in two places at once. I'll be there, visiting Petula, then I'll decide to go to Austria, and I'll end up here. Two Hop's in the same place. I'm surprised the universe hasn't imploded. That'd be just my luck."

Although you would consider this peculiar, the people of this world were accustomed to abilities of all forms. This Nurse could create plasters from her fingertips. Thank God she wanted to be a nurse!

"You're from Defence E, aren't you?" she asked. "There's not a chance you'll be ready to return to work tomorrow. You've had a fatal accident. You're not in a stable position. I'd be surprised if you could even walk. How much can you remember about the accident?"

He had forgotten the truth for starters. The clash between elation and trepidation that emerged after being reunited with his father. Only patches came back to him. The remembrance of the throbbing pain that followed his tumble off the crest. Luckily, most of the pain went unfelt, since he had blanked out halfway through his fall.

"Not much at all," he answered. He attempted to pull himself from the bed, but his legs wouldn't let him. They were straining, heavy like boulders. "Maybe you're right," he hated to admit, because Hop was a stubborn chap. "Ethan won't be happy."

"Is Ethan your boss?" The Nurse asked.

"Guessing he's the one who got me to the hospital. It wasn't Petula's daughters, because I've never met the lassies. Ethan's a bampot. The No Man couldn't put out a fire in an ocean, and Isla's got better things to worry about."

"He'll have to be alright with it, as you're in no fit state. Thank you for your service, by the way. Defence E is having a rough time at the moment in the news at the moment, so I expect you're feeling useless."

"I always feel useless."

"Well, you're not. All of you are heroes. Your reputation doesn't deserve to be tarnished."

"I blame Carim. He should have followed Ethan's orders right."

"The Knight is a hero too. You all are. The press may say otherwise, but they forget how much you've all sacrificed.

"I suppose you're right," he replied, half-humbled, half-reluctant to accept the compliment.

"Just you rest. You deserve it, and you need it. I need to talk to the other you!"

"Let another nurse do that," Hop responded. "It'll get too complicated otherwise."

Hop was left with his bare thoughts in a mind scavenged of its former contents. The truth was distant once again. Sometimes he heard his father's susurrations, but he blamed any inexplicable noises on the humming machines. It was easier to disregard the ghostly presence of the parent he once lost to time. With the next turn of the wind, the ghoul would leave him once again.

19.   Hop's Story

My origin story begins when I was a wee nipper of nine years.

First I'll speak about my Mother. She was the stereotypical fifties mum, anachronistic from her time, with cheeks pampered until rose, an apron almost always tied to her waist, dark curly tied-back hair and a vivacious grin. Housewife, loving wife, all to the spoiled brat in the highchair and the man of the house; a tall, firmly built, brown bearded fellow with warmed icicle eyes. Every day would play out the same. He'd return home from working for Defence C, he'd plant a kiss on her forehead, then rub my shoulder. Sometimes he'd get home at 5, on other days at 8. He was one of those 'men have to be men' types, who'd probably accept very few occupational pathways for me other than construction, branding cattle, or saving the world.

Our home was one you wouldn't want to leave, so why did he? A detached three-story home, close enough to the city to make contacts, far enough to avoid them if necessary. You could be alone with the birds as they chanted a chorus of their morning tune. This was a perk of the job, as Defence C rewarded him with a home that had a swimming pool we could bask in, a master suite for the adults, a playroom for yours truly, a garden that stretched beyond its two-acre confines, neighbours who grinned and always greeted, and a wife and son who always returned the courtesy.

I'll tell you why he wanted to leave. I was nine, still in my smiling, everything's perfect phase, before the novelty of life wore off, thrilled even by a ride on a swing or a sweep of a kite. Mother made us spaghetti that night. I remember, because it was my favourite meal, and I haven't eaten it since. Father came in. Kiss, shoulder rub, some inaudible Scottish dialect greeting that I couldn't understand and haven't heard since. It was Friday evening, and as always, we watched TV. A snap of whatever movie was on that night, followed by a chat show. *Jurassic Park*, a film about an archaeologist called Alan who brought back dinosaurs using his powers of resurrection, was the picture debuting that evening. During an advert break, Dad became accustomed to channel surfing. That was when he found the report.

Six miners had been stuck underground in Columbia after an excavation went wrong. I came to hate them. Father killers, husband killers, who were best off dead. That was forgetting they probably had families too, but dad shouldn't have thought it was his place to rescue them. Defence C didn't call him, but he had to be the hero, didn't he? Landslides had been resolved before. Maybe the Columbian police should have stepped in instead. Then he never would have had to die.

Any sudden movements and the mine would collapse. Water would flow from the dam and shower them in liquid. Nobody could rescue them except my father, he believed. Time traveller, teleporter, future maker.

Knowing these may have been his final moments (yet he went anyway), he explained everything to Ma, and bickering ensued. She tugged on his arm repeatedly, but he pushed her aside and made me his next target, kneeling, embedding the possibility of me becoming the man of the house into a mind too young to understand the gravity of the situation. He transported himself upstairs to equip himself with his regalia. Defence C uniforms were different at the time. Mustard, bordering on gold, with a large 'C' covering the breast pocket, and a cape draped over his back. I didn't know that would be the last time I'd see his face of oystered goodwill. He blasted away, and the next we knew, he was on the television screen with bodies hung over his shoulder, resting on the rocks by the dam. I cheered. Mum cried. She knew what I didn't: Wesley's act of heroism would be the end of him.

Unfortunately, the embankment which held Wells together was provoked when he tapped his feet against the wrong rock. I can't give a detailed description because I wasn't there, and when the reporters realised how certain death was if they remained, they fled like the cowards they were. Other superheroes emerged at the scene and tried to hog my father's limelight, but all of them failed because Hop Sr. was supreme.

Only flocks of screaming waves crashing against the rocks alerted forces to the fate of the three remaining miners who had not yet escaped, and my father. Mother didn't cry because she believed there was a way he could have survived. The bodies of the others were found, but not Hop's. Some say that he was lost to time, and that the incident was so damaging that his abilities had been confused to the extent that he was thrust in every which way to the point where he became a ghost on the cusp of reality and not just another dead man. All this time later, I know that was not the case. I'd rather think of him as dead than being experimented on, tortured, stuck, or as a coward, and as an abandoner of his wife and son.

Ma refused to have a funeral and neglected to wear black. Seeing her in her flamingo pink dress without the bonus of her smile was odd, to say the least. I didn't stop crying for months. I wanted to know when he'd come back. Man up, he would've told me, so I did. That meant losing my innocence, my joviality, and my blissful childhood of being so easily pleased, but he would've been proud if he saw me for overcoming everything.

Let me speak about Petula Wednesday. She wasn't the most obviously beautiful person. No, she was haggard, bent-backed, with youth lost long ago. There was something about her, though, which was hard to deny. A grace which only I saw, and I constantly struggled to define. Her limp was beaten down by a constant skip of the step and eagerness of the eye. To me, even her shadow looked gracious in the moonlight. Meanwhile, my colleagues commented that she was looking her age, and I could never see what they meant.

Ma, despite her features being damaged by run-down makeup from sneaky tears, let Petula in when our leader rang the doorbell. Ma didn't want me to know she'd been crying, but I made no effort to hide the tears that shattered my optimism. Petula arrived when I was in my weeping phase, refusing to break her 'no hugs' policy, instead offering a few wise words to me and some flowers for Ma.

She kneeled down to me - I was 4"3 at the time, though considerably taller now, and she claimed to be sorry and insisted we both sit at the living room table that revolved around the mantlepiece. I remember glimpsing ripe generosity in those eyes. Looking back on it now, maybe the altruism was artificial. She revealed that, as a reward for Dad's service, Defence C would be willing to pay off the mortgage and take care of any outstanding bills. Petula suggested she had a duty of care for us, which meant they'd bring me up and give Ma whatever money she needed. She refused at first, insisting that Wesley would return, but Petula was unwilling to take 'no' for an answer, aware that Dad was gone for good.

Looking back on it now, they had an ulterior motive: me. The old Hop was gone and they needed a substitute. That was why Petula paid for me to take boxing classes, exercise workshops, gym sessions, even from age ten. Ma took on extra hours at work as a receptionist for a primary school, but any effort she had withered away. Alcohol became her comforter, as did tobacco and, consequently, her super senses became much less super.

The same was the case for me. I completed a sandwich degree in psychology and law at Edinburgh Uni, under Petula's orders. I'd always dreamt of being a chef or something, but Petula pushed me in another direction. She paid for my tuition fees, my nights out, my living costs, and that was probably why I fell for her, on top of all her wisdom and concealed beauty and charm. Ma never knew about us. Ma still doesn't. She's still living in that same home, believing that nothing needs to change, looking at that picture of Dad on the mantelpiece in his work uniform and maintaining that the real Hop will come home one day. She was never happy that I was his replacement, considering that, apparently, he was still out there, and ready to start saving the world again. I became their investigator, using my abilities to travel back through the personal histories of the criminals we caught to figure out their motives and desires.

One of my first missions involved the supervillain known as Eclipse. I explored his backstory to discover why he intended to cake Carlisle in shadows, wiping out the city's population, and found out that he didn't - he couldn't control his abilities, they controlled him, so we locked him away in a mental asylum. I almost felt sorry for him, but he was a threat to society, as well as himself, and he incidentally wiped out the entire population of Carlisle.

I didn't interfere in any of the lives of the criminals which I investigated. Sometimes I'd have the opportunity to help my colleagues rough up a few rotten eggs, but I'd usually be kept away from the practical side of the business.

My services were in Petula's name as much as in Dad's. I believe she liked me too. No nights were spent on moonlight river walks or candlelit dinners, but we often talked extensively. I never overstepped the boundaries. Our relationship remained platonic, but I cannot deny that I loved her. Adored her, even, for what she'd put on the line for me and my mother. The least I could do was rescue her from the mountain accident, but I failed at that too.

Time is like Jenga. Remove one block, and the rest collapses. Add another block on top, and everything will be fine, as long as it doesn't make the other pieces tumble. The guidelines are therefore simple: I can't cheat time like my acquaintance, Isla, nor can I break it, but I can make myself a part of time if it feels as though I have always been there at that particular moment. People believe time is a linear track that starts and ends, but it's really a loop which spins and darts in all kinds of directions. I could be in two places at once, or I could encounter myself, as long as I encountered myself the first time. Do you understand? Probably not.

I became Hop to continue the legacy of my father and the work he so majestically accomplished. Since then, his accomplices informed me that I was doing his legacy proud. Everything I do is done for justice, just as was the case with him. He'd sacrificed his life. This was the least I could do. I've never been the hero type. I did my job for him, but that's not to say I wanted to. It gave me money and respect, and that's all I wanted.

I was not a hero because my past made me. I couldn't even call myself a hero, not really. If I was, then I was a hero because Petula made me so. And no, I don't mean that in the way I thought. She wasn't the perfect altruistic specimen that I thought she was, and it makes me question whether I ever should have loved her at all. I look back on everything and think about where I would have been if my life continued on the trajectory it was once headed on. I've never liked my job, but I've been good at it, even if I've rarely put in the effort. Now I know most of what I did wasn't for a just cause, I'd like to think of a life where I was happier. Maybe then I could have done what was right. If not for others, then for me.

20.   Protest
Cameras snapped outside the fire station like ticking clocks. Demonstrators equipped their megaphone voices to shatter the sound barrier. Isla chose the wrong time to arrive, approaching with steely steps in her customary turnout: white top, gold cape, 'E' chest.

Written on the signs in deep bold black: *Down with Defence E*! On another: *The Knight is a murderer*! On a third: *Justice for the One Percent*! They waved these banners in Isla's face to the soundtrack of eager exclamations.

Questions were bombarded at her from inflamed marchers and the journalists recording them: What are your thoughts on The Knight's actions? Would you defend Carim for what he has done? Are you and The Knight an item?

"Jesus," she blasphemed. Ethan had instructed her to ignore her critics, so she pushed them aside and raced into HQ. Once she'd passed the automatic doors, she entered the expansive void where the corridor seemed to be the only item in existence. Beth the receptionist was there, negotiating with an ambassador from Zimbabwe.

When Isla entered, she noticed Ethan was wearing earphones to shield his fragile ego. From his pugnacious persona alone, one would picture him as a gentleman of great resolve, but the headphones implied weakness. He stamped his army boots once to greet her. She was about to salute, but she remembered that he considered saluting to be a sign of weakness. Truth be told, she didn't even know how to look at him without sparking his vexation.

Ethan had also placed earbuds in a birthday cake situated on one of three chairs. On the second chair was a tablet screen which held Hop's image. Hop appeared bedraggled, and not because of the wavy signal that pixelated his features.

"Alright?" The No Man asked Isla as she blew out the lone candle atop the fondant gateau he had shifted into, setting in motion a birthday wish that never came.

Ethan removed the muffles, realising the ear protectors made little difference against megaphone mouthed Meg. The strength of his composition had been lost somewhat. "My years in the force equipped me for a great deal. My best friend died in my arms when I was only sixteen. I was shot at by every nationality on the map. I have tough skin, but that's difficult to maintain when you experience as much disrespect as we have from those crowds. They antagonise us despite all we have placed on the line. Carim's actions averted disaster. Why can they not understand that the unblessed are the villains?" His glare turned to fury. He could tell Isla wasn't certain he was right. Her eyes were too narrow, and her croaky breath derided him. "Defence E isn't good enough. It's falling apart, and all my soldiers are to blame. Carim's left us. Hop's in hospital. The press cannot latch onto that. Journalists take weakness and they run with it. Petula's in a coma. Chrissie's causing trouble."

"Chrissie's causing trouble?" Isla questioned while attempting to drown out the gnawing groans of dissenters. "Have I missed something?"

"I hope you're not saying anything important," The No Man said, still wearing earbuds lodged in fondant. "I don't have hands, so my ears are blocked and I'm useless to do anything about it!"

"You're always useless," Hop grumbled quietly. "Pretty bloody useless, too" Hop grumbled quieter.

"Did Hop just make some wiseacre remark?"

Isla removed the earpieces from the fondant. "There you go."

"I can hear the voices in my head again! Oh wait, those are just the voices of the people outside. They're flipping loud, aren't they?"

"Megaphone Meg's back at it again."

Ethan graced his ears with his palms. Their honesty brought him pain, but his indifference must persevere. "Chrissie published a different version of Carim's story to the one we published this morning," he growled. "Clive Mannering from *The Manifesto* had to make edits to preserve the sanctity of our operation."

"I'd be careful what you say," Hop warned. "If you can hear the protestors outside, then it's likely they can hear you."

"So you're doctoring this story?" Isla said.

"Martin's right," Ethan barked. "Be quiet!"

"Martin? Do you mean Hop?"

"We're not children playing superheroes in the park. There's no time for silly little names and sillier little costumes. This is real life."

"We've got nothing to hide, but if you keep interfering, Ethan, it's going to look like we do."

"I know what I'm doing," Ethan snarled. "Are you questioning my competency?"

"No, sir," she shuddered.

"I should hope not. Hop, when are you due to return? In a matter of days, I should expect. We need you back on our force."

"Weeks, possibly," Hop's dwindling voice commented.

"Not weeks. Days," Ethan declared.

"I still can't feel my legs. They'll have to teach me how to walk again."

"They'll have to get moving, won't they? I've made sure you have the best healthcare. Now more than ever, we need as many people on our side as possible, and that includes you."

"I'll try my best to get better."

"That's the problem with you, Hop. You rarely try hard enough."

Isla could sense the awkwardness within the room, which was why she changed the subject back to Chrissie.

"Do you think people don't know you brought out *The Manifesto*? I picked up a copy this morning! One minute they're slagging you off. Next minute, they're singing your praises. Journalists may be fickle, but they ain't that fickle."

"I beg to differ," groaned Hop.

"Plus, their motto is now, '*The Morning Manifesto*: Official paper of Defence E'," The birthday cake interjected. "Bit of a giveaway."

"We'll make sure Chrissie gets put in line," Ethan replied.

"What's that meant to mean?" Isla squinted.

"She'll be publishing another story tomorrow. I'll have a discreet word with her beforehand."

"Like you had a word with us when you first arrived, you mean?" Isla inquired. "Lord help her."

"Have either of you been able to speak to Carim?" Isla's scornful expression looked at Ethan as if to place full blame on him for Carim's incarceration.

"I spoke to him," the Northerner responded. "He's repenting. Meant to be a bit scummy in Woodville. Says he's got a stabbing pain in his arm but other than that, he's all fine."

"What about Petula?" Hop asked.

"She's not our boss anymore," Isla responded.

"We're making sure Petula's being well looked after," Ethan promised.

"I heard about that," Hop said. "Who are her daughters? Royalty?"

"They belong to the gentry. Lila and Tegan Wednesday are very important individuals."

"I'm surprised they aren't called Tuesday and Thursday!" The No Man said.

The gentry were not only upper-class snobs who owned too much land and too much money to know what to do with it. They were upper-class snobs who owned cupboards of superpowers known as 'lockers', as well as too much land and too much money. They used the light from leftover atoms to create any ability imaginable, thanks to Edward the Third's pursuit of the flame. The gentry would be looking down at Ethan, and that thought made him squirm.

Tired of Megaphone Meg's slander, he stormed out of the windowless room so he could reach one with a considerable aperture. Shortly after he left, Isla marched after him, slow enough so that her leader didn't notice. One birthday cake and one pixelated tablet remained. The former clicked his teeth to cure the boredom.

"So, how's the hospital?" The No Man broke the silence.

"You don't have to fill every silence, you know?" Hop asked.

"I'm not particularly good at silences. Leads to lots of awkward man chats. Men aren't built for conversation. Particularly not you. No offence."

"I'm well aware I'm useless! Haven't I said that enough times?"

"Let me guess...you're gonna say that I am too."

Hop would have smirked, but the pain made it difficult to express any animation.

"Hospital's absolutely terrific," Hop enunciated his sarcasm.

"I can never tell whether you're being sarcastic. You're always so bitter that I can't really tell."

"Jesus!" Hop snarled. "Have you ever stayed in a hospital?"

"I grew up in a mental institution, dear!"

"And was it nice there?"

"No."

"Then why would my answer to 'how's the hospital' be anything other than 'bad'?"

"Hospitals are different from mental institutions. They're a lot less mental, for starters."

"They both share in common the fact that you'd rather be at home."

"I'd rather be at home than at work," he replied, "But it doesn't mean work's a hospital."

"I think you need another lobotomy."

"I think I need a slice of cake! Problem is, I'm inside of it."

"How come I can't remember what I had for dinner last night, but I can remember you?"

"Because I'm that darn memorable," Silence again. "How long are they going to take?" asked the shapeshifter, bored of boredom; chairman of the bored.

Ethan threw open the window next door, and Isla's shadow drifted behind her. He observed the protestors before deducing what unified them. All genders, ethnic groups, cultures, and sexualities were present. All they had in common was a tedious nature which characterised most journalists.

Defence E were used to journalists. Recent pay cuts, strikes and accusations of prejudice had brought the reporters flocking. They also had to worry about gossip columnists, who tried making Defence E into celebrities. Ethan hadn't been there long enough to be used to them. Defence J, his former place of work in Orkney, lacked the might to possess the same status as Defence E, and his vicious snort was enough to indicate his impatience. Ethan made his first press conference on the first day of his time as leader, to a crowd of a dozen, and this felt like his second. Whereas Petula used passive tongue to gauge the cues of public speaking, critics believed Ethan came across as overly aggressive.

Isla felt like his guardian, prepared to reign him in if she had to. She thought he didn't know she was there, but this was Ethan, who had (metaphorical) eyes on the back of his head. The stress in him was evident from his dilated pupils and flushed colouring. His face looked like it felt a considerable deal but strayed away from remorse. The protestors' heads tilted to face him.

Paparazzi flickers blasted into his fragile irises like the sun's lurid flame. He held his face under his uniform, vampirically, to shield himself from the light. Down to Defence E!, decried the demonstrators. The Knight is a murderer! and every syllable enraged Ethan. Ethan panted and paced back and forth, without once making eye contact with Isla. His blood looked as though it was boiling from the rush of scarlet on his veiny face and the unruly vigour of his bloodshot eyes. He stormed to the window, grabbed several pound notes from his pocket and flung them into the crowd.

"What's that for?" Megaphone Meg asked as her accomplices swarmed around the money fountain like parasites.

"It's so you can buy yourself some respect," Ethan blasted. A ripple effect of exultation emerged as the leeches collected their profits. They may have wanted the money, but Meg ignored it. She wouldn't give into Defence E's games. She looked on at her accomplices, capricious enough to accept the money, in shame. "Your behaviour is almost scandalous."

"You must be the new leader, I take it."

"Petula informed me that you were one to worry about."

"I'm glad I've made an impression!"

"Too much of one. Your protests are breaching the law."

"What have I done?"

"The rules state that anybody with your ability must not extend beyond the sixty-decibel limit."

"Do I look like somebody who cares about that?" Meg was quieter than she had been. She didn't need a smart suit or a posh voice. Her presence was enough, even with jogging bottoms and a Yorkshire accent.

"You will care when you receive a £20,000 fine," Ethan said.

"That will prove my point."

"Your point is to antagonise yourself, is it not?"

"Defence E is built on a structure of prejudice and discrimination, and they remove anybody who seeks to expose that fact."

"What do you want?"

"For the unblessed to be freed!"

The chanting rippled across the crowd like a Mexican wave: *Free the Unblessed*!

"Free them? Is that what you really want? You say that now without weighing up the consequences. If we free them and live among us and touch us and touch the things that we will also touch, all superpowers will be lost. People will find somebody to blame. They always do. Do you want to be the one who receives that blame?"

"I'd be willing to be the one to blame if it means the one percent get what they need."

"Pah! There are 76 compounds for the unblessed in England alone. We spend approximately £44 million on each of these compounds every year. That is over three billion pounds of England's money spent on feeding, clothing, and maintaining the unblessed. What more can we do?"

"Release them into the free world."

"Now who's speaking about them like they're caged animals? You're nothing but a blessed saviour. You want to liberate the unblessed without allowing them agency. You believe playing the martyr will provide you with status. You wish to capitalise on their alleged suffering for the gain of your image."

"If I don't do it, who else will?"

"If the unblessed live among us, they'll be outcasts. They will ruin everything, and the public will learn to despise them. In their compounds, they have the opportunity to be content. We give them all they need, and they can do what they want with it. All of you believe yourself to be so heroic. You must realise, Megan, that every other member among your crowd was capricious enough to accept money from the man they condemned."

Meg turned around to the guilty expressions and tugged-at collars of her fellow demonstrators. Some purple and orange bills remained on the floor, but the reporters had buried most of the cash in their bustling pockets.

"Do you think we'd lock the unblessed away if we had a choice? No, they'd be living out here with the rest of us, and we'd return to a completely equal society, except it's not plausible. Look at what happened to Carim, who you will know as the Knight." Journalists were snapping and jotting at meteoric speed. "Once, he lived a life of relative pleasure as a completely free national hero with the power to fly and shoot lasers from his eyes. All of that has been stripped away and replaced with a life of misery and want because he touched Winona Barton. Should that become the fate of the majority? The minority are able to live in comfort. As I'm sure the Prime Minister Phillip Letter will inform you, the fortune of some must always come from the misfortune of others. I hear there are protests up and down the country. Why? Aids packages, supplies, comfortable housing. What more could the unblessed need? Chrissie Young published a story on the matter in The Manifesto. You should read it."

"The paper you purchased?" One journalist interjected.

"*The Manifesto* chose to alter their standpoint. Ask Clive Mannering if you need to. Clive is still very much in charge of what's published and what's not."

"Should we expect you to attempt to buy out all papers who dare to act as opposition?" asked the North coast reporter.

"As I say, The Manifesto's decision to fall under our ownership was a product of free will."

"How much money did you pay them?"

"I think that's beside the point."

The flash of fluttering lenses continued to flare up in Ethan's vision, so he shielded his eyes with his arm and his movements started to shudder.

"Certain sacrifices must be made so you can sit at home with your glasses of wine and your television box sets. You can go on your holidays and relish what your abilities offer you. Do you think of the unblessed when you relish in these indulgences? You accuse my mindset of introversion, but can you claim to be any less ignorant? You slander me while taking my money, but none of you are any less vain than the rest of us."

"The difference is, we're not part of a 'perfect police force'," Meg ranted, "who kills completely innocent members of society. A schoolteacher and two security guards were killed because they sought freedom."

"They were criminals who would have damaged the fabric of our society as much as a serial killer would after escaping prison."

"Difference is, they were innocent, and they had families, friends, and lives."

"I have to admire you, Ringleader, but I'll have to restrain you if you continue with these protests."

"How are you going to do that? Are you going to kill us too?"

"Our heroes will arrest you if you do not vacate the property. We hope that what happened to Winona, Kenny, and Elijah will never have to happen again. Our duty is to uphold the law and one of those laws dictates that the blessed must remain in their communities. Any strategy, no matter how extreme, must be employed to restrain them. If you wish to blame anything, do not blame the institutions that carry out the laws. Blame the laws themselves. However, said laws have been introduced for a reason. We are responsible for the safety of the people of the North. Letting them go would break the promise we made when we joined Defence E."

Censorious signs hesitated to surrender, apart from those who were vain enough to snatch Ethan's money and run. Ethan pulled a phone from the wall, dialled a number he had memorised and waited for the vibrations to sound.

"I'd like to report a crime that is more befitting of your duties," Ethan spoke to a member of the street-level police force. While Defence E skidded across the North in search of physical activity, other agencies dealt with the day-to-day, ennui sides of crime. "Megan Lorton has exceeded the decibel limit and I wish to install the necessary fine as punishment."

"You don't have to do that," Meg warned him.

"You're not in a place to demand anything from me. My suggestion is that you return home. Do whatever you do. Catch up with bills, or your TV box sets." From the way Ethan spoke, it was clear that this was not how he enjoyed spending his own free time. "If you step back onto the property of Defence E or any of the adjacent organisations, then I will ensure you are punished."

"Is that a threat?"

"I'm not dictating what you should think. I am only dictating the way you think it. You may conduct your slanderous riots elsewhere, but you must not do so here." Ethan returned to the call. "Forget I said anything. They're leaving now."

Ethan looked at them with lips locked in a cocksure pose. He restored the telephone to his place and Meg clapped her hands, leading the others to follow. Then, Meg pivoted and snarled as Ethan preserved his impassive manner. There were people out there who could read minds. If somebody read his, he would be in hot water.

Meg may not have ceased her protests - therefore he may have achieved very little - but she was out of the way - for now. Freedom of speech was one element of life he couldn't oppose.

"I know you're there," Ethan said as he closed the window and faced Isla.

Isla's back lay against the adjoining wall, but a lock of her vermillion hair unravelled her. Ethan returned his hands to his pockets. No longer was he enraged, not that his face ever altered to exhibit any emotional fluctuation.

"How did you become so tough?" Isla questioned. "Was it your stint in the army?"

"The job accustoms you to difficult tasks such as these," responded Ethan. "I have come to learn what needs to be done to ensure people don't become obstacles."

"You would do anything to protect your standards of what's right, wouldn't you?"

"Absolutely anything, as long as I deem it to be moral."

"Do I have to worry about you?"

Ethan released a brief laugh, but even his chuckle possessed brutish attributes. "I hope you're not questioning my competence."

"Is this a dictatorship? It's starting to feel like one!"

He didn't once look at her. His staunchly composed back refused to yield. "I sense that you believe you could have conducted my affairs better than I have."

"That's not what I meant."

"Being the leader of an organisation like this is more challenging than it may appear."

"I'm sure it is," lied Isla, finding it easier to conserve her issues with his leadership. She didn't stammer. She wasn't afraid. She wouldn't have gotten this far if she didn't have pluck.

"You best return to the others. We were midway through a meeting."

"Are you coming?"

"I'll be there shortly."

Isla left her boss with his hands clasped ahead of him and his gaze fixed through the window. For a brief time, Isla intended to turn in the direction from whence she came. Back left, to Hop and The No Man, who still suffered through their endless silence.

Isla should have gone left. She didn't go left. She turned right.

Ethan was hiding something. She was sure she'd find out what by navigating the labyrinthine corridors of the Deansgate fire station. Once Isla turned right, she acknowledged that it would be too late to turn back.

21. <u>The Truth</u>

Most of the rooms in the fire station had very little to say for themselves. They were empty and bare like the ones she knew better and hardly screamed *clandestine*. Some rooms contained fireman uniforms, left behind on makeshift pegs by Patrol D.

The corridors never seemed to end as they writhed to mimic a cobra. Every step Isla took revealed another twist or turn in the passageway. At least if somebody followed her, she would receive a warning from the vinyl croak of the floorboards. The issue was, sneaking around herself was nigh on impossible. At the corridor's end - finally - was Ethan's temporary office. Breathlessness suggested she needed the exercise. Skipping time made walking unnecessary, but recalling non-existent strolls preserved her nimble figure.

The rusted unkempt bronze door took her by surprise, considering that Ethan struck her as the fastidious type. He was the sort whose shoestrings never went untied, whose uniform never went unbuttoned. A nameplate sagged from the frame: 'Ethan Song' in block Garamond lettering. Given the torn paint beneath it, another name plate must have once occupied this position, only for him to have snatched it away. Isla remembered how much easier it was when Defence E had a base of their own. Back then, they had a staff room, a sauna, and a coffee machine, presumably all funded by Petula. No longer. Sure, their new base was closer to home, but distance wasn't so much of a worry for her. She could skip time and be done with rush hour, no matter how far she travelled.

Isla turned the knob on the office door. Locked. A locked door wouldn't stop Quickfix. It never had before, anyway.

The mechanics of her abilities astounded even her. Swinging forward her wristwatch a few minutes placed her inside Ethan's locked office. She avoided the tetanus-infested door handle by flicking forward time. She was there because she had pushed forward time from moments earlier, meaning she had never completed the task of opening the door. However, the door had been opened by her skipping past the moment in which the task had been completed. Paradoxical, nonsensical, and if you thought about it any more than Isla did, your brain would implode, so don't even try.

Isla had a rummage around an office which, like the fire station itself, had very little going for it. Another white room with a few single tables topped with stacks of notes. Ethan's handwriting on said documents was broad and sure of itself, filled with 'Y's' that flicked and 'K's' which kicked.

Amongst these accounts was a name, a telephone number, and an address, belonging to Petula's daughter, Lila Wednesday. Isla flicked through the desk compartments to grab her own piece of paper. Following this, she snatched a nearby pen, still equipped for use from where blue ink had marked these details, to construct her memorandum. She leaned over to copy the details, distracted only by a chorus of *Down with Defence E*! from outside.

Isla slid behind a desk to protect herself as the ghosts of the past emerged via the clock's next rotation. She grazed her fingers against the details while keeping her eyes situated on her pocket watch. This allowed, using the weight of her mind, to push the hands of the clock to their necessary positions. The room shifted and jolted until Ethan emerged with his back against the seat which Isla was only metres away from. If Isla ever doubted that Ethan had anything to hide, the way he spoke to the adult acne sufferer on the screen would have put any uncertainty to bed.

"-With everything?" Francis Swallow asked. She must have arrived midway through a conversation. "You've left no trail?"

Ethan was playing with something in his hands. What looked like a boiling tube? Those notes Isla had found were on his desk. "Once I've shipped the serum off to the locker, there will be no trace." Lila Wednesday had enough power to almost be a member of the gentry, so it was obvious that she'd own a power locker. What was Ethan shipping there? Whatever was in his hand, Isla assumed. He continued, "I know what I am doing,

Francis. What about you? Are you keeping an eye on Carim?"

"Of course I am. I must have secured Defence E's trust by now."

"Petula trusted you, and your father, so I hope I can do the same."

Isla felt a sneeze coming along, but it was one she managed to resist. Never had she been the clumsy type, but her kneeling stance caused her to wobble.

"You've been as faithful as you could be," Ethan said. "Noticed anything that the Naylors haven't picked up?"

"I'm cautious about Eva and Maeve Croft. They know there's a spy here. Only a matter of time until they realise it's me."

"You don't remember, do you?" Ethan asked, recalling a note strapped to his freezer.

"Remember what?"

"Nothing," Ethan sighed. "Will anybody believe the Crofts? You're a teacher. An upstanding member of your community. People will trust you. They've got no way to prove your allegiances. If they become a threat, you'll need to remove them, although you'll need to think innovatively. I'm sure you're capable of that."

"Innovatively?"

"The press is already attempting to brand Defence E as xenophobic. If we remove the Crofts in such an abrupt way, who knows what might happen?"

"I wasn't going to suggest killing them. I thought that move was too brash when it came to Winona and the two guards." A subtle criticism. Francis must have been missing his friend and colleague, since he had known Winona since Kindergarten.

"No wrong moves," Ethan twiddled his fingers across his keyboard, extracting information onto the studied note.

"You need to trust me, Ethan."

"I'm your boss. Do you refer to superiors on a first-name basis?"

"No…boss."

"I'll get the serum transferred to Lila's locker right away, then we'll have cleared all evidence of the extraction."

"I've got a plan to get rid of the Crofts."

Isla felt another sneeze coming along, but she pinched her nose to prevent her nostrils from exploding with phlegm.

"I can push the Crofts into becoming enemies of the community. Nobody will believe them if they attempt to spread their message about a spy if I discredit them through the right means."

"And how will you achieve that?"

"Swift, subtle moves. Suzie and the North family are my best bet to start with, if I make it clear that Hex encouraged their insurgency and caused their deaths. I've already tried, but I can try harder."

"You really don't remember? I see. Carim must not be harmed further by these allegations, since any condemnation of his actions could come back on us. I'm being blamed for the unblessed murders as much as they are. Unlike Carim, however, I feel no shame."

"I'll be careful. My abilities have remained hidden for this long. I think you can trust me to be discreet."

"Do what needs to be done."

The commotion of protestors from outside had only recently begun. Isla became irritable, since she thought she had escaped Megaphone Meg and her band of hooligans.

Isla couldn't claim to be stunned. This was quite what she was expecting. A spy in Woodville and a lie in Defence E. Still behind the desk, a declarative from familiar lips snapped her into the present. The note was gone, as were all signs of the past. She was still in Ethan's office, kneeling with raised shoulders and bent kneecaps and looking completely suspicious. The present-day Ethan presided over her, expelling a cough of acknowledgement. Her sight wobbled, focusing first on Ethan's squeaky clean combat boots.

"Last time I checked," said Ethan, "You weren't allowed in my office."

He approached the desk, tore the slip of paper into shreds, and chucked it in the bin. He washed his hands on a little corner basin to remove any residue. Isla had to glide upwards to make it look as though she hadn't travelled back in time to spy on him, but his suspicion was unmatchable.

"What are you doing?" he asked in a calm growl.

"Nothing," Isla replied as she returned to her feet. Travelling through time always made her dizzy, and this instance was no exception. "Are the demonstrators gone?"

"Gone for now, but we've presumably not seen the last of them. The world's turning against Defence E. Get back to the meeting room. We'll discuss this matter further."

"Indeed, boss," Isla replied as she entered the office. She would never see Ethan in the same light again, and she was glad. At least she understood his true colours, but she didn't yet recognize his shades.

As she trotted back to the room, she glared back at him with contempt. When she turned her back, he issued a similar scowl. Isla was onto Ethan, and she was sure that Ethan knew that. She would have been worried but - again - she hadn't gotten this far just to give into fear. She had to stay strong. She had to know more.

22.   Feel my wrath

Chrissie Young was furious. Angrier than she had ever been, and her discovery of the cover-up at Edgehill was no exception. Her story was unworthy of the front page, and that couldn't be true, because she was Chrissie Young.

Unworthy, even, of every page. Doctored, edited, butchered, whatever verb you can think of to describe it, her boss had done it. A condemnatory article about the repression of the unblessed twisted into a piece conforming to rigid mentality. Chrissie was sick of the gaping inertia, and incandescent at the prospect of Ethan rejecting her story. To describe her as an egomaniac would be a disservice. Her status as the best journalist in the North was objective, well-deserved. She had won the Packer prize in 2008 - the most esteemed media award there is - and the Journalism society award two years later. He, Ethan Song, personality peasant, military brute, had the cheek to reject her!

This was a woman who got a job at the Edgehill power station just so she could shut it down. This was a woman willing to stand up against the blatant misogyny of her former boss. Journalism required risks, and she was willing to take them.

The year was 2008. Meet a woman - a girl then - who had always wanted to be a journalist. She had remarkable abilities, and abilities mean everything in this world. How does one discover they can access memories by placing a memory stick in their gullet? The answer: stupidity and chance and nothing more than luck. Before Chrissie turned five, the doctors struggled to identify what made her unblessed. Could she fly? Could she read minds? Abilities have a habit of revealing themselves, but none were being exhibited. Some professionals believed she was an anomaly - unblessed but born to the blessed. Others speculated that she was idiosyncratic.

At school, her teacher left a memory stick holding photographs from a school trip on her desk. Chrissie, intrigued by the contraption, stuck it up her nose and her mouth. There was a stinging sensation, and an ocean of foreign memory consumed her. She found the stories that mattered and from there, her passion for human affairs was born.

Like all good journalists, her origin story lacked a linear trajectory. She spent three years writing for a university newspaper which only three students read. The years afterwards may have been spent in a newsroom, but only so she could make the coffee. It meant she had to keep her ears to the ground to become more than a secretary, and the office's therapeutic clamour could facilitate that need.

Not unlike her current boss, Chrissie attempted to leap on stories before anybody else could. If her memory stick alerted her to chaos on the tube or a mugging on Acasta Way, she'd be there. Often, she'd be too late. Her abilities let her discover stories and predict crimes that no other journalist could. It took her until the age of twenty-four to equip them well.

Her vortex of imagination enlightened her to radiation leaks which a walk past the power station confirmed. Rot on the edge of the cooling towers implied that all was not right, so she took on the job of Clive Sutcliffe's secretary. He was a gruff, rumpled troll of a man lazy enough to allow the breach of protocol to go unchecked. Messing with a powerful man with invulnerable skin like Sutcliffe was a suicide game that she nevertheless played. Calling out the violation made her a hero, and the Packer prize was hers.

Chrissie had sacrificed her parents' aspirations so she could become a journalist. Her mother was a nurse and a very good one at that, while her father was a dentist and a very bad one at that. She believed she needed to be somewhere her abilities to scout information needed to be put to use. Lodging a memory stick into her throat would hardly save lives, but there were places such an ability could benefit society, and especially herself.

Chrissie had even been an ambitious child, who built her own swing when she was three and launched her own pirate radio station at twelve. An office job here and an award there attracted the attention of Alan Pye, a chubby, stubby man beset by a pork pie figure. His penchant for gluttony was the only continuity between Pye and his successor. Unlike Mannering, Alan possessed generous attributes which led him to hire Chrissie for more than her abilities. He saw her as a rising talent and not a bomb to detonate. Alan saw people for more than their abilities, apart from Ruth, hired only thanks to her dictionary mindset - too lazy to stand out, but too useful to let go.

Clive Mannering had been accepted into the fold three months earlier. His cheating and spying at Firefox made him a controversial figure, using his superhuman hearing to steal stories. Yet, Alan gave Clive another chance. Clive had the potential to be more than he ever managed to fulfil, and Alan became determined to prove it. The Manifesto was very much his paper, and he hoped it always would be, but as they say, all good things...

Nobody knew where Alan was in the present day. Whether he was alive, dead, abroad, or missing, was beyond them. He'd vanished off the face of the Earth and Chrissie rarely thought about anybody else. The most important man in her life - much more than her father or boyfriend - because he was the first man to see her for who she was, not what she could be. At appraisals, he'd tell her what she was doing wrong, rather than sucking up to her. When editing, he'd offer constructive criticisms she could build on in future.

Whenever she became unsure of what to do next, she would ask herself: What would Alan Pye do? Such a scale of conundrum approached her in her fury. If Ethan had refused to publish Alan's story, he'd find a computer, contact a rival paper, tell them all about Ethan and the unblessed. So that is what she did.

Part of her pondered whether to take Ruth, but she let her friend capture some sleep in a monotonous, growling snore. It was better that way, since Chrissie worked best alone, when there was nobody else to worry about.

This was mid-afternoon. Chrissie pressed on the buzzer beside the iron-clad gates. Midnight's storm clambered over her, so she wrapped herself in tight hazmat. While she waited, her gaze met with the domineering decay of the sign above her. 'Woodville Estate', characters as unkempt as the neighbourhood within.

Carim picked up her image on the screen, eyes and knees baggy from exhaustion. The noise of a brief alarm relented once Chrissie scanned a barcode against the doors to prevent the reminiscent shrill shriek. The gates wheezed open onto an orchard camouflaged by opaque light.

"Is it time for my interview already?" asked Carim, suited up and eager to go, without a weapon in sight. "It is midnight."

"I'm aware of that," Chrissie whispered, even though the nearest apartment complex was minutes away.

"I thought you said our conversation would commence when my shift was complete."

"It will," Chrissie promised. "I fancied another look around."

"At midnight? There will be nobody to interview."

"Uh-uh," Chrissie responded. After a jolting skip, she twisted around. "You haven't read the most recent edition of *The Manifesto* by any chance?"

"I can sense frustration in your voice. Have you tried Xanax? I expect Ethan forbade the article concerning the unblessed from being published."

"You're right. How did you know?"

"He despises the unblessed," Carim said. "He believes the lies that they are otherworldly monsters that deserve subjugation."

"Did you believe that before you lived here?"

"I thought my next interview was scheduled for the morning?"

"Say what you like. I won't be recording this."

"I never thought of them with the same obsessive hatred that Ethan does. I often neglected the recognition of their existence, as the majority always have."

"Is there any reason why Ethan thinks of the Unblessed in the way that he does?"

"Any answer to that question would revolve around mere theories. Perhaps it would be best to ask him yourself."

"He's not the most approachable of people…"

"I thought you were supposed to be fearless. What you are doing is admirable, Chrissie. Saving the Unblessed when nobody else has the courage is an incredible achievement."

"Thank you! Must dash! Are you bored yet?"

"Waiting in the freezing cold for something to shatter a possible eternity of unending nothingness? Tedium defined."

Chrissie moved like a spider, scurrying, difficult to swat.

"Do you happen to know where I would find a computer around here?" she asked when she paused. "Telling me where would help me continue to do admirable things."

"Yes, of course, in the cafe downtown. You know the place?"

"Affirmative! There's only one!"

The cafe had internet and coffee, but like all coffee shops, closed well before midnight. Caring not about who stole what, the barista left the door unlocked, as one croak of the handle revealed. Sometimes the starving and the thirsty would break in to take what they could.

Chrissie flicked on the switch and the lights revealed themselves in succession. She tightened the lapels on her attire, dropped to a nearby seat and launched into a typing frenzy on a nearby laptop. No password was required, but patience was necessary to suffer through the computer's monotonous speed.

Intrigue convinced her to type 'Ethan Song' into the search engine. The only articles that appeared were about Ethan leaving Defence J, and the press conference for his Defence E initiation. Then she typed in 'The Knight Defence E', but her article about Winona's murder wasn't discoverable. She speculated that the internet had been censored and doctored so only pieces that favoured the unblessed could be found. Twitter, blocked. YouTube, blocked. Comments sections, blocked. Advertisements about a flight to Rome for only £15 would bombard the sidebar of any article on the outside world. Here, 'pop-ups were blocked'. Aspirations can kill, remember, and nobody could book a vacation for love nor money. Even if they could leave the country, being unblessed and abroad was no desirable feat. In France, they were locked away in chateaus. Shanties in Spain, and concentration camps in Russia.

Moira Standerton from *The North Coast* was her reporter of choice. A furious email typed at a relentless pace insisted that Defence E had bought out *The Morning Manifesto*, and she wrote an article about the plight of the unblessed which had been doctored and exposed the gruesome conditions of the compound she had been secluded in, meaning that Ethan does have biases against the unblessed and that the world had not yet heard the complete truth. The same email was sent to *The Salford Bulletin*, and *The Yorkshire Press*, and any other paper she could think of that had not yet been bought out by Ethan. Fuel to the fire would follow publication. Megaphone Meg would have everything she needed for her tirade. Stay-at-home mum, political activist, wannabe reporter, but Meg was exactly like Chrissie - a strong woman hoping to be stronger.

Journalists would be pounding on the story like packs of ravenous dogs. Chrissie let an earnest grin rise to her lips. The door groaned again, announcing the presence of another alongside vigilant footsteps, identified as those of Francis Swallow, retiring behind the counter to grab a complimentary coffee.

"This cafe's closed," Chrissie announced. "I expect you know that already."

Francis, the secret superpowered spy who could relay his thoughts to any person he so chose to, detected her snarling thoughts. The more emotive the thought, the easier it was to hear. All thoughts have flavours and textures. Hers were oily and thick. Francis made himself a cappuccino and towered over her. As he did, she was about to press the 'enter' key. Press send, and there would be no turning back. Declaring war on Defence E, the organisation that had provided her with the 'opportunity of a lifetime,' a promise they had failed to deliver. Then the unblessed would be free. Then Ethan Song would be exposed as the fraud that he was.

Francis fixated his side-eye on her. Should she do it? The consequences would be catastrophic. She should do it anyway. Francis shoved his solid framed glasses back to his glabella as he leaned over the back of her chair. A phenomenal performer, very different from the disinclined teacher Winona once worked alongside. Francis slammed down her laptop lid before she could press 'send.'

"Almost looks as though you're hiding something," Francis said with as much nasality as ever.

"What are you doing? What's on that screen is my business!"

He rolled up a rock-hard chair opposite her on the two-seater coffee table. He clicked his knuckles and leaned over her, snatching the computer to delete every copy of the email before it could be sent. Then, he returned the device, by which stage every version was gone.

"You're the reporter, aren't you? Aggie was saying you spoke to her in the Newsagents."

"What gave me away?" she groaned, observing her own journalistic blouse and journalistic expression.

"I expect you'd like an interview, given that you've just deleted my work. Did you read what I said? I expect you knew already. Defence E couldn't have gotten away with what they've done if they didn't have a half-decent spy nestled in their community."

"Nonsense! I don't want to speak to you! I know somebody who does though."

Francis prised a phone from his pocket, taking his time, expecting her to be afraid. This was a Nokia Brick boasting only megapixels and kilobytes. Ethan's mumbled voice picked up on the other line.

"Do you recognise that voice?" Ethan asked.

The voice was low and droning, intercut with a guttural, masculine laugh. There were several male utterances over the line, but only one she recognised. Declan Dalton, her beloved blonde-haired partner, an emergency planner at the local council who worked from home. Francis held the phone against her ear. A gulp reached her throat.

"Do you?" Ethan's tone became more impatient.

"Yes," Chrissie gasped as if she predicted what was coming. "That's Declan."

"Yes, it's Declan, and Declan's been having an ordinary day. He's got friends over. They've ordered a takeaway. He's missing his girlfriend and doesn't know when she'll come back. I doubt he knows he's being observed behind the hedges by his girlfriend's boss."

"Clive's my boss."

"Wouldn't you rather I was?"

"No."

"How many years have you and Declan been together now?"

"Four."

"Four! I expect you care a lot about him then."

"Of course I do."

"Usually people who care about one another as much as that would be married by now."

"My career always comes first," Chrissie stated with conviction, "We agreed that marriage could become an obstacle."

"Sensible move, I suppose. Love is the most inexcusable weakness. It's the only one we can do anything about."

"Has it ever become a hindrance to you?"

"You're not compiling an article about me, remember!"

"I'd certainly like to!"

"You find me that interesting?"

"The lengths you go to so that you can get your own way are astounding. You're watching my boyfriend through the hedges. That's quite frankly disturbing."

"Your career comes before anything, does it? Does that include your morals?"

"I'm a good journalist. Of course a good story comes before good morals."

"You're admitting you're a bad person?"

"I'm admitting I'm a person with questionable morals. I'd say that's different."

"I've had a long day, Chrissie, and I'm doing whatever I can to hold together Defence E while the foundations fall apart around me. When Francis told me that another obstacle had approached our infrastructure, I wasn't best pleased. I put my faith in you, Chrissie. You let me down."

A rustle of nearby bushes intervened with his composure.

"The heroes behind Defence E aren't the corrupt ones," Chrissie replied. "Carim's trying his best to change things. I'm sure the others would if they knew your true colours."

"They're afraid of me. I can see it in their eyes and hear it in their voices, but you are not. I cannot recall the last time I met somebody who was as unafraid as you."

"I've faced your type before. You're the sort that needs people to get in your way every now and again so you can prove that they can't. What was it, a career in the army? That's what I guessed when I first met you."

"Very perceptive."

"The medals were a giveaway. You threatened people in conflict, I bet, like you're going to threaten me now. To get your own way. So go on, make your move."

Declan's husky laugh infused her with pain. He annoyed her, as any boyfriend would. He didn't like how into her career she was, even though he was allowed to be consumed by his own. He flirted with other women, and he liked to drink all too much. But he was a good man. Committed, like her. Flawed, like her. And she loved his good heart.

"Declan can fire bullets from his mouth. I can mimic the abilities of anybody I come into contact with. Say I enter his home and threaten to kill him. He'll fire. Nothing will happen. The bullets will ricochet off my body and into his, and then who will be to blame?"

"He's a pacifist," her inflexions became increasingly unsteady. "He won't use his abilities, and you're powerless then, because people have to use their abilities for you to mimic them. Unlike you, he believes there are other ways to deal with a problem than killing it."

"Are you accusing me of murder, Miss Young?"

"Considering that you threatened to kill my boyfriend, you at least have the opportunity to be one. I bet you killed plenty of people in combat."

He squirmed. He couldn't let himself remember what he'd experienced when he'd been used as a weapon by the army.

"His life would be endangered the moment I stepped through that door and, trust me, I could get in there if I wanted to."

"Don't you dare," Chrissie murmured, edge of tears.

"Lovely place this one. Nice neighbourhood. Two-bedroom houses, a spacious garden. Not the epitome of fortune, but you could do worse. Do you miss it?"

"I've worked hard for my fortune. Anything's preferable to the place I'm living in now."

"I can imagine you in your hazmat suit, in that cafe, believing you're doing the right thing, but you're not. You save the unblessed and the blessed die. Not only Declan, who I'm looking at through your window, but your parents, your sister, Ruth's family. I know where they all live. I know everything about them. Do you want their blood on your hands?"

"No."

"Look how it's made Carim feel. I appreciate the content you wrote about Carim feeling remorse for his actions. We need more of that, and less of all this about the unblessed being subjugated. Their lives are fairer than they deserve."

"What have they done to deserve this?" Chrissie spat. Ethan didn't respond, as if he had no answer, or was too afraid to provide one.

"Francis will be keeping an eye on you. If you make one wrong move, I will know. Your victims will know too because they will be yours. You are property of *The Manifesto*, so you do what *The Manifesto* demands. Otherwise, *The Manifesto* demands compensation. If you continue to pursue the path you are currently following, it will become clear that you care more about your job than anything or anyone else. I expect you're human enough to want to avoid that."

"Of course I do," Chrissie gave in.

"I hope we won't have to speak again anytime soon. Make sure you keep any mention of the unblessed being unfairly treated out of tomorrow's article. Focus on redeeming Carim. You will be rewarded with the lives of your loved ones, and Ruth's. Her mother's in a retirement home, isn't she? I hope she's doing well. It's about time I paid her a visit to find out. That's if you don't do as I demand."

Chrissie's mask left only her stark eyes exposed. Francis poked at his glasses as if to make a point. His smirk was enough to motivate her to punch the table in fury. Her weapon against Ethan Song was no more.

Remember when Chrissie was angrier than she had ever been? Times change, because she'd just reached the next level of anger. Embittered, she stormed out of the café and resisted the tears which wished to drown her well-composed features in sorrow.

A knock at the cabin. Expecting this to be Ruth, she answered, only to be faced with a brown-haired lady. She recognised this to be Quickfix, minion of Ethan Song, so she slammed the log door. Isla's boot prized a gap open and she barged inside.

"Lovely place," the cockney swung her arms around and knocked Chrissie's papers to the floor. "Not enough room to swing a cat, though. You look red. Something wrong with you?"

Chrissie groaned deeply and her knees clicked as she kneeled down to pick up her papers. Before she could, the wind rushed around the cabin and the papers were returned to their former position. Isla vanished for a moment until she returned with flushed breath and the need for a sip of water, stealing one of Chrissie's bottles.

"It was me who dropped the papers, so it should be me who has the responsibility to pick them up," Isla remarked. "You must not be the biggest fan of Defence E after we've put you up here. At this moment, neither am I. I suspect you've got a few problems with Ethan Song. We might be able to help one another out."

"Count me intrigued," Chrissie's expression suddenly lit up. "It's not a trap, is it?"

"No, it's not a trap. Do you think that little of me? Don't answer that! I've discovered something. There's no such thing as the disease that strikes when the Unblessed touches the Blessed. No, that was made up a long time ago. Carim didn't lose his powers because he made contact with Winona Barton. His abilities were taken from him by Ethan Song."

"Tell me everything you know."

Eavesdropping on the cabin was Francis Swallow, about to call on Ethan Song, ready to take whatever action was necessary to keep their secret as Chrissie and Isla debated the cruel truth.

23. <u>The Stranger</u>

Sunflowers to the left. A blank canvas to the right. A paintbrush in her left hand. Other students behind her in utter silence but not in awe. Their works put Maeve's to shame, and they were only children.

Maeve's art had too many imperfections to be anywhere close to faultless. The leaves looked like jets and the petals like dandruff. It was either the fault of the dying flower which draped over thanks to its unnatural hunchback or the way she had mixed up the paints. The green was more brown than viridescent. The faded mustard yellow failed to appreciate its sparkling amber blossom. The vase, too, was too hollow for the glinting structure. One had to be a mess to be an artist, but she was a mess of an artist.

Who could blame Maeve, when she had taught herself? Her education had been poor, and her unenthusiastic teachers had been poorer, and for that, her insufficiency became understandable.

Her students were squashed together in a rotting cube that fought for character with glitter and colour. Notice boards in red and yellow overstated the scribbled messes of younger pupils' artworks. Ranging from five to fifteen, her tutees all employed the same eager commitment to copying their chosen items. Some drew flowers, others chose fruit, but none of them did justice to their subjects, even if Maeve informed them otherwise. Maeve could be too encouraging sometimes, but their proud grins made it difficult to spurn their 'masterpieces'.

Maeve herself became transfixed by the image while she constructed it. Eyes slightly away from reality, mouth on the verge of indifference, fleeting breaths only. A raised hand caught in the mirror glass snapped her out of her peak of concentration. She shot around to meet the eyes of an eleven-year-old girl with pigtail hair and narrow spectacles.

"Finished," the girl gloated. Bishop Tomlinson's Granddaughter.

Maeve retired from her seat, approaching the faded scarlet gala apple. It would be the child's tea that night, and the painting failed to mimic it. It captured neither the abrupt surface bumps nor the slight patches of dwindling green that obstructed the ruby pigmentations. Maeve still patted the girl's back and pretended she thought it was great. Her reaction may not have even been fake, because Maeve didn't know better.

The paint palette on the girl's desk contained vague sachets of red and black. Only the scarcity of materials could be blamed for the inadequacy of these paintings. Hands darted up across the room and Maeve, a short woman who lacked the weight and height to infuse energy, darted in zigzags.

Another reason she showered them all with praise was Hex, her son, who made her fear accusations of bias. Hex was in Class B, and this was Class A, but Maeve always complimented his artworks. After all, he was her son, and she'd never hear the end of it if he didn't. Therefore, she had to complement everybody else's work to avoid being branded chauvinistic. Some of her students were teenagers, others had barely passed toddling, and she had to treat them all the same.

Her artwork summoned her like a pirate to the song of a siren. To her, it was something more than the inconsequential and, quite frankly, subpar piece that it happened to be. Pupils, meanwhile, found the classrooms of their irises stimulated by the task ahead. Nothing could distract Maeve from this work of triumph. Nothing, except...

A knock at the door. Then there came a stranger.

A somewhat ferocious elderly stranger swapped what must have once been a handsome visage for one of cruel seniority. His bald head alone was curiously aggressive. His soul was darkened by the sacks beneath his eyelids and his limp saunter implied that he required a cane which he refused to wield. The dull colouring of his eyes and face accentuated the wrinkles on his countenance. Additionally, scars marked the left-hand side of his face, blotches of skin burned away from long ago.

"Can I help you at all?" Maeve asked, forgetting in her hallucinogenic inattentive state that this was a classroom of students and that was a stranger. If she remembered that, she would have fought harder to keep him away when he barged into her teaching quarters. She groaned in defeat once he made it past her to watch over the class.

He wore a tweed jacket with elbow patches fit for an English lecturer. On his side was a satchel which comprised belongings Maeve never discovered. A trilby hat sat on his naked head. Something was comfortable, if not comforting, about his presence, as if he felt like he belonged there, as if he felt like he belonged everywhere. The old man sat amongst the children as if he believed the classroom to be his own. He was out of breath, worn by experience, although the nature of these experiences remained unknown.

"Maeve," the stranger said as he moved his index finger to Maeve's lips to prevent her from asking the obvious question, accompanied by a shushing sound. "Don't ask who I am. We both know I won't tell you." He turned to the students, most of whom refused to turn their heads from their feeble artworks. "Hello, children." No response. Stranger danger. Maeve had taught them well. "Suit yourselves then," he murmured.

"I'm not allowed to ask who you are?"

"As I say, I won't tell you."

"Do you work here? Are you allowed to be here?"

"I won't cause them any harm."

"I'm not sure I can let you be here."

"Come over here, away from the kids." He stood again. "I don't want you to think they're in any danger. I have no reason to hurt them."

This guest made a gesture with his right hand to welcome Maeve to the box room's dim corner, away from the brief candle at the centre. Maeve kept her distance, but the man hushed his husky, withered voice to avoid being heard.

"Hopefully I arrived before it was too late," said the enigma. "You and Eva are currently trying to deduce the identity of the superpowered spy in this compound."

"How…How do you know about that? I haven't told anybody that."

"Maybe I'm a mind reader, like the one you're after."

She gulped. "You're the spy? I've never seen you before."

"Wouldn't that explain both so much and so little? To tell you the truth, I'm knackered. I've been through the wars and back and I've got so much to tell you. I'm not allowed to. What I can tell you is that a blessed man resides in unblessed territory. I need you to know so you can try to stop what happens next. I think it might be too late already."

"Carim, you mean? Or the journalists my wife claims arrived this week?"

"None of them. The spy who claims to be Unblessed like you."

"It's true then? There's a superpowered spy?"

"You didn't believe that?"

"Of course I didn't. Touch the unblessed, and you become unblessed."

"It's difficult to see you with your naivety so intact."

"How do you…"

"Shh! Don't ask the obvious. It's boring, Maeve, and you should steer clear of predictability. You believe that the unblessed can make the blessed like them?"

"I believe in what I've always known," Maeve replied.

"Isn't that what Winona said? Moments later, Winona was plotting her way out of here. Why is that? It was out of character, don't you think? Same with Kenny and Elijah. They were subdued by the system, only for a rebellious thought to kick in, as if from nowhere. It's as if there was a switch at the back of their mind which had been turned on. At that moment, they remembered."

"They remembered what?"

"That people had escaped before, and people had gotten away with it. I saw it every single time. Some even lived amongst the blessed without the blessed knowing."

Her mind felt numb. She sweated profusely. "This is a lot to take."

"Don't you want to know who the spy is?"

"I don't know how you know.

"As you say, I could be him."

"I've never seen you before. I know everybody who lives here. Woodville isn't exactly huge."

"I'm not the spy, but you could brand me an observer. I know the name of the man who lives among you, who claims to be one of you. Do you know Francis Swallow?"

Francis Swallow. Not a friend, not an enemy. Nothing more to her than a man on the same plane, like this stranger, or any other. It made sense. A teacher was the best shot at uncovering information. Think about it. Who does an adult open up to when they think nobody else is listening? A child. Where do adults come every day between 9 and 3? A school. Perfect place to figure out who needed to be put in line. Maeve's expansive cheeks opened her silky muzzle.

"How do you know this? Why are you telling me of all people?"

"Everything I do is done for justice. You may believe your existence to be trivial, but you are the most important of us all."

"Don't give me that."

His voice contained gravel and effort, so complimenting her was not something he would have done if he didn't have to.

"You're the one who started this," he declared. "Now you're the one who must finish it."

"I'm not the one who started anything! Outrage. Perplexity. Heady emotions rushed at her and made her giddy. "My evenings are spent watching game shows and washing and playing cards with Hex. I'm important only to my wife and son, and the children who I teach."

"You're not teaching them particularly well."

"You come here to baffle me and insult me?"

"My eyes might not be what they used to be, but I know a good picture when I see one, and nothing in this room strikes me as such. Maybe, however, you are a better artist than you think. You've made a perfect design for the person you believe you want to be. You've managed to fool them, and yourself, on countless occasions. Maybe your true talent is hidden at the back of your mind like the rest of it."

"Stop speaking in riddles!"

He sighed longingly. "I'm not as young as I once was, nor am I as important, yet I hope I have done what is right. Expose Francis, and you expose the lies at the centre. There's lives at risk."

"What lies? Whose lives?"

"That's what you need to find out for yourself. I'm under strict instructions not to tell you anymore."

"Who by?" No answer. "Please tell me who you are."

His mouth hinted at a smile that it never delivered. "There's so much you don't yet know, but you will know it in time." He saluted his trilby, not a charming man, but charming by artificial choice.

"Bye, kids! Farewell Mrs Croft!" Then, he left the classroom as if he had never been there at all.

Maeve returned to the easel and engaged herself in art to distract herself from the nagging concern that her whole life had been wasted. Was she a poor artist? Was the truth about the unblessed not the truth after all? Was she living on the foundations of a broken lie that would be best left forgotten? The answer to all these questions, of course, was yes. It frightened her to acknowledge that.

24.   The Body

It was a few hours earlier, and the event that the stranger warned Maeve about had already played out. Chrissie had spent so much of her night gossiping with Isla that she had spared no time to catch up on sleep. Exhaustion was getting to her so much that she became dizzy while she stood, so she did her best to get some kip. It was one of those 'If I get to sleep now, then I'll get four hours of sleep' kind of nights, and fear of her boyfriend's fate only got her forty winks further.

She phoned up Declan at what must have been seven, relieved to hear his native Geordie vocals on the other line, insisting he was busy, declaring his readiness for her to return home. Realising she hadn't heard from Ruth for some time, she knocked on the cabin. No response. Ruth tended to wake early, but perhaps she was walking across the expansive field that lay outside Woodville's orchard. A heavier knock, and the door opened itself.

Chrissie didn't know how she'd missed the commotion despite being so close, but spilt blood was rampant over the ripe red floor, and there were very few signs of life. She raced over to Ruth, covering her boots in a layer of human blood, shook her over, but there was nothing. One kiss of life later, and Ruth was still very much dead. Chrissie sobbed and shrieked at the sight of her colleague sprawled out on the floor with stab wounds across the body.

Rage forced her to barge out of the hut, wiping the tears from her face and propelling herself beyond the gates with a tap of her ID badge. Carim had finished his shift, as exhaustion retired him to his bed. Bishop Tomlinson, taking his granddaughter to school, noticed her striding, camping out in the bushes to wait for the apartment complex which housed Carim to open. The Bishop asked her how she was, but she refused to favour him with a response, instead racing into the open door and up the stairs, knocking enough times that Carim might answer.

Her phone buzzed. It was Ethan, insisting that she was still watching over Duncan, a cause for concern, because Ruth had been her warning. When Carim answered, she pushed him aside and grabbed the propped-up rifle. She forced it into the face of this now powerless specimen and left right away, in quite a hurry. Carim tried pulling her back, but she kicked his shin to slow him down when he inevitably tried to chase after her. Chrissie shot at Carim's stomach when he pursued her, and he tumbled down the remainder of the stairs, while she left with little trouble and very few doses of remorse. She thought about stopping, but she persevered, raw red with rage and targeting the rifle at anybody who looked at her.

Among these observers, Francis, wide awake despite their encounter the night before. Francis raised his hands to act oblivious and she thought about shooting. Francis was merely a puppet, and shooting him would solve very little, but she knew he was patching through to Ethan at that very moment, preparing the forces to amass against her. She rushed through the orchard and out of the gate, where another click of her ID badge opened the gates with a grinding alarm.

Suzie, having been witness to this confrontation, entered the apartment complex to find Winona's killer out cold with a gagging hole in his stomach. She contemplated leaving him there, but instead she called for help, and Francis and Gordon rushed in to help him up, taking him one arm at a time. Suzie smiled to herself at her virtuous act of goodwill.

Chrissie kept on running. It was then that Ethan received the information about a fugitive and called on Quickfix to apprehend the escapee. Quickfix booted and suited up and clicked her fingers to arrive at the community in no time. She spotted the body with the heaps of blood first, then Chrissie, racing with the rifle touted first at Isla, then to the grass.

"Come on, Chrissie, you're smarter than this," Isla remarked. "You've worked so hard to get to this position and now you're just going to throw it all away."

"You're smarter than to hurt me, because you know what harm it's done to Carim."

"We need to bring Ethan down, Petula too, but we can't be brash about this. Ethan's taken a life. That's your friend, isn't it?"

"Ethan gave the order. Francis killed him. When I saw his face in there, pretending that nothing had happened, I wanted to fire. I need to find Ethan, and force him to confess. You're going to take me there. We're going to make him tell us everything."

Grasshoppers ricketed frantically from adjacent vines. Chrissie's rifle clicked into gear. She couldn't be labelled a dab hand, given her inexperience with firing guns.

"I took a shine to you when we spoke last night, Chrissie. You're headstrong, assertive, and in many ways, you remind me of myself. This isn't you, though. You write incredible stories and that's how you express yourself, not with a silly little rifle. Your friend's dead in there, right?" Another stream of tears formed for Chrissie. "I don't peg you as the type for waterworks, either. You've lost your senses, so let me take the gun." She held her hand out, but Chrissie refused to yield. "The best way to take Ethan down is through words, not action."

"I shot Carim," Chrissie shuddered. "I won't hesitate to shoot you too."

Aware that Chrissie was more of a hindrance to her intentions, she clicked her fingers when the bullet assembled in the gun, and before it could reach her, they were at the police station. Isla whispered into Chrissie's ear: "I need to earn Ethan's trust. You're not exactly helping me, Chrissie. I'm sorry about your friend, but I'm afraid I'm going to have to sentence you. Hopefully by the time the trial comes, we can minimise your sentence. I'm sorry it had to end this way."

Chrissie's rifle had been confiscated and her hands were in the chains that Isla had rushed her into. Isla shot back to the community in no time, aware that without the disease to hold her back, she could enter and exit the community at will. All she would have to do was imagine being beyond the walls that read 'Woodville', and she would be able to see Carim again.

25.   Yes, Prime Minister

Phillip Letter did nothing that a politician should do, except lie, cheat, scandalise and womanise. So, Phillip Letter did everything a politician usually does, but nothing that they should do.

The rest of it - Passing laws, addressing the nation, attending parliament, overseeing the government - came as a secondary priority. His robotic clones completed these tasks for him while he surrendered to a life of indolence.

You can imagine it now. Several identical, slicked-black-haired, round pointy-faced buffoons, dashing around Downing Street in matching suits like mad things. Each of them completed a different task while the days drifted away for Letter himself. For the parties and jamborees, of course, Letter would show, but the more important parts of his profession came second.

Like any person with an ounce of status, the Prime Minister possessed an ability locker. The origins of lockers had come from King Edward, who syphoned off the light from Stonehenge to prepare for potential catastrophe. Upon induction, a world leader would receive access to a cabinet of developed abilities. Some powers - like Chrissie's more distinctive capabilities - scientists found impossible to replicate. Others - flight, mind control, matter manipulation, and, most importantly of all for Phillip, matter duplication, could be constructed by the greatest scientific minds the country had to offer.

One of these allowed him to construct as many copies of himself as he wished, who could all co-exist with him without existing at all. So, while he lazed around on his sofa with his Jack Russell watching television and eating cake, his minions completed all the dirty work. Seven versions of him currently existed, each with distinctive purposes, each one with the same blank canvas of a mind. One was in the kitchen preparing a banquet; another was busy plunging the sinks.

Their only job was to exist and to work. Phillip could create as many mindless replicants as he needed. He didn't need to hire anybody, and that meant not paying anybody, and that meant more money for him. The only staff on site was the servant who ensured the clones never spiralled out of control or gave away his act. Additionally, he had people write speeches for his clones and people to choose what they wore each day.

Splashing out on his girlfriend wasn't a problem. He didn't have to step outside and risk his life. All he had to do was flick a button, issue a command, and his clones would function. Sometimes they became bodyguards, or public speakers, or drivers. Letter didn't have to risk his life by stepping out of the Downing Street doors.

Residing on the chaise in a museum-style living room that defined the bourgeoisie lifestyle was a lifestyle fit for a monarch. The only downside being that he was putting on ten pounds a day, massacring his eyesight, demolishing his mental health. None of this encouraged him to stop whiling away the day on subpar television.

The clones also had access to the powers that he did, as long as he instructed them. At the end of the day, they would be deactivated, so their powers weren't problematic. One clone, for example, leapt down the double staircase using their abilities of teleportation. He'd instructed them to arrange a meeting with Ethan Song, and it needed to be done quickly. A press conference was coming that evening, but unbeknownst to the rest of the world, Letter wouldn't be conducting this himself. He reserved that role for one of his duplicates, who was as slippery and plastic as he was.

Letter possessed enough abilities in his locker that with the right mindset, he could take over the world. Leading Britain took enough effort, so he never tried.

One ability from his locker forced him to retire from his comfortable home at the centre of the couch. This allowed him to alter his measurements to whatever quantity he deemed fit. Being a prime minister meant the whole world judged him - or his image. He couldn't risk being overweight. The locker squeezed the fat and allowed his stomach to retreat to a comfortable status. Then, he would return to his lounge to laze in dormancy. Often his weathered eyes would grow tired of screens so he would idle to the radio instead. Eyes shut, always.

Rarely did his sleep comprise eight-hour shifts, since little activity meant there was nothing to tire him out. He would shut his eyes whenever he could, to Beethoven, Mozart, or sometimes even Beyonce. Inertia exhausted him.

Gloria stayed with him despite the scandal about his night in a university dorm with the Philosophy lecturer's pet sheep. She adopted a more active lifestyle and encouraged him to do the same. Whenever she wasn't marketing for Glorious Gloria's (her makeup brand), she scrubbed surfaces and babysat Phillip's many children on their days away from their many mothers. Her large-chested, lingering-legged, perfect blonde stature was akin to the models who often graced Phillip's television screen. A former reality television star, well above his league, so he often suspected she was gold digging. Around the house, she often wore jogging bottoms and gym wear. On evenings away from home, there was the pleasure of coiffed hair and trumpet gowns.

Gloria heard Phillip's voice coming from the conference room. She knocked, greeted him, and was met with a monotone timbre, rather than her husband's usual rambling resonance. This was not her husband, nothing more than a facsimile, who was preparing to impersonate the Prime Minister once again.

"What did I tell you about not interrupting me during my meetings?" The doppelganger asked. Gloria groaned and opted to flee upstairs to her real husband clattering along in her leopard print and high heel boots.

Gloria had pampered the fake Phillip in so much makeup that his plastic skin appeared authentic. Fake

Phillip didn't smile unless he was told to. Cue cards matched with his eyeline held by the one servant who directed every move. Natters from the real Letter family were almost inaudible thanks to the thick ceilings.

The ceilings, though, were not soundproof. Slamming doors and vehement rows were still transparent for Ethan to hear. Whenever Gloria appeared in public, she had the obligation to grin. In private, rarely did her lips invert from their resting frown.

"Do I have to do everything around here?" Gloria erupted in a voice distant from the faux cockney she pursued on TV. When the cameras were on her, she needed to be somebody else. Perfect. Glorious Gloria - make-up that can make you heal, exactly like her. She could have been a Nurse, but she chose to waste her life on Phillip bleeding Letter instead.

"The kids need to be picked up from school in half an hour," Letter groaned. "Send one of the clones if you need to." Feeling like he was in one of those grape-eating-Roman paintings, Letter was hesitant to move. He leaned over the adjoining table and clambered about for keys, sparking discordant jingles. He grasped the key, chucked it at Gloria, and she caught it without any struggle. "Keys to my Range Rover. My programme's getting to a good bit. See you later, sweetie!"

She grunted at the lack of enthusiasm in his 'sweetie' and the door nearly detached from its hinges. Every time she felt like leaving him, she'd return to her room, and remind herself of all the pretty items her patience brought her. When the screen was ready, it exhibited Ethan's familiar profile. Ethan appeared in mint condition, polished livery to boot. Phillip called through at 6.29PM.

"You said you would call at 6.30," Ethan said.

"Early is better than late or never," Phillip - but not Phillip - bumbled. His register carried natural stumbles, although most of these cues were for show. The duplicate interlaced his fingers and observed the autocue with care. "I expect you know what this conversation is about."

"About Defence E. I expect you believe my leadership to be inadequate."

"I appreciate all you and your staff have put on the line to protect the people of Hull. You know that you have my gratitude, and the gratitude of Great Britaim, yet recent events..."

"Great Britaim?"

The writer of the autocue dialogue must have made a spelling mistake. In response, the servant slammed his palm against his face while the other duplicates exchanged a flavourless glare. A brief flicker consumed Phillip's face as the writer programmed fresh words to recover from this glitch.

"Great Britain," the twin corrected.

"You don't have to hide from me," Ethan said. "We have earned the perks of the job. You're not the real Phillip. I know what's in an ability locker. You're an AI mouthpiece. You're a duplicate who's been programmed to reel off declarations and pause only when somebody else speaks. I don't care about that. People are pulling the strings, watching this conversation. They'll pass on what I need to say."

The copycat persevered. "...Have let the British public down. The Knight's actions have not only corrupted the reputation of your team. The other police forces have all had to pay the price. We've received many accusations of institutionalised discrimination. Following Queen Victoria's edicts, nobody will stand for discrimination against the unblessed. Jackson Lorde from Defence A got in touch and asked what should be done. There were protests outside his house today."

"I can't apologise enough for the mistakes I have made."

"I hope you are learning from them already!"

Ethan, usually intrepid, felt stamped on by the boot of power. "Of course I am, sir, as is Carim, in the compound, as you may have heard. He's feeling remorseful for his actions."

"What he did was right. The way he did it was wrong. The unblessed are a problem, in that the people are starting to see that the unblessed, apparently, don't have enough. It's deflected onto your team, and to my government. We'll soon be expected to pass laws in line with the unblessed."

Phillip kept bleating on, injecting tone into the cue cards. "I dread to think how much of a strain that will have on our party. If people start to believe the unblessed deserve equal rights, or better rights, and we fail to deliver, we'll pay a price. You underestimate how far-reaching the effects of your recklessness are."

"My recklessness, sir?"

"You gave Carim the order to suppress the unblessed fugitives through whatever means necessary. Those means cost us considerably. You've seen the protests, haven't you? Some took place outside Downing Street today. I hear you faced similar demonstrations."

"Yes, I did, sir."

"I'm putting you in charge of sorting this out. You seem committed to your cause, Ethan. I hope I am justified in keeping you in this role."

"I will go above and beyond to prove it."

"Excellent," the duplicate responded. "You're better than what you have been. I've seen your team achieve incredible feats. Our defence forces should be guiding our world."

"I'll do better."

"Better is necessary, Ethan. I'm sure I can trust you. You've been nothing but dedicated to your cause. Prove to us that putting you in charge of Defence E wasn't a mistake."

When the call finished, the servant deactivated the duplicate by flicking a switch on his nape. The clone even had the same eyelash flicks and moustache gaps.

Upstairs, Phillip entered such a state of languor that no other human could aspire to. He'd ordered a takeaway pizza during the call with Ethan and reflected on how he wished his life would never change. A knock at the door from his speechwriter gave him the minutes from the meeting. Phillip's wrist shooed him away and the Prime Minister gorged on the next slice.

The press conference that night would entail a bumbling heap of bubbling propaganda. He'd claim it was "tragic that the unblessed must sometimes pay the price of death". However, he'd also claim that the escapees were criminals who endangered their very way of life. He'd praise Defence E while condemning the deceased security guards. He'd go on about Viva La Vida, conforming to the sort of nonsensical idiolect which politicians often did. He'd promise to pass a bill in their favour, and he'd hope the world would forget the whole ordeal.

Many wouldn't forget. Meg's ilk was no longer few and far between. None of this was fair, and England blamed their Prime Minister. No matter how much he internalised himself, Phillip couldn't escape the warning that his way of life was under threat. The opposition would weaponize this ordeal against him. Parliament would pressure him to make concessions. No MP could judge him. They all had their clones do the dirty work, and none of them even tried to care for the unblessed. There was no unblessed party or unblessed representative. Phillip's rule was falling apart, and something had to be done.

He'd rather recline on his sofa, eat pizza, watch television, and forget all about it. So that is what he did.

26.   Saving Lives

That's what Suzie had always wanted to do: save lives. She remembered whenever Winona would come over for playdates. They'd known each other for some time, which was why Winona's death hit so hard. They always went to Suzie's house, for whatever reason. Perhaps Suzie's parents were kinder. Winona brought her precious second-hand sindy-doll her parents gifted her from the Newsagents, while Suzie gazed at a poster loaned to her of the superhero Grace Magnificent, her idol, in the sequined golden cape with the perfect complexion.

"When I get older, I want to be just like Grace Magnificent," Suzie squeaked, unusually shrill even for a child aged seven. "She's incredible! The best hero in Saviour Corp!"

Saviour Corp was a precursor to Defence E, in Michigan, and they were much better at tackling their fame than their contemporaries. There were movies about Saviour Corp and their real life and fictitious ventures. Suzie had them all on cassette, gifted to Woodville for free and snatched by her Dad when they were in sore need of a way to pass the time.

"We're gonna be superheroes one day," Winona said. She'd become a teacher and her friend would be a Nurse, and Winona would end up dead. "We're gonna get superpowers and we're gonna save the world, just you see!"

Now, Suzie had the chance to save a life, ironically that of a real-life superhero. A stretcher pushed an ailing Carim through the streets of Woodville at the fastest possible pace to get him to Suzie's medical shed. Once Gordon and Francis dropped him off, Suzie searched for medicines that could come in handy. With her gauze, Suzie applied pressure to the wound. Then, with exclamative panic, she insisted Gordon grab antibiotics from the shelf while she reduced the swelling and held the blood dripping from the wound. Rolling up his sleeves, she ensured there was no damage elsewhere, revealing only needle marks which appeared recently indented. Steven, another loved one of Carim's victims, watched on with disdain as Suzie healed the man who murdered her best friend.

After a click of her finger, Isla joined them there too, incidentally obstructing Suzie from bringing Carim to health, since Isla wanted to kneel down and hold Carirm's hand and be there to tell her friend that everything would be dandy in time. Gordon took Isla aside, surprised that she didn't so much as stammer when the Unblessed touched her Blessed body. By the time she turned around, Francis was gone, after discovering his identity the night before. Francis must have been contacting Ethan as they spoke, to declare that Isla was not where she should have been. Isla's phone started to ring. It was Ethan. She rejected the call.

"Isla," Carim muttered as his eyelids fluttered. He figured out a smile when he saw her. Joy turned to surprise when Suzie was also hovering over her. He feared for a moment as he saw a great deal of Winona in her, but she tapped his arm and promised him that everything would sort itself out. "You saved my life, Suzie. Why would you do that?"

"It's my duty," Suzie replied. "You're Winona's killer, but I'm a better person than you could ever be and I got to work and decided to be a hero."

"That is what you do on a daily occurrence, Suzie Barlow. You get on with life and you save others. You are in some ways more of a hero than Isla and I could ever be."

"Oi, I'm right here, you know!" Isla exclaimed. "Although, for the purpose of not inflaming this situation, I'll decide to agree with Carim's comment."

"How are you here, Isla? You should not be this close to the Unblessed. You will catch their disease. You will become just like the rest of them."

"I'm here to liberate your new friends. Are you the Mayor? You look important?" Gordon nodded when she asked him. "Ruth's dead. Chrissie's been apprehended. It's Ethan we need to worry about now, and his little minion, Francis. There's no such thing as a disease that turns you Unblessed. It was all made up. I'm here to spread the word, and see Carim, naturally."

"That must be a lie in itself. I am aware my powers were taken from me after I made contact with Winona Barton." Suzie squirmed at the murderer mentioning Winona's name. "I woke up in the mirror the following morning and lasers no longer stemmed from my eyes."

"Wait a minute, did you say that Ruth Mayor was dead?" Gordon asked.

"One of your people is a spy. Keep up. There's other things to worry about right now."

Blood continued to pour, and Suzie intensified her hold over her body, but the blood was becoming too loose. The harder she pulled, the tighter Carim's screams became. Isla had never heard him in so much distress.

"I revisited that night, when you took Ethan's orders," Isla elaborated. "The Naylors barged into your home and took your powers from you. None of you are infected. You've been spun a lie. You can leave Woodville Estate and nobody will be harmed so long as you keep it that way."

The haggard creature that had recently come from visiting Maeve's classroom stormed into the tent, asking: "Are we too late?" He dropped a pen from his pocket which presumably held The No Man encased within it. "You've told Carim and the Unblessed everything, haven't you?"

Isla squinted. "Is that you, Hop? I wouldn't have recognised you there for a second."

"It's me. He sees now. I can tell he can see everything that's been hidden from us. It's time."

"What do you mean, it's time?" Isla asked, and Carim was starting to see something in his final moments, and he said: "I see it now. I see my true history."

One side of the old man's face was put to ruins. The other, perfectly blonde and blue-eyed. Who else could it have been?

Carim saw something then. The memory of his brother was fading in those final moments. He couldn't remember Abbas's face, voice, or the way he smiled, and this had been all he had thought of since Abbas's death six years prior.

Carim remembered wearing a green apron, an olive-coloured bakers' hat, and grungy black trousers caked in flour. A swing faucet wiped away excess debris built from wheat. He remembered this life as a supermarket pastry chef as if it were his own. He remembered the freezer that was cold enough to burn the prints from one's finger, and the oven so warm that it risked achieving the same effect.

He'd spin dough like a circus artist spins plates. When he imagined this, he imagined himself. He would rush and clean and dance to grace the shelves with pizza, and people would crowd around the dough as if it were divine, desperate for more. He used laser eyes to release the ingredients from their packers and would waste no time in showering these ingredients onto the bases where they belonged. The kitchen would always smell of red onion and burnt cheddar, but it would feel like home.

Like in Woodville, every day was the same until it wasn't. An incoming cane made a spitting noise and revealed a oman grey enough to camouflage with the store's mundane colour scheme and the dull items which graced each shelf. Carim was making a pie at the time from fresh batter and a sprinkling of ale, before distributing his prized work onto the shop floor. The piranhas pounced, and Petula used this as a means of reaching Carim without distraction. Petula, on the first occasion he encountered her, appeared not too dissimilar from the present. He, however, was without his war-torn eyes and guilt-rattled physique. She placed her ice-cold index finger on his temples and he froze with a fright.

The final signs of life faded from Carim as the bullet wound got to him, and he spoke his final words to Isla: "Look after yourself, Isla." That was all. The Knight faded into the night, just as he had come to the day.

<u>**PART FOUR**</u>
<u>**LEAVE THIS PLACE AND**</u>
<u>**NEVER RETURN**</u>

27.   <u>Castle of the Mind</u>

Hopefully this freak won't stay here for long, thought Suzie. Unbeknownst to her, Francis the mind reader heard it, but it brought him no pain. He knew what people thought of him - potty-faced, greasy-haired - even Winona deemed him an aberration. He learned to stop caring, hence the dead shark eyes equipped when nobody was watching.

Francis played one act in the oyster of another. One minute, he portrayed the buoyant teacher in front of the kids, naturally energetic. The next, a begrudging teacher to Winona, who taught just for a means of filling his free time. Now, a sinister schemer with legs crossed and knuckles clasped, and a coward banking on the impulses of others to remove Maeve and Eva Croft.

The kettle roared as water spat with vehemence from the spout. Francis awaited the cup of tea promised to him, devised from a recycled tea bag, lukewarm water, and a dash of what he hoped was milk, but couldn't be certain. Suzie entered with the mug, almost scorching her hands, but placing it on a coaster before she could. Tweeting magpies functioned as background music for a day caked in the sun's gorgeous golden gleam. Despite restoring her former glow somewhat, Suzie's mood failed to match the weather's bright disposition. The sunlight collided with Francis's eyeline, though, emanating a glow hidden amidst his venomous exterior.

Thoughts made him feel how emotions did for anyone else. Negative ones were a prang to the soul. Positive ones made butterflies race to his stomach. Unfortunately, grief and misfortune plagued Suzie and that meant her mind was a dungeon. While she pretended to be welcoming, her musings were almost always cynical. *What does he look like, with his monobrow and his glasses hanging from his nose?* More took place in her mind than even she knew, and that was why Francis crawled inside. Suzie had not yet been informed of

Francis's hidden superpowers, only that Francis despised the Crofts as much as she did, for whatever reason.

"Do you miss her?" He asked, choking down the tea in reluctant gulps. "Winona, I mean. I know you cared about her. She bemoaned your company frequently, but I got the impression that she admired you too."

"Of course I do," the hint of a smile, "She was my best friend, my housemate, and waking up to fetch breakfast, or going out on my evening run, it doesn't feel right when she's not there beside me. Of course I was angry with Carim, but I've let the past go. He wasn't to blame. He followed orders. He followed them well."

"You called me for a reason, I assume," said Francis. "Our last conversation was about the Crofts, if I remember correctly. You'd best hurry. I need to be off to work in a jiffy." This was forgetting that he had recently killed someone, a poor red-headed journalist, whose blood was still as red and undiscovered as when it had been spilt. "I assume you've heard the latest?"

"Chrissie, Ruth, yes? Carim's dead and we're no less stuck here than this time last year, so what reason would there be to hate, other than to keep on hating? I called you here because I'm having new memories. I know that's not possible. Memories are recycled. New memories are called experiences, but these are not experiences from the present. What I remember are moments from a history I feel I never lived through."

Francis delved into her mind without permission: a battleground where memories were the soldiers at war. He viewed the brain as an ornate building which needed to be preserved. Renovations come in the guise of exercise and meditation. The more renovations, the more coherent the structure will become. As the building grows older, it becomes infested by mould and damp that strips away what was once present. Over time, that structure will decay, and in time it will collapse.

Francis felt himself inside that cascade that resembled, to him, a castle with tall spires stemming from the iver. Stormy seas were gushing away at the motte, commonly referred to as the synapse sequence. Wind lashed against brick as Francis wrapped himself in tattered clothing. The structure of the castle shifted with every blink; the size and shape contorting without warning or reason. Wooden palisades and artificial mounds submerged as the ground rose and swallowed up the structure. The grass, as fresh and viridescent as God made it The sky, clearing from winter, now humbled by glorious azure.

Francis grazed his palm against the freshest pillar while very much being in the room with Suzie. Suzie felt a numbing pain in her temples as he infiltrated her subconsciousness. She threw her palms to his ears to stop the incessant and shrill ringing of the thoughts which fought for a place in her mind.

Years earlier. Suzie and Francis both saw it. A guard dressed all in black with a plastic pass on a lanyard and a taser on his belt. He entered Apartment Block C and rotated a key into the circular lock of Suzie's apartment. A sable mask covered his mouth and nose, and steamed goggles looped around his frigid eyes. Suzie had been wrapping her needle around a feline-fit sphere of orange fabric when this man's knock hammered heartily on the door. She promised she'd only be a moment, setting her cross stitch aside, but a half-finished cross stitch infuriates the creator as much as a never-resolved thought.

Her brown hair was a softer tinge of hazel then, unlike its matted contemporary cousin. Her cheeks were rosier and warmer, and even the counters sparkled better. Pictures of Winona's late parents graced the mantle, who died at such a young age that they could not be there to mourn her. Suzie's brother, too, not an only child like Winona, left her alone to face the dark. They'd died of tuberculosis, typhoid, diseases the outsiders had ensnared. Suzie limped from her chair and the rough sofa creaked with her as she answered the door.

Without the benefit of a peephole, she received little warning that the masked man would bombard the premises by grabbing her diseased paws with masked hands. He wrapped her hands behind her back as if he was arresting her, gagging her mouth with a piece of cloth. An infantile scream carried past a baby monitor. The man's head jolted as he released the glove from his hands to touch her neck, causing her to slump into his arms. He draped her over the sofa as he investigated the shelves, discovering nothing more than rags and photo frames. Suzie, out cold on a rare day off, while Winona worked at the school, would remain oblivious to the intruder, as they always would.

Another two men entered wearing complete protective gear. They made as few changes to the setting as possible to make their presence untraceable. They dragged an unconscious Suzie out by her arms, letting her legs drape ahead of her. Hardly inconspicuous, one could question how they entered unnoticed.

Next thing Suzie knew, she occupied a dentist chair in a darkened room. Eyes bore into her, over her, like headlights, but her vision was too foggy to discern who they belonged to. A sliding door shifted open, revealing brief hints of light. The bounces of a silver cane followed as the door slid shut and the lights came to life. A flock of matted grey hair arrived and towered over her, revealing the harsh wisdom of the figure Francis knew as Petula Wednesday, who he had heard legends of, but had never had the displeasure of meeting. Suzie would have wrestled against the chair's grip, but she felt too faint to resist. From another room, a baby bawled. The last time she checked, Paul, her son, had been asleep. The older woman murmured something with her croaky voice, although Suzie was too dazed to distinguish what, or to even are.

"It's all coming back to me," Suzie became frazzled, returning Francis's lost gaze to the present. "Are you even listening to me? I'm getting these memories back, slowly, like it's being drip fed. I remember being happy, happier than I have ever been since. Holding that baby in my arms and calling him my own." She swiped away a tear that bloomed. "They took my baby away from me."

She remembered being in the small pregnancy ward in the shed outside. The ward was so cramped that it barely constituted a ward at all. The pain was unmatchable, indescribable, but worthwhile, for a few moments later, a hand softer than any other she had felt before clasped her own, and there came an innocent, untainted smile from the specimen born.

"You're implying that the Crofts took your son from you?" Francis replied, feeling like a physiatrist masquerading as a teacher. "Except I thought you chose to give Hex up."

"Paul, his name was back then. I'm not sure. Urgh, my mind's a mess. He was named after my father. I wouldn't give him a name like Hex."

"And what about the father of the baby?"

Francis pictured him as Suzie remembered what may have been the love of her life. A silver fox, with dashing good looks and unmatched charm, a decade older than her. He was the father of her current colleague, Arnold Walsh, but a respected doctor in his own field, if anyone trained under Woodville guidelines qualified as such. Drawn in by his appearance, Suzie spent one night with Nurse Mateusz after they shared a drink (of water. Who do you think they are?) after her mother's funeral. A slight peck of the cheek turned into much more.

Mateusz made up for his inhuman attractiveness with completely human flaws. When he noticed the irregular bump on Suzie's stomach, he made a run for it. He was the one to identify she was pregnant, holding a stethoscope to his ears and picking up on more than one heartbeat. He had already had two children, and it was too late in his life to start again now. Maeusz, a ladies' man, allergic to commitment, even with his wife, spent his final few weeks on a hospital bed in his own intensive care ward, looked after by Suzie and Arnold.

It hadn't been Suzie's choice to get pregnant, especially not with a father who would not commit to her, even if she did love him. He'd been there for her entire life. She'd been to school with Arnold so he'd always been there. His son still worked for her, after all.

Suzie visited him on his deathbed, plagued by tears, with her bump about to burst. She rested a jug of chrysanthemums by his bed, planting a feeble kiss on his forehead, while Mateusz's son and wife watched on with disgruntlement. Suzie watched as the heartbeat monitor dissipated into a resounding chime. Wavy lines collapsed into a linear passage when Mateusz's respiration ceased.

"I don't know if he was the love of my life," Suzie commented. "Or whether he just happened to be there. I don't believe in destiny. If one of us lived in Hull and the other in Swindon then I don't think we'd have been destined to meet, and if we were, that would have been true love."

"You believe in fate? Chance?" Francis asked. "I believe everything plays out the way it must."

Francis did not have a tragic upbringing to motivate his introduction as Defence E's spy. His father had done it before him, but Francis played this dangerous game for the same reason Archie Swallow had, for the money, and for the hell of it.

"They snatched me and Paul from our home," Suzie returned Francis to the room. "Three men, all in black, protective gear, not like us. Blessed, I'd assume. They strapped me to a cosmetic chair. A woman leaned over me…"

"You don't have to explain. I know already. I can…guess. Yes. You'd been told you couldn't have children, then by some miracle, you became pregnant, but these people who barged into your home took your only chance to have a child away from you, and gave that child to Maeve and Eva Croft."

"That's right. How did you even know that? *She* took them away." She, here, referred to Petula Wednesday, dagger-mouthed when messed with, gentle-lipped when appeased. Anybody with a weekday for a surname was destined for eternal misfortune, Francis thought, and Francis's last name was Swallow, so he'd know misfortune better than anybody else. "I heard the grotesque skips of the spitting cane, with steady, subtle footsteps, and it brought me so much pain."

Another figure revealed itself in her memories. Tall, sullen, late twenties, dry around the eyes but soft around the cheeks. She shut the narrow chestnut–coloured eyes which formed her olive-shaped head so that she could concentrate./ Suzie shot to consciousness, her expression wired, no longer sedated/ She jolted from side to side, leading the seat to rattle rhythmically. One masked man held her down. Suzie kicked him away and leapt out of the chair, hurrying for the doorway, but the woman, a younger version of Maeve, clicked her fingers and Suzie's memories turned to dust. The next moment, Suzie woke up on her coffee table following an aimless sleep. From the looks of the faded sun, morning was soon to be ripe.

"Winona asked me how I was, and she made me a cup of tea," Suzie said, as Francis returned to the room again.

"As nice as this one?" Francis gurned. The quality of his refreshment made him convinced that

Suzie only gave it to him because she despised him. "Do you know why Petula took the baby away?"

"Petula? Who's Petula?"

Francis had said too much. Suzie must have heard of Petula, though, from the many news reports she had a starring role in. "I best be going," he said, and he made his way to the door after slamming the half-full cup of hot liquid onto the table with abundant relief.

"Aren't you going to ask me about why I called you here?"

"You said. Maeve took your baby away. She is blessed, but even she has forgotten that."

"That's exactly right. I know why I hate the Crofts. Why do you?" Francis paused, pushing his glasses back to the bridge of his nose. "You really should invest in a better frame."

"I'll get you what you want, Suzie. The Crofts will pay."

It surprised Francis to hear Suzie say. "I don't want that. Like I said, I'm beyond wanting revenge. You want it, for whatever reason? Fine, but I'll have no role in your games."

"You've got to help me," Francis begged. "We can get Hex back."

"The worst of us are defined by our pasts," Suzie replied. "The best of us, by our futures. If I'm destined to get Paul back, I will. If destiny doesn't allow it, I won't get him back. That's fine. He belongs to the Crofts now, more than he was ever mine."

The Crofts were about to expose Francis, and waiting was all he could do. So he waited, and the waiting felt as though it would never end.

28.   Ruth and Lester

It was a few years earlier and the superhero met the journalist for an interview to remember. Neither of them could stand silence so they opted for an internet cafe setting, with the background music of a cafe jazz version of an old Stevie Wonder show they both very much liked. The No Man took the form of a mug containing hot chocolate sipped on by his invisible mouth. Ruth steadied her notes and placed her recording device in check, while people glared at the cup which miraculously spoke fluent Northern English, somehow an attraction despite these observers possessing abilities like the power to communicate with the deceased, or obscure ones like the power to know the lyric to any song which came over the radio.

Sweet Caroline by Neil Diamond came on and everybody started singing, except Ruth, including The No Man, and she had to wait for the mug to finish before she commenced her interrogation, and the soundtrack shifted into some downbeat dirge from the 1960s.

"For the record of this observation of your triumphs in defeating the notorious arch criminal, Napoleon Estafa, I'd quite like your full name, name," Ruth said. "I'm producing an article on you, after all, so I think it'd be best for you to give it to me, me."

"I've spoken to you before, I think," The mug said. "I was with my colleagues, and you were with yours. I came with Hop, and he'd do nothing but moan. You arrived with Chrissie, and I think the fella's name was Alan. Me and Pye respected one another. Where is he now?"

"Missing, MIA, A. They've brought on Clive Mannering, the big fella, to take his place, but I've always thought Chrissie deserved the job more, after all that she did for the Edgehill plant, plant. You'd never forget me, would you, with my scarlet mop of hair, hair?"

"Never! You're a beautiful lady too, if I do say so myself." Ruth blushed. Very few people had complimented her good looks before. "I'd rather you didn't know my name, or see my face. I'm ashamed of what I once was. As you know, I spent my early days in The Institute. I made very few friends there. It's why I never take conversations like these for granted."

"Well, I'm always here to chat, if you need me, but the entire purpose of this interview is to build up a profile of you, you. You're one of Defence E's greatest heroes, yet you don't let anyone see you, you. Why is that, that? You're ashamed of yourself, self? Well, you shouldn't be, be! You're an incredible man with great talent and an astonishing resume, me. Be proud of that, that."

"You can't understand what it's like to be an anomaly like me. I'm an aberration, and that's the only reason why I'm respected. Sure, I can become whatever form I want, but I wish I was normal. Sometimes I wish I wasn't born blessed at all."

"Your Mum and Dad, Dad? Where are they these days, days? What do they think, think?"

"Pa…I don't want to talk about him, and Mum, well she's been admitted to hospital again, like she always is, hogging off the supplies that others need because she's too lazy to do a single thing herself. It's always me and Auntie Jess dragged into her ploys."

"I do understand what you've been through, through. I have a Mum, she's in a nursing home, and she does deserve the help, help. That's where most of my wages go, go. I have this speech impediment, which always makes me repeat the last word I say, say. People say I'm lucky to know everything there is to know, know. I could build a car just as well as I could write a headline, but that's forgetting that people can't bear to speak to me because the conversations will lose their interest, trest."

"There's an ordinary person deep inside of me, but he never wants to come out."

"You're not some rich snob living it up in Villa Aurora, Aurora - I only know what that is because of my dictionary mind, mind! You're you, you. You're vulnerable, ble. Accept that, accept that."

"Except what?" He suddenly realised what she meant, and in a bid to avoid sounding stupid, changed the subject. "I've got somebody who I can set you up with. Somebody I knew from The Institute. One of the few friends I made. I think you'd like one another."

This was Declan, the man who could fire bullets from his mouth, and therefore his abilities disadvantaged him enough that he needed to stay inside The Institute until his powers were kept on a leash. The pair did not hit things off as well as The No Man thought. Ruth could not stop thinking about Defence E's most tragic recruit, and Declan ended up with Chrissie eventually, and they planned a keen future with one another.

Ruth agreed to meet with The No Man, in the form of a houseplant escorted there by Carim, at *The Morning Manifesto* offices. Clive had already set up his podiums to make himself at home and Chrissie was busy searching around for stories with her memory stick chipped into her mouth. The No Man felt he could trust Ruth, so much so that he told her his name was Lester Haggard, and he showed her his face. It was nothing to be ashamed of - a pale, stick-thin being with grungy black hair and worn brown eyes. He presented the deepest of smiles and the pair locked lips.

They agreed that relations between a superhero and a journalist would be talk of the media if anybody found out, so they kept schtum. Nobody knew, not even Chrissie, that they met up every Friday night. They never fell out, never crossed a word, and they could be themselves with one another, so when Lester found out that Ruth had been murdered behind the walls of Woodville, which he learned from a phone call with Isla, he wasn't bound to be happy.

"How did this happen?" The No Man asked. He'd learned to be in his own form even when Ruth wasn't around, just not when he was in the company of others. "Who did this to her? This was before Carim passed away?"

"Give the phone here," the older Hop demanded of Isla, which was a request she immediately accepted. "There's a spy buried within these four walls, sent here by Ethan Song. His name is Francis Swallow. It's believed that he killed her, but he hasn't yet been caught. Isla will do the job. Ethan issued the order."

"He can't get away with this," Isla said when the phone was passed back to her. "You need to get here as soon as possible, No Man. We need all the help we can get. Are you going to tell us your own name now?"

"It's Lester. Lester Haggard." He wiped away a tear, and got to work.

29.   Hidden Villains

Maeve dragged her ankles down the momentary corridor as if such an activity was arduous. The school was small enough that a corridor such as this ended before it began. For once, she couldn't wait to return home to nothingness. Never did she dread seeing her sunshine blonde son and frizzy-haired wife, but rarely was she anxious to leave. She passed Francis Swallow as she made her way to the entrance which she'd use as an exit. Francis looked her up and down, squinting in his narrow, distrusting little way. She pulled the door towards her. Francis pulled her back, tugging at her arm with his wrist. A meek and weak looking chap, he didn't seem the type for exertion.

He twisted her around, snapping her arm before it could release the door. The break room was nearby, only a shove away, and a shove he issued her. She tumbled into the pathetic cube of three tables and a broken coffee machine. Empty. Her bag on her back, her hair over her face. Francis, red with rare rage.

"You're planning on telling Eva," Francis said.

Yes, she'd intended to leave. To the Newsagents, to tell her wife about the spy. Instead, she'd remain, rubbing her arm with unease. She found great discomfort in knowing he was inside her mind, crawling about her mental passages like a spider. Only this knowledge led her synapses to snap at the mosquito bite of his intrusion.

Francis placed a mug underneath the coffee machine, desperate for release from Suzie's tepid contraption. He hammered on the machine, leading the spout to sputter in nervous trickles.

"Would you like a cup?" He asked.

"Nuh-uh."

Every time he swerved round a corridor in the abyss that was her mind, she felt a slight twitch. Numbness of the brain, a jolting sensation. Like Suzie's, her mind contained chambers. Not a castle, but a mansion. Francis approached the vast gates. It was night-time, and the manor twinkled in its towering estate. He knocked on the door, but the door was open. It creaked open, revealing a dining room of chandeliers and a banquet table that stretched around a spacious square. Dotted around the table, in gowns much fancier than their true selves could afford, were those closest to Maeve. Eva, Hex, in wedding dresses and suits.

"It's weird how the mind presents itself," Francis noted, eyes closed. Maeve rushed for the door, but he stepped to the side to obstruct her. No windows, no other ways out. The two of them, in a locked room, as he clawed through her mind.

In the hallway was a staircase. Below the staircase, the hidden chambers of the palace. The spiral staircase seemed eternal, contorting with mismatched steps in shapes and sizes. There was a lone bronze door at the bottom which a twisted handle could not open. His boot went before him, back and forth several times until the wood was no more. Planks remained scattered across the ground which he stepped over. Light blasted with obnoxious rays akin to the entrances of heaven. Into a room he went which even Maeve refused to enter.

"Get out of my head!" she demanded, snapping him out of his haze.

"Oi! I was just getting to the interesting part."

A gallery of identical doors approached him in the dazzling light. He'd need to enter one so he could escape the blinding gleam, any one would do, so he picked the first one to his left. The floor around that door rumbled as if a beast lurked inside, adamant about escaping. He'd forget that his body was in the break room while his mind was inside hers. She'd thrown him aside, extracting him from his state of utter concentration. He grabbed her again, pulling her inside, bolting the exit. He cornered her by the coffee machine, and her hands danced around behind her back, in search of a knife, or anything.

"Stay back!" she exclaimed as she wielded the cup of coffee he had left behind. "I'll throw this in your face if you come any closer!"

He burst out laughing in his hidden, obnoxious giggle.

"Put the coffee down. Bravery doesn't suit you."

Tremoring hands diminished any courage she believed she could possess. No matter how much she tried, she couldn't play the strong woman role. That was her wife's job.

"I'm not going to hurt you," Francis promised.

"Isn't that what they all say?"

"If you'd excuse me, I'm exploring the basement of your mind."

An odd vagueness defined the cellar where Maeve's darkest and deepest thoughts remained hidden. The top floor, the mansion itself, held the people and memories that Maeve chose to retain. Beneath that were more suffocated components, obscured by obnoxious light or flashlight darkness.

There was a phone in the break room, but Eva was at work. Their home phone was all they possessed in a community which could not afford data or contracts. Anytime they needed the internet they could use the cafe, free of charge. Anytime they required a telephone, those shoddy contraptions in public spaces like the break room would do the job.

"What are you gaining here?"

"Shh," Francis placed his finger at his lips. "I'm concentrating."

A torch formed in Francis's fingertips. Metaphorical, of course, like the structure of Maeve's mind which unfolded. The light unleashed onto tucked away memories. First, those he'd already experienced; Suzie, dozy on the dentist chair, too listless to consider retaliation. For Maeve, it was like he'd prized open a locked door. The tide had been out for so long that she'd forgotten what it was like when the waves lashed against the shore. Paul. Suzie. Petula. Many doors to unlock, and they were flying open.

"Make it stop!" she cried, forced to sit down. The pressure of forgotten memories returning to her was too much to handle. Francis chuckled. She'd remember the faces of Lewis Shepherd, Kelly Summerhill, Arthur Trent. Lewis, lithe and skinny. Son of Gordon Shepherd and Agatha Churchill. The son she'd taken away.

She remembered watching it on the television screen. The howling alarm as the gates rushed open. Lewis, hurrying across the grass as he failed to escape the ambitious snares of Carim's laser eyes. Closing her eyes and making everybody, even her wife and son on the sofa behind her, forget the whole ordeal. Forget, under Petula's demands, that Lewis Shepherd even existed.

"You remember what you did now?" Francis asked.

"Stop!" Her ears were ringing. She clasped her palms against her ears to halt the raging tumult. A wind washed through her mind and tore her apart.

"Winona wasn't the first person to try to escape this place. Even I forgot that. Even you."

"Stop! Please!"

"The exact same event played out before. Three people escaped from Woodville, got further than Winona did. Same as Kenny, they showed their escape on the television. Same as Winona's lot, Carim arrived and slaughtered them all. The difference is, Carim's reputation never suffered. He forgot, as did everybody else, because somebody wiped all of our minds of the incident. It's only when I explore your memories that I remember that. Defence E forgot they had the option of using somebody like you because they forgot you even existed. You made them."

She recalled the brutal dispersal of ashes as Arthur Trent fell to pieces as his friends became consumed by smoke.

"Make it stop!" she screamed, but all he did was open more doors. More memories that she'd rejected.

Winona wasn't the first time she'd cradled Hex in her arms to shield his eyes. That time, Eva had cried. Maeve shut her eyes and with a storming bellow, made everybody forget.

"I'm not the only one in Woodville with abilities, Maeve," declared Francis.

"Stop!"

This time, when Maeve roared "Stop!", smoke released from her mouth and made her words boom. No longer did she speak in passive, hushed ways. Her exclamation carried such volume that the glasses shattered and the tables rattled and Francis left her temple mind, but not by choice.

Maeve's stormy state settled, allowing her to release her arms. She jumped to her feet, approaching Francis, who sneered. Maeve remembered her grandma informing her of her duty. She remembered the first paycheck, the first call with Petula.

"You and I are the same," Francis announced, looking cocksure. "In every way but one. I remembered, and you didn't."

"What am I?"

Maeve had never been particularly comfortable in her own skin but never had she been afraid of herself. It was an odd sensation.

"Concentrate, and you'll be able to retrieve the memories you've hidden."

"Can you read my thoughts?"

"Both the pedestrian, and the extraordinary."

"I'm like you?"

"They hid you well. So well that you ended up hiding from yourself."

Maeve shuddered, feeling like somebody had ripped her brain in half. "My head…"

"You don't remember how it feels to have powers. They've remained hidden from you for so long."

"I can't be..."

"It's how you wiped Lewis and Kelly and Arthur from the face of history. It's how you took Suzie's son and made him your own. We're cut from the same cloth, Maeve. Either you're the government's backup spy, or I am, and I would never let myself be *just* the backup."

There came a memory of a different time, a predilection for nostalgia for the days without Francis, without the break room. Eva is sitting opposite her around the table in their apartment. It is too small to contain them both, but it manages to. Maeve felt as though she was there. A door unlocked, a room entered. She smelled the unrelenting urine and rough fabric that prevented her house from becoming a home.

Maeve wraps her hands around Eva's. Eva looks raw and empty from revelation. Her palms are arctic like the apartment.

"Where's the extra money coming from, Maeve?" Eva's expression drops. Maeve observes herself in the mirror, stern but on the borders of blubbery.

"I can't lie to you anymore," Maeve declares.

"Go on then. Spit it out."

Maeve graces her eyes with her palms, every tear shed swept away. "I'm one of them."

"Blessed, yeah?"

"A spy."

The croak of a floorboard. Hex, from the bathroom. The door creaks open. A blonde head reveals itself. Maeve pulls up a chair to encourage the child to sit down too. Hex is too curious to resist the opportunity.

Hex's bearing brightens because they have involved him in their conversation and that makes him feel like a grown-up. Eva puckers her delicate lips. Laughter from the orchard from some celebration the Crofts are not invited to.

This is the aftermath of Eva discovering the payslip. She finds that Maeve, like Francis, is earning more than she should be. Maeve does not want to hide from her wife and son any longer.

"I need you to write it down," Maeve demands as she hands stray strips of paper to Eva. "All of it."

"All of what?" Eva asks, readying a pen.

"Lewis Shepherd. Arthur Trent. Kelly Summerhill. Write down what you need to." Eva proceeds to scribble down these names. "Do you remember them?" asks Maeve. "Those names. They should be familiar to you."

Eva shakes her head, as does Hex. Maeve continues, "I'm the only one who still remembers. They used to be our neighbours. Our colleagues." Maeve looks as though she will drop into a fit of tears. So does Eva. Eva feels betrayed. Eva's wife is not who she thought.

"What are you talking about, mummy?" chirps her eight-year-old son.

"I'm sorry I had to make you forget. These were the orders I received."

"From who?" asks Eva.

"Anybody at the government who needed to administer the orders. They institutionalised me, trained me to become their spy."

"You're having a laugh!"

"I can wipe the memories of anybody I wish to. If I concentrate hard enough, I can wipe an event off the map. That's what happened when three of the unblessed escaped this place weeks ago. I erased Lewis, Arthur, and Kelly from the minds of every person on this planet apart from my own."

Eva wheezes. Her talons claw at her eyelids as she pulls them down her face in excruciation. "I don't know how you expect me to respond."

"Anger."

"Yes."

"You believe me then?"

"That you have abilities? That you're blessed?"

"What you going on about, mummy?" young Hex inquired.

"You'd have lost your powers by now. You've touched me, and if the blessed touch the unblessed then they become unblessed."

"That's a lie," Maeve said. "The disease, no such thing."

"No, it can't be."

"What would I gain from lying to you?"

"You've been doing it long enough," Eva responded. "You tell me."

"I have powers. Do you believe me?"

"Show me."

"Think about something," Maeve demands. "Tell me what you're thinking of."

"You're putting me on the spot here."

"Just think of anything. Literally anything."

Hex turns to Eva. "What about a bird, mummy? You know all about those from what I was telling you."

"I was definitely listening when you told me," Eva murmurs with scathing sarcasm. "Okay, what bird should I think of?"

"A black kite. Bird of prey, member of the Accipitridae tribe."

"Remember the black kite," Maeve says.

"Black kite, black kite, black kite," Eva repeats.

With that, Maeve closes her eyes. As she does so, images of a brown bird flapping across a desolate sky sweep into her thoughts. Images of the bird, swooning and gracious, until it nested on a branch clashed with photographic reflections of her own wife. Eva's face, then the hawk's, a transformation that speeds up, becoming a collage. Shapes twist in her mind with frenetic rotations. Her outstretched tongue is baked in purple.

"Awesome," remarks Hex, underestimating the gravity of the situation.

A flurrying wave brushes across the apartment when ashen smoke projects from her tongue.

Only does the wave reach Eva, as if it pinpoints her glabella. Eva swerves back her neck and shakes herself off after the blast collides with her forehead. Maeve's tongue returns to its usual powder pink. Maeve detects a headache, which her abilities often produce.

"What is the name of the bird which Hex talked to you about?" Maeve asks.

Eva looks over at Hex. It is almost as though his excitement at his mother's superpowers means he wants Eva to forget. "I…" It is as if somebody had drawn over the memory in black ink. A stutter, as if she finds it hard to admit because admitting it would render it true. "I don't remember."

"Mummy has superpowers!" Hex proclaims.

"Shh," hisses Maeve, "The less people that know the better."

"That can't be possible," Eva says. It isn't that she doesn't believe it. It's that she doesn't want to. "Everything we've ever known is a lie and you just expect us to forget that?"

"No," Maeve responds, enveloping Eva's hands again. Eva, incensed, returns her paws to her lap. "I expect you to remember."

Eva rises from her seat, traipsing back and forth down the room, ignoring the dripping tap of the ceiling.

"Do me!" Hex cries.

"Don't you dare do anything to my son," Eva mutters with her back turned.

Eva storms over to Maeve, pulls her up, and grabs her by the wrist. Eva's face itself is rage alone. "Leave him alone, okay?"

"I needed you both to know."

"What did you expect us to do? You've made us fools, Maeve."

"I've written that note. It's securely kept inside of that book. When the time is right, you show me that note. I intend to wipe my memory of all this. I need to figure out the truth myself. We don't have to live in this compound forever, so we won't. We'll escape. I covered up people's deaths. I helped to cover up this lie. I can't know about my abilities because they only bring people pain. The superpowered can coexist with people without abilities and we can be the ones to strike that harmony. It's compensation for all I've done."

"Do you think we'll forgive you for this?" Eva inquires.

"I've forgiven her already," Hex interjected.

"No, you haven't."

"You can't tell me what to think, Mum!"

"Mummy," she corrected.

"Like I said in the note, I know you've had that feeling of urgency to escape this place," Maeve says. "Like an itch at the back of your mind. We'll get out, but to do that, you need to trust me."

"But the urge isn't there because you wiped it from our minds," Eva grumbles.

"I understand you're upset. It's a lot to take. This is beyond us. The timing needs to be right. Everything needs to go down without a hitch." Maeve grazes Hex's knee after sitting down again. "Both of you, I need your help, so I can make up for all the pain I've caused."

"I'll do what I can," Hex winks, rocketing over to the bed with excitement.

"Don't tell anyone," Maeve demands. "Please, Hex. I know you're a good boy."

"Yes, mamma," Hex responds. "My lips are sealed!"

She turns to Eva. "And will you?"

"Will I do what?"

"Keep quiet."

"Your bosses won't be happy about that."

"I'll make everybody forget. Everybody, apart from you two. That includes myself."

"Tell me everything," Eva commands, and Maeve explained every sordid detail. Her tongue lights up again and she makes Petula forget about her powers. She makes herself forget.

One day, they would escape that place. That day had come.

"When the time is right," Maeve said to her wife. "You'll know. Then, you'll tell me everything. Or I'll remember. For now, I need to forget. My powers only bring harm. The least I can do is throw them aside."

One moment, Maeve was in the living room with her family. The next, in the breakroom with Francis. Synapses surging, veins racing. Closing her eyes allowed her to harness untapped potential. Her tongue, protruding, illuminated in violet. Her eyes, bolted, crawled into their sockets. A gust of wind swept across the room, closing in on Francis. His eyes shut too, overwhelmed by the vigorous wave.

She roared, and moments played out in flashes. The storm shattered more mugs, and the coffee machine went apoplectic. Francis fell to his chair. Cut to black. Francis was unconscious, neck draped over his chair. Cut to black.

Everything returned to focus. Francis clicked to life again.

"I must have nodded off there for a moment," Francis remarked.

Maeve didn't respond. Fear paralysed her enough to forbid vocal formation.

Francis observed the time on his wristwatch with an expression of alarm, immediately escaping his seat. Back to his ordinary downbeat self. Every word a grumble, every syllable laborious. His shoulders sagged into an everlasting shrug.

"What just happened?" Maeve trembled. By that point, Francis was already out of the room. Maeve had never felt so distant from her own body. Her legs trembled with a collation of shivers.

Sick to the stomach, hazy in her crumpled rags, so distant from the present that she had failed to notice that her boss had joined her in the break room. The headmistress coughed with vigour. That stabbing pain in her glabella had returned, unparalleled by any other agony she could recall. A ping of the microwave brought her back into focus.

"Are you alright?" The headmistress asked as Maeve wept into her coffee. Francis pounced out of there, ready for his next class, only to find Isla in the hallways ahead of him, tapping her wristwatch, with chains in her hands. Their eyes met, and the amnesiac faced some inexplicable cause for concern, but not for long, because Francis ran in the direction from which he came, back into the breakroom once Isla targeted him. "Francis, what's wrong? You look shaken."

Isla's face appeared in the window frame. She knocked once, and with a tap of her watch, she materialised in that very room, and blew a punch to Francis's stomach. Maeve giggled, as Isla grabbed him at the cusp of her handcuffs, and flashed them both away to the nearest prison cell she could find, allowing Maeve to drink the remainder of her coffee in peace.

30.   <u>Wrinkles and Ennui</u>

Two evenings had passed. As soon as Woodville's Mayor greeted his wife on that fateful day, he announced to her that Carim and Ruth were dead. Agatha said "Okay" and got on with her day.

With no children, two incomes, and a mayor in the household. Life for Gordon and Agatha must have been cushy. Don't be mistaken, because their lives were as tedious as anybody else's. Their apartment may have been a little larger than the others, but that didn't make them exceptions to any rule. It still smelled of fusty mildew. Rats still scurried in every waking hour and mice still scratched at the walls in every sleeping one.

Despite that, their joint income, combined with Gordon's status, provided them with greater luxuries. For one, Gordon could afford to opt for a bath over a shower. He'd spend most of the nights following Winona's death in his porcelain tub, pondering whether it was all his fault. If he'd kept a closer watch on his neighbours, he may have been able to deter them from their fates. A mass of bubbles converged over his unmentionables and enclosed his grey fluffy chest. He sighed as his thoughts never left the subject of what to do next.

To distract himself from self-deprecation, he'd hum. Tunes from his childhood that had kept him content even in the darkest of times. The position of mayor was hereditary, but never had a mayor been so fortunate. Every April, the government offered him a bonus check, some of which he'd spend on himself and his dear wife, who he cared about dearly despite the quietude of their company, the rest on the community.

Back as a child, he'd been as impoverished as the rest of them. He and his father would spend nights in the aching cold lifting their mood by singing the very few tunes they knew. In the bath, he whistled a hit from The Four Tops, and Agatha wondered how he could remain so upbeat.

A similar reflective state had reached Agatha, who glared out of the window, gazing at the grassy expanse. The gate covered any sign of anything beyond home. Home, meanwhile, was not enough to keep her satisfied. There was emptiness in her soul, but beyond those steel gates, there were prospects. She wanted to seize them, but Gordon refused to believe what Isla had told him, because he would be painted a fool if it was ever known that he believed the lies.

A starling landed on the thatch roof of the adjacent building. It did so every day, same time, same spot. Its apricot beak stretched before it, pecking itself, making it look as miserable as her. It flapped its delicate wings with little certainty. It tilted its fragile neck from side to side. Then, realising there was nothing for it, it left the rooftop behind. Agatha's vague hope dropped into a morbid grimace.

Sometimes she would glare at the abyss for hours on end, as the day faded into the night. The sun's fading glaze would promise the moon and the patches of clouds would dissipate as if they had never existed. In the place of the starling, a minuscule bug crawled along the glass surface of the window. Agatha could have swatted it away, killed it, but she knew she could do with the company, so she left it alive, and observed its aimless movements with empty fascination.

A longing groan met her thoughts. How could Gordon croon in a jovial fashion when reality prevailed? The inertia was killing her - well, maybe the tumour was killing her, but the misery may have caused the tumour. Every day was the same. Wake up, open the shop, run the shop, close the shop, go home. Look out of the window, hopeless, fantasising about what more there was to see. There was no turkey at Christmas, or fireworks at New Year, because they couldn't afford those luxuries.

She could spend hours draining her thoughts through the window. Her legs crossed, her back arched, cramped. Conducting the same life on a daily basis provided little capacity for fresh musings. She'd mistake feelings for notions or notions for feelings, but she'd never have both.

After everything, she had lost the capacity to derive pleasure from simple things. After several decades of running the newsagents, of all the same niceties and cliches. After forty-five years of marriage, the same conversations and kisses. After sixty-eight years in that pigsty of a village.

The humming halted. Gordon wrapped himself in his towel and changed into his pyjamas. A jolt of the bathroom door revealed the dapper senior looking cosy in his turquoise square shirt. He noticed Agatha hunched at the windowsill with her knuckle resting against her chin. Yesterday's damp dripped onto her at a steady pace.

"Be careful where you sit, dear" Gordon warned, noticing his wife was becoming drenched in drainage. "The sewage pipes run through the area."

"I was so lost that I forgot to notice."

Gordon left her to veg while he prepared their ravioli. The dining table was fit for one but seated two, where Agatha parked herself in front of a meagre plate. She prodded at hers with her spoon, rarely letting the pasta touch the sides of her mouth. She decided she wasn't hungry and handed the rest to Gordon, who was ravenous from the stress of the day that had been, and the press conference to follow.

"Are you sure I can have it?" He asked, gobbling it away after she shook her head. Agatha, weepy and dead-eyed, looked in a way that Gordon had rarely seen from her.

"The Journalists have gone. Defence E arranged for Francis to be carted off and incarcerated for Ruth's murder just this morning." Agatha issued no response. "Lovely ravioli." Again, nothing. "Moira Lambert is ill," Gordon announced. Confidential, but it filled the dinner silence that marked the gap between mouthfuls.

"You were at the choir recital with her only yesterday, weren't you?"

"Mmm."

"Osteoporosis, the medics believe."

"Oh," Agatha grumbled. "What a shame."

Most of their conversations revolved around death, their own, or others. In a community where proper medics remained untrained, there were plenty of deaths to discuss.

"Did you get the appointment, in the end, to talk about your back?"

"They've got enough on their plate. My back's not important."

"It might be if you don't do anything about it!"

The community only had two medical professionals, although neither had been sufficiently trained. They'd had their lessons over conference calls and training videos sent to them across the internet. Home to around a thousand people, the compound needed medics, but Gordon failed in the recruitment process. Still, Gordon maintained a bounce in his senior drawl.

Once dinner was done, Gordon did the washing up while Agatha returned to the window. She sported a shift dress which a fellow resident had made her, but it was falling apart, and the measurements were all wrong. Gordon took his time to clear the debris from their meal, knowing there would be no other way to occupy another evening that would stretch ahead eternally. He swiped his bare hands around the plates in dirty water until only a few spots of rogue sauce remained. Their favourite show was on television in two hours but until then, nothing, and Agatha wanted to do nothing other than waste away cross legged atop the windowsill.

Something slammed against the table and a turn of her head revealed a chess board which exposed a grin amongst her melancholy. She retreated from her sedentary pose in a saunter wilted by age to seat herself at the dining table.

Chess had united the childhood sweethearts decades ago. They had been the titans of the strategy game, in a school that was no different then than it was now. Of course, it wasn't like 'the good old days'. They coped better with what they had back then, and they never once moaned. That was what Agatha claimed, anyway. Gordon knew it reminded Agatha of better times, and that would be enough to lift her spirits.

At 1500 Elo, impressive for the experience-excluded type, Gordon and Agatha could play the French defence and queens' gambit with ease. A heated game of precise movements and deep stares ensued which distracted them from the overwhelming decay of their milieu. Agatha won the game. Elated at first, although her expression almost immediately sagged into despondency.

Their double bed held them both as long as they squished tight. Lights out at nine, often because their age made them too exhausted to stay up any later. Gordon failed to notice that Agatha had not slept since the night of the incident. Instead, she ensured she slept closest to the door, creeping out of the covers when he reached internal darkness. To deceive him, she padlocked her eyes and rested on the pillow until she was sure he was asleep. Then, she would park herself by the window, unleash the curtains, and glare into the darkness until the sunset beckoned. Ever since her conversation with Kenny at the Newsagents, she had pondered what was beyond those gates. Honesty had to be preferable to silence.

"I've had this feeling...that I'm missing something. A piece of my mind. Don't you?"

Everybody in their community had that sensation, at one point or another. Their minds were jigsaws with pieces not yet joined into place.

"I hate to say it," Agatha was about to...and from there, she could never go back. "Winona may have been right."

"Right about what?"

"Right to escape. You know the government. They're serial liars. If the Prime Minister were Pinocchio, he'd have a nose the size of Belgium!"

"Belgium isn't really that large when you think about it, compared to some places..."

Agatha clasped at her spine when a twinge of pain thrashed her back. Gordon propped some pillows behind her and a blanket over her, all without moving from his tucked-up position to her left. Gordon rubbed her stern gently.

"I lied," Agatha declared; catching his attention, her icy exterior penetrated by a soft trickle of tears that she soon swiftly swept away.

"You lied about what?" Gordon asked, refusing to be angry, because he had been lied to too many times to care anymore.

"I said I had a good night's sleep last night. I lied. I've been up looking out the window and staring, pondering what lies beyond the gates."

"There's nothing out there for us."

Gordon pointed at the bookshelf beside them. *The Pickwick Papers* was already reserved to his side, and she had already eyed up *Little Women* to read when sleep didn't come. Beside them, Britain in pictures, A History of the Unblessed, and Around the world in eighty photographs. These were gifts allocated to every household to exhibit the outside world they would never get to see. It helped to quench the rebellious urge that the incarcerated were bound to feel.

"They gave us these books so we could see what was outside without endangering ourselves," Gordon claimed. Gordon wasn't a good enough liar to lie about this, so he must not have known the truth. He was in charge no more than Agatha was. "They made a world for us because the one outside will not accommodate us. We can see the world through photographs, and on the news." Gordon pointed to the dusty black electronic box to their side, which required a neck tilt to survey. "Should I switch on the television?"

"No," Agatha insisted. "You're trying to avoid the tricky conversation, because you know there's a chance what I'm about to say could be true."

"I'm denying that it's true, my love."

"Of course you are. You've run this place for decades. Too long to know any better. To see through their lies. They've treated us well, you say." She planted a kiss on his forehead. "You poor naive thing." A gasp of pain marched into her lips when she twisted her posture in the incorrect direction.

"Keep still," Gordon demanded, bolstering her back onto the headrest. "Any sudden movements could provoke your pain." He stroked her cheek, beaming at her, still seeing as much beauty within the wrinkles as when her skin had been pure.

It was time for her to declare it. The moment felt right. "I went to the doctor."

"Oh, I see," Gordon gulped, detecting the emergent disquietude across her outline.

"I know I said that I didn't, but I lied, because I didn't know how to address it. Sometimes when matters are difficult, it's easier to forget."

"There's nothing you could do to bring me pain."

The next words proved him wrong. They'd bring him physical pain. Like daggers in his gentle heart.

"It turns out you were right about my back. They say I have a vertebral tumour. I didn't want to tell you because saying it aloud would make it feel real but keeping quiet isn't going to make it go away. Walking's harder than it once was, and there's a constant pain, but they say it's bound to get worse. They say it could spread into other parts of the body if untreated, and there's nothing they can do. I'd need chemotherapy."

"We…" He froze. "We don't have the resources for that."

"Anybody with a malignant tumour in this town has died. I suppose I've been lucky to get to my age of sixty-eight. What's the average age here? Dad died when he was forty-two, and mum when she was fifty-three. I've had a good innings."

Gordon wept like a little girl, clasped onto her, pampering her face with several tearful kisses and gasping often.

"I need to see it, Gordon," Agatha announced.

"See what?"

"That's why I brought up Winona escaping. I see why they wanted to. I look out of those gates, and I know I need to see it all before I go. Unlike them, you've got power. You've got contacts. You can get us out of here. "

"I can't let you do that."

"Why not? I'm going to die anyway. The blessed only become unblessed with physical contact, if you're still adamant on that being true? I'll keep my distance, and I won't hurt anybody."

"They simply won't let you."

Gordon shed a tear, then he shed many more tears. Agatha, having lived with her diagnosis for days, tolerated the knowledge that death was unavoidable. As long as she could see what was beyond the walls, she'd be happy.

"Look at the books," Gordon said, as if they would be enough. He chucked them at her, losing control of the rhythm of his motions. Affection may have been for the youthful, but they couldn't resist an embrace. He nestled her armpit around his head and stroked her silvery scalp. His cries belonged to those of a whimpering puppy.

"It's not enough," Agatha declared.

"How long do they say you have?" Gordon asked.

Agatha shook her head. "Anywhere between six months and two years. No way of telling because it depends on the person. If it's not treated, it will kill me."

"We don't have anybody or anything capable of chemotherapy."

"Out there, they have powered people who could pat me on the shoulder and I'd be okay. Because the blessed can't touch us, natural death can come for us and there's nothing we can do. Even if they could do something, I'd feel like a cure would be a lost battle. This isn't a battle I want to lose. I'm bored of this world, Gordon."

"Are you bored of me?" he blubbed.

"Never. Your heart is too pure. I'm sick of this place. I need to know what it's like out there before I go."

Hence her crows' feet and jagged jowls, not to mention her impaired spine, age had hardly ignored poor Agatha. Now, she was looking more wizened than ever. A new travelling companion had found its home in her back and would eat away at her until it completely devoured her. The gaps in her mind provoked urges for rebellion like they had for Winona. She hadn't realised before Winona's escape that those once immovable gates could open. With Gordon's authority, she could open the gates, breathe in foreign air, and see the cars and the clamour and the rage of the world. She gazed into Gordon's soul with begging eyes too desperate for him to resist.

"Please, let me have this."

He fired another bombardment of kisses at her forehead. "I want to give you the final days that you want. It's a huge risk, but if it's for you, I'll think again."

There wasn't anything he could think of that he wouldn't do for her. Their marriage may no longer have excited them, but their mutual adoration was intact.

"...I'll see what I can do." He bobbed his head, almost in shame for his surrender. It was choosing between his duty and his wife's wishes. It was an ultimatum he never thought he'd have the option of facing.

"And you'll come with me?"

"I must remain at my post. Woodville needs its Mayor in these precarious times."

"I can't live my final days without you," Agatha could never remember being so saccharine. Agatha, not usually the crying type, fell victim to his own tears. Gordon glistened in the vague moonlight, painting his face with sorrow. There would be a last time he'd touch her, and a last time he'd see those eyes and those lips. That time was soon, and that sickened him. She glared at the chessboard, then at him, and they spent the rest of the evening reminiscing on all the memories they had made together, forgetting that they once had a son, taken from them by events they would never be able to recall. At last there was something to occupy time other than silence.

A slight prang of guilt hit him, knowing what he'd have to place on the line for her, but it was for her, and she was all that mattered.

He remembered that Isla was still wandering about the community and thought it best to put the controversies hanging over him to bed. When they were done, he and Agatha could leave Woodville behind them. He marched to the community gates, watched on by Isla, and gave Ethan a call on the video phone.

"What is it?" Ethan growled. "I'm trying to catch up on my sleep."

"Ethan, I need you here in Woodville. Isla's living among us now. There's no such thing as the disease, and I'm hoping to prove to you that the Unblessed are no better or worse than you."

Ethan rubbed his eyes and promised to be there soon. Isla grinned, informing him that he was doing what was right, but Gordon wasn't so sure.

31.   He Arrives

Sunrise bled across the dry horizon. Lights flickered in occasional stammers. These were the moments in which loneliness was almost guaranteed.

When the rest of the world slept, landrovers came bright and early in the morning to drop Ethan off at his destination. He let the doors slam behind him as he showed off his military ensemble. His mouth was covered by a mask, as was that of the man in the passenger seat, Clive Mannering.

It had been a difficult few days for *The Morning Manifesto,* what with Chrissie's arrest and Ruth's death, both of which Clive had refused to disclose to the press, yet Clive persevered as if nothing had ever happened, and kept his mind solely on the pack of doughnuts front and centre in his office. Ethan, meanwhile, used gloved hands to tap on the entrance of the community, causing the gates to grind open. Greeting him on the other side was Isla, standing beside Gordon and Bishop Tomlinson as if there were no such concept as the Unblessed.

"I thought I told you to bring people with cameras?" Isla asked, and Clive tapped his pocket, onto which a camera must have been hidden, just in case.

"That was never going to happen," Ethan declared. He'd made sure to visit this early in the morning so that none of Defence E's stalkers would follow. Meg would lap his visit up to Woodville like crazy, as would the papers. He refused to remove his mask or gloves as he strided through the community, taking notice of the ramshackle school and Newsagent combination, while admiring the orchard he considered too fine for their needs. "You should get away from them, Quickfix."

"Nuh-huh. The way they've behaved since Carim's passing is astounding. Are you not going to comment on that?" The Knight's death had made front page local news, but Ethan hadn't known the chap long enough to mourn. "I knew him for six years. He was a wonderful man, and he knew what you did to him before he was sent here."

Isla clicked her fingers and all of a sudden she was behind him, glinting the best smile she could muster, exposing her pearly whites. A net engineered the night before by Caleb and Steven North, in teamwork between the father and son who had too been victim to Ethan's games, flew down from the roof of the building Isla had lured him underneath and caught him in its grip. He tugged at the fibre but the material was too dense to rip. Clive attempted to run away but Isla flashed up before him and used a pocketed pair of handcuffs to imprison him. She ordered that the Norths take Ethan inside, after a brief high-five, to the community centre, where Gordon watched on as Isla used Ruth's tape recorder, gathered from her shack.

"We haven't yet cleaned up Ruth's body," Isla said. "She's dead, you know, and I used to like her. My friend Lester very much did. Francis may have killed her, but she's just another one of your dead, isn't she? Winona Barton, Elijah North, Kenny Farrow, they're just the start of it. You could use my powers to get out of here, but if I don't use them, you don't stand a chance."

"What exactly are you accusing me of?" Ethan asked, to which Isla clearly stated: "Multiple counts of murder, because I don't have to be afraid of you anymore."

Eva intervened. "I'm sorry, Gordon, but he was complicit in wiping your son off the map. Lewis Shepherd. I seem to think you loved him dearly."

Gordon gulped. "I don't remember him." He couldn't cry for somebody he didn't remember.

"We're going to keep you here, and I'm going to stay here with this recording device until you decide it's time to confess to the truth," Isla explained. "You, Clive, are just as complicit as Ethan. You let Ruth die. Tell me, Ethan." She said, as the whole community gathered around to watch, aside from a few noteworthy exceptions. "Did you know the disease wasn't real?"

Ethan expectorated. "Out of all my time, you were the only one I could count on to do what was right. Hop's lazy. Lester's a joke. Carim was…I've been told not to speak ill of the deceased, and manners are a priority of mine."

"I phoned The No Man this morning and told him everything. He believed it right away. He'd never liked you, or even Petula. He asked if there was anything he could do to help, so he arranged to get Chrissie a memory stick. She's done her research on you from behind bars. Carim's death was her doing, not yours, I know that, and she'll pay, but she's a useful asset in bringing you down."

"What charge would that be? Manslaughter? I've killed nobody. I *am* the police. I have the power to wipe all your names through the dirt."

"How much dirtier can their reputations get? Me? Like Megaphone Meg said, I don't care as long as the right thing happens. That's what I came to Defence E to do. That, and to pay my dues to the parents I let down. You wouldn't believe some of the information Chrissie's found on you. Go on, tell us the whole story. Your little minion isn't here to defend you anymore."

He narrowed his eyes on Eva. "You're Eva Croft, aren't you?"

Isla snapped her fingers before his eyes. "Back in the room, Mr Song! You're talking to me, not some poor lady in the audience."

"Francis was my spy. I admit that. As Chrissie is bound to discover, I have my reasons to distrust the Unblessed. Francis wasn't my only spy, however. I knew this could happen and I needed reinforcements. She doesn't even know it. She's such a good actor that she's made herself forget."

Maeve sat in their home in Apartment Block A with her knitting needles and created a jumper for herself. Hex twiddled his thumbs opposite with music blaring through his headphones. Maeve was none the wiser that she had been the one to wipe the minds of everybody in Woodville of some of their closest friends. Her abilities had been so in tune that she'd made herself forget that she even had superpowers in the first place. Ethan sniggered as Eva watched on in terror. She needed to get back home.

32.   Ethan's story

I sit here having just ordered the murder of an innocent journalist, who found herself enrolled in this situation out of obligation, just like I did. I confess, Father, to my sins. I was told to do so, though I must not get my hopes up. I do not believe in your God.

To amass great power requires the inheritance of fortune from birth. My father was a renowned author of detective fiction. His father was a politician in the higher echelons of Parliament. In my youth, I lived in a house larger than I needed. I swore that if I ever had a child, I would not provide them with similar substance. Substance taints a person. Even Father believed that.

I do not have time for children, or for lovers. They invoke feelings, and I shy away from emotions if I can help it. They are innate to the human condition, yet I strive to avoid the weakness they bring. I felt anger when the protestors arrived. I had to fight to prevent that anger from bubbling to the surface, as it had in the greatest battles of my adolescence. I wear my badges with pride and serve my duty with honour. My feelings do not stretch any deeper.

It has been a week since I became the leader of Defence E, and the public have already dismissed me as their salvation. I strive to prove them wrong. The Song legacy and my work down in Orkney gave me status, but not preparedness. There is no way to prepare for slander on the level I have faced.

Forgive me, father, for I have sinned. Can God forgive me when I never once acknowledged his existence? I have taken a life, yet I have no shame. Did God not command the Israelites to destroy for the sake of his divine plan? We deem God to be a hero, his actions necessary for the greater good. I do not believe in a god, but the concept of sin and subsequent persecution is one I subscribe to. I confess my sins to process their reality.

Ruth Mayor died so that we could win, so the unblessed could pay. The Bible never spoke about the unblessed, for they had not yet come to exist. I mourn for the days before the impure when all were the same. Don't mistake the fact - the unblessed are all the same, no matter their deceptions. Ruth's death - murder is too harsh a description - brings me little sympathy. That's because I know her sacrifice saves countless more. If she and Chrissie exposed my lie, we would find no way to prevent the liberation of the unblessed. The results of such a situation would be catastrophic.

I wished to justify my decisions, and how I could ever consider my actions to be moral. My commanders taught me that God was our greatest friend on the battlefield, our one true confidant. We could tell God our sins and God would not answer back. I'm not a believer in God, but that sentiment remains true. It's the least I owe to Ruth Mayor. I will forget this confession, so will you, and if God exists, so will he. He has other people to care about. Its nature is confidential - that's guaranteed - and God has already proved he cares little about me. Why does God work in mysterious ways? That's how he punishes us for original sin.

I bring us back to Christopher Song, my father. You may know him as the creator of Emmanuel Stanton, a university lecturer turned hard-boiled detective. He earned a fortune from his father's legacy and his newfound fame retained said fortune. He'd divorced the mother I never knew and took up with Stepmother at a time that predates my memory.

I have no complaints about my upbringing. While our country estate may have been indulgent, I was far from spoiled. Father placed me under a stringent routine from a young age. Bed at 9, curfew after 6, no strangers in the household nor visits to friends he deemed strangers. Father taught me how to fire a rifle and skin a deer. We'd spend Saturday afternoons hunting and

Saturday evenings roasting. Private tutoring trained me in elocution, posture, and, most importantly, tuning my abilities. I'd complete five straight hours of exercise each week across the vast fields near my estate. I'd follow a strict diet which would build me up while forbidding empty calories. I'd only interact with my siblings, tutors, and house staff. He'd never allow me to do what the other children did. We wouldn't watch television, since it wasted time. I wasn't even allowed to read Father's novels, since fiction distracts the mind for too long. He expected me to read, of course, but my mind was instead boggled by the work of intellectuals and academics.

Father did all this because he remembered how much good his time in the military had done him. He aspired to make me like him: unafraid. A grumpy miser of a straight-backed man, but one who did not allow emotions to enfeeble him. Stepmother enjoyed lavish silks and expensive liquors. Father, meanwhile, controlled his intake of luxuries. He believed that fortune was enough to corrupt a person. He didn't drink, he didn't gamble, and he gave much of his money to charities helping those who did. He'd encountered children of equal wealth who became pompous and arrogant thanks to their riches. Father didn't want me, or Dustin and Burnette, to be amongst that crowd.

He sold our estate to a family much richer than our own and moved us to Shetland. There, we'd be out of the way enough to avoid falling into the traps of affluence. You'll wonder why somebody like me speaks with an eloquent tongue. It's because I received the best education, better than most military men do.

We moved to a three-bedroom cottage, enough for us. Father didn't like me attending an ordinary school, with normal children, so I only spent three weeks at the local academy. Father wanted me to be ordinary, so I'd learn the hard lessons that life deals. He didn't, however, wish for me to be average, which community schools run the risk of breeding. Romance, friendship, sin, would all become temptations. These were all weaknesses.

A boarding school would put me into shape, Father resolved. I'd spend several terms there, practising archery and economics, before returning home at Christmas. In Summer, Father encouraged me to attend military school. I learned everything there that my parents couldn't teach me. Many believe that in a soldier, abilities are more important than character. If somebody has bulletproof skin, it doesn't matter whether they are valorous or vain. Many are wrong. Character is vital. The way you hold your weapon and direct your spine is pivotal.

Of course, my powers gifted me with natural advantages. Words were had between General Scott and my father, both of whom controlled my life more than I controlled it myself. Weeks later, they'd agree to ship me off to battle, at the meagre age of fourteen. I was too useful a weapon to waste. When bullets approached us, those bullets would ricochet from my fingertips. When flames erupted, I could become a human fireball. Whichever enemy we fought would stand no chance against me. There's always a war going on, even if nobody knows it, even if the soldiers don't. I'd always be fighting, always. They took me out of school, and I'd spend all year as their weapon. I wouldn't need any more training than Father gave me. All I needed were my powers. I was the youngest on the squad and amongst the most valued. Nobody wished to mess with me, and I put anybody who tried in their place. I never got given a nickname like most superheroes do. To name me a Quickfix or a Knight would undermine me instantly. Nobody dared to undermine me in the way an alter ego would, because I had made examples of my formidable nature.

For example, we had bunk beds following initiation. When I took the top bunk, a boy who could form any weapon he wished in his fingertips created knives on each finger. I stabbed him in the shoulder when he fashioned a finger knife, before claiming self-defence. He spent three nights in the hospital and transformed into a meeker version of himself. The more people I put in their place, the more consumed I became by my potential. It's why I'm taken aback by people believing they can dictate my actions in the present. It's not what I'm used to, nor what I should have to grow accustomed to. They pushed me to the limit in training drills, so I didn't get cocky. I'd work hard, every day, and never stopped fighting, and that meant I deserved a reward.

For my fifteenth birthday, General Scott allowed me to return home. Over the six previous months, the military sent me anywhere and everywhere they needed me. Iraq, Lebanon, Ethiopia. I lost count of the number of people who died at my hands. Those who came at me with bullets, I fired back at them. I console myself with the knowledge that they had to die. Like Ruth had to die.

This is a world where you must kill or die, yet we all end up dead regardless. Your God tells us that's a good thing. I'd dispute your dreams of paradise.

Father never spoiled me, but when I returned, he believed I deserved a break. We went to Lyon, and we'd spend two weeks there. The holiday happened to coincide with Christmas, but Father had never allowed Christmas in our household. Not only was Stepmother Jewish, but he considered materialism, and faith, damaging to our mindsets. He'd judge me for speaking to you now. Let me make it plain - Father is dead, as are my siblings. Their names were Dustin and Burnette. He gave us strong names to set us on the right track. Ethan means "Firm" in Hebrew. Dustin means "Stone". Bernette means "Brave bear". Compared to me, they were weak. She could turn anything she wanted to ice. He could do the same for gold. Who knew how I inherited my abilities? I expect my power to mimic came from the mother who left when I was one. Father only had flexible skin, so I doubt they came from him. Father was a difficult man to get along with - a prescriptive bore who only expressed passion in prose - so you could see why mother left, especially if, like me, her abilities gave her untapped potential that she wished to explore. Stepmother's barrister credentials allowed her a stiff backbone, but it was not her place to raise me. She left parental duties to my father while she followed his rules.

The opportunity to be abroad wasn't exciting since I'd gotten used to hopping from one place to another. That's why I didn't mind travelling from Orkney to Manchester, and many locations between, in the years that followed the crash of Flight 482.

I hadn't travelled by plane before, and I resolved to never do so again, if I could help it. Eventually I gave into my fears, but that took time. Planes aren't necessary when people can transport you by hand. In the military, soldiers with the power of flight could pick you up and drop you off, so there'd be no need for planes. One of our drivers could even speed up time to twice its pace, but part of the ride involved relishing the experience. People built planes for comfort and ease. Being up in the sky provides an unmatchable quality. I remember the pop of the ears and the rush of the engines. The memory would haunt me every night so long as I let it, and you should be aware of my resolve. I would not let it define me.

Dustin, the youngest child, geared up for a life like mine, took the window seat. I, meanwhile, received no exotic sights other than the loaded drinks trolley escorted by the flight attendant. Father, wishing to separate us from those with the possibility of corrupting our well-curated souls, treated us to first class. TV screens ahead, desks to ourselves, roll out beds if we required them. I hadn't ever sat down and watched television. The first programme blasted into my pupils was a French children's programme which Dustin enjoyed, but I could think of nothing worse than sitting through it, and that included the crash that followed.

Father wanted to distract us so he could write in peace. He laid out his pen and paper and let the air move him. The raw aroma of coffee beans marched down the aisle, coating the nostrils. He refused to let us surrender to stimulants. Chocolate and coffee and alcohol weaken a person, in spirit and body. Stepmother stopped following his rules. She was furious with Father for signing Dustin up to a military academy without her permission.

"Look at the boy," he'd insist. "Straight-backed, always attentive. The perfect warrior."

"I don't want my son to be a warrior," Stepmother replied.

"You've got a daughter to raise the way you want. I know how to turn a boy into a man."

She didn't like that I didn't show much emotion. It creeped her out. My experiences had beaten all my feelings out of me. One of my closest crewmates died in my arms when I was twelve, gunned down before I could return the favour to the enemy. His blood stained my paws for days to follow. I'd explode into a range of bullets and destroy the nemesis who destroyed my best friend. It crept Stepmother out that I'd look into her eyes and exhibit indifference. She wanted her children to have a more ordinary upbringing. She wouldn't want to spoil them, despite their fortune, but she wanted them to choose their own paths. Father believed with abilities such as ours, we needed to mean something more than the average person.

"Oh yes," Stepmother would mock, "A novelist is the most butch profession there is."

"It's a dangerous world out there," he'd reply. "I'm not saying they can't choose their paths. I only want to prepare them for what they will have to face. If they wish, like Ethan, to put their powers to use, then so be it. Never do I claim that it's an obligation."

I was not yet old enough to drink or smoke but I was allowed to fight in wars. Father rejected the offer of a free meal. Stepmother did not. Lamb chops, high in cholesterol. Father tutted. He liked keeping us all in good weight because he controlled everything. It would have hurt him to know he couldn't control what happened next. Father scowled at Stepmother, who was thin enough to afford to gain a few pounds. Father encouraged her to exercise, but she never built muscle on purpose like us men. He retreated into his own corner of our airborne lounge to launch Emmanuel Stanton into a fresh farce. I inherited any fastidiousness I am defined by from him. He'd lay out his ink in perfect rows, refusing to use technology for ease. He'd click his knuckles and set Emmanuel into action. He wrote for half an hour before we heard screaming erupt for the first time. We shut our cabin door, which only opened when we needed to step outside, so as far as we knew, it could have been the clamour of ordinary folk.

I'd seen limbs blasted off, men caught in engine fire, children blown up before my eyes. That's why it didn't shock me when we received an explanation for the noise. High squalls in response to deep bellowing commands. A knock at the door.

Stepmother slept. Dustin observed the French television show which was getting more intolerable by the second. Father wrote, ignoring the distraction. The knocking didn't relent, so Father stormed over to the cabin door. He rotated the lock. Three men entered wearing balaclavas and holding pocket knives. My head turned from the vacant expanse of mountains to us passengers in danger. They forced us out, threatening to gut my sister if we didn't move into the plane's hallway. Father issued a blow to the mugger's cheek, his legs contorting in flexible motions. A knife formed at my fingertips. They waved about the weapon, grabbing Burnette by the throat. Any sudden moves and the hijacker would cut her throat open. We couldn't take the risk. Burnette's screams escalated beyond control, as one might expect a threatened seven-year-old to howl. The rest of them, flush cheeked from a disaster so far removed from their lives of secluded luxury. Turbulence settled in and the stowaway holding Burnette jittered. No harm would come to my sister if we stayed back, he claimed. I didn't trust the masked man, who suffered from a tremor. These were suicide hijackers, willing to crash a plane to prove a point.

There were enough people with the ability of foreknowledge to predict a disaster like this. We'd gotten so good at predicting disasters that this happened to be the occasional anomaly. The incident preceded future crimes units, which the government introduced after the attack.

The culprits were in the cockpit, throwing the pilots into the aisles. They had knives they were unwilling to use. They came from Kirkwall's 'Winterborn Estate' and somehow made it all the way to the airport. I never knew how they escaped but Major Green informed me how the fugitives hijacked the plane. They'd kidnapped a teleporter and forced him to bring them onto the vehicle. This teleporter was a coward, unwilling to act when it could have been easy to stop them. The pilot wasn't. He'd snapped into minuscule size, so he vanished, leapt behind my sister's captor, and issued a blow to the terrorist's stomach. The captor swiped the knife, gashing my sister's throat. What I did then remains a blur. I remember Father running towards the hijackers, throwing them to the floor, with nothing to lose. I remember Father snapping one of their necks, in the way he'd taught me with the deer. Stepmother cried, so did Dustin.

Only a dozen of us remained on the plane. None of us could fly. We wouldn't be there if we could. The other two hijackers murdered the pilots, leaving nobody to rescue us. Signs flashed and alarms buzzed. Light and speed and a loss of control. The sky became the ocean in seconds.

Nobody had time to attach the oxygen masks to their faces. We guzzled water as waves crashed into the vehicle without sympathy. I could no longer see Father or Dustin. I grabbed Stepmother by the waist and pulled her from the wreckage. We swam through violent gestures of waves, rising to the surface, containing our breath.

I remember persevering through miles of water until I reached the surface. I pushed back and the waves washed us to shore.

I woke up on an Island wearing only half my moist clothes. The ocean drenched Stepmother's perfect hair and left her makeup in ruins. She shook me awake. We were alone. We twisted around to face the sea; the wreckage hidden, their bodies consumed. We became the only survivors. I didn't cry, but I mourned, in my own way.

We live in a world of superheroes, yet disasters still happen. Freak blips like these. It might be a higher power teaching us a lesson. No matter how safe we make ourselves, we remain mortal. Government agents arrived on the beach to rescue us. They could have rewritten time, but they chose not to. They used it as an opportunity to learn from their mistakes, and as a warning that any future incidents would not go unnoticed.

They informed me and Stepmother about the Kirkwall escapees. They told us we couldn't tell anybody about the unblessed status of these hijackers. Petula expressed her sympathies. Major Green wiped all evidence of the incident from all minds other than my own. He believed I had the right to remember, as compensation for my service. I promised to stay quiet. He wiped Stepmother's memories, and she became a stranger. Everybody in Kirkwall forgot about the three fugitives. There were many reasons why they kept the matter under wraps.

If people knew that unblessed people had escaped, hope for greater insurgency would be born. Violence would get people talking and enlighten them about the outcasts they'd forgotten. It would have acted in the government's favour, in a way. They wanted the unblessed locked up, and this incident proved why. The unblessed could be dangerous. I know Winona Barton and her friends could have killed people if they escaped. If that meant they'd get their way. The government couldn't risk the unblessed being relevant again. They did what they needed, to keep people safe. I wish they wiped the unblessed off the map, but the government didn't want to be killers. Exposing what happened to my family would risk their grasp of power over the unblessed. They touched me, they touched Stepmother. We didn't become diseased. If people found out about the incident and watched it back, they'd see that. The lie was in place to keep people safe, to prevent similar incidents to the deaths of my father, my siblings, and everybody else who died on Flight 482 on that fateful Wednesday morning in the tail end of December. My family had to die so we could learn what the unblessed were capable of.

Those who told me the truth knew I'd understand. Powered by the knowledge of the unblessed being guilty, I made it my priority to control them. I enlighten you about the lie, and my motives for keeping it, so I can justify Isla's death. I will forget Isla soon. Then I'll wonder why I ever entered this confessional. If we free the unblessed, the disease may not spread, but more innocent families will die. Chrissie and Carim claimed they are normal, like the rest of us, but many of them are like the hijackers - evil. I could have been angry at the government. They worked behind the scenes, doing what they had to. In time, so did I.

There may have been a time when the disease was not a lie. The plague spread through physical contact in the thirteenth century. Now, it was a fiction that needed to remain intact. The lie became the punishment I administered to the unblessed for what they had taken from me, and in the knowledge of goodness, I am able to sleep at night.

I thank Petula Wednesday every time I see her for enlightening me. She trusted me because she knew I'd never surrender to shallow emotions. I'd follow protocol. I'd ensure no unblessed people ever escaped again. I'd do anything.

I get up every morning and I do what I have to so that I can maintain the lie. Your God teaches us that liars are sinners, but we must lie sometimes to protect what is right. I rifle through rows of navy jackets before selecting the cleanest of the dozen. I pamper my wounds, button up my shirt, comb my hair, and get on with my day. I had to cut the problem from the source. I had to make sure Chrissie knew where she must stand. If I didn't, the unblessed would escape. If they ever did leave their compounds, more innocent families like mine would die. They have a better life than they deserve. They could be in prison camps, for all I cared. It's what they deserve. I sit back and I let them live their lives of comfort, even though I know what it costs, both financially and ethically.

Isla summons me to Woodville tomorrow morning, on advice of Jake Latimer and the Naylor twins, and I fear I am being led into a trap. I think of the end of it all and whether it really matters if this is my last step on life's long journey. Can you look me in the eyes, and call me a true sinner now?

33.   Mighty Hath Fallen

Ethan found himself wrapped up in the chains he had welded for himself, with Clive by his side. Clive wrestled for freedom from the rope that bound him, but flabs of weight stood in the way. He stopped when the exertion led him to sweat profusely, and he turned to Ethan, tilting his neck as far as the restraints would allow.

"Tell me, then, we have time," Clive wiggled. "What did they do to make you hate them?"

"The Unblessed. They killed my family. The three who escaped would have caused chaos if they succeeded in their mission. They're lazy and cruel."

"That's why you hold a grudge with them? They can't all be like that, can they?"

"It takes a few sour grapes to rot the punnet. I fought for my country so that the blessed could keep on living, and the unblessed joined them. My best friend died in my arms and many best friends of my enemies died at my hands. Was that just so the Unblessed could sit on their behinds while we worry about rotting away if they escape from the compounds that we have risked everything to put together?"

"Megaphone Meg arrived outside of my office a few days back. She demanded to speak to me, so naturally, I let her in. She said there's no such thing as the disease carried by the Unblessed. Is that true? The blessed are guaranteed salvation? Nobody's listening. You can tell me."

Ethan's paranoia led his head to dart all around him, in case there were spy cameras dotted about, but the Unblessed lacked the technology, even with Isla on their side. "You've entrusted me with your paper, Clive, so I can trust you with the truth. There's no such thing as the Unblessed contaminant, but we need to keep on living as if there was."

"Why have they been in compounds since, I don't know, 1347, if they're not really diseased? Do your soldiers at Defence E know all about this?"

"You're referring to them as soldiers now too? I taught you well. The lie has been passed on through generations and my soldiers are expected to act accordingly. Why? The Unblessed are dangerous, but the Blessed wouldn't believe that unless they had something to gain from the others being locked up, so my ancestors created the concept of the infection, and that concept has passed on down the line like an infection in itself."

"What about my journalists? Naturally I was among the first people to be informed that one of my subordinates had been arrested and the other murdered by one of your puppets. Naturally, I am aware they were a nuisance, but I don't understand why they had to die."

"Chrissie has been vying for your job ever since Alan Pye's disappearance. Where did he go?" Ethan asked, and Clive shrugged. Clive genuinely had no idea where his former boss was, nor did anybody else. "She stole a rifle belonging to Carim, at the time he had been entrusted with guarding Woodville's gates. She used it to shoot Carim, and the wounds amounted to his death. She was a liability, and you cannot tell me Ruth wouldn't have been either."

"Ruth was a decent person," Clive responded. "That's why I kept her on, because she was decent, and she was kind, or so I'd expect. You're confessing to ordering Francis to terminate Ruth Mayor's life?"

"What else was I to do? I speak as if I had little choice and that's exactly right. The Unblessed are a pox on civilisation, but Chrissie threatened to expose that it was all fiction. She needed to know I was in charge, so I settled the scores by removing someone she cared about. I didn't anticipate her next rash move, after I threatened to do the same to her loved ones. Look where she is now. Declan and Ruth's mother are still alive, and Chrissie's in a prison cell."

"You threatened the lives of Ruth's mother? She said her mother lived in a retirement community. Declan was Chrissie's boyfriend. They cared greatly for one another."

"*Cared.* You use the correct tense there. I'm sure you understand we can't let Chrissie get away with badmouthing our organisations and spreading dirt on our names. I have contacts who have arranged for Chrissie to be terminated too, before she can get that far. It will be made to look as though it was internal, by one of the more violent prisoners."

Isla surprised him when she appeared at his back. "Thank you, Ethan. That was great. That was all we needed to know." She began to unwrap Clive from the rope, but not Ethan. "You should see your face right now, mate, it's a picture." Luckily, she had a pocket mirror which exposed his stunned profile. "You told us when we first met that we were wasting the potential of our abilities. We've learned from that mistake."

Every bone in Clive's body shifted and changed until it vanished entirely, dropping down not just to pencil-size, but to become a literal pencil, from which a Northern voice sprouted. Isla collected a recording device which The No Man had stored in his pocket when disguised as Clive.

"I cared a lot about Ruth. Things were getting serious between us, and then you took her away. Clive's in his office right now, indulging on fruit fancies. You won't see him again. With all the confessions we have on that tape, you won't see many people again."

Isla opted to take Ethan away, and she bounced him to the police station, handing over the recording chip and pushing him away into a guards arms before he could equip her abilities to escape. For a moment, back at base, the pencil became Lester, taller and thinner than Clive could ever dream of being. His phone rang, and Jake Latimer was on the other end.

"You got him?" Jake asked, and The No Man replied: "We got him."

"That's good at least. The news I bring isn't all positive. Chrissie was found dead in her cell this morning with a memory stick in her mouth. The future crimes unit investigated, and found Ethan played no role. It was rapid aspiration pneumonia, following her first meal after accidentally swallowing the memory stick she equipped to help us."

"Make sure our respects are passed on to her loved ones. Declan will be gutted."

"The Naylors have gone haywire. Something's very wrong. Is there anything wrong with you?"

Come to mention it, Lester's mind had been playing up, as if he, like Suzie, like Carim, had gradually been developing new memories. The Naylors' heads bobbed in too quick a motion to catch up with, and it was then that Lester knew that he must set aside the tragedy of recent revelations to visit his good friend in hospital.

34.   Gait Testing

You may have met some very stubborn people in your life, but it is quite possible that you have never met somebody as stubborn as Hop.

Bedridden for days, with half a face torn off, every move instigated grinding pain. When the nurses insisted he should embark on gait testing, he claimed there was little requirement. It wasn't that he claimed to be fine. If he feigned good health, the hospital would no longer have him. He'd no longer have his complimentary meals and the excuse to stay in bed from one morning until the next. Problem was, if he wanted the luxury of idleness, he'd need to prove his willingness to cooperate, so he allowed the nurses to strap his harnessed body to what appeared to be a treadmill. Wires sprouted from every which way and connected to parts of the body seen and unforeseen. Screens bleeped with wavy lines and a belt pushed him along the accelerating surface. Extending his aching arms and swinging his stiff legs wasn't exactly possible, but the sliding mechanics of the machine got him closer.

Being the self-confessed pessimist he was, Hop fitted in with the hospital's pensioner majority. He'd moan about everything - the meals, the staff - and his fellow patients would moan with him, about him, and moan on his behalf. Even though he moaned, he felt as though he was living the high life. Sure, the dank musk was sometimes difficult to take, as were the night-time bellows of his comrades, but he'd take it over a life of effort. Most people hated hospital, but hospitals were a sloth's dream.

Gait testing was another step closer to life with added effort, but the nurses forced him into it, keen to get him back to saving the world again. They were not keen on the grumpy man who occupied the bed 24/7, but they knew he had to be saved, for Hull's sake.

He'd spend most hours asleep with his blinds drawn and his nightmares ripe. His single room allowed him the peace, distant from the din of his peers, that his consciousness did not. Except these were more than nightmares. These were memories from a life unlived that only emerged in the perpetual abyss of the nighttime. He'd remember the protests, the accusations branding his father a coward, and the crocodile snaps of camera lights bombarding him and his mother. Remembering his father, and the damp last kiss on the child's forehead before Wesley left. He'd dismiss these memories as mere concoctions of the mind. He'd be wrong to do so.

With every step he took on the treadmill, the line following his heartbeat would incline. A screech of white noise erupted in his eardrum. A nurse remained behind him at all times as he skidded along the treadmill's shifting corridors.

"Guess who?" whispered a Northern voice that seemed to be coming from his chest and which only he could hear.

"Bloody hell. The numpty is here. How did you get in here?"

"I'm a shapeshifter! I can get in anywhere. That includes your buttocks. God knows why I said that! Now I'm imagining your buttocks. What a grotesque thought."

"Stop talking about my buttocks and get out of my heart!"

"I'm always in your heart, dear!"

"Shut it."

"Are you alright?" remarked the nurse in response to what appeared to her either as a one-sided conversation or a spate of unprompted impoliteness.

Hop, at the time she asked this, was attempting to swat at his chest with his restrained arms to remove the man who currently resided inside. "Did you hear about Carim?"

"No I didn't. What didn't I hear about Carim?"

"Carim's dead. Ruth too." This hardly affected Hop. "Isla's settled down in the community to pick up the pieces, and Ethan's been arrested."

"A lot's happened then, since I've been forced out of the loop."

"Stop being in a grump with us. It was you who decided to rescue Petula, and boo-hoo, you've been left with one half of your face charred off."

"The Nurse can't hear you, can she?" Hop asked.

"No, she can't," replied the shapeshifter. "It might be because I'm inside your monitor, or because I'm whispering."

"You're not as quiet as you think, you know?"

"I'm not talking," responded the nurse.

"I know you're not! Ignore me. I'm a nutter."

"No longer do I have to be bound by the confines of visiting hours," cried the Northerner, "I can just show up here whenever I like, and nobody needs to know."

"Oh goodie," grunted Hop.

"Something wrong with my company?"

"I would say you should use your time for something useful, but you're about as useful as a pair of chopsticks for a guy with one hand."

Hop wanted to stop, but the machine wouldn't let him. Knowing that The No Man was spinning around like he was a cloth in a washing machine made him squirm. It was unpleasant enough knowing The No Man was nearby, let alone inside of him.

"I can detect the measurements around your heart, and they're not good," The No Man diagnosed as if he were the nurse.

"Alright, Doctor Zhivago!"

"Do you know anything about Doctor Zhivago?"

"Nope!"

"Why do you need a heart monitor anyway? You're learning to walk again, aren't you?"

"They're giving me a once-over. I'm getting back into shape."

"You better be! I can smell the cholesterol! When did you find the time to stuff all those doughnuts in your gob?"

"I'll be back at Defence E in no time, don't you worry."

"That's what I'm worried about!"

"Looks like you will be," replied the Nurse. "While it would be unwise for you to walk without support for some time, your legs appear to be coping with the pressure."

"That's the first time anyone's ever said anything's suitable about you," mocked The No Man.

"It's a greater compliment than you'll ever get, laddie!" barked Hop.

"I don't admire your tone," grumbled the nurse. "I am *not* your 'laddie'."

"I didn't say you were! There's a man in my heart!" The Nurse tutted. She left him with the machine that continued to whisk him away. "Oh great. She's upped and left because of you, and now I'm stuck on this infernal machine."

"That's dandy, because I need to talk to you."

"About Carim? That Jake Latimer visited this morning and told me everything."

"Good, because that's not what I came here to talk to you about. Have you, by any chance, been getting new memories?"

"New memories? Memories can't be new. They're recycled."

"That's what I thought."

Hop would have been lying if he claimed that everything was ordinary. Sometimes, he'd hear one breath too many in the hospital room he inhabited. When he was alone, a groan sounded on top of his and the respirator. It didn't come from another room, nor his own. It would come at night and leer over him, with a hand that tried to touch him but couldn't quite reach.

That was forgetting the premonitions that came to him in his sleep. The wet kiss from Dad. The prick of Petula's index finger as it scraped against his temple when they first met. Hop's memories, of his father's heroism and his mother's grief, all faded away, replaced with fresh recollections.

Here is the lie: Hop Senior sacrificed his life to rescue half a dozen miners. The truth: Powered by the drunken grief and guilt surrounding his failure to catch a killer, Wesley lacked the strength to hop to Columbia and rescue the miners whose lives were on the line. Contrary to popular interpretation, he instead spent the night drinking and ignoring calls and arguing with his wife. When the press found out, they labelled him a fraud, and he proved them right. By the time his wife and son woke up the next morning, he'd left a note explaining his absence. The moment Petula touched his temple with her magic index finger, he'd forget all about it.

Hop remembered the moment his memories altered. He was twenty at the time, lazing ahead on the television watching repeats of Ellen. Jobless ever since his six-month stretch at the coffee shop, without any qualifications behind him. Unambitious, so he had never considered training like his father once had. One of the world's few time travellers was willing to waste his potential. He hadn't even travelled through the colour vortex since his adventures with his dad when they'd been younger. When they'd been happy. Imagine that - Hop, keeper of a perpetual frown, happy. Unimaginable.

The only time Hop used his abilities was to hop to the fridge for another beer. Mother was upstairs, snoring for two, out like a light from the previous night's bender. There came an urgent knock at his door, and he knew he'd have to answer. He clicked his fingers, ended up at the entrance, and twisted the handle. He'd discover a pallid woman with a walking stick, far from his type, with wrinkles thick enough to repulse.

"Do I know you?" Hop grunted at the woman who had not, in fact, been present his entire life, but which the new memories made him believe she had been.

Hop's father was still out there, somewhere, living life in the shadows and lost to eternity, swinging from one end of time to the next, boundlessly. Wesley's boss snorted, consuming the stale tang of rough air.

Cereal boxes everywhere, TV rarely ever off. Hop, still in his dressing gown. She rammed her cane against the wood, forcing open the ajar door which Hop resolved to keep closed.

How was Hop only remembering all this now? For so long, he'd thought his first encounter with Petula came when she offered his mother the house, rent free. He should have acknowledged that as fiction, as too good to be true, but his stubbornness prevailed.

She didn't waste any time in grabbing him, dropping the cane she only used for show, and planting her index finger on his temple. Her finger, like ice, a cool glaze trickling against his scalp. Everything wobbled and his memories reconfigured. Hop Senior became a deceased hero; his mother became more than a drunken slob, and so did he.

"I'm having strange nightmares," Hop noted. "That's all."

"I thought you had too much pride to admit that you had nightmares."

"We all have nightmares."

"Not you, chief! I remember you bragging about it. 'Oh, I don't have dreams'. 'I'm pathetic, I have no imagination'. Trust me, I've been there."

"Have you been having nightmares too?"

"Not nightmares. New memories. Petula lied to us...Martin, can I call you Martin? I heard the doctors call you Martin."

"Those were nurses. You're...you. I don't even know your first name."

"Nor will you ever!"

"What are your new memories then?"

"You could sound a little bit more interested!"

"You should know by now. I'm not the type to be interested in stuff."

The Nurse returned with a paper and pen, power walking as if in a constant rush. Hop, or Hop's harness, still moving, no sign of stopping.

"I'm a bank clerk, and I'm being all Northern, and charming, you know, because that's what I'm like, and I'm laughing away, and I'm helping people out."

"Sounds like a nightmare for the customers."

"The way I remember it, Petula found me from The Institute. I spent most of my childhood, or so I thought. My memories of the mental hospital - prison, whatever you want to call it - are fading away."

"What's to say they're not just nightmares like they are for me?"

"Because they're coming to me in the day, when I'm wide awake, and you're too stubborn to admit the same has been happening to you! My past ain't what Petula made me think it was. No way. She touched me with her finger of death, and it was icy cold like the claws of death, and everything changed then. I'm not a superhero. Not really. I'm a bank clerk from Yorkshire and she took that away from me. She moulded me into the soldier she wanted me to be with whatever kooky powers she has, and I think she did the same to you."

"No."

"No?"

"Petula wouldn't do something like that."

"Oh yeah, I forget about your whole secret love affair with Petula. Weren't she old enough to be your gran?"

"It wasn't like that."

"You haven't got faith in anyone or anything, but you've got faith in Petula. Why is that?"

"Because of everything she did for me and my mum after dad died."

"Petula made our backstories and characters up. We're who we are because it fits her agenda. You think you owe Petula everything and that's why you're working for Defence E even though you don't have to be."

"Where's that voice coming from?" The blonde nurse intervened. "It sounds Northern."

"Oh, so you can hear me now? Hola! I'm The No Man. I'm in the hand sanitiser because Hop, *Martin,* was fed up with me being in his heart. I'm usually a right laugh, but I've had some news that indicates everything I've ever known and lived through is a lie, so don't expect me to be too chipper today. I want to get off this treadmill."

"I may have had vivid dreams in my time - when Henry the Eighth punched me so hard he gave me a nosebleed, for one - but I know a dream from a memory when I see one. Think about what we all have in common. Petula came to visit us when we were at our lowest points. We felt like we owed something to society, or ourselves, and to Petula, so we accepted her offer to become superheroes. We all had some exciting, turbulent origin story which kicked us into place. What's your origin story?"

"Dad saved those miners in Columbia. He put everything on the line."

"And let me guess? Your nightmare says that isn't true."

"I have nightmares..."

"Do they ever become daymares?"

"...Imagining that he didn't save those miners. But I remember it."

"I remember growing up in The Institute, but it doesn't mean those memories weren't inserted. Aren't the memories you thought you had going hazy?"

Hop wouldn't admit that he was wrong. It wasn't in his nature. Come to think of it, though, something had clouded over his mind.

The Nurse removed the harnesses and grabbed both his arms and helped him off the machine. She lifted him and distributed him into an adjacent wheelchair. His powers were as limited as they had been when he was a child. He couldn't hop from place to place any longer; those luxuries were reserved for his future. With every day and every gait test, he'd get closer to being freed from the prison that was the hospital, whether he liked it or not.

Hop's mouth and mind were numb from the crash, but he motivated his lips to persevere. If he could move his arms, he'd clap his hands together and demand the nurse to wheel him along. Instead, he barked, "Get me out of here."

"I'll follow you!" The No Man cried, leaping from the hand sanitiser dispenser into a mop. The Nurse dragged Hop's chair down the corridor, and the Northerner followed. "Get a grip, Hop, and start believing me."

"There's a flaw in your logic," said Hop on the way to his bed. "If Petula chose the perfect set of heroes, why did she choose you?"

"You're still finding time to insult me even amidst an existential crisis!"

"Petula isn't the sort of person to cheat history. She always made sure I didn't."

"Who knows what anybody is anymore? It's easier to run away from the truth, but you're learning to walk again. Walk towards the truth. Treat it as a metaphor. I remember everything, and it's about time somebody did something about it."

Hop insisted the Nurse speed up, which she did, to the pace she could manage. Hop looked over his shoulder to the corridor where The No Man remained, somewhere, hidden.

When he reached his room, Hop noticed the curtain twitch. Only for a second, but a shadow lingered. The shadow of his father. The shadow of the lie. Hop shook away the notion and reminded himself that his father was dead and that Petula would never do anything to hurt him, but that may have been his stubbornness talking. The Nurse popped him back onto his bed, and he hoped something would come along to prove the daymares were nothing more than machinations of the mind.

Later that day, Isla arrived with a dignified stride and a protein shake which the Nurse feared could mess with Hop's diet. Rather than drawing up a chair, she remained standing, having read that standing is always better for health and posture.

"Are you here to talk about your new memories too?" Hop grunted.

"As welcoming as ever!" Isla remarked. "I'm here to see how you are, because you're my friend."

"*Colleague.* There's a difference, and it's about time people acknowledged that."

"These new memories you talk of. I'm assuming from that, Lester's been here, and has told you about what we discussed."

"The No Man's name is Lester? He told you and not me? I would care if I had any respect for the laddie. I'll be out of here in a few days, you know. I'm not looking forward to it."

"You'd rather lie in a bed all day and watch the world do the hard work for you? That sounds like you, but I couldn't think of anything worse."

"It's not just me who's enunciating the insults here then! You think these aren't daymares? They're real life? Like The No Man, *Lester,* sorry, you think Petula lied to us? She created new identities for us that shouldn't have belonged to our names."

"Correct. I'm remembering my real past so vividly now. Petula's in this hospital, right?"

"If I'm still in the damn Manchester Royal Infirmary, then yes, that's right. Three doors down from here, I believe, but I've not got a chance to see her since I've ended up like this, with my face torn to pieces."

"I bet that's killing you. You've always been so into your good looks, except even you have been letting yourself go of late. You came to New York with your hair quiffed on day one, then you ended up a bit of a mess by the time Petula left. Speaking of Petula, I need to pay her a visit."

Hop would have called Isla back, aware that her meeting with Petula would carry repercussions, but truth be told, he had better things on his mind, namely what was on his television set that day, so he put the TV on, and watched the programme with little awe other than the knowledge that it was able to pass the time.

35.   The Crofts

Eva had never run so quickly as when she went to Apartment Block C and smelt the mildew of every opened door and rotten ceiling that she passed, but she ran so fast that it barely mattered. She stopped with a bang at the door where she found Maeve and Hex in a malaise, but they answered the door together.

"Ethan knows everything," Eva said, as she made her way to her belongings, grabbing a carrier bag stolen from the newsagents she worked at, and piling all of her belongings inside. "The disease is a lie. We can leave this place, and we're going to have to. Everybody knows, better than even you do."

"They know, do they? About Mummy?" Hex asked, and Maeve got the impression that she was the only one who had been kept out of the loop.

"What don't they know? Who don't they know?" Maeve asked the questions, and Eva turned to her to provide a brief summary: "Francis isn't the only spy hired by Defence E to go undercover in Woodville. You are too. While Francis has the ability to relay information back to the government and the police, you have the power to wipe minds. You erased Gordon and

Agatha's son off the map, and many other friends and family members of ours. You stole Hex from Suzie because you knew we wanted a child and we couldn't exactly adopt when we had the chance. Everybody knows. They'll want to organise a witch hunt."

"Why don't I remember?" Maeve asked, but Eva only stopped to pick up the bags with the bare essentials they needed, and dragged wife and son along in either hand. Maeve watched through the window as Isla carried Ethan away, before swiftly vanishing. "That's Ethan, isn't it?" She pointed at a now blank area. "He's gone. We don't need to worry."

"Everybody's mad at you. They'll all want answers. We need to sneak you out of this place before they find out that me and Hex knew too. You were so equipped for your task that you wiped your mind of the knowledge that you even had these abilities."

Maeve resisted Eva's hand briefly, but Hex tugged on the other to pull Eva away, aware of how urgent their situation was, a situation which Maeve misunderstood the gravity of. "If this is true, if I've been complicit in whatever corruption I'm hearing about, with Francis, and everything, then why are you still helping me? That means our entire existence is a lie."

In 2006, Maeve's Grandmother, who she had lived with until the age of twelve, and who was secretly blessed in the same way as her, was the one who informed Maeve of her abilities, first time around. She claimed it was necessary to do whatever those in power said, for the sake of her family, her friends, but that nobody must know who she serves. Miriam owed a great deal to the government - the men in charge.

When Maeve's mother came down with the inexplicable, undefinable condition that later killed her, Miriam used government money, handed to her as compensation for her spywork, which she was never caught out for, to fund Maeve's existence. Gordon was the one who told Maeve that Miriam Croft had died, but he too was none the wiser to them secretly being blessed. Their powers had been passed down through the generations, and only Woodville's first Mayor, in 1486, was any more the wiser. Maeve let Government orders rule her, with no parental influence to tell her otherwise, aside from Bishop Tomlinson, who took her under his wing until she was old enough to go out on her own, six years later.

"You're still my wife. Hex is still my son. No matter what happens, I'll still do anything for you, because that's what I promised when we made our vows."

Eva pushed at Maeve harder and Hex agreed to come along. Having worked in the Newsagents for years, Eva knew how to balance a lot in her hands, so she managed to simultaneously collect her two bags and two human beings and tug them down the staircase, although Maeve and Eva eventually decided to push forwards of their own volition.

Waiting for them outside the Apartment were Suzie and the Norths, the most reliable victims of Defence E within the Estate. Suzie was bound to be seething, and that showed on her ever-vexatious expression. She had crossed arms and when she approached the Crofts, Eva thought they were due a punch in the face or a few expletives, but all they got was an "I forgive you", a statement that hit home how important their new situation was. She elaborated: "There's a whole world out there for us to explore, and we can go out and explore it. Hex is your son, however much I hate to admit it. You go your way in life, and I'll go in mine."

Gordon had already made his way to the gates, and the Crofts opted to follow. People still looked at them with obnoxious glares, and Eva wondered how Agatha could even dream of forgiving Maeve for taking her son away. That's because the infirm seventy-seven-year-old had not yet been informed. There was so much Aggie had left to do, and this was freedom. Steven, Elijah's brother, tapped Maeve on the shoulder, and shook her hand.

"I understand that you aren't the villain here," Steven said. "It was Defence E. You were a puppet, just like my brother. He killed our father, when Caleb planned to escape this place. You didn't make us forget that. I'm not sure why. Apparently you aren't sure either. Ultimately, I forgave him. You should have heard the rows we went through in the redemption process."

"We heard every one," Eva murmured. She clasped at Hex when he approached the gates and the true fresh air made itself known as the first symptom of freedom.

"You weren't on their side, were you?" Elijah asked, and Maeve nodded, because as far as she was aware, she had always felt guilty siding with the likes of Petula Wednesday, still in a coma, as she possibly always would be. "You were brought into this against your will by the people who came before you, introduced to this act when you were only a child. You weren't like Francis, or Carim, or even my son. You didn't spill blood in the name of good."

"That's why we've decided to forgive you. The world's too big a place to stay in the present. Aggie doesn't know what you did. She can never know. I'm loud and she's still too hard of hearing to understand what I'm saying."

"Thank you, Elijah, I appreciate that," Maeve said, then swiftly corrected herself. "Sorry, Steven, I mean. You're just so much like him, in his mannerisms, and everything."

"That's okay. I could sort of be flattered by that. It means we'll never forget him, even if we get to venture into that bright and bountiful world out there."

They stood at the gates, all of them, as Isla and Gordon took turns to pull them open. The alarms went howling, but it did not matter, for beyond those gates, they could find freedom.

36.   <u>Comfortable in your own skin?</u>

The pastoral podium outside Bishops Heath has been home to some of the most influential speakers in history. It was where Paddy Ashton announced his victory over Tony Blair. It was where veteran Troy West spoke about how his powers of flight rescued the Triple Entente.

A few miles away, somewhere in Hull, was a park bench. On that park bench was Ethan Song, opposite Moira Standerton, reporter of *The North Coast*. Moira's wrists danced over her notepad as smugness frequently met her face. Ethan chose to dress down in his overcoat, no longer dressed in medals and badges. A look of constant shame marked his downcast face. Only days before had he been arrested, and he fell to his hands and knees in shame at the prospect of his failure. This had still, to this date, not been made public knowledge, and right now he was sitting on a park bench in Hull.

"I confess," Ethan declared with a bowed head, "that I am the one that the world can blame for locking the unblessed away."

Already, there had been protests on either side. People like Megaphone Meg demanded that the Unblessed should be housed in proper communities so they would no longer be isolated from society. More extreme demographics demanded that the diseased should be shepherded back to their compounds and forced to remain there until eternity reached its final second.

The emancipation of the unblessed brought many complications. Not only were the blessed rendered powerless by the loss of their abilities and, therefore, their identities, but there would come overcrowding and overpopulation, and a lack of adequate space as the Unblessed moved into cities and towns in search of freedom. The unblessed may not have carried disease but the world became so used to branding them inferior that it forgot how to regard them as anything better.

"I announce this live on television, that if it wasn't for me, the Unblessed would still be locked away. The blessed can hate me for being reckless enough to let our secret go: That there is no disease, and the Unblessed and Blessed are just the same. Those who support the

Unblessed can hate me too, because I was the one who kept up the lie on Petula Wednesday's behalf.

Ethan was acting out of character. Not only did he resort to being humble, dropping his militaristic resolve, but he also twitched too many times and left too many gaps in his sentences.

He confessed to Moira that he and world leaders had lied about the infected and that lie had passed down the generations. He confessed to issuing the order for Carim to kill the unblessed insurgents. He confessed to ordering the deaths of Chrissie Young and Ruth Mayor.

Moira's lackey, Megaphone Meg, clicked the red square button on her camera with glee as the confession concluded. Moira turned with a smirk.

"We've got it," Moira exclaimed. "It looks like our plan is going to work."

Ethan smiled. Not a sinister, empty smirk like those he usually offered. Instead, a buoyant, triumphant grin, as if his defeat elated him. There was a reason Ethan was off-kilter. Why his eyebrows quivered, and his top button went undone. Once the camera stopped rolling, Ethan's chair became vacant, and Ethan vanished.

"Did it work?" The No Man asked, having become the chair.

"That's as close as we're going to get to a confession from Ethan while he rots away in his prison cell," Meg declared. "There's no way for him to prove that's not him confessing on the video, and this will lock him away for good. He'll be out of our hair forever."

"Ever since I found out Ethan brought *The Manifesto,* I became keen to expose his lies," Moira said. "Thanks, The No Man!"

"No worries, my journalistic friend!"

They waited for the trial to take place and for Ethan to try to dispute the indisputable. They didn't get that far. Ethan Song slit his wrists at the first chance he got.

38. <u>The Hotel Newton</u>

By day four, it was no longer true that every day was the same. At least, there was nothing to say it had to be.

For Agatha Churchill, relative inexperience provided the greatest of pleasures. For most, having freedom of activity was a luxury taken for granted. For Agatha, freedom was something to cherish, after a life of constancy.

All she and Gordon could afford was the Hotel Newton, a cheap four-storey inn. Fifteen pounds a night. Breakfasts were served with stray hairs and the bargain rate drew in drunkards, but the change of scene and the charging rate provided little to turn one's nose up at. Her room may not have been special, but a balcony was a welcome novelty. This balcony overlooked a park, dull at day but quaint at night. Gordon had researched the location and promised to meet her there when their ordeal was over. With a flippant leap, the unblessed had entered the world, providing Gordon with ample opportunity to meet his wife. She'd paid for the hotel with his money - his treat - and savoured every moment.

By day two, she'd already been bird watching and park walking. She'd saved the luxury of a well-cooked meal for when she could be with her husband. Until then, she'd bask in foreign lands with the comfort of the little money she had. She avoided the television which announced that the unblessed were free. Instead, she purchased a cup of tea from the vending machine and took it to the parapet. Only the crashes and bangs of cocktail drinkers passed the vacant pasture her room overlooked. The promise of midnight settled in the skies during a rainfall that seemed to never end.

Fast asleep on their bed - uncomfortable, but preferable to their former haystack - Gordon promised to wake soon. His eyes flickered as the last morning of their stay dawned. Within time, they'd return to Woodville, and they'd settle down in Woodville Estate, which was set to become just like any other district in Yorkshire. They'd worry then about money and jobs, which were concerns they had left behind them.

Gordon's wife was on the balcony, her frail legs crossed in tights. Gordon doddered over to her, taking a groan with him. Her feet were bare against the dirtied cobbled patio, but she did not care about the grime from the unclean budget hotel. As long as she had these moments, she cared about nothing more.

Their stay had been far from perfect but also far from inadequate. Daytime strolls down the town, as far as they could go, or as far as their lumbering legs would take them. Evening meals down in the all-you-can-eat buffet, plagued with grease and pink meat. The proper, undiluted coffee scent effused from the canteen. They met, for the first time, those with abilities. There were a lucky few, after all, who retained their powers. People who snorted fire from their nostrils and smoke from their lungs were treated no differently by the couple. Agatha considered everyone with a slight tint of cruelty, while Gordon provided nothing but courtesy.

Seeing the world gave Agatha everything she wanted. She may have forgotten about the son Maeve took from her, or the friend in her back that would take her away. She could see the world now, and it would harm nobody for her to do so. Agatha smiled; a novelty on a face where a smile should not fit. When she was alone with the trees and the wind, she forgot all her troubles. Damp light glistened on her wrinkled face and her mind felt at rest. Her diagnosis did not matter anymore. Only nature mattered now. Nature, the cup of tea in one hand, and the man who held the other.

39. Lady Not Waking

By the time Isla saw Petula again, Wednesday was hardly at the peak of health, with a respirator and an IV tunnel and so little life that it was a wonder she had ever been alive at all. Isla had never liked Petula much, even though she was the most admired of their little clan, and Petula looked at her with platonic appreciation.

She saw Petula's eyes were shut and her body immobile, so she clapped her hands, with her eyes fixed on her wristwatch, so time passed forward and the clock in the left-hand corner went haywire. It was five in the evening when she began - she was Petula's colleague, and a superhero, so she didn't have to adhere to visitor's guidelines - and four in the afternoon when it ended, as night turned to day and back to night again. She stopped clapping her hands when Petula woke, by which time Hop had been set free.

Isla flicked on the television, and there was a report featuring Defence B member and social media icon Nancy Bradshaw, recorded live at the scene of Woodville Estate. A young boy called Hex said they should dance, so they all started dancing outside the gates: Maeve, Eva, everybody, flamboyantly and merrily, setting their grudges and grief aside so they could be happy, just for this moment.

"Look at it," Isla said as she leaned down to face Petula with a smirk. "That's the first sign that you've lost this game you've been playing with us."

"Isla-" Petula quivered.

"Don't play the meek innocent role! I'm not too convinced that you haven't been faking this coma the entire time just for attention. Hop believes you wouldn't do anything to harm us, but Lester and I know better, devoid of the biases of infatuation."

Petula saw the headlines shift. She read out what she discovered. "Carim Shafiq and members of the Manifesto paper are dead. The Unblessed are free."

"Chrissie and Ruth would have loved to be where I'm standing right now, talking to the mighty Petula Wednesday. They'd have loved to see the Unblessed escaping from their compounds, dancing with merriment. It fills me with glee."

"Tell me everything that's happened since I've been in this coma."

"Quite a bit. We got a new boss, Ethan. You always liked him, probably. I didn't. Hop sacrificed his life for you, and ended up in a hospital bed with half a face off. Your daughters brought you here to this Hospital, and tried to build the Wednesday name back up, but they failed as much as Ethan did in raising Defence E to glory. Defence E has fallen."

"That's not possible. I planned everything so precisely. There was a certain way that everything needed to be."

"That's why you rewrote our histories? For your distorted dreams of paradise? Tell me candidly, what were the lives you took away from Carim and I? You never got to tell him you were sorry for destroying your life. You wrote the scripts to our lives. You introduced Carim's brother to his life and then you killed Abbas off. That was cruel."

"You're smart, Isla. No matter our differences, I hope you know that I always admired you."

"I know I was your prized pig. It doesn't make any difference to be the criminal's favourite, though I am no exception."

Petula inspected the balloons and cards left around the room. "Lila and Tegan turned this place into a temporary home. I'm looking forward to getting back to my permanent one. It never felt like home, after George died, but I can appreciate it now. I don't have to keep on running. Running was what led me to Kitzhubel in the first place."

"Don't try it on with the sob stories! You're the villain of the piece. I ain't gonna feel sorry for you, with your mansion and your history corruption."

"Fine. You want answers? I'll explain how I turned you from inadequate to extraordinary overnight. Carim Shafiq was born in Manchester, not Damascus, to

Haya and Akil Shafiq. He was a supermarket chef, always had been, not a Syrian refugee after all. That backstory was manufactured for tragic relief. So many lives were consequently saved."

"What about the events on the dinghy that he said made him? Abbas Shafiq?"

"There was no such person. I implanted him in Carim's mind to make him strong. A pizza chef is no origin story for a superhero."

"That's right. Why did you pick us then? There are plenty of people who would have been eager to save the world. Why did you select a handful of people who really weren't?"

"This may sound selfish," Petula said. "But I wished to receive the credit for building you up."

Isla chuckled, unamused. "How's that going to turn out to be anything other than selfish?"

"It worked wonders for you. You get to live out your dream."

"It's only my dream because you made me think it was. I don't remember my real childhood, so who knows? I might have wanted to be an air stewardess, or a taxi driver, you know, something random like that? You had no place to take that away from me. We were so damn ordinary that we became your targets."

"Ordinary was the right way to go. You were untainted. You were perfect templates."

"What about me? I know the answer. I entered Defence E because I didn't save my father from the man with the knives in his fingertips. I thought I had so much to make amends about, and society, so I enrolled in Defence E and I became one of your soldiers."

"You ran towards villains like the one who attacked your father," Petula said. "Forgetting that you were one of those villains yourself."

"Nine years old, I started sneaking out of the house. I found some friends in primary school who were a bad influence on me. I started getting these rebellious urges. It started out as me stealing a few things, pickpocketing, you know the type, but then things got serious. I remember now that my Dad wasn't assaulted. You introduced that so I'd have a sob story to bring up to the journos whenever they asked how I became Quickfix. I left a young woman, three years older than me, in intensive care, when I was twelve, and I kept going with my descent until you arrived on my doorstep and designed my backstory. You destroyed so many lives, and as soon as you get out of here, you and your daughters are bound to cause so much more. You want the Unblessed locked away and for time to play to your tune, but we're not standing for it anymore. *I'm* not standing for it anymore. I'm out."

"What are you going to do about it?" Petula called Isla back as she approached Hop, who played witness to the conversation, entering the room with a broken expression, asphyxiated by the truth about his lover. "I'm sorry, Martin."

"You're not sorry about anything," Hop grumbled. "I sacrificed everything for you."

"You put your life on the line. I appreciate that, my love."

"Excuse me while I heave," Isla interjected. "Don't listen to her bull, mate. If she didn't interfere with our pasts, who knows what we'd have been. We'll never find out. Carim would probably still be with us right now."

"You wouldn't have even met Carim if it hadn't been for me." Hop sort of nodded.

"Don't take her side!" Isla begged him. "She's the one who made all of us who we are. She probably made Ethan into the Unblessed-hater that he is."

"*Was*," Hop announced. "I came here with a purpose. You've been standing here unconscious since the day you last visited me. That was four days ago now. Ethan Song was found dead in his prison cell last night. He slit his own wrists."

"Oh. What a disappointment. I was hoping he would rot in his cell for the rest of eternity."

"So was I, but the world's too cruel to work out that way. That's been proved by me loving a woman that turned out to be my worst enemy, sacrificing myself so she can keep on breeding her lies, losing my powers as I hop from one time to the next with no way to control it."

"She doesn't have anyone to play her games with," Isla continued. "The great Petula Wednesday has a lot of hard work to be doing and her daughters haven't been making her proud, from what I can tell. They've been sitting on their backsides waiting for you to come along and save their skins."

"I'm not averse to hard work," Petula replied. "You should know that because I made you."

"You aren't Frankenstein and we certainly aren't your monsters."

"You could kill me. Lock me up. I expect your intentions aren't to leave me in this hospital bed."

"As a matter of fact, they are. I find it so funny that you were once a woman who used her cane for show, and now you're gonna need more than a cane to walk around. Kill you? That would be a breach of the hero's code, and we've broken enough rules on that because of you. Arrest you? Then you wouldn't be able to see the world that the Unblessed build for themselves, and I want you to be able to see that, so you know that you have lost. I was a criminal when I was younger. There's no escaping from that. I put a young person in hospital fighting for their life, and I have to own up for that and pay for that, now that my real memories are coming through. First of all, though, I want to go on one last trip. I'm coming with you, Hop. Wherever we go, we're going far away from here, where Petula can't get us."

"You choose. I must be able to muster enough power to get you where you want. Anywhere in time, past or future, make your wish."

Isla made sure Petula was watching as she waited for the beats of the heart monitor to settle before she made her decision.

Printed in Great Britain
by Amazon